Praise for

BONNIE HEARN HILL

"Engrossing, provocative and haunting,
Intern is a riveting combination."
—Mary Jane Clark,
New York Times bestselling author

"A real page-turner. Hill gets the reader's attention
with a contemporary issue (is slim the only way to
be?), intriguing characters and clever plotting."
—*Publishers Weekly* on *Killer Body*

"Bonnie Hearn Hill's *Intern* is a book to pick up
and not put down."
—M. J. Rose, bestselling author of *The Halo Effect*

"*Intern* is a thriller
that reads as if it's ripped from today's headlines."
—Alex Kava, bestselling author of
At the Stroke of Madness

"Fans...will appreciate Hill's skill in combining
first-rate suspense with glamorous characters and
a topical story line."
—*Booklist* on *Killer Body*

Bonnie Hearn Hill
"...creates more than enough suspense to keep
readers intrigued [in]...this page-turner."
—*Publishers Weekly* on *Intern*

Also by BONNIE HEARN HILL

INTERN

*And watch for BONNIE HEARN HILL's
newest thriller*

DOUBLE EXPOSURE

Coming April 2005

BONNIE HEARN HILL

KILLER BODY

MIRA®

ISBN 0-7783-2127-4

KILLER BODY

Copyright © 2004 by Bonnie Hearn Hill.

All rights reserved. Except for use in any review, the reproduction or
utilization of this work in whole or in part in any form by any electronic,
mechanical or other means, now known or hereafter invented, including
xerography, photocopying and recording, or in any information storage or
retrieval system, is forbidden without the written permission of the publisher,
MIRA Books, 225 Duncan Mill Road, Don Mills, Ontario, Canada M3B 3K9.

All characters in this book have no existence outside the imagination of the
author and have no relation whatsoever to anyone bearing the same name
or names. They are not even distantly inspired by any individual known or
unknown to the author, and all incidents are pure invention.

MIRA and the Star Colophon are trademarks used under license and registered
in Australia, New Zealand, Philippines, United States Patent and Trademark
Office and in other countries.

www.MIRABooks.com

Printed in U.S.A.

To Laura Dail.
For making the dream come true.

ACKNOWLEDGMENTS

Killer Body and I want to thank the following for their contributions to this book:

Amy Moore-Benson, whose superb editing and suggestions humble me.

Laura Dail, the best agent on the planet.

Tania Charzewski, for the wise counsel and the Cinderella stories.

Donna Hayes, Loriana Sacilotto, Alex Osuszek, Gordy Goihl, Ken Foy and Fritz Servatius, for making it happen.

Weight Watchers International; also, the members of the *Fresno Bee* Weight Watchers at Work Program and its inspirational leader Annie Hickman.

Debra Winegarden, the ultimate Killer Body, who gave me a glimpse of another world.

Bev Medina, Dennis Lewis, Ph.D., Dr. Regina Shay, the experts.

Larry Paquette and Hazel Dixon-Cooper; YCs forever.

Jennifer Badasci, I love you.

Genevieve Choate, Jared Hinson, Sheree Petree, Meg Bertini, Jay Crosby, Linda Nielsen and the Tuesday Night Writers. Ditto.

All of those with weight issues who shared their stories with me. We're owned only by that of which we cannot speak. Thank you.

Left Coast Crime, 2003, for auctioning off, for charity, one of the names in this novel, and to the person with the winning bid: Only you will know which character has your name, but, as promised, you *do* have a killer body.

Dianne Moggy and MIRA Books. For believing.

ONE

Rikki

If it had been anyone else but my cousin Lisa dying like that, and anyone else but Aunt Carey doing the asking, I wouldn't have gone to the funeral.

I'd escaped from the life we'd shared, shrugged off my childhood, as best I could, put myself through college and landed a job at the paper. I didn't want to be reminded of those long days and longer nights in Pleasant View, California, when I was just another kid without a father, taken in by relatives whose sense of duty outweighed their own good judgment.

"I knew you'd come, Rikki Jean," Carey had said when I met her at her hotel. "You're still a pretty little thing." Then her lower lip trembled, and she let the tears take her.

If there's anything I hate more than my name, it's my whole name, but the only rules Aunt Carey plays by are her own.

Now I hold her hand in the back seat of the limousine, and look out on Belmont Avenue, once a main drag, today an urban danger zone. The limo inches past the freeway, beyond the outskirts of this conflicted, basically angry Valley town. We head for that leftover geography cut off from the city, like dough from a cookie cutter, the part of town now occupied by only the very poor, the very transient and the very dead.

Lisa Tilton is no longer my cousin, but *the deceased.* No, make that *the victim,* brought down by a heart attack just months before her wedding. And Carey Tilton, my aunt, has faded and shriveled since I last saw her right after she moved to Colorado, following her surgery. She's the one who's supposed to be dead, but not even cancer could stand up to her.

"She left you her crystal," Aunt Carey says.

"That's nice." I've always felt Lisa's crystal was too fragile. We couldn't even clink it when we shared a glass of wine.

As our limo follows the car that is following the car ahead, I shift in the back seat and squeeze my aunt's limp hand. Her peach-fuzz hair is a shaggier version of mine, but longer, with spiky bangs and fringe around her ears. People always said I looked as if I could be her daughter, which both pleased and embarrassed me back then. And Lisa? Other than a brief, roly-poly moment as an infant, Lisa always looked like herself. Perfect.

This is not one of those block-long, bar-included limos Aunt Carey reserved for Lisa and Pete's wedding, but a short, stout vehicle that tries to scuttle, unnoticed, through the streets on its way to the part of town most residents visit only when they have no choice.

"Valentine's Day. We're burying her on Valentine's Day."

Aunt Carey sits like a statue next to me. All that I can see of Pete's black suit in the back seat of the car ahead of us is caved in, his shoulders rolled toward the window.

During the funeral in the church where he and Lisa would have been married, Pete sat between Aunt Carey and me, gripping his knees so ferociously that I finally reached over and clutched his hand. Grief and emotions I could only imagine wiped his handsome features into a gray slate.

Fresh air. That's what we all need. But none of us dares to say it. We walk through a ritual, written lifetimes before, procedure approved, as is this final ride we're taking.

Finally, we pull into the memorial gardens where Lisa will be laid to rest, as the euphemism goes.

I touch Aunt Carey's stiff shoulder.

"I've got to stay in the car during the next part," I say. "I can't watch it."

"No, honey. You can't stay here. She wouldn't do that to you."

No, she wouldn't. Lisa would do what was expected, and do it better than anyone else. Aunt Carey would see to it.

"I'll go with you, then."

"I knew you would."

Once free from the car, I take her arm, and we walk to the fake grass and the very real dark rectangle of earth I've been trying to avoid.

The minister approaches us, but Aunt Carey waves him away. She grips my wrist, as if she has just awakened from a dream. "I've got something important to tell you," she says. "Something very important." It's the voice she used back then, when she asked me if I'd done my homework. She moves her lips close to my ear. "They killed Lisa, those people at Killer Body."

"Of course they didn't." I step back from the harsh words, so rancorous I can almost smell them, like alcohol on her breath. "I don't even know why Lisa insisted on joining Killer Body. She didn't need to lose weight."

"She wanted to, for the wedding, and those bastards gave her supplements, bad food." Her blurred blue eyes bore into mine, begging me to believe her fantasy, assuage her grief.

"That's not what did this to her. Heart disease runs in the family. It killed Mom, remember?"

"I remember, all right." Her face goes pink, as if someone just pinched her cheeks. "Nan's illness was her lifestyle," she says. "Lisa didn't smoke *or* drink."

"No, she didn't." My mother did, and we both know it.

"She was in perfect shape, Rikki Jean. And there's something else. A man from Killer Body was meeting her in L.A., coaching her, she said."

"Coaching?"

"To be on television. He'd promised her she could be in one of their TV commercials. You know how Lisa loved to be in front of a camera."

"I know." That does it. Tears finally begin to squeeze out. I fight to hold them back. If I don't, I'll be lost forever, afloat in a sea of grief and guilt. "No one but Julie Larimore is ever in their ads," I say. "The man lied to her, or she misunderstood."

"She didn't misunderstand. He told her Julie Larimore might be quitting."

"I don't think so," I tell her. "If that were the case, we would have read something about it. Julie Larimore *is* Killer Body."

"You've got to help me, honey." Aunt Carey grasps my wrist tighter. The blind pain in her eyes makes me want to turn away, but I don't. "For Lisa. You're a journalist. This is what you write about, what you win awards for."

My award was for a series of articles on bulimia, but I don't bother to correct her. I look into those eyes, jolting blue, brimming with tears. I can't tell her that what she wants won't bring her daughter back. I've never been able to stand up to her, and I'm not about to start now.

"What do you want me to do?"

"Get that man. Get Killer Body." Tears course down her cheeks, melting their powdered perfection. She makes no attempt to wipe them away. "Please, honey. I've never asked you for anything."

And you raised me, took me in when my own mother didn't want me.

I look past us, past the softly gathered friends and family, to the rectangle. To the grave. The grave that will hold Lisa, just four months before her wedding. Death by heart attack. Death by Killer Body, Inc. Or so her mother would like to believe.

The minister moves close to us, like a dark memory. I put my arm around Carey's shoulder. How brittle it feels, how frail. Is this how it happens? Age? Death?

"I'll try. I'll do everything I can," I say, hating myself for wanting the approval I see gleaming beneath her tears. Needing it, damn it.

Then we walk past the minister, past the people in the cold, beige folding chairs someone has arranged far too close to the grave and the heavy fall of soil that will follow this brief ceremony of farewell. I can feel the strength drain from me; I feel liquid, like water.

"Promise?" It's that homework voice again. "Rikki Jean?" she asks. "Promise me?"

And I nod.

TWO

Lucas

Ellen Horner had a killer body. Everyone who worked in the inner circle did. It was one of the old man's sexist ideas that persisted, as Bobby W persisted himself, in this otherwise politically correct world.

"Sorry to break in on you like this, but some reporter's trying to reach Bobby W," Ellen said.

Lucas guessed that Ellen would have looked this good regardless of where she worked. She didn't have to flaunt what was obvious in spite of her respectable black-and-white jacket, striped like an awning, and her white skirt that stopped just above her knee.

Her fine blond hair, mostly bangs swept across her brow, was tucked behind her ears, making her look both innocent and professional. But not happy. Not at all happy.

"Female reporter?" he asked.

"Yes, and not a friendly one. Her name's Rikki something." She grimaced. "Rikki with an *i*, as she was quick to point out."

"He'll charm her," Lucas said. "Always does. Might as well set up an interview."

"Okay." Ellen didn't move toward the door, the expression on her face pure dread. This was worse than a reporter. "What is it?" Lucas asked.

"He's at it again." She gestured with her folder at the ceiling. "This time it's Rochelle McArthur."

"Here? Right now?"

"Upstairs. Door closed. It's all we need."

Lucas's internal sigh stopped just short of being audible. "Where'd he find her, anyway? That TV show was canceled how many seasons ago?"

Ellen grimaced. "She found him, I'm afraid. You *know* what that means."

"She wants something."

"But just try telling *him* that."

Lucas got up from his desk, took a fleeting glance at the Santa Barbara coastline, imagining the sailboat where he'd hoped to spend the day. Maybe he still could. Maybe this wouldn't take too long. He opened the door of his office and nodded at Ellen. "Shall we?"

The walls of Killer Body, Inc. were plastered with photographs of Julie Larimore, the company spokesmodel. The walls of Bobby Warren's office were plastered with photographs of Bobby Warren. The shots of the iron-pumping man in the posters had little in common with the Bobby W of today, who, although he still worked out, had to do it around the good-size paunch beneath his windbreaker. Sitting on the chaise across from his cherry-wood desk, he held a glass of bourbon in one hand and Rochelle McArthur's thigh in the other.

"Come in, come in," he said, as if greeting a visitor to his home. Apparently forgetting Rochelle, he rose to shake Lucas's hand and greet Ellen with a kiss on the cheek that turned into an appraising gaze of her body. He smelled of expensive cologne, like the ones that arrived embedded on the glossy papers accompanying Lucas's credit card bills each month.

And bourbon. Yes, he smelled of that, too. And it wasn't even noon yet.

"Care for a cocktail, Luke?"

Fifties word, fifties attitude toward liquor in a health-oriented organization.

"No, thanks. It's a little early for me."

Bobby W grinned, bringing his eyes, the same color as the bourbon, to life. Lucas couldn't help giving in to a smile. He hoped he had half the old man's stamina when he was his age.

"We were getting ready to have a little lunch out on the balcony." Then it obviously hit him he'd forgotten the other half of that *we.* "Oh, please. I'm sorry. You know Shelly, of course."

Lucas nodded, although they'd met only once in passing.

"Lucas is our marketing director," he said. "My right arm. And Ellen here is my left arm."

"The rest of that body belongs to you, I hope." With an unstated defiance, Rochelle McArthur crossed her legs and didn't bother to pull down the skirt of her shimmery knit dress, green as the contact lenses she wore.

Her voice was the way Lucas remembered it from her tele-vision series. The face and body hadn't fared as well. Either hard living or plastic surgery left her looking drawn beneath her ironed-on tan and bleached-to-the-point-of-brittle hair.

Still, to a seventy-year-old widower, his vision dulled by Crown Royal and loneliness, Rochelle probably looked like one of the hotties draped like fur coats around Bobby W in the photographs on his wall.

"I'm always in the market for takers." The old man sat down next to her on the silver-gray chaise, and Ellen and Lucas followed suit on the other side of the coffee table. Ellen perched on the edge of her chair, as if whatever had afflicted Rochelle were contagious and she didn't want to catch it.

"So what we're discussing is the Ass Blaster," Bobby W continued, as was his way, as if they'd all been in on the conversation from the beginning. "This aerobic stuff is shit, if you'll pardon my French. I'm not denying what it does for the heart, but what good is your heart if you're hauling around an assload of lard?"

"My point exactly, Bobbo."

Damn. No one but his oldest buddies called Bobby W *Bobbo*. Yet, he didn't seem to mind.

Lucas glanced past Rochelle's crisscrossed high-heeled sandals, her long white-tipped toenails, at the pearl-inlaid coffee table and its conveniently available coasters. She'd barely touched her drink. Catching his eye, she reached down and lifted the glass to her lips, deliberately. "You know, Bobbo, someone needs to say it just like that. No mincing words."

Now she'd done it. If anything glazed Bobby W's eyes and good sense more than a semisexy woman looking his way, it was someone, anyone, agreeing with him.

Lucas winced as Bobby W shot him a look of pained superiority and ran his hand across the fraying remains of what had once been a full head of hair. "I've been trying to tell that to my good friend Luke, here, but every once in a while, we fail to see eye to eye."

"But I'm sure not very often." Without moving her

gaze from Lucas, Rochelle reached for her glass once more. "Killer Body being your business and all."

"Good business is good people, and I have the best." Bobby W frowned at his empty glass, as if it, and not this troublesome conversation, were making him uncomfortable. "Ellen, honey, get me the Ass Blaster file, will you?"

Ellen stood, as if glad for an excuse to flee. "Which Ass Blaster file?"

"The marketing file. The photos, endorsements. Hell, why not bring in the prototype, too? Maybe Shelly would like to try it out, see if we can improve on perfection."

"Sure," she said in a voice that sounded like a sigh.

As Ellen left the office, Lucas hoped she wouldn't return with her written resignation the way too many others with similar degrees, and similar good looks, had.

The door drifted shut behind her, and Lucas looked back at the sofa to see that Bobby W had moved to the window overlooking the harbor, a miraculously full tumbler in his hand. How had the old bastard wrangled that?

"Mr. Warren," he began.

Bobby W turned from the window. "No need for formalities, Luke. We're all friends here." He smiled at Rochelle. "Isn't she a beauty? Wouldn't anyone kill for a body like that?"

Then Lucas realized what was going on, what the poor old bastard was thinking. Julie Larimore was bad enough. Bobby didn't need two of them. And neither did he.

He moved toward the window, trying to pretend the woman in the emerald-green dress and matching contacts was not in the room. "Could we discuss this later?"

"Later's an excuse for those who can't take action now." Bobby took another swig and stared past Lucas's shoulder at Rochelle, smiling so hard he could injure his jaw. "What the hell is so wrong with having a spokes-body—what do you call it?"

"Spokesmodel, Bobbo," Rochelle said from the sofa.

"Spokesmodel, right." Then, he turned his gaze on Lucas, and the burn of those still brilliant brown-black eyes and the legacy they carried was stronger than any argument in the room. "Why can't we have Julie Lari-more for Killer Body, Inc. and another spokesmodel for the Ass Blaster?"

"Because, with all due respect—" Lucas shot Rochelle a look that he hoped conveyed just a smidgeon less than that. "Because we can't confuse the public. Julie Larimore *is* our Killer Body. She's in our ads, on our products, our posters. Bobby, it just won't work."

Not now. This was the last thing he needed. Lucas's collar felt suddenly stiff and itchy. How bad could this timing be? They'd been to the mat, as Bobby W called it, before, and they always came away better friends. Damn, he loved the old man. He could already see the sadness filling the brown eyes. Could see Bobby W, like a kid in grade school, trying to remember a speech, get-ting ready to explain away this pseudo offer to Rochelle.

Then Lucas glanced at Rochelle and knew, just like that, as sure as there was sun lighting up the water of the Santa Barbara harbor, that she realized there was only one way this little meeting of her-against-him could possibly end.

"All I want is the Ass Blaster," she said. "I love, love, love it, Bobbo."

"That's a lot of loves." His grin bordered on giddy; the eyes were way too smitten.

"That's how they say it now in Hollywood—New York, too. No one loves anything. They love, love, love it. And I love, love, love your wonderful Ass Blaster."

"Sweetheart," he began, tapping on her thigh with his pale fingers.

"You two talk, and we'll catch up later," Lucas said. Then he left the room before he had to embarrass either of them one more minute. On the balcony, breathing that sea-fresh air, he tried to control his temper. So easy to tell the old man to stuff the job, to walk out the way he had on his own father.

No, he could never deal with that kind of guilt again. It was Bobby W's company, and Lucas could do no more than offer an opinion.

He heard the glass door slide open. Smelled her perfume.

Lavender. Lots of it.

He didn't bother to turn around. Just looked out on the ocean that calmed him as no person ever had.

"I'll join you two in a moment," he said, meaning that she could leave him the hell alone.

"I'd rather stand out here."

She slid up beside him at the railing. "Besides, Bobbo's in the john."

"He'll be out soon, I'm sure."

He was trying to be cool, but he had a nasty feeling he wasn't going to get out of this one unscathed.

She nudged him with her elbow. "So what *were* you?"

"What *was* I?"

"You know. Mr. Rose Bowl? Mr. Long Beach, maybe? The jacket's nice, but it doesn't cover the obvious."

"Thank you," he said.

"It's not a compliment."

"I didn't think so."

"Then why'd you thank me?"

"Just trying to give you the benefit of the doubt, I guess."

"Don't get all testy. You were a body beautiful, weren't you, in spite of the getup?"

"The jacket," he said, "was a gift from Bobby W." Damn, he didn't expect her to be a label reader, but he should have guessed. She no doubt dressed her husband. "Bobby's a generous man, as I'm sure you know."

"But you're a Mr. Beautiful who didn't go to pot when he hit thirty." She poked a finger at his arm, and he automatically flexed. "See what I mean, big boy?" She flashed a Marilyn Monroe pout that made him smile in spite of his irritation.

"You should be a comedian, Rochelle."

She tilted her head. Showed him a dimple as seductively as someone else might show her navel. "You can be my friend, Lucas. Just don't be bad to me."

"Wouldn't dream of it."

"You don't want me to get the job. I know it."

"At this moment, there is no job."

"And when there is, you still won't want me to get it."

"When would that be?" he asked. "When do you think there will be a job?"

The dimple again. Hollywood was crazy to write off this woman as over the hill. The few lines in her face worked for, not against, her. "I try to think positively."

"You really want to be a spokesmodel?" he asked. "You want to do infomercials showing you on your back, in a leotard, or less, attached to some machine?"

Her eyes went bright—anger, maybe, tears. "Since when did you become my agent?"

"Sorry," he said. "Someone should have pointed it out, though. Being a spokesmodel for exercise equipment is a far cry from your television show."

"You telling me Jesse isn't doing his job?"

"I'm sure your husband's doing a great job as your agent." He wanted to squeeze her arm, tell her it would be okay, but he felt touching her would be like punching the wrong code into a burglar alarm, something he'd done once in Bobby W's office. He never wanted to hear that sound again.

"You don't respect Jesse."

No one in the business respected her husband, but Lucas wasn't going to say so. "Let's not get into that," he said.

She pressed a finger into his shoulder again. He turned, hoping to hell she wasn't going to come on to him. "I respect Jesse's work and what he's done with your career. The posters were a stroke of genius." He turned to face her. No, it wasn't a come-on. It was desperation. "For now," he said, "we need to get back in there, especially if you want to stay on Bobby W's best side."

"You think I'm stupid, don't you?" She grabbed his arm, and he looked down at the white-on-white fingernails that matched her toes. "That's what people think when you look the way I do, or the way you do, for that matter."

"I don't think you're stupid, Rochelle." He had to grit his teeth to get it out.

She reached for his lapels, grinned again and pulled him close to her. "You think you've judged and juried me, but you aren't even close. I'm not some chick whose bust measurement is higher than her IQ. You might be looking at tits and ass, because that's how Jesse markets me. But I'm a hell of a lot more than that."

At that moment, staring at the energetic, face-to-face beauty of her, he wondered if he'd been wrong. He tried to give her the same fair assessment he wished others would grant him. Maybe she wasn't just another too-thin, top-heavy opportunist, looking for Bobby W to be a sugar daddy.

"Whatever works for you," he said.

They were still face-to-face when he heard a flinty, scraping sound from behind, and both of them backed away from each other.

The patio door flew open. Ellen burst through the door, her eyes panicked. Bobby W followed her.

"I just talked to someone from the police department," she said. "Julie Larimore's gone, disappeared. Her housekeeper reported it. Julie was supposed to be back from her San Diego trip five days ago."

"I talked to her last week," Bobby W said. "Damn, maybe it was the week before. Jules always calls me every day. I thought something happened to her cell phone, even wondered if she was mad at me, but Jules wouldn't be mad at me, would she?"

Lucas didn't bother to answer him. "What do they think happened?" he asked Ellen.

"I don't know, but she's missed appointments, including a photo shoot. The housekeeper tried to reach her at the hotel where she was supposed to be staying. She never registered, Lucas. And now the police are coming over here. They want to question us."

They all returned to the office. Tears shimmered in Bobby W's eyes as he lowered himself onto the chaise.

"Not my Jules," he said. "She wouldn't go away without letting me know." Lucas wasn't surprised when the dark eyes narrowed on him. "Find her,

Luke," Bobby W said. "Don't you dare bring your butt back here until you do."

The Interview

What would you do for a killer body, Julie?

You don't do it for the body, of course. You do it for what the body represents. Let me be frank about this: There's a down side, and considerable setbacks. That's when you have to persevere. Do so, and suddenly—and it will seem sudden to everyone else—you're this wonderful walking testament to self-discipline, accountability, control. The ability to continue when most people give up.

That doesn't mean it's out of reach, not at all, only that the price is as high as the achievement is rewarding. Driving a Maserati costs more than taking a bus, but which way would you prefer to view the landscape of your life? You're the only one who can decide which way you want to travel through this tenuous bit of time on earth.

I made my decision, and I'd make the same one again, even knowing what I know on what may be the darkest of all the dark days.

What would I do for a killer body? What wouldn't I do? What haven't I done?

THREE

Rikki

I force myself to go into my office at the *Valley Voice* the next Monday. I must steel myself against the flowers on my desk—flowers so fragrant that their scent will forever remind me of tragedy. The department secretary does this each time an employee takes off a day or more for a grievance leave. I remind myself it's not personal. I need to move past the flowers, past the funeral, past matters too dark to conjure just yet. Move into facts and what I can do next. I am a reporter, and this is what I do. I only hope I can remember how.

Dennis Hamilton's door is open, our tacit signal that he's had the requisite caffeine and nicotine to enable him to communicate with his staff. A little early for his door to be open; for my benefit, no doubt. He's like that. I step through the door, trying to push away the too-vivid memories of Hamilton and me.

He turns from the computer to face me, his expression even more grim, more flooded than usual with the flushed evidence of his excesses.

"I was there," he says, and I know the *there* of which he speaks could be only one place. "You probably didn't see me."

"I felt you." Aware of the embarrassment heating my face, I try to backtrack. "I mean, I kind of saw you. It was frenzied."

He stands, and for that moment, I want to run into his arms, where everything will be safe, secure and handled, but that's a lie. He's my boss now, only that. His appearance at the funeral means no more than the flowers on my desk. I can never run into his arms. And nothing in my life will ever again be safe.

Rotten tears. Just when you think you have them under control, they rush to the surface like embarrassing relatives, claiming you as one of their own.

"Sorry." I wipe my wet cheeks, try to stop the flood.

"It's okay." Something close to dignity shows through the harsh light of Hamilton's eyes. "Take as much time as you need."

"I'm not trying to get out of work," I say. "I want an assignment."

He turns toward the door. "Maybe later, after you've had time."

"No, you don't get what I'm trying to tell you, Den. Let me say it in two words. Julie Larimore."

Hamilton nails me with that damned intense gaze of his. "What about her?"

"She disappeared."

"No shit, Sherlock. Sure, she disappeared. But what could you know about that?"

"I don't *know* anything."

"Okay, then. What do you *think?*"

"I think," I say, "you need me to cover this story."

"Why?"

"Because there could be bad stuff going on at Killer Body, Inc."

Hamilton's coffee cup stops on the way to his lips. "Bad, how?"

"Someone telling women they can be stars, that they can be the next Julie Larimore."

Hamilton's coffee cup settles on the desk, forgotten. "They're doing that?"

"So I've heard." I force myself to look into his eyes and just speak the truth. "I know of only one time it happened, Den, but it's a starting place. Please let me cover this."

"It's not going to bring your cousin back." He speaks softly, but his pale eyes don't give an inch.

"I know that, but it might help another woman, lots of other women."

"And if I don't give you the assignment?"

I don't answer. No need to mention that I've already tried contacting Bobby Warren.

"No response?"

I feel my lip quiver, try to fight it. "Nothing, I guess."

"You ever visit the Killer Body place here?"

"No. You?"

He pats the coarse fabric of his shirt. "Are you suggesting that I should?"

"Of course not. You know how I feel about those places, that one in particular."

"Want to take a run out there?"

That easily? He is giving me what I want this easily? I stand straighter, trying to look taller, and not too surprised. "Right now?"

"Why not?"

Damned Hamilton. Just when I think I can forget our short history, write him off as my only one-night stand, he does something nice, and then, I don't know what I want. But he's my boss now. He pretends that the night—that we—never happened, so I pretend, too.

"Den?"

"Yeah?"

My throat tightens, but the pain is farther down, deeper. What is wrong with me?

"Thank you." I turn toward the door before my tears can further embarrass either of us.

"You owe me lunch," he calls as I rush out of the office.

That's what I'd told him that one night we shared—that the next time, I'd buy lunch. Then he got a promotion, and our lunch never happened.

Because I can't deal with his comment, I pretend I didn't hear it.

"Bye," I shout, and let the door swoosh shut behind me.

Rochelle

Dr. Hauschka was one of her very best friends. It was a secret affair, of course. Sometimes, but not always, the secret ones were the best. This one was.

She carried him in the cell phone compartment of her bag for days like this, when she'd been doubting herself, feeling old and fat, and she love, love, loved him. She parked before the Santa Barbara condo she and Jesse had rented, and before she even checked her face in the mirror, she pulled out Dr. Hauschka's translucent makeup and began applying it to the backs of her hands. She'd called Jesse from the road to tell him about Julie Larimore, but he'd already heard.

Like magic, the bluish lines and smatterings of age

freckles blended into a monochromatic study in beige. *If your hands are young, you are young.* That's what Jesse always said. Truth: hands were the first to go. One day you look down, and there's your mom, the sad fingers, all those spots. Depending on your genes, the face follows, and then the butt. Or was it the other way around?

Jesse sat at a table in their room, his laptop flipped open, the television across from him playing without sound. She stopped even before she closed the door to admire him, his face tilted up from his task, the sun off the water reflected in his gray-black hair pulled back in a short ponytail. He was a man of extremes—hot looks, cold heart, easygoing outside, tough inner core—a man she had once loved with her life. And now? She couldn't bear to think about now.

"You talk to him?" That was the extent of his greeting.

"And then some."

A smile lit his eyes, then lingered, almost decadent. "Oh?"

"What do you want me to say? That one hand job later, I'm his spokesmodel?"

"Turn off the drama and trauma, okay? And close the door, if you don't mind."

She did as he instructed, then pulled up a chair on the other side of the table. "Bobbo did come up with an idea, Jesse. It might be good."

"Good how?"

"He can't just hand over Julie Larimore's job to me, especially now that she's—that she might be—"

"Dead?"

"Yeah. Dead."

He frowned at the screen of his laptop, keyed in a few more commands. "And so," he said, still clicking the keyboard, "since she might be dead, the old man's afraid to give you the job?"

"Not afraid, exactly. He cares about Julie. Her safety is his first priority."

"His profit margin is his first priority, and you know it."

"Don't take Bobbo for granted. He's not that easy to figure out. And he can be cagey."

"But he does have the hots for you. Even after all these years."

"That would bother most men."

He snapped off the computer and directed his gaze at her. "I trust you. Although when I think back, I don't know why I should."

"That was a long time ago, Jesse, before I ever knew you. Damn. It's bad enough that you try to control my present. Don't try to control my past, too."

He repeated the frown, this time directing it at her. "You seeing that shrink again? You always talk like this when you're seeing a shrink."

"I'll see anyone I fucking please."

"Little girl, talking big."

"Try me."

He stood, unzipped his pants. Oh, no. Not now. Not with what was going on, not with this battle in her mind. "I said he can't just hand the job to me. He has a better idea."

Jesse's hand stopped at his zipper. "Such as?"

"He thinks he should announce an open competition for spokesmodel for Killer Body, Inc. Invite pros and nonpros to enter. Then, after top media exposure, pick the new Killer Body."

"You?" Jesse shook his head as if trying to clear it of a dream that had suddenly become real.

"I hope me," she said.

"Of course it will be you. He's setting it up so that it will be you. You're going to be the next Julie Larimore, babe."

"I could be, yes. Not that I wish her any harm."

"You hate her guts, and you know it."

Hate? No, that wasn't the right emotion. She said it the way she hoped Julie would. "Whatever our personal differences, I hope she's okay. But I want this job. It's my chance to reinvent myself."

"You'll get it." He crooked his finger and rubbed the bulge in his pants. "Now, come to Papa."

Something stopped her. No, more than that, chilled her. She couldn't do this, not one more time.

"I might need a little space, honey."

He rolled his eyes. "The space cadet needs space."

"I am not a space cadet. I'm not stupid, Jesse."

"Whatever you say."

"I mean it."

"You too smart to get naked?"

"I'll get naked. Will you?"

"Fucking A." He began unbuttoning his shirt. "We can do it right here, on this great table."

She went to him, let him slide her down on the table. He stood, running his fingers beneath her. "You're skin and bones, but you still have a great ass," he said, beginning to knead it. "Maybe just a little on the fleshy side."

She jerked away from him. "My ass is perfect, and there's not a damn thing about me that's fleshy."

"Take it easy. I was just kidding. Hey, what are you doing?"

She pushed him away and swung off the table in one smooth gesture. "I'm out of the mood." Damn, she wanted a cigarette, but she couldn't do that. She could already detect tiny vertical lip lines when she pursed her mouth in the mirror.

"Baby, come here," Jesse called in a singsong voice.

"I need some exercise. I'm going to take a run on the beach." She dug through the open suitcase and pulled out a pair of white shorts.

"I'll give you some exercise."

"I mean it, Jesse."

"I was just kidding about your ass."

"That has nothing to do with it." Damn, he was irritating today. She put on the shorts against her smooth skin. Yes, it was still smooth where the tan abruptly went white. And there was nothing wrong with her ass.

"Then, come back here."

"Later."

She sat on the bed and started putting on her shoes. Jesse stood before her. "You're really sensitive about your looks lately."

"You'd be, too, if your looks were the way you made a living."

"Your looks *are* the way I make a living, but you don't see me all jittery."

"No, not jittery." Critical, she felt like saying, judging, but she wasn't sure about that. Maybe the insecurity she felt lately didn't come from Jesse but from within. A run on the beach, and she'd feel better. That's what she needed. Maybe skip dinner. She wasn't hungry, anyway. "I'm just tired," she said.

She looked up at the television set. Julie Larimore's photograph smiled back at her. It was a coy pose—head tilted, one arm crossed in front of her, blond-streaked hair lit from behind. The Killer Body pendant—a red-enameled woman's silhouette on a silver chain—hung from her neck. "This whole Julie Larimore thing has me freaked."

"It could be the best thing that ever happened to your career, so why do you care about her?"

"I don't know. She lived this perfect life. No scandals, no secrets, no enemies."

"Everyone in this business has enemies. Secrets, too."

Julie's face left the screen, and the television camera swept a tree-lined condominium complex. "That must be where she lived." A shiver fluttered through her.

Jesse reached for the remote and flicked the television off.

"Hey, I was watching that."

"I thought you wanted to go run." His gaze dropped ever so slightly. Checking out her ass, she'd bet on it. She stood abruptly and brushed past him on her way to the door. She could still see Julie Larimore's face, her barely there smile.

"How does someone just disappear in San Diego, of all places?"

"Stop being morbid." Jesse swatted her on the ass. "And try not to be so nervous. You'll get the job. The old man still digs you."

"We'll see Friday night. He's invited me to a party."

"So, we have to stay here until Friday?"

"I do."

"Maybe I'll go back to L.A. Unless you need me at the party."

He flipped on the television again, this time with sound.

"…no sign of a disturbance," the announcer said. "Larimore was believed to have been visiting friends in San Diego, according to her housekeeper."

Rochelle stopped, her hand on the doorknob.

"Jesse," she said. "Do you have a cigarette?"

The Interview

You and Rochelle McArthur are old friends, aren't you, Julie?

Indeed, we are. Rochelle knew me when, a whole lot of whens.

How do you feel about her as a spokesmodel for exercise equipment?

I'm thrilled for her, and I think Rochelle will get whatever she wants. She always has. I respect her drive.

Conversely, I don't know that I'd choose a youth-driven product such as exercise equipment. Plastic surgery, perhaps, breast augmentation, or any of the many areas that would inspire people in her age group might be an easier match.

Old friends? Right. Spokesmodel? Right. Exercise equipment? Even a small scrap of my job? Right, Rochelle. I'd die first.

Lucas

"You didn't."

Bobby W had been bleary-eyed since noon. Now he just sat in the boat's galley, sitting straight up as if he thought someone was photographing him.

"We have to go forward. She'd want us to do that."

"But a contest to replace a woman who might be dead, Bobby?"

The ocean between Santa Barbara and the Channel Islands never looked as luxuriant, never felt as endless. Ellen Horner had tried to invite herself along. Now

Lucas wondered if he should have included her. Somehow, he couldn't picture Ellen's perfect little black-and-white awning jacket awash with seawater. More than that, he needed to have a heart-to-heart with his boss.

Bobby W tried to stand, and the moment he did, a wave hit and he crashed back into his seat. He slammed his hand over his glass just in time.

"Bobby?"

"Keep the fuck away from me."

"I'm just trying to help."

"I don't need help." He pulled himself to his feet, and Lucas forced himself to stay put.

"Talk to me," he said.

"I'm talking."

"Then tell me how to explain to the media that we're replacing Julie less than a week after she disappeared."

"We're not replacing her. We're enhancing her. Tell them that."

"*Enhancing* is a euphemism," Lucas said. "The media will know that."

"Euphemism, huh?" His eyes, the part of him that had stayed miraculously young, lit from within. "That's why I have a smart, well-educated man such as yourself working for me, so that you can separate the euphemisms from the bullshit."

With that, Bobby navigated his way to the galley, where he kept his Killer Body supplements. His gait was stiff. Lucas winced in sympathy. Stubborn old bastard, but who could judge him? How easy is it for any man, especially one who has been a fitness legend, to admit to himself that walking would be less painful if he used a cane?

"Great stuff." Bobby began counting out the tablets and gel caps. "If you can't live longer, you can still live better. Are you taking yours?"

"Whenever I remember."

"Not good enough." The old lion's roar, familiar from all of those television commercials, was only slightly diluted by age and the sounds of the sea. "I don't have to tell you that good health should be your number-one priority."

"I know." He sighed. "So, what shall we tell the media, Bobby?"

"The truth." He looked up from the pills he was shaking into his palm, as if to say he was insulted to be asked.

"Which is?"

"That we're looking for a second spokesmodel to enhance, or whatever you want to call it, Julie's efforts in our weight-loss clinics. Someone to represent all we hope to achieve with the Ass Blaster." Bobby W gave him a look of disappointment, his eyes glistening.

"Why don't you just hire Rochelle and get it over with?"

"You don't have any idea why I'm really doing this, do you?"

"Apparently, I don't, so why don't you tell me?"

"Friday, my house." It was the voice he used when Lucas had gone too far, a voice he didn't use on anyone else, because when anyone else went too far, he simply fired them.

"Friday," he repeated. Then he placed the pills in his mouth and swallowed them with his bourbon and water.

FOUR

Gabriella

The princess always took the high road. It wasn't easy, but in matters of character, one had no choice.

This situation was especially embarrassing. Gabriella was grateful for her brown-tinted sunglasses—rimless and Ralph Lauren and *très chic*. But more important, right along with the UV protection came eye-contact protection, which she needed—at this moment, very much.

She had the damned dress in her hands, and it was perfect. How could the Killer Body people ignore her in patchwork and lace, so retro it made her want to break into tears for a past she'd never visited, except through clothes, of course?

Not to mention the bandanna. Damn, if she were a shoplifter, as many in her strata were, she'd stuff that two-hundred-plus-bucks baby right into her bra. But that wasn't the way she was raised.

That the shop girl was a fan made it worse. The girl had gushed through the sale of the marvelous dress, the bandanna, the cute little flip-flops with their silver buckles and stacked wood heels. Now her sunny face was a wall between the two of them. The princess knew there was a problem. She stood on the other side of the counter, head dipped slightly down to avoid eye contact, but in an aggressive stance in her crochet cardigan, camisole and jeans. She might be on the verge of up-chucking, but this one would never know it.

"There seems to be a problem with your credit card."

Oh, no. This was what she'd feared most, and now here it was, delivered to her on a tiny, black, rectangular platter. But the princess always took the high road.

"I can't imagine what the problem would be."

"It was declined."

Declined, such a polite word for what she was suffering. She'd made a payment, maybe not the full amount, but everything she had.

"I made some purchases earlier today. Perhaps I exceeded my limit. Can't you just add it to my hotel room bill."

The girl gave her an embarrassed smile; her slender fingers edged toward the wonderful dress, reclaiming it for someone with better credit. "I'm sorry. If it's declined here, it will be declined at the front desk, too."

"It will be fine by tomorrow. As I said, I probably just exceeded my limit."

"That's probably what happened." She drew the dress closer.

"I have other credit cards."

"I'd be happy to try one of them for you."

Try? Not *process.* More fear invaded, each rush more threatening than the last. She'd been honest about her life on national television. Had talked to Larry King and Edd Forrester, damn it. Why was this stopping her?

The answer came to her in the private part of her brain

that she reserved for herself and maybe two other people. *Because you haven't beaten the food thing yet. Because you were a bad wife. Because you don't have enough money to buy this dress that could make you the next Killer Body. Because you can't even afford a freaking olive-green bandanna.*

The shop girl, who of course, couldn't hear the voices, gave her the professional version of a droopy look, holding the bad plastic between two manicured fingers.

Gabriella yanked it back, shoved it in her bag.

"I'm sorry," she said. "It's obviously a foul-up with my husband. Would you give me a moment to get my driver?"

"Of course."

Gabriella went out to the lobby to get Christopher and dragged him back in before any of the greedy shoppers could as much as spot her dress. The dress would be hers now. It would transform her, maybe even make her look as if she had boobs. Bobby Warren was supposed to be a boob man. She hoped he discriminated between real and fake ones. If he did, Rochelle McArthur wouldn't be in the running.

Christopher was at his Banana Republic best, his body reflecting his hours obsessing at the gym. His tan was baked on, and his exposed flesh, from his arms to his shaved head, simply glowed.

"My credit card isn't working," she said. "That's all I need."

"Don't worry."

The shop girl let the dress she was in the process of removing slip back onto the counter when she saw him. Christopher had that effect on people.

"I'll take Princess Gabby's parcels," he said.

"But—"

Parcels! Gabriella hid a smile. He'd learned the term when he'd been her real driver back when she could afford to pay him. He whipped out his wallet and shuffled through his own credit cards like a magician. "You can use mine for now." He glanced at the dress. "Very nice. You're taking the bandanna, too, of course."

Gabriella nodded. Poor guy. He'd just spent more than he earned in two weeks.

"If there are angels on earth, you are truly one of them," she said as they left the store.

"That's because all the homophobes are in heaven."

"They can have it," she said. "I'll pay you back as soon as I can. I should be getting some money from Alain next week."

Christopher frowned. "Don't worry about that. You'll be gorgeous for the Killer Body party. That's all that really matters."

"Thank you for knowing that. It's one of the reasons I love you." She started to kiss his cheek, then noticed a woman standing outside the store, holding a notebook.

"Gabriella Paquette?" An autograph-seeker. And absolutely charming. Life wasn't so dismal, after all. It would probably be rude to tell her she preferred to be called Princess Gabby.

The woman, younger than she, was a lovely little thing, with fine bones, short-cropped strawberry-blond hair and large blue eyes. Still nervous, that was all Gabriella could see—the long neck, the prominent collarbones above the black top and lacy traces of a blouse beneath it.

"Hello," she said, and reached for the book to sign it. "I'll need to know your name."

"Rikki Fitzpatrick, *Valley Voice* newspaper." She held fast to the notebook, and Gabriella felt a flush warm her cheeks.

"So, you're not…"

"I'm a reporter." Her voice stopped just short of a drawl.

Christopher stepped forward. Goodness, what would she do without him to look after her? "Then don't pretend to be looking for an autograph."

"I wasn't pretending to be anything I'm not."

"Princess Gabby doesn't give interviews unless they're prearranged."

"*Princess* Gabby?" The reporter's lip twitched, and Gabriella caught a hardness in her eyes she'd missed before. "Weren't you born in Texas?"

"I am a princess," Gabriella said. "You don't lose those titles because of domestic changes."

"Such as divorce?" The reporter asked it as she scribbled something in her notebook. Gabriella had dealt with her type before. The best approach was openness, honesty. That's what tamed the press. They absolutely adored candor.

"Yes, I was born in Texas, and yes, I'm separated from my husband. Is there anything else you'd like to know?"

"Why do you want to be the next Killer Body?"

The question stunned her, partially because of the way the reporter's eyes went from inquiring to fiery. "Considering the problems in my own life, the weight issues with which I've had to deal, I'd say I'm a natural candidate, wouldn't you?"

"Some say it's because you're trying to get your own talk show."

Christopher touched her arm.

"It's all right," Gabriella said. "In fact, it's a good question." The reporter didn't smile. "It's a darned good question," Gabriella continued. "I've come forward about my own problems."

"Such as the photographs taken of you when you were married and having an affair with one of your husband's friends?"

She'd heard this before, and she knew how to respond. Open. Honest. "Just so you know, they were barely acquainted, and my husband and I were having some pretty major problems. If anything would motivate you to lose weight, it would be seeing photos like that and having the press dub you Flabby Gabby." She paused, then remembered something else she'd never before said, wondering if she should just go for it. Why not?

"You know something else?" she asked. "I felt beautiful when those damning photographs were taken. I felt loved, and wonderful, and all of the things a woman must feel to take off her clothes in front of a man. When I saw what I really looked like, what he must have seen, I saw only ugly, and I resolved to change my life."

"And to get your own talk show?"

What could make anyone so young this embittered? "You don't get me," she said. "Do you? You think I'm an opportunist, when it's quite the contrary, really. I want to help other women, motivate them to change their lives as I have."

"How did you find her?" Christopher demanded. "Do you just follow people around so you can accost them?"

The reporter's cheeks colored. "The desk clerk said you'd asked if there was a boutique on the premises. I thought I'd take a chance. I'm interviewing all of the candidates for Killer Body."

"I'd be happy to give you an interview," Gabriella said, "but not out here on the street."

"Shall I meet you back in the lobby?"

She didn't like the reporter's attitude, but an interview was an interview. And the *Voice* was a major daily, San Joaquin Valley or not. "Around three o'clock?" she asked. "I have some other errands."

"Three is fine."

"Not very friendly, is she?" Christopher asked as the reporter strode away. "Quite a chip on her shoulder, I'd say. You'll melt it, though. You always do."

Standing out there in the chilly air, Gabriella found herself starting to tremble, and all of the old fears seemed to be crashing in on her. How stupid must she have looked to that shop girl, standing there with that credit card, trying to lie her way out of a situation the girl witnessed on a daily basis?

"Christopher?"

"It's okay."

He opened the car door for her, and she slid into the back seat, hugging the shopping bag to her. "I feel damned sheepish letting you continue to drive me around," she said. "Now that I can't pay you."

"Forget it. We're friends. I'll drive you anywhere you want to go, anytime you want to go there. Now, where to?"

It had been a hellish afternoon, and the prospect of the reporter wasn't wonderful, either. "You know. Don't make me say it."

"Oh, Gabby. Do you really want to do that to yourself?"

"Only once this week, so far. Come on. I'll treat you."

"I wouldn't touch the stuff."

He did agree to a burger, though. They ate in the car, he in front with his burger, she in back with her fries and Frostie. Christopher handed her the bottle of Baileys she kept in the glove box, and she poured a little over the Frostie before she dipped her fries.

Christopher shuddered and shielded his eyes with his hand. "I can't even bear to watch this."

"Sweet and cold. Hot and salty. And alcoholic." She dipped another fry, loving the hot, greasy feel of it in her fingers, anticipating the chilling relief. "It's everything good. The ultimate comfort food."

Gabby was glad she had enough in her purse to buy lunch. Christopher refused. She insisted. The princess always took the high road.

The Interview

Do you think you were harsh regarding Gabriella Paquette?

I'm the last person in the world to pass judgment on anyone. I've thought a great deal about those comments, and I have to say that I can't answer yours or anyone's questions with less than the truth.

Princess Gabby used poor judgment. We've all used poor judgment. I can't imagine the horror she must have felt seeing those damning, grotesque photographs in the tabloids, and I commend her honesty with the media, her take-charge attitude toward her weight. *Flabby Gabby* was a cruel label, true. The press is good at punchy, honest prose, and I don't think their cruelty is necessarily personal.

My heart goes out to her husband, however. Prince Alain had to see those photos, as well. How will he ever forget the sight of his wife romping in nothing but a tiny thong, on his own estate, no less, with the man he considered his friend? How much comfort can it give him that her candor and weight loss have won her a following, of sorts, on talk shows?

Was I too hard on Gabriella Paquette? Was I? No more so than I'd be on myself.

FIVE

Tania Marie

Word of the day: *Ugsome:* Frightful, loathsome

They chased her again. They were always fucking chasing her. Cameras, voices attached to tape recorders. She'd wanted the limelight once, and now she was being punished for that, for everything, especially for what happened with Marshall. Why was the woman always the bitch and the man the saint? She was the one who'd lost her job. He was still America's most trusted newscaster.

She'd hoped she could slip through the gates of this Mission Canyon place for what old Mr. Warren promised was going to be a private party.

It didn't feel private. It felt like the usual. How long and how hard did you have to pay for loving the wrong man?

And what about her clothes? The white silk vest under her matching jacket was just low enough to reveal an intriguing glimpse of her only decent attribute. Pants were in right now—black and white—black on the butt, white on the boobs. *Oh, God, please let me still have boobs. And diminish the butt while you're at it, God, if you're at all in a charitable mood.*

She made sure the black silk pants covered the shamrock tattoo on her ankle. Every time she looked at the damned tattoo, she remembered Marshall's lips on it.

She'd never get to the party before the media caught up with her. Never. She slid her fingers into the side pocket of her bag, shoving the foil-wrapped stash of chocolate chips out of the way. What the frigging hell did women do before they were able to carry their phones with them?

Mr. Warren answered himself. That surprised her.

"It's me. Tania Marie Camp. The press is everywhere."

"You poor child. They must be dogging you."

"They are, kind of."

"I'll have the guard lift the gate. You go through. If they try, they'll be stopped right there."

She pressed the phone against her ear. He sounded like a kind man, kind enough to give her a chance, she hoped. At least he'd been willing to talk to her press agent. Nobody else had. "Thank you, Mr. Warren. I can't wait until I meet you in person."

"Any lady with your track record is a friend of mine."

That didn't settle too well. "Listen," she said. "I know Marshall Cameron claimed I was a psycho when we got caught, but I'm not a psycho, okay?"

"If he allowed that to happen—" Mr. Warren's voice rasped as if he were already defending her honor "—the gentleman deserves whatever he gets."

"I agree."

"You'll be safe here. I'll meet you at the gate, sweetheart."

She looked behind her—at the cars and vans, everyone who wanted to link her to Marshall Cameron, the love of her life, the reason she no longer had even a lowly job in television.

"I'll be there right away." She forced herself to turn off the movie channel of memories and tend to the task at hand. "Just have them shut it fast, okay?"

The Interview

You called Tania Marie Camp a scheming manipulator, did you not? How do you feel now that she's joined the Killer Body family?

What I meant to say was that this is a young woman who told everyone from her mother to her hairdresser that she was going to marry an already-married newscaster who personifies public trust and integrity.

Now, because Marshall Cameron's housekeeper told the press she discovered them in bed together, Tania Marie Camp is humiliated, and Marshall Cameron and his wife are even closer than before.

Scheming manipulator? I don't recall saying anything that insensitive. I sincerely hope Tania Marie's acceptance of the Killer Body program is genuine and that it will help her to control her yo-yoing weight. A yo-yo is either tightly wound or all the way down, and we can't live rewarding lives when we're always in such destructive motion.

I hope I've addressed that topic once and for all. Next question?

How do I feel now that Tania Marie Camp has joined the Killer Body family? My family? If you only knew.

Rikki

Lisa would have loved this room and its glass, its treetop views.

I hate it.

Most of all, I hate the posters of Julie Larimore that have been situated among the priceless art.

Lisa would memorize how these people are dressed in this historic home, and she'd try to replicate it. She'd look across this room and see Princess Gabby, and her cleavage-skimming dress of patchwork and lace, her retro olive-green bandanna gathering the loose dishwater-blond curls that fall to her bare shoulders.

And what would Lisa think of Rochelle? Would she see the tight, yet tired lines around her lips? Would she feel a compassion I cannot quite muster? Would she smell the spiraling scent of despair?

Rochelle's dress is sexy, though, although trashier than Gabby's love-child ensemble. It both conceals and reveals Rochelle's age in a parchment-colored crochet. The front ruffles of its matching duster fall gracefully around a body that still refuses to quit, the top part, especially.

I've played it safe in my jeans, a soft lavender shell and a violet suede coat Lisa bought me at Christmas. Our last Christmas. I'm a reporter, not a contender, and I can dress any way I damn well please.

I slip into the room, unnoticed, and I just stand there at the bar, grabbing a drink I don't want, some kind of liqueur that, although it tastes like rotten peaches, won't matter the moment it numbs me into a less painful state than this.

My interview with Princess Gabby yesterday didn't

reveal anything that wasn't in the press kit. I'd come on
too strong, and she appeared to be rattled, distracted.

I look around and realize that, for all its elegance, this
is an old man's home, a home maintained by paid help.
If it were not for the paintings, which may or may not
be real, and the sweeping view of the city below, it
could be one of the sprawling farmhouses that dotted
the central California valley where I was raised.

For a quiet gathering, which Bobby Warren's marketing man told me this was going to be, there's plenty
of noise, most of it coming from a frenetic African-
American man at a baby grand. He has a strong, Broad-
way kind of voice, enough to attract the attention away
from the tiny knots of conversation sprouting up around
him.

A good-looking man with too-short dark hair and a
New York-formal suit stands with a winsome blonde by
the door to the balcony. They appear in unsmiling conversation with Robert Warren—Bobby W to his friends,
and he appears to have many of them. He also appears
to have aged since the last time I saw him on television.

Rochelle McArthur slides next to the piano man.
Damn, I hope she's not going to sing. Maybe not.
Maybe she's just flirting with him. Her husband-slash-
agent seems to be hitting it off just fine with Princess
Gabby.

Behind me, I hear Gabby telling him and two other
men about a play she saw last week in Pasadena.

"It's *so* California," she says in her accent without a
country, and I wonder where the hell the lady in the
most California patchwork-quilt ensemble this side of
Rodeo Drive thinks she is.

I hold in my rage, grateful for anonymity and whatever I'm imbibing, which has slowly become friendlier

to my palate and my brain. I'm thinking I'm safely incognito, trying to continue my eavesdropping. Then someone grabs my arm.

"You're the reporter, aren't you?"

I turn around and just cannot believe the childlike face shining up into mine. In spite of the cobalt-blue John Lennon glasses, the short, heavily gelled black-cherry flip, and the baby bangs that had to be cut with two fingers above her eyebrow, this chubby little thing is so innocent-looking that she almost glows.

"Tania Marie?" That's who this creature in the flowing black silk pants and white jacket and vest must be. Tania Marie, the honey bee. Marshall Cameron's nickname for her was almost as embarrassing as her confiding the fact to too many people she thought she could trust. How the hell did she get in here, and what is she trying to prove? "How can I help you?" I manage to ask.

"You're writing about all of us, aren't you?"

"All of who?" No, it can't be. Killer Body, Inc. couldn't be so cruel as to make this poor baby believe she has a chance against the others.

"Well, *us*. Bobby Warren's picks."

"You're in the running for Killer Body's spokesmodel position?"

She takes off the glasses and nails me with her cool blue-green gaze. "Why wouldn't I be?"

"Good question. I was just—"

"I know what you were *just*. I don't know how you media people sleep at night, you know that?"

You don't sleep at night when your cousin drops dead, when your aunt, the woman who raised you, more or less demands that you find out why. You don't sleep at all.

I could tell Tania Marie all of that and more, including how rotten I feel about the way I tore into Princess Gabby. But I am not sure if I can say it without tears. And besides, Tania Marie is a documented bimbo, a psycho chick who tried to bring down one of the most respected news commentators in the country. What can she ever understand about anything?

I dig up my reporter voice from the attic of my mind. "I am just a little surprised. And, yes, I do hope to interview the finalists for Julie Larimore's job."

"It's not *her* job."

"No one's clarified that for me."

"It's just not." Her gaze holds mine then drifts, bouncing over my shoulder, past me, for anyone to rescue her. "Not one of us wants anything that belongs to Julie. But there's room for more than one Killer Body on the planet." She smooths limp white hands down her shantung-covered hips, as if hoping her touch will melt away the fat there.

"What do you think it takes to be a Killer Body, Tania Marie?"

"Passionate desire. That's more important than anything, the passion." I've already gotten down her answer when she slams her hand over her mouth. "You know what I mean about desire, not that it's sexual or anything. *Drive* is probably closer to what I meant to say."

"Drive?"

"Yes. To be the best. And Killer Body is the best. It helps people metamorphosis."

She has a difficult time getting the word out, but once she does, she pats her short, spiked flip and flashes me a jittery smile.

"So your weight—" I pause, not even sure I can be this cruel. "You're not concerned that your body type will be a factor in the final decision?"

"Put away your fucking notebook, lady."

I try to raise a questioning eyebrow, but I can't say that I don't understand her anger. "I wish I could do that, Tania Marie, but I can't."

"You don't wish shit." Tears streak her powdered face. "You just want good copy. That's what you media bastards call it, right? You don't care about me, and you don't even care about Julie Larimore."

"Do you?" I shoot back.

"Damned right I do." A handsome server approaches us, shaved head, starched jacket, big-time attitude. His tray of drinks glistens. Tania Marie grabs for a crystal stem. "You take one, too, just so I don't feel so guilty."

"Sounds like a good idea to me." I lift a flute that twinkles like a baby lava lamp with what looks like champagne. The taste confirms my guess. It's not my usual bottled Fiji water, but it will get the job done.

I study the waiter's name tag. "Thank you, Christopher," I say, then look again at his face, more closely this time. Before I can ask if we've met, he moves away.

"Who is he?" I ask her.

"Beats the hell out of me." Tania Marie makes short work of the flute. When she sees that I'm watching her, she adds, "Booze isn't my thing. I just have to numb myself somehow. I'm scared shitless."

My hand creeps into my shoulder bag for the notebook.

"Why?"

"You think I'd tell you?" Her voice rises, probably in proportion to the amount of alcohol she's just inhaled. "I know about you."

"No, you don't."

"Yes, I do. I have a Ph.D. in media, lady. And I learned it the hard way."

My itching fingers can't help themselves. I attack the notebook, scratching down every word.

"I'm sorry," I say, "but this story is important to me. I'm not trying to hurt you."

"The hell you're not." She wraps her sad white jacket around her, as if trying to squeeze off inches from her formidable shape. Not an unattractive woman, I think, in spite of the newspaper cartoons that make a caricature of her short legs and chipmunk cheeks. I begin to see what might have attracted Marshall Cameron to her.

"Do you know Julie? Have you met her?" She waves a fist at the poster. "You're trying to stir up all of this shit, and you don't even know her, do you? You have no idea what she's been through. You're just trying to ruin her life."

I move closer to the poster, tuning out Tania Marie as I study the pose, arms crossed, brown hair streaked blond—the same as Lisa's had been. The tank dress, with its wide belt at the hip is identical to one Lisa wore frequently. The ensemble, the Killer Body uniform, even has the same side slit, the same ankle-high boots. And that red pendant that is supposedly modeled after Julie Larimore's body; Lisa had one just like it. As I look at her there on the poster, I realize that Julie Larimore could have *been* my cousin.

And my cousin had wanted to *be* Julie Larimore. Why didn't I ever realize it before? And when had it begun? Before she joined Killer Body? After she'd been promised the possibility of a television commercial?

Tania Marie has run down, like a clock.

"Not fair," she finishes.

I try to reverse my spiraling emotions, pull away from the pain. I have a job to do. "How well do you know Julie?" I ask.

"We've met." She crooks her finger at the champagne server, who leaves Princess Gabby's side, almost reluctantly, I think.

Tania Marie's features are far more refined than they appear on television, her lip color a pinky-brown blend that matches the subtle blush on her cheeks. It's a little-girl look—kooky with the spiked-up flip and baby bangs, for sure—but this woman is not the psycho she's reputed to be. For a moment, I feel almost sorry for her, but I remember my promise to Aunt Carey.

"Are you and Julie friends?"

"Everyone's Julie's friend." A prim smile. She gives me a blank, vague look. The waiter approaches with his tray. Her arm shoots out. The tray moves toward me. I decline.

"What do you think happened to her?"

Her exaggerated grin doesn't erase the fear in her eyes. "Julie's always been loyal to Bobby W. I know she wouldn't do anything to harm the Killer Body family."

Killer Body family. The wrong combination of words said to the wrong person, a person whose family is one person less, possibly because of someone at Killer Body.

I swallow my anger and ask, "So, you don't think she just took off?"

"Of course not. She's not like that."

"But she's missing. Gone. How do you know her, anyway?"

Tania Marie gulps down the rest of the glass. For someone who claims alcohol isn't her thing, she is demonstrating an amazing capacity.

"What business is it of yours?"

I swallow a little liquid fuel of my own. "Everything about this story is my business. I don't want to hurt you or anyone else, but I have to know the facts."

I expect her to flip me off. Instead, I can see from her eyes that she buys it. I start to feel guilty again, start to question what I believe about the whole Marshall Cameron/Tania Marie Camp scandal.

"It's personal. But what happened—it made us close, in a way."

My fingers tingle, but I don't dare try to write this down or do anything else to derail her fragile thought process. "You met through Killer Body?"

"No." Innocent little-girl eyes, eyelashes like gold-tipped black spikes. "That's all I'm going to say. Can I go now? I'm supposed to meet my bodyguard here."

She is asking me for permission to leave. A nause-ating wave of guilt damned near fells me. "I didn't know you had a bodyguard," I say, a bit too shakily.

"Virginia, my mom, just hired him. I don't even know where he is. The whole thing is ridiculous, but if you knew Virginia, you'd understand that some things you just don't argue." She shrugs, feigning more hap-piness than either of us can possibly stomach at this mo-ment. "Let me know if you see a short guy in cowboy boots walking around. I hate short men, don't you?"

That strained, breathless tone in her voice makes me feel put off, as if she's asking about the bodyguard to distract me.

"Must be tough for you having a famous chef for a mom," I say.

She tosses her head. Her gelled hair doesn't move. "Virginia's cool."

"Do you always call her by her first name?"

"Doesn't everybody?"

I get the point. Virginia Camp, like Oprah, Elvis, Madonna and God, doesn't need a last name. Icons sel-dom do.

"This guard of yours—does he work full-time for your mother, or is this a special assignment?"

She shoves her hands, champagne flute and all, to her hips, and I can see the true, top-heavy form the expensive ensemble almost conceals. It isn't pretty, and witnessing it doesn't make me feel any better about myself.

"He works at her San Francisco restaurant, okay? I don't even know the man, and I don't need him or anyone else for backup."

"What's he supposed to do, exactly?"

She gives me a bleached-white grin—good, even teeth—reproach, maybe even disappointment, in her eyes and voice.

"Protect me from people like you, for starters." With that, she turns her back on me and disappears into the body-to-body crowd. I get the feeling she's fighting tears, and it bothers me more than it should. For a moment, I wish I could run after her, take her arm and tell her to get the hell away from Killer Body. But I'm a reporter on assignment, a reporter who's promised her aunt she'll uncover the truth. And I will.

The woman walking away from me has been exploited by the media more flagrantly than anyone in a long time, but I don't dare allow myself to dwell on that now. Tania Marie is a source. That's all she can be.

SIX

Rikki

Once Tania Marie stalks off, the room is mine. I check out Bobby Warren, who has left the good-looking couple and is involved in an intense conversation with Rochelle McArthur.

He's tall, craggy and older than he appears—surprise, surprise—in the Killer Body literature. His hair is a brittle gray pressed flat to his head. His posture is as attention-getting as Princess Gabby's, only on him, it looks natural. Although his attention is focused on Rochelle, he stands like a Thoroughbred in the winner's circle. Yet this Thoroughbred is not aware that the prizes have already been given out and that the crowd left for home years ago. Nor is he aware of the muscles that no longer ripple to attention and the spread beneath his shirt that, like a snowball gathering speed will very soon, if it isn't already, mushroom into a potbelly.

He stands, caught in a memory of what he was, looking into Rochelle's smile for a reflection of it. Only in his dark eyes do I see a trace of what, many years ago, made him Mr. Universe and drew the country's attention, much as Schwarzenegger did later, to what could be accomplished by weight training.

As they talk, I can see the hard points of Rochelle's nipples poking through her crocheted dress. She cannot possibly dig this old man. She *can't*. She must be a better actress than I guessed.

"Excuse me," I say.

Bobby Warren gives me a bright-eyed smile. "I don't believe we've met."

"I was cleared through your marketing people."

"I'll have to speak to Luke." He takes my hand and draws me closer to him, as if trying to read my name tag. Only I'm not wearing one. "Luke knows I like to be alerted when there are lovely ladies on the premises. I trust you've met Shelly."

"I spoke with her husband briefly." I glance around for Jesse and spot him across the room, captivated by something Princess Gabby is saying. Rochelle sees him, too.

"What is it about royalty?" She shakes her head and turns to Bobby Warren for an answer. Her scent is as strong and overpowering as her voice. I feel it is covering something; I can detect another scent beneath it— cigarette smoke, I'd bet.

"It has its charm," the old man says.

"How else could someone with nothing but a phony accent get invited to every talk show in the country?"

"You surely don't mean Princess Gabby?" Bobby Warren throws her a look of chastisement, although his voice remains friendly. "Gabby's a wonderful talk show guest, so refreshing and honest about her past difficulties."

"I heard she's trying to get her own show," I say, hoping to stir up Rochelle once more.

"And if she's lucky, she just might. I certainly hope so," Warren replies.

"No question that she's lucky." Now Rochelle's husband is laughing at something the princess has said. Rochelle turns her back on the scene.

"A major reason she'd want to be the Killer Body spokesmodel?" I ask.

Rochelle nails me with an emerald-green gaze that matches the stones around her neck. Contacts, for sure—not just a subtle tint but blatant color, as fake and in-your-face as her jewelry. "Who are you, anyway?"

I tell her my name, including my famous last name, the name that got me in the door: *Valley Voice* newspaper, Pleasant View, California.

"You've invited a reporter to take part in this?" she asks the old man.

He stands even taller, his smile—in spite of his age—all John Wayne and Gregory Peck, a man who can make you believe that he's one of the good guys, and that, whatever happens, anything he does is okay.

"Absolutely. It's a major undertaking for Killer Body, and we welcome the media's interest and support."

Rochelle takes his arm. "We need to talk, Bobbo."

"Of course. But first I need to greet some of our other guests. I'm afraid I've been monopolizing you, dear Shelly." In spite of his tenderness, there is something dismissive in his tone that neither of us misses.

He drifts off in the direction of Tania Marie, leaving the two of us facing each other. Rochelle glances over at her husband again, then back at me, and I feel as if she's trying to decide which is the lesser of two evils.

"Why do you want to be the Killer Body spokesmodel?" I ask.

"Is this on the record?"

"Always."

"Then, let's just say that I respect the way Mr. Warren runs the company, and I want to serve as motivation to the many who have been helped, as I have, by the Killer Body program and the fine example set by Julie Larimore."

I grind my teeth and don't even bother reaching for my notebook.

"Do you know Julie?"

"I haven't seen her in years."

"But you have met?"

"Yes. Actually, I introduced her to Mr. Warren, so in a way, I was responsible for her getting the job."

"You didn't want it?"

"Heavens, no. I was involved in my film career."

"That would have been six, seven years ago, right?"

"The show's only been off for three."

She doesn't say more. We both know what that can mean to a woman in Hollywood.

A server with a tray of appetizers approaches. This is definitely Killer Body food—not even a morsel of anything fried or salted in the lot. Lox comes closest, a smidgeon of it dotted with capers and resting on a small bleached wafer.

I reach for it, Rochelle shakes her head, and the server moves on. "Mr. Warren must have picked the menu," I say.

"Oh, yes. Mr. Warren's a one-man show. Absolutely amazing. Don't you love, love, love him?"

"And you can say you knew him when, right?"

"Well, his *when* goes back way further than mine. He was already a success by the time we met." She signals the waiter. "At least he allows booze at his parties."

"But not cigarettes?"

"Never." She frowns. "You're not a smoker, are you?"

"No."

"I didn't think so. Your complexion—" She lets her words trail off and absently brushes her fingertips across her own face.

The waiter appears with a full tray. This time I recognize him. He lit into me earlier in the week when I'd waylaid the princess outside the hotel boutique.

"You get around," I say, reaching for a glass.

"You, too."

"From chauffeur to waiter?"

He gives me a fey smile. "It's been done. Last I heard, it was called moonlighting."

"Me, too."

Before I can say more, he turns and moves to the next group of people, leaving me with unspoken questions about why he would just happen to be moonlighting at this party.

Tania Marie

Word of the day: *Tartarian*: Of or relating to Tartarus; infernal

No matter how busy she was, she always checked her computer, right after her e-mail, for the Word of the Day. It was the only thing she still shared with Marshall. He'd gotten her in the habit; building his vocabulary was a compulsion with him. What was today's word? They hadn't been good ones lately, and this one had something to do with hell.

She was living it right now. Not a damned piece of

meat in the whole place. If she looked at another tofu roll, she'd have to tear the chocolate chips out of her purse and down the whole bag right here in front of God and everyone.

Tartarian. That was the word. A place in Hades where the worst souls did time. Now it just reminded her of the raw steak Virginia served at the restaurant—filet ground up with raw red onions and spread on toast. Damn, she could gobble it by the fistful right now. Instead she followed Mr. Warren onto the balcony and joined him at the table. He carried a glass, but there wasn't a smidgeon of food in sight. Before them, the lights of Santa Barbara twinkled.

"I'm glad you came tonight, so pleased."

From the way he slurred the words, she knew he'd hit the sauce hard enough that he wouldn't be thinking about food.

She sucked in her stomach, pulled back her shoulders, praying she didn't look fat. "Thank you for inviting me. I love Killer Body. I sure hope this works out."

"And Killer Body loves you." Icy fingers dug into her left thigh. Mr. Warren didn't as much as look at her. She knew her spongy flesh felt like mush in his hand and tried to contract the muscle. Tears threatened to spill down her face. Humiliation. That's what her life was now.

"I could do a good job," she said. "I'm working really hard."

"That takes courage, especially considering what you've been through." The fingers softened but stayed locked in the death grip.

"I know I can rebuild my image."

"*And* your weight. You're looking trimmer."

"Killer Body's really helping," she lied. He didn't

need to know she'd been visiting another center, paying next to nothing, yet she hadn't eaten a bag of Milanos for at least a month.

Mr. Warren squeezed her again. "If you work the program, the program will work for you. That line was my idea, you know."

She wanted to cry. She wanted to eat. Most of all, she just wanted out of here, where she was the laugh of the night.

"It's very catchy," she said.

Just then, the French doors opened and the server stepped out.

"I hope I'm not interrupting anything, Bobby, but there's been a delivery—from Julie Larimore."

Mr. Warren shot up from his seat. "From Jules? Is she here?"

"No. She had something delivered to you."

"I knew it. I knew she couldn't stay quiet for long." He darted through the door as if she weren't even there. Tania Marie followed.

A deliveryman stood just inside the door to the main room, holding one of those padded mailers. Whatever she was sending, it couldn't be much. For some reason, that gave Tania Marie comfort.

The rest of the group continued to laugh and talk, all except for the reporter, who caught sight of what was going on and turned from her conversation with Rochelle.

Mr. Warren grabbed the package from the messenger and directed someone to show him out.

"It's her handwriting," he said to Tania Marie. "You see, I told you." She wasn't certain he'd told her anything.

"I'm glad," she said. "Glad she's all right, honest, Mr. Warren."

He yanked open the packet, dark eyes glittering with anticipation. At first Tania Marie thought it was a packet of papers, but no. It was fabric of some kind. Black fabric.

"What the hell?"

Mr. Warren gathered the material into his hands, letting the envelope fall away. It was a dress, long and black and split up the side. No, not just split. Ripped. Torn. Somebody had slashed Julie's Killer Body dress to ribbons.

"No." Mr. Warren held the dress away from him, and then he had no words left, only his anguished moan filling the now-silent cavern of a room. Then, someone—the reporter—cried out, as well.

Rikki

Seeing that dress, so similar to Lisa's that it could have been the same one, almost topples me. As everyone in the room rushes toward Bobby Warren like a human wave, I cry out, unable to move.

The next thing I know, someone grabs my arm.

"Are you okay?"

I nod up at the tall man in a sport coat and glasses, the one I saw earlier with the well-built blonde in the conservative black suit. "I'm fine."

"I'll be right back. You stay with her, Ellen," he says to the blonde. And he is gone, weaving through the bodies, to Bobby Warren. His face is familiar, almost too handsome, the dark-rimmed glasses like a prop, his voice the type that is used to giving orders.

I know, even in this blurry moment, that it was he who made it possible for me to be here. Lucas Morrison, Bobby Warren's marketing director. I'd expected

older. I'd expected sleazier. I'd expected longer hair
and short sleeves and gold chains and paunch—in short,
a younger version of Bobby Warren. I hadn't expected
Brooks Brothers with muscles. I sure hadn't expected
sex appeal.

I turn to the woman he called Ellen. She's trying to
evaluate my situation.

"I really am okay."

"You're sure?" she asks in an unconvinced voice.

I nod and fake a smile, my skin still clammy. "Yes.
It was just a shock."

"I know," she says. "Now, I've got to go check on Mr.
Warren."

She gives me a quick once-over, followed by a
look that says I pass inspection. Then she, too, works
her way through the people separating her from the
old man.

Now, hours later, Ellen brings me another glass of
water. I'm sharing a table with Lucas on the balcony.
She asks him if he'd like one more Corona.

"I'm fine," he says. "Why don't you sit down?"

"I'd like to go home, if that's all right. I can't get
Bobby to eat anything. He doesn't look well."

"Go, and take your time coming in tomorrow."

"I just want Bobby to be okay." She shudders. "You
need to get him to rest, Lucas. You know how tenuous
his health is."

He gives her a sharp look. "He's fine. He's just tired."

"I just meant he's already upset. He doesn't need
this. And what did you make of Rochelle McArthur's
little display of emotion? I just hope the poor man
knows that she's milking this whole deal before we
have a chance to as much as hear from Julie."

"We can talk about it later." Lucas looks from her to

me, reminding her again with his eyes what I do for a living.

"Sure. Sorry. See you later." And she scampers off to wherever good little children who work for Killer Body go after they've served their purpose for the day.

Lucas and I sit breathing the late-night air from the balcony, where I blatantly hammered out the story on my laptop and e-mailed it to Hamilton at the *Voice*.

Lucas tried to intercede, but Bobby Warren, back in charge, said, "No. Leave the little girl be. Someone's going to write it. Might as well be her."

The air between Lucas and me has been charged with animosity that would probably have exploded by now into a full-blown argument, if we weren't still both so numb from what we witnessed tonight.

Bobby Warren joins us on the balcony now, his posture perfect, his taupe fleece jacket zipped up around his sharply boned, still-handsome face.

"Ellen went on home," he says, and pulls out a chair from the table where we sit. "She wants you to call her later on, let her know how I am." His hoarse chuckle is buried in a wavering voice. "I told her I'll be fine."

"You *will* be fine," Lucas says.

"How can you be so sure, after what happened tonight? You didn't have to touch that dress, didn't have to feel it."

As he moves closer, I can see that the color is drained from his cheeks. It's clear Lucas is concerned, no, more than that—genuinely worried about him.

"You need something to eat, Bobby W."

"A cocktail will be fine."

"You haven't touched your last one."

He looks down at the weathered teakwood table, chuckles. "Now, that's a first." He turns to me. "I had to call the police. That doesn't mean I think a crime's been committed."

"You did the right thing," Lucas says.

"That dress." The old man runs his hands through his hair. "It still smelled like her. That wonderful perfume, like baby powder. Oh, God."

"Bobby, don't."

He takes away his hands. Tears smear his face.

Lisa also wore a baby-powder scent. I can barely speak, but I try. "It could be some kind of prank," I say, although I can't imagine why someone would want to play a trick of this magnitude on anyone.

When Warren returns to the bar, to "freshen" his drink, as he puts it, Lucas asks if he can get me anything.

"I need to be going," I say.

"You live in Santa Barbara?"

"I'm staying here while I cover the story."

"Which story?"

Narrowed eyes behind the glasses. Noncommittal voice.

"The only story."

"Julie's disappearance?"

"For sure."

"Or the new candidates for Killer Body spokesmodel."

"Both."

"About Julie." He pauses as if not sure how to continue. "This is really hard on Bobby W. At his age, he doesn't need any more heartaches."

"There've been others?"

"His life hasn't been easy. Julie's like a daughter to him."

"I'm just writing articles," I say. "I can't change the

facts. And daughter or no daughter, he sure couldn't wait to run out and replace her."

"He doesn't see it that way." Lucas shifts in his chair, and in the dim light from the room that was once full of party and people, I can see him changing his approach. "One thing perhaps you can clarify for me. Why is a central California newspaper so interested in this story?"

I feel myself tense, but I don't make a move. "Many newspapers are interested in this story. A national spokesperson has disappeared."

"But those newspapers aren't sending reporters to Santa Barbara."

"Not yet." I push back my chair. It scrapes on the balcony.

He stands, too. "Everyone was upset about what happened in there, but you were trembling all over. I was afraid you were going to collapse."

"Well, obviously, I'm fine," I say. "And I do need to go now."

He reaches out for my arm again and brings his face close enough to mine that I can read the suspicion in his dark eyes. "Is this thing personal for you? Do you have some ax to grind with Bobby W?"

I pull away from him. "No," I say. "No to both of your questions."

As I cross in front of him, heading for the door, he says, "I want your contact information, the name of your supervisor at the newspaper. Everything."

I stop in the doorway, take out a card, write Dennis Hamilton's name and e-mail address on the back of it. "I'm staying at the El Cerrito," I say. Then, in a final rush of words. "Look, I'm just a reporter trying to do my job."

"If that's the case, you'll receive complete cooperation from us."

His voice makes it clear that I haven't quelled his suspicions.

"That's the case," I say.

I leave, still seeing the black dress in my mind—that hideous, hateful rip. Julie Larimore's dress. Lisa's.

The Interview

How does it feel to have caused this kind of commotion?

How do I feel now that the black dress has commanded their attention? The fat girl, the haggard hag, the phony royal without a family? See how they run, how they worry, how they consider, for the first time, their own precious garments and the bodies that display them.

Even the reporter has taken note. She will sleep less smugly tonight. She will rise to tell her story in the morning. And she, along with the rest of them, will begin to reconsider.

Hear this plea, Santa Barbara ocean. Swallow the dawn and fold these secrets into your waves. It won't be long now, and everything will be right again. Strong again. Strong and safe.

How do I feel? I feel vindicated.

SEVEN

Tania Marie

Word of the day: *Supercilious:* Arrogant, condescending, haughty

"Four frigging headlines for one frigging evening."

Tania Marie piled the newspapers and their lies in the wrought-iron bistro chair beside her. Jay Rossi had brought the good news with him, driving up that morning in a black pickup she'd die before she set a foot inside. Virginia had to be out of her mind.

In the plus department, Rossi had a nice-enough face, more sneer than grin, and hair a soft brown color that only those who were blond as children possessed. Not that it mattered.

Strike one, he worked for Virginia, which translated *flunky.* Strike two, he had short-man attitude to the max. Strike three, that horrendous truck he called "Blackie" was an accident waiting to happen. The passenger door wouldn't even open. If she hadn't been so upset about what happened at the party, she never would have subjected herself to the short ride down the street.

She'd known better than to have coffee with the supercilious punk, but it beat the hell out of dinner. Now, after poring over the stories, she never wanted to see another newspaper, or another bodyguard again. She took a final swallow of her latte—nonfat sugar-free vanilla, thank you very much—then got up and tossed the cup, cardboard collar and all, into the bin.

"Why do you read those stories about you if you hate them so much?"

"Why do you look when you pass an accident?"

He laughed, then cupped his espresso in both hands. Short man; short drink; short date.

"I can walk back to my apartment," she said. "It's been nice knowing you."

"Same here."

The prick stood up and pulled his windbreaker around him. "Not even Virginia has enough money in her coffers to put me though this crap."

"I told you I don't need a fucking bodyguard."

He flinched. "And I don't need to take any more lip from you." And without waiting for an answer, "I'm not here by choice."

"No?"

"Hell, no. I'm just trying to do a favor for your mother."

He threw a bill on the table and started for the truck.

"How much did Virginia pay you for this gig?"

"Enough. I'd do it for nothing, just to learn from her."

"Another ga-ga wannabe chef? I should have known."

His defiant eyes went cold as limestone.

"So, she's a lousy mom," he said. "I grant you that. She shouldn't have had kids."

Tania Marie didn't know how to respond to that. People either adored Virginia or they didn't. This was the first time anyone had spoken the truth without judgment.

Before she could respond, Rossi said, "She's a hell of a chef, though, and I intend to learn everything I can from her."

"Even if you have to baby-sit her errant daughter?"

He moved closer to her, and maybe because she wasn't used to being this close to anyone but Marshall, she was startled by his lack of scent. No cologne. No hairspray, no mousse, no gel. What man on earth had the guts to wear no cologne, use no hair products? To just smell like himself?

"Get this straight. I'm doing it for Virginia because she's giving me a chance. If it were up to my dad, I'd get an MBA. I already got the bachelor's degree for him. But Virginia knows I can be a chef, and whether you know it or not, she's worried about you."

"As much as she can be." Tania Marie met his eyes, wondering if he would opt for the truth or the easy answer.

"As much as that," he said.

Another point for the short man with the arresting eyes.

"What'd she tell you to do?"

"Just be here. Hang out with you."

"And report to her?"

He gave her a steady gaze and picked up his keys from the green table. The man wasn't a liar, but he wasn't coughing up the truth, either.

"She wants you to report to her, doesn't she? She can't be bothered to check up on me, so she wants you to."

"Can you hold it down?" He walked along the sidewalk, his jacket flapping in the breeze. "People are going to think I'm hurting you."

"You might as well be." The familiar rage coursed through her again, leveling her senses. "Get out of here, or I'll scream."

"No reason for that." A mirthless smile crossed his face, and he leaned toward her. "I can't wait to get away from you."

That parting shot had made her feel stupid, like the foul-mouthed fat girl nobody could stand. But at least she'd managed to get rid of Jay Rossi and spend the rest of the day in semi-peace. Now she was safe. No one would recognize her here, the one place she could blend in. She'd tied back her hair, anyway. These women had seen it all. They *were* it all. The arms that dripped fat by the buckets, the thighs puckered with cellulite. Hell, she was skinny by comparison, especially to the ones in the heated pool, the only place to hide at all.

This was the fourth night she'd come to the gym and the first she'd ventured into the separate room and its large pool of warm water and thrashing mountains of flesh. At least she'd work off some hunger, and when she finished, she could sweat off her past sins in the sauna. She'd brought six of the Killer Body bars, lemon meringue flavor, and chewed through a couple in the car. Nothing at home but Virginia's care packages, neatly labeled and dated. And the secret stash of Milanos, of course. She couldn't think about them, though, or she would be lost. One night, she'd actually dipped a whole bag, cookie after cookie, in tomato soup because Virginia had made her promise to eat something nutritious for dinner.

"Your name?" The instructor had entered the pool area through the back door and stood with her clipboard, looking at Tania Marie.

"Mary." Damn, what was the last name she'd made up when she'd registered, paying for a whole year in cash? Oh, that's right, a private little joke with herself, using the old man's last name for luck. "Mary Warren." She felt exposed. The other heads bobbing in the water turned to look at her.

"Is this your first time?" the instructor asked.

She nodded.

"Cool. I'm Betty. If you need anything, just ask, okay?" She smiled at Tania Marie and stepped down into the water. Even she was chunky, not one of those tushless anorexics they had at the clubs in New York.

"Okay," Betty called out. "Let's start with an easy little jog."

Water splashed around them as on the CD player, a male voice, the only one in the place, sang "Kansas City."

Tania Marie sloshed, almost happily, right through the warm-up, nodding to the others, all of them older than she, all but one far larger. If she weren't so desperate, they'd be kind of cute. An extremely overweight woman had tucked her hair into one of those plastic shower caps, the kind some hotels still had in their bathrooms. Another slipped and slid in purple plastic shoes. And when they looked at her, it wasn't to gawk but to grin, as if they were all in this together.

All were squeezed into one-piecers, like hers, maillots, as Virginia called them, in a voice that made it clear they ranked right down there with falsies in her estimation. Tania Marie jogged harder, trying to eliminate that voice and the expression that accompanied it. For a moment, she was free, flying to the surface of the water with little effort.

"Now, Cross-Country."

She mimicked the woman next to her—one leg behind one in front, arms cutting through the water like scissors.

"Left arm, right leg," the instructor called. The other women turned to look, still continuing their routines.

Tania Marie tried. She stopped, put her right arm forward, her left leg back, and started walking to "Kansas City." Except she couldn't make it happen. Betty, the instructor, approached, pushing herself through the water, blond bangs pasted to her forehead. It was PE class all over again. High school and fat and uncoordinated, to boot. This time she couldn't run to the locker room and cry. Couldn't screw the football coach to get even.

Whatever made her think she could do this? She should have skipped this bullshit, headed straight to the sauna.

"Here." Betty took her hand, pulled it through the water. "You're doing fine," she whispered, but Tania Marie knew better. Shit, her first day in fat class, and she was going to flunk out.

"Now, Skateboard." Still standing in front of her, Betty showed her how to lift her knee to her chest, then kick it out in back. Tania Marie tried to get into it, but then, it was time for Cross-Country again.

The class lasted little more than an hour. By the time the other women climbed out of the pool, she felt better. Betty bobbed through the water toward her, and Tania Marie pulled the scarf tighter around her head. Without makeup and hair, she was just another fat girl.

"It'll get easier with that Cross-Country, Mary. It's just like skiing."

Tania Marie didn't dare mention she'd been lousy at that, too. That was one of the stories about Marshall and her that had become a public joke. The ski weekend when the only skiing that took place was in the bedroom.

"I'll get the hang of it."

"Just keep coming back. You can stay as long as you want. This is our last class of the day."

It always was. And she was always one of the last to leave the gym, when there were few people to recognize her. How long would she have to continue this deception?

"You think I can really lose weight doing this?"

"Sure." Betty patted her own ample hips. "Of course you can't lose weight doing any one thing if you eat more than you burn off. You doing anything else, going to Weight Watchers, LA Weight Loss or anything?"

"Killer Body." She almost whispered it.

Betty shrugged. "The Julie Larimore diet. What do you think happened to her?"

"I don't know."

"She's perfect, isn't she?" Betty lifted her arms from the water. "I know she'll be fine. You'll be fine, too. It doesn't really matter what you do as long as you stick to it. See you tomorrow night."

"Yes," Tania Marie said, and for that moment, she believed she could stick to a program, maybe this one and the nice, not perfect woman who hadn't made her feel like a clumsy ass for not being able to coordinate left and right.

She slid into the water, up to her neck, sinking into its warmth. She needed a plan, like Virginia had when she'd opened her first restaurant. As the water momentarily liberated her from her girth, she let herself bob about like a cork and thought about what she should do next. Maybe join a program like Weight Watchers. The one meeting she'd sneaked into hadn't been bad, but it could take forever. Besides, she'd have to be accountable.

Maybe she ought to look into one of those alternative measures she'd heard about. Epsom salts. Temporary, for sure, but it would clean her out, maybe knock off five pounds; that's what Marshall said his wife did. If his wife, why not his mistress—okay, fucking ex-mistress. Why not?

All she needed was to demonstrate a considerable drop in weight in the next week or two, something to rivet the attention of the press. Then she could do something sensible, find a weight-loss program that worked. *After* she was the Killer Body spokesmodel.

She'd had it with the pool. Tania Marie pulled herself out of the water, grabbing on to the rail parallel to the slippery steps. Her weight hit her like a wet, heavy towel, and she almost retreated back to that warm, buoyant place. But, no.

In the sweaty sanctuary of the sauna, she climbed up on a bench too narrow for any normal human and let herself absorb the steam-filled air. Damn, it hurt good. As she lay there, wiping the sweat from her face, she could almost feel the fat evaporating.

It was too late, and she was too tired to think. Maybe she should just go back to her place and pig out. Damn, she'd worked off a German chocolate cake's worth of calories in the pool. And if embarrassment and feeling like a dork made you sweat, she'd probably earned at least a wedge of cheesecake.

Sweat drenched her body. Heat filled her nostrils. At least she'd look skinnier until she did something stupid like drink a glass of water.

Should she find a grocery store on the way home and buy one of those shitty mixes in the box, or one of the frozen second-rate cakes she wouldn't have time to thaw? Or should she just suck it up, and walk into Trader Joe's, bigger than hell? Eat the whole damned cheesecake in the car if she felt like it? How late did Trader Joe's stay open?

None of the options sounded all that good. She was still considering them when the lights went out.

Black. Pitch black. Only her own sounds and smells. Her own self in a small room sucked dry of light.

Her breathing accelerated. What the hell was going on? How much time had passed since Betty and the class filed out?

She started to rise from the skinny bench, then realized that she could barely breathe. The heat had flattened her, little by little. Now she felt too weak to move, losing strength and air by the moment.

She sat there only seconds, then knew no one was coming to her rescue. No one would. She had to get herself out of this. *Think, damn it.* Her bag, in the locker, had her cell phone in it. She could make it through the darkness, feel her way along the hall, and get to it. Then, she could call for help.

Call whom?

That was a depressing thought, but shit, even with no one to care about her, she could phone 911. She could phone Virginia or her best friend, Sheree, back in New York. If she were really scared, she could call Marshall's assistant, say it was an emergency. No, she couldn't lie to herself. Marshall hadn't taken a call from her since the day the first story appeared. He hadn't even talked to her after she was fired.

Tania Marie hobbled to the door, pulled the slippery

handle. It didn't budge. Her hands were too wet. She moved back through the darkness and wiped them on the towel she'd brought in with her. Scampered back to the door, the handle. Holy shit. It wouldn't open. It was locked or stuck or— She didn't even want to think about it. She wanted to scream.

That wouldn't work, either; it would only drain her energy. She needed to think. The darkness seemed to slither toward her, crawl up along her bare arms, her neck. The hot, moist air threatened to suffocate her.

Someone would come soon. This would be okay. It was probably just a power failure. The thought gave her no relief. She was alone in this dark room, fighting for every wet breath, alone the way she'd been, one way or another, her entire life.

Holy shit.

Dizziness set in. She felt like a wet, heavy rock sinking into an ocean of sweat. She banged on the door, tried to scream. She was going to die.

No, don't think that.

Yes, do think that. It's what's going to happen.

She was going to die.

Just like Julie Larimore.

That was the last thought she registered before she slipped away, into the dark, wet, roaring place, the place so heavy on her chest that all thoughts and fears were pressed out of her.

Only one thought bubbled to the surface. *Tania Marie Camp died today. She is survived by her parents and Marshall Cameron, the love of her very short life.*

The noise came from outside, barely rousing her. A scrunching, sliding sound. Tania Marie tried to fight the heavy stone on her chest, her tight, closed nostrils. Could it be? The slide became a screech. A burst of cool air blew in. She gagged on it, grabbing herself around the waist. Oh, yes, it was sweet, pure air, and she was drinking it.

How long? A minute? An hour? Who cared? She breathed now. She'd almost passed out, and now she could breathe. Perhaps the door had just been jammed. The creepy feeling along her arms told her otherwise. Someone had locked her in; someone had let her out. Like a rat in a cage. A rat being observed.

It was too dark here. But she could find her way to the door, she must. Already, her eyes were adjusting to the dim light. Better than pitch-black hopelessness.

Once out, she felt her bare skin prickle in the cool air. The fucking heater must be off, all except the hot air forced into the sauna. Everyone must have gone home. The towels hung from hooks on the wall closest to the door. Find her towel, and she'd find her way out.

She dragged her finger along the cold wall. There it was. She could have kissed the soft Egyptian cotton. Instead, she wrapped it around her like a fur coat. Make that *faux* fur. She'd never wear the real thing, never again. She'd never sleep with another married man, never. Oh, God, just let her get out of here, and she'd do her best to turn her life around. Just please let her get out of here. *Please.*

The door must just be steps away. Yes, she felt the raised molding around it. Scrambled for the knob. Turned it.

Nothing.

She turned and twisted.

Nothing.

All she needed was to get out of this cold, frigging tomb, get to her locker, to her clothes, to her cell phone.

She jerked the door, screamed, twisted the knob again.

Nothing.

"Why me?" She sank to the floor, still pounding the door. "Why fucking me?"

She would die here, in this place. Whoever had taken Julie Larimore—and, admit it, someone had taken, kidnapped or, damn it, killed her—that person had her now. No way could she escape. She began to sob. A big, fucking baby. A loser, crying for her mama. That's all she'd ever been.

"God," she said. "Why?"

Then she felt the harsh pillow of the door shift and soften. She looked up. Yes, it was opening. Pure light flooded the room. Wonderful light, blinking, flashing light. Human voices.

"Tania Marie. Look over here, baby. Give me a smile. Yes, that's right. Good girl. Another one, okay?"

"Tania Marie. How long have you been coming here?"

"Hey, Tania Marie. Where'd you get that swimsuit? What size is it, anyway?"

Reporters. Every shape, every breed, every medium, closed in on her as the darkness had just moments before. She had thought someone was going to kill her in the sauna. Now she realized what was really going on. Here she was, barely able to speak, and looking like the Battle of Pork Chop Hill. And every frigging reporter in town was here to witness it.

She put up her hand between them and her, not much of a shield. She was not going to die. She would only wish she were dead, and that was far worse than what she had imagined when the lights went out.

"I can't talk right now," she said.

"Just tell us how you got locked in here, Tania Marie," demanded an aggressive male reporter.

"Men aren't allowed in this club," she said. "I suggest you and your photographer get the hell out of here."

"Aw, Tania Marie." The reporter tried to get flirty on her, but she'd had lessons in flirty from the champ.

She motioned toward the hall, where her locker, her clothes, waited.

"Out," she said.

The reporter hesitated at the doorway. "Just a few questions."

"Out," Tania Marie repeated. Then, looking beyond him, she saw the arrogant reporter who'd gotten pushy with her at Bobby's party. Rikki, whatever her name was.

Braver now, breathing easier, Tania Marie got in her face. "You did this to me, didn't you?"

"I didn't do anything." Color tinged Rikki Whatever's cheeks.

The others turned to look at her. Good. Now the bitch knew how it felt.

"Sure, you did." Tania Marie raised her voice as she thought about the indignity of it, the naked fear. *Turn it around.* That's what Virginia always said she did when she was battling her way to success in the restaurant business. Probably the only parental advice she'd ever received came to Tania Marie the moment she needed it: *When someone comes after you, baby, turn it around on them.*

"You locked me in here, damned near snuffed me in the sauna. Then you come waltzing in, pretending it's just a coincidence. Did you call these other assholes, too?"

Murmured voices mulled over her questions. The reporter's pale cheeks blazed.

"I didn't call anyone," she said.

"Well, then, it's pretty amazing that you just happened to be at Bobby Warren's party last night when Julie Larimore's hacked-up dress got delivered. Even more amazing, you broke down when you saw that dress."

"Everyone in town's following *you.*" Rikki slipped so close to her that Tania Marie could see the variegated blues of her eyes. "Anyone could have followed you in here and called the rest of us."

"Somebody called you?" The information derailed her for a moment, and she pulled the towel closer. She'd been so sure it was this one.

"Left a message for me at my hotel," the reporter said. "Believe me, I'm not interested in embarrassing you, though. I just want to talk about Julie Larimore."

Her eyes almost looked honest, but Tania Marie had been tricked by honest eyes before. She'd been tricked by cameras, flashing as these did, by friendly voices saying, as these did, "Tania Marie, look over here."

Oh, shit. What was she going to do, standing here, freezing, with her thighs hanging out of her suit and only a towel to protect her from the frenzied reporters?

"If you mean that," she said, "help me get out of here. Help me get to my cell phone, so I can call my bodyguard."

Yes, Virginia was right, as usual. She really did need a bodyguard.

EIGHT

Rikki

Maybe it's the eyes, large and frightened.

Maybe it's the pathetic way she tries to cover herself with the sad blue towel.

Maybe it's something deeper, the realization that we are all no more than our lowest common denominator, and that this shivering creature deserves better than she's getting from my colleagues and me at this time in her life.

Or perhaps I'm just greedy, and I see an opportunity for an exclusive. I am capable of that; I am capable of anything right now.

Before I can question the reason for or the wisdom of my decision, I take Tania Marie by the arm. Then, before anyone figures out what's happening, I guide her through the cameras and the questions, with a posture of authority I've learned to imitate by being on the wrong side of it since my first newspaper job.

"Let us through, please. Excuse us."

At least a dozen reporters follow us past the lockers into the main club. We're in luck. Someone has turned on the light, and several manager types hasten toward us.

"What the hell is going on here?" asks a short-haired blonde with a gym-teacher voice. She flies past us, raging at the reporters. "Didn't you read the sign? There are no men allowed in here."

"Run," I say to Tania Marie, and we bolt to the door. My car awaits on the other side. She scrambles into the passenger side, and I get behind the wheel and take off.

"My clothes," she wails.

"They're the least of your worries. Be glad you're out of there."

"My cell phone."

"I'll go back and get it for you."

"Damn, thank you." She wipes her eyes with the towel. "You can't imagine how it felt to be trapped like that. I'll be all over the news. Everything will start up again."

I don't tell her that it never really stopped. That's what it must feel like, being a top news story, the subject of gossip. Being out of the papers for even one day must seem like the beginning of normalcy once more. But I know as I glance across at this woman in the black bathing suit and the blue towel, that normalcy is years away, if ever.

When a newsman of Marshall Cameron's reputation is involved in something as sordid as the Honey Bee Affair, the public will find reason to blame the woman—especially if she's young, and okay, especially if she has a weight problem. America doesn't want its trusted analyzer of the news to stray from his path of dignity. But if he did, even once, it's the woman's fault.

I stop at Hollister Avenue and ask, "Where to?"

"Home," she says. "I need to get some clothes. Can I use your phone to call my bodyguard?"

I hand it to her. She calls and immediately begins swearing. Hangs up in a huff.

I start driving in the direction of her complex.

"Let me drop you off. Then I'll go back and get your things."

"I used a different name at the gym," she says.

"I can understand why."

"Now, I can never go back." Her voice trembles, and she wipes her eyes.

"You probably can, after a day or two. This will quiet down in no time."

She turns to me in the car. "You really did get a phone call that I was there? You didn't make it up?"

"I really got a phone call," I say. "A message, actually, at my hotel."

"Man or woman?"

"I don't know. It was left at the front desk. I'll find out."

"What did it say?"

"Just that you were at the gym." And that it was a good photo opportunity, I add to myself. Just enough information to intrigue the Tania Marie spotters.

"And now I'll be on the front pages of all the tabloids again. And I'll never have a chance at Killer Body."

Anguish resonates from her. I have to ask, and not just because I'm looking for a story. "Why do you want it so much?"

"I can't tell you." She crosses her arms over the towel. "You might have helped me back there, but you're still a reporter, and you'll still screw me over if I give you a chance."

"You have a low opinion of the press."

"What would you have if you were in my position? What did I do that was so fucking horrible that you or anyone else wouldn't have done?"

Fall in love with the wrong man. I'd done that once, just much less publicly than she. "I'm not trying to judge you, Tania Marie."

"No, you're just trying to get a story out of me, like everyone else."

I stop at Patterson and steal a look at her. "Exploiting you isn't my goal. That's not the kind of stuff I write. I told you I wanted to know about Julie Larimore."

"Why her?" She hugs the towel tighter, as if trying to protect herself from what I am asking. My instincts tell me that she might know something.

"Were you friends?"

"Not friends, exactly. No one could get too close to her."

"How did you know her?"

"Don't pretend you don't know that I got on the Killer Body program after everything broke loose."

"After the stories about you and Marshall Cameron?"

"I was trying to take charge of my life. I needed something that worked fast. Someone at Killer Body thought there might be a place for me in the organization—not a position like Julie's, of course. Just some kind of PR job. I'd lost some weight, and we thought I could be a Killer Body success story. Good for them, good for me."

"And what happened?"

"Somebody screwed me over, of course. I never even got a chance to meet with Bobby Warren. His people told my people that I wasn't right for the Killer Body image."

"Perhaps that's all it was."

"No, it was sabotage. Everything was a go, and then it just stopped."

"Do you think it was Julie?"

"At the time, yes. Then, later, I wasn't so sure."

"Why?"

"Nothing you'd understand. You're not the kind of woman who understands anything she hasn't experienced."

"That's a pat assessment." I feel as if I've been physically attacked. I want to stop the car and tell her to get the hell out and walk her fat ass home if she has such a low opinion of me. Instead, I say, "I expected more of you."

"I expected more of you, too. I told you I didn't want to talk about how I met Julie. Why can't you respect that?"

She has a point. I'm crowding her on the one night she doesn't need to be crowded.

"Okay. I hear you." I drive for a moment, and the stillness in the car is louder than our arguments have been. "Who else at Killer Body did you have contact with?" I ask to break the silence.

"Just her. And hunky Lucas Morrison. He's the one who finally said it was a no go. Then, after Julie disappeared, my agent tried them again, just for the hell of it, and it was Mr. Warren who said okay."

I try to make sense of the scenario. I'll need to talk to Lucas Morrison again, that's for sure. And I'll need to dig up everything I can about Julie Larimore.

"Did they give you any material about Killer Body?" I ask. "Something beyond the usual press kits?"

"I have a ton of stuff."

"Could I look at it?"

"You can have it. After what happened today, I don't stand a chance."

"You never know."

"Yeah, right." She leans back into the seat. "I'm starving. Put that in your story, too."

"I'm not trying to hurt you," I say. "This is the right street, isn't it?"

"Take a left, and I'm two blocks down." She shudders. "You don't suppose anyone followed us here?"

"I'll drive around the block, if you want. I think they got the story they were after."

"They didn't want a story. They wanted what they always do." She counts them off on her fingers. "They want to look at my thighs, which they hope have grown. They want to look at my butt, which they hope has spread. And they'll run those fat, ugly photos across their newspapers, so that everyone can laugh at Tania Marie, the honey bee."

I can't argue with her, because she's right, and, again, I wonder how intriguing this story would be if she were thin.

We reach the gates of her complex which, to my surprise, isn't some little beachfront condo Mommy picked up for her. The fact that it's not makes me like her better. The fact that I surmised it would be makes me like myself a little less. "Would you mind if I came in?" I ask. "I would like that information on the company."

"I don't think so. I don't want to see my apartment described in the paper. You'd better wait outside."

We weave through an entry drive, and I park outside a fenced-in courtyard. Although she hasn't moved, I can almost feel her anxiety suck the air from the car. My head begins to throb. I can't imagine how hers must feel.

"Want me to get out first and open the gate?"

"Thanks." She puts her hand on my arm. "I don't know why you helped me, but I appreciate it."

"I told you," I say. "I want to learn everything I can about Julie Larimore."

"Well, good luck. No one really knows Julie, not even old Mr. Warren."

"What makes you so sure of that?"

She starts to speak, changes her mind and gives me a grim smile. Finally, she says, "You're really clueless, you know."

"Then why don't you enlighten me?"

She shifts in the seat. "Hey, I was just trying to help you. Don't give me the fucking third degree."

"Calm down," I say.

"I can't." She starts to sob. "Do you know how fucked up this whole thing is? Can you imagine how my life is right now?"

I want to tell her it could be worse. That she could have lost a cousin, that her aunt could be demanding results she might not be able to deliver. That instead of a wealthy, famous mother in San Francisco, she could have a grieving mother in Colorado, a mother who has no answers to the question that haunts her day and night: *Why?*

I open my car door. "It looks pretty quiet. Try to pull yourself together. You'll be inside in just a minute."

"That's easy for you to say." She tugs at her short bangs. "No one tried to kill you back there."

"No one tried to kill you, either." My voice is harsher than I intend, tears close to the surface.

"They did, too. They locked me in the sauna. I nearly passed out."

A tingle spreads along my arms. Is she overreacting? Imagining something that didn't really happen?

"Perhaps the door of the sauna just got stuck."

"No way. It was locked. And then unlocked. I heard the sound when it happened."

The tingle becomes a full-blown chill. Car door

open, I study her face in the dim light: the wide eyes, the straightforward manner that has already gotten her in enough trouble to ruin a good chunk of her life.

"Somebody locked you in the sauna?"

"And then turned off the lights."

I think back. The lights in the place had been blazing when I arrived with the other reporters. The door to the club had been open.

"Then somebody unlocked the sauna?"

"And I stumbled out, got my towel and found you people waiting for me. I tell you, somebody locked me in there, then let me out just in time."

"Who would want to do something like that to you?"

"I don't know," she sobs. "If they tried it once, what are they going to do next?"

I try to follow up on Tania Marie's story back at the health club when I pick up Tania Marie's phone and clothes. The woman with the gym-teacher voice informs me that she's the night manager. She doesn't like my questions and especially doesn't like my invading the privacy of her members. When I ask if I can speak to the employees who were responsible for locking up that night, she says certainly not. She mentions attorneys. I tell her I'll be checking with her. With her still berating me, I walk away.

Tania Marie refuses to see me, so I leave her phone, jeans and T-shirt outside her apartment as she has requested.

I know what I have to do next, but I don't want to. I try to invent excuses, reasons why I must remain here in Santa Barbara, living out of a motel, talking to the other Killer Body candidates. It doesn't work. The knowledge of what must happen next keeps me thrashing most of the night. I leave a little after six the next morning.

It's close to eleven by the time I reach Pleasant View. Pete Lewis's office is located in the rapidly developing northeast part of town, on the twelfth floor of a bank building. I asked if we could meet here because I didn't think I could bear being in the home where he and Lisa were going to live. Now I'm not so sure I shouldn't have opted for something impersonal, like a coffee shop.

We sit in his conference room, with its view of the hazy day. Pete doesn't look as if he's slept, either. His jeans and fisherman's knit sweater look brand new, as does everything I've ever seen him wear. I remember that I told Lisa he was too perfect, asked her if she didn't ever want to just reach over and muss up his hair. But then, she was that way, too. Perfection personified.

Although his hug is warm, I know he'd rather do just about anything than meet with me today. After he asks about my trip, which was uneventful, and lunch, which is impossible, he sits on the edge of the conference table, his eyes so intense I have to turn away.

"I went to the cemetery this morning," he says.

"I'm stopping on my way back."

"After the funeral, I spent that first night out there, all night, in my car."

"Oh, Pete."

"I couldn't stand for her to be alone."

The ragged pain in his voice mirrors what I feel, what I try to hide from others. There is no reason to hide it from him. I let the tears fall. He leans down, puts his arms around me, and I know that he is crying, too, into my hair. Turning abruptly, he walks to the window, his back to me.

"What are we going to do, Rikki?"

"I don't know. Work, I guess. That's what I'm trying to do."

"On that Julie Larimore story?"

"Yes," I say to his back.

"You get anything?"

"Not much, so far. That's why I'm here. I need your help."

He turns. "I don't know anything that can help you with that story."

"You might." I sit straight in my chair, trying to pretend he is a source and not the man who loved my cousin, not the man who spent last Saturday night at the cemetery because he didn't want her to be alone. "I need to talk to you about Lisa."

"She had a bad heart, like your mom did. A young woman can look healthy, and then, just like that." He snaps his fingers.

"She'd lost a lot of weight."

"That was for the wedding. She had this crazy goal. I told her she looked great, that she'd be a beautiful bride."

"A lot of weight, Pete."

He glances away, as if he can visualize her, standing there in the space between us. "That wasn't what killed her. You just need to believe it. You have to blame something."

"She idolized Julie Larimore."

"That's a pretty strong word for it."

"She wore her hair like Julie's. Streaked it blond. Bought that black dress with the low-slung belt. Even the locket."

He pulls out a chair from the conference table and sits stiffly. "A lot of women admire Julie Larimore. I caught her on some of the talk shows. She sounded okay to me."

"Discipline and accountability." I sit to his right, forcing him to look at me when I speak. "Those and a Killer Body membership can fix anything, right?"

The doubt registers in his eyes. Then the lawyer in him comes back, fighting. "Rikki, tell me. Would Lisa want you asking all this?"

I've wondered the same thing myself. Maybe it isn't the lawyer in him that's making him resist my questions. Maybe it's just the man who lost his woman and who doesn't want to endure one more second of pain. I tell him what I know. "She'd want me to if it would help find out what happened to Julie Larimore."

"You really think it will?"

No point in lying to him. "I don't know, but it's all I've got. Someone had Julie's dress, or one that looks like it, delivered to Bobby Warren Friday night. I was there. It was torn to shreds. The police have it right now."

"God."

"Something else happened last night." I decide not to mention Tania Marie by name, knowing how he'll react. "Someone else connected with Killer Body could have been hurt, maybe killed. I need to know how involved Lisa was with the organization."

"It was her thing. You know that. She'd go down there every day, to weigh in or whatever they do. A few times, she went to L.A. to consult regarding some television spots. They never happened, though."

"Did she ever meet Julie Larimore?"

"Are you kidding? You would have been the first one she told. She worked with people who did." He pauses as if trying to decide how much to say. "Like I said, she went down south a few times to audition or whatever."

"For whom?"

"Somebody down there told her she had Julie's look. That if she lost a few more pounds she might be able to be in some of their ads. I didn't think it was important, or I would have told you sooner." His eyes darken, and he gnaws his lower lip. "She was going to be my wife, damn it. I trusted her."

In his eyes, I see something else that connects with my own, still-nameless emotions. And all I know before I turn away is that he's not telling me the whole truth.

NINE

Rochelle

She met Blond Elvis late that day at the club. She hadn't been able to schedule him in earlier, and Lord knows, she needed him.

He was in the posing room, doing a back double biceps, staring intently at his back through the mirror in front of him. She knew how it felt after a good workout, to make that mind-muscle connection so that you could really isolate and flex.

"Am I early?"

"I'm just finishing." He turned away from both mirrors. "Now you're going to think I'm one of those stereotypical narcissistic assholes."

"I already know you are," she said. "Because I'm one, too."

"Well, just take me out and shoot me if I ever get fat." He took a final, lingering look at his back. "I mean, Christ, if your belly is so big that you can't even see your own dick, what's the point?"

"A man after my own heart," she said. "Now, let's keep me from turning into another Tania Marie."

"No worries there," he said, reaching for the door. "At least you don't have to sneak into a fat ladies' gym and wind up with your ass plastered all over the newspaper." *Ass,* she thought. Not boobs, not abs. "You should have given Tania Marie my phone number, especially since she appears to be in the Killer Body family now."

"Not on your life. You know too many of my secrets."

The floor was quieter than usual, only the clank, creak and groan of the weight machines. Rochelle lifted two fifteen-pound weights from the rack and began her traveling lunges, motivated by the ass comment as well as by the Nordic picture of perfection beside her.

Blond Elvis, as everyone at the club called him, was the ideal personal trainer. He knew how to coax extra reps out of her, pushing her beyond her limit while keeping her form perfect. And he didn't judge.

At the end of the session, she wiped a towel across her forehead, patted down her neck, feeling more animal than human, a feeling she relished. Her body ached from within, and her head spun in a whirlwind of endorphins.

Her hand trembled as she filled in the check.

"Here," she said, handing it to him. "You might be as expensive as a shrink, but you're a hell of a lot better."

"That's what I tell everyone."

Then she caught a glimpse of herself in the mirror. Her damned ass, and in navy blue, at that. How the hell did it look in street clothes? To Bobbo? Jesse, for that matter?

"What's wrong?"

"My ass." She met his porcelain-blue gaze and tried for a comedic, scrunched-up grin.

He frowned and walked around her, shaking his head. "Looks pretty good to me."

"Don't stroke me, Blond. With Tania Marie out of the way, assuming I'm that lucky, the Killer Body job is between Princess Gabby and me."

"Damn." He couldn't hide the doubt dimming his eyes. "Princess Gabby is pretty hot."

"I don't want to hear it, okay? I just want to know what I can do. I need something now, and I need results right away."

"What are you eating?" It was a Jesse question, but before she could conjure a Jesse answer, he said, "Don't lie to Blond Elvis."

She laughed. She should never underestimate this man. "Actually, with that new cut, you look more like Billy Idol."

"But we aren't talking about me, are we, Shel?"

"Minute Rice. Are you happy now?"

He put a hand on her shoulder. "Don't bullshit a bullshitter. I did the same thing when I was competing."

Jesse would have chided her. Blond understood. "A whole cup for one-third the carbs."

"And zip nutritional value, but this ain't Nutrition 101. What else are you eating? Let me guess. Baby food vegetables?"

"It's Survival 101, and yes. Tuna sometimes, though."

"By the tablespoon?"

"Quarter cup." Damn, it felt good to talk like this.

"Taking Clen?"

Clenbuterol, Clen, for short. She leaned so close that his sweaty, husky scent burned her nostrils, like smoke. "Sounds like a venereal disease, doesn't it?"

"It works in the short run, and that's what you're concerned about, isn't it?"

In that second, she realized something that hadn't occurred to her before. Her entire life, from the time she'd left home, had been the short run. Every role, every goal, had been the short run. Jesse and Megan were her only constants, her only long-time commitments. Her husband. Her daughter. And her damned, betraying body, of course.

"I've used it before. What's the price these days, after you take off the trip to Mexico? About a dollar each?"

"No way." His voice was as quiet and full of whispered conspiracy as hers. "I can probably get you fifty for around twenty bucks."

She hadn't expected anything this reasonable. Jesse had scored the first Clen for her when her series was still going. That was almost four years ago, and Blond's price was better. She tried to remember the dosage.

"I can take, what? Six a day?"

He grabbed his hair as if pulling it out by the roots. "That is just so ballistic."

"Calm down. I did it before."

Something new, an emotion he hadn't exhibited previously, set his face as if it were a photograph. "Who told you to take that much?"

And before she could reply, "Don't do it again, Shel."

She nodded. He was right. The last time she'd been so shaky, so jumpy, she'd had to take way too much Valium just to claim a decent night's sleep.

Blond had this way of making you feel it was just the two of you. As she looked around, she realized that, for once, it was true. Few people remained on the floor.

"Guess we'd better get out of here," she said. "I'll pay attention to what you said."

He gave her a hug. "You're in great shape, Shel. You're wonderful."

"And Princess Gabby?"

He had to look away before he could face her.

"She's hot, but that doesn't mean jack shit. Stuff like this always comes down to who wants it, and you want it more than anyone."

"You'd better believe it."

"The Clen will do the rest."

"And if the Clen doesn't work?"

"It always works."

The club felt more like a warehouse. For the first time, this young boy trainer looked like a neophyte with all of his directives and platitudes.

She squeezed his thick arm. "What if the Clen doesn't do enough, Blond? What if I can't lose what I need to?"

"Then," he said, "I can get some toys that will."

"Toys?"

"That's what the bodybuilders call them."

The word intrigued her, as did the thought. "Toys," she repeated. "Why don't you look into that for me? Just in case."

Rikki

After I leave Pete, I call Dennis Hamilton and tell him I'm going to be spending the night in town and am going to drop by the office in the morning. He asks if I want to have a drink or dinner. Translated: Would I like to drink with him or eat while he drinks?

After my short visit with Pete, I don't feel like talking to anyone, so I decline Dennis's invitation. I need time to think and plan. Tania Marie actually lived up to her promise and gave me all of her Killer Body literature, but I learned little from it that I didn't already know.

Bobby Warren, world-famous bodybuilder and inventor of revolutionary exercise equipment, started the program when he was trying to help his wife, Dolores, lose weight. It worked, Dolores lost, and Killer Body gained.

Crazed with success, Bobby Warren went national. Now Killer Body is the top weight-loss program in the country, in dollars, at least. Jenny Craig, Weight Watchers, LA Weight Loss don't even come close. The secret is the spokesperson. *Was* the spokesperson. Julie Larimore.

It's her image that dominates the centers' walls and windows, although constant videos feature "real people," as Killer Body calls them, who've achieved major weight loss with the program. Members meet daily with counselors, taking responsibility for every morsel they put into their mouths.

In the fitness center, they ski on elliptical machines, run on treadmills and submit to what the literature describes as "dynamic body-changing sculpting classes." Julie Larimore's motivational tapes are piped into their ears via the ever-present CD and headphones. In short, they are immersed in a program of self-absorption that works, or works for a while. "You've got to want the body" is the slogan, and they do.

Hamilton and I didn't learn anything when we went to the local Killer Body center last week. I decide to try it again, alone.

Unlike the lavish Killer Body headquarters in Santa Barbara, the local place could have easily been a dentist's office or a photography studio in its past life. It's jazzed up now, though, with nonstop videotaped success stories and counselors who could be described, with a straight face, as "svelte," another term that keeps popping up in Killer Body jargon, usually in a reference to Julie Larimore.

As I enter, I hear the music coming from the back. That must be where the workout center is. Once they get you in here, they don't let you go. I recognize the song, "Personality," which is "Bobby Warren's trademark tune." Because that's all that matters, right? And that's why the big ladies ahead of me in line are spending the big bucks. Personality.

The one ahead of me, about the age my mother would be if she were still around, says, "You're too small to be here. You must have hit goal."

"I had a weight problem once," I tell her, which is true.

She nods and moves closer to the glass-topped counter. "Once a problem, always a problem, right?"

Another Killer Bodyism. I wonder how I'd feel if I were her size—or even myself when I was overweight. Would Killer Body intimidate me, or would it offer me the hope I couldn't find within myself? I shut off the questioning reporter in my brain and the questions that are hitting too close to home. Two more women, and it will be my turn.

The tiny reception room, with its mirrored back panel full of Killer Body bars, shakes and jars of supplements, has room for only one chair. On the wall behind the chair is a floor-to-ceiling poster of Julie Larimore against a glossy red background. She's wearing the red-enamel pendant, the black dress, with the slit and the perfect legs. Above her is the slogan, printed in black against all that red: *You have to want the body.*

I turn my back to it, wait for my turn.

The receptionist must have wanted the body, because she has it.

"Welcome," she says, then frowns, as if trying to remember my face. "I'm filling in for Joyce today, going to be your counselor." She reaches for a large file. "What's your number?"

That's a new one. How could Lisa have paid for membership in an organization where she was a number? What could have made her that desperate, that self-demeaning?

The girl does everything but drum her fingers, waiting for my reply. They're nice fingers, too, with shell-pink polish that matches the stripe on her navy tank top and pants. Her face, in dimmer light, might be attractive. Here, with sun streaming through the window, she's no Julie Larimore, but she does have a killer body.

"Your number?" She strains for a smile, just about makes it.

"I can't remember."

"That's okay. What's your name?"

"Lisa Tilton." I say it before I can reconsider this biggest of lies. In my wildest dreams, I could never be Lisa Tilton.

She surveys me for a moment, taking me in, and I'm scared. I've just pretended to be my cousin, and I'm scared.

"Oh, Lisa. Here you are." She pulls out a plastic-clad green card. "You're eighteen forty-five, just so you know. Let's go back to a private office where we can chat. Want me to weigh you in first?"

I'm not sure how to answer that. Finally, clutching the card, I say, "Sure."

We go into a private room off the reception area. She motions to the scale, a flat, black bed on the floor, a digital device on the table beside it. I experience immediate recall of everything I've eaten in the past week, maybe longer. That salmon at Bobby Warren's party collides with the cheeseburger I ate yesterday, the Heineken I had with it.

Immediately, I step out of my clogs. Not enough. I remove my watch, too clunky, really. I ought to get rid of it. Damn, I need to get rid of everything except the fillings in my teeth.

She witnesses my frantic removal in silence, as if she sees it every day, which she probably does. Then it's just the two of us, the piped-in music and the scale.

I drank a beer last night, I want to say. *Ate a burger.* Instead, I suck it up and climb on that big, black teller of truth. Digital numbers flash all over the place. I look to her for guidance. How the hell long should I keep standing here?

She touches my arm in answer to that unspoken question. I all but leap off the scale.

"You're up a little bit." She whispers it, although there is no one to hear.

"How much?"

"Just a couple of pounds. Fine for your height, really." She grins. "Your goals are even more ambitious than mine. Makes it tough sometimes. But you've done great, amazing, really, especially considering where you started."

"Which was?"

"How soon we forget." She taps the plastic-shrouded paper. "We're looking at some serious weight loss here."

I study this revealing sheet of statistics, see the dropping numbers and get angry all over again. How could any professional think this kind of loss could be normal?

At the end of each week, someone had scrawled time, date and initials next to Lisa's stats. I don't want to give away anything, but I have to know.

"I'd like to talk to my regular counselor," I say. "Could you set me up with an appointment?"

"Joyce? Sure thing." She takes the card once more. "Let's see. You started about a year ago, right?" Before I can answer, confusion clouds her eyes. "What are you trying to pull on me?"

Sweat breaks out on my neck. I'm caught, and I know it. "What do you mean?"

"Tell me." She slams her hands on her hips. "Are you from Corporate, one of Mr. Warren's spies? 'Cause if you are, lady, you can tell him I do Killer Body by the book. I'm a good employee, a great employee. You tell Corporate how good I am, and you'd better not lie."

"I'm not a spy for Mr. Warren," I say. "What could possibly make you think that?"

"This." She shakes Lisa's chart in my face. "We always initial the forms after every meeting. Your last five were stamped in by Corporate. Explain that, why don't you?"

I'm angry by the time I get to the newspaper. I don't care that I'm wearing only sweats and a T-shirt. Or that my unruly hair is sticking up like feathers. Or that makeup hasn't touched my face. I can only see the Killer Body woman's know-it-all sneer, her smug indifference at the information on the card that should have screamed danger to anyone who can think. Through the roaring in my ears, I keep hearing that damning word. "Corporate."

Dennis Hamilton's office door is closed, meaning he'd prefer not to be disturbed. I storm in. He's working on his computer, back to the door, but whirls around when he hears me. I know how it feels to be taken by surprise and know in that flash of his pale eyes that he hasn't gotten over what happened with us that night any more than I have.

"Sorry. I didn't mean to startle you."

"What's wrong?"

Only now do I realize my hand is shaking, and that I am clutching Lisa's Killer Body card.

"I yanked it out of her hands," I say. "It was my cousin's. I just took it."

"Sit down. Tell me."

The simple commands, his raspy voice, connect with the sane part of me, the part that feels buried. I let them guide me out of the pitch-black cave where I've been lost since my visit to Killer Body.

I do as he says. I sit. But my hands still tremble.

Trying to explain them away, I say, "I am so damned pissed."

"Can I look at that?" He gets up and comes around the desk, closes the door. Standing next to me, he waits. I hand over the card, and he sits in the chair beside me. He doesn't just look at the card; he reads it, both sides. Then he glances up at me, his pale-green, bloodshot eyes almost the same color as his faded khaki shirt. "How'd you get this?"

"I went back to that place. Didn't say I was press this time." I force myself to say the rest of it. "Said I was Lisa."

"Shit."

"I know. But look at the last five entries, Den."

"Quite a drop."

"Not just the weight, the signature."

"It's not a signature. It's a stamp."

"Exactly. Killer Body Corporate, the counselor said. She was pissed, thought I was some kind of spy for Bobby Warren."

"It doesn't surprise me that he has spies."

I take the card from him, look at the KB stamp again. I can't sit still. I want to confront Bobby Warren, make him tell me what he and his people did to my cousin.

"Come on." Hamilton nudges me. "You want some coffee?"

"One more ounce of caffeine, and I'll be swinging from this acoustical fake ceiling."

"A walk, then?"

His face is too close, his smile too decent. He stiffens and removes both.

"Den."

"I know. Just trust me on this one." He opens the office door, and somehow, we're moving down the polished floor to the stairs. He goes first, and I follow, watching his khaki back as his scuffed shoes take the stairs ahead of me.

The front office is relatively quiet. Since management installed an automated teller in the lunch room, employees no longer line up in the front lobby to get cash at the classified counter.

One of the classified reps, a pretty, prematurely silver-haired woman, gives me one of her brilliant smiles as we pass. I know that she's heard about my cousin's death. I try to smile back.

A security guard barely looks up as Den and I head through the gate and out the front door.

"I shouldn't have come here," I say. "I ought to have waited until I thought it out a little better."

He frowns and tells me what I need to hear. "You did exactly what you should have done. You know that."

Yes, I do.

In spite of the hundreds of employees who occupy this building, there is a feeling of family at the newspaper. The kind of family whose members donate their sick time to a circulation department employee when her husband is dying of cancer. The kind of family that adopts a school in an at-risk district, and backs up the commitment with both hands-on time reading to kids, and with money. The kind of family that, in this age of corporate cutbacks, has an annual holiday lunch for employees and retirees so crowded it has to be served in two shifts—that produces its own corny talent show, on company time, to raise money for United Way.

Often dysfunctional, always connected, this family of almost eight hundred who work here share more than a job.

I know that's why I came back here, to Hamilton, to the paper. Because going through the motions in this building of otherwise-occupied co-workers is somehow more healing than spending time with my aunt or Pete, whose hell of tears and guilt is as fierce as mine. And, yes, because being here—pretending that I'm still part of this buzz of motion and commotion—telling myself that I matter, is a little bit better than being alone.

A jolt of cold air hits as we walk out onto the steps, and I realize I am not dressed for the weather. I also realize my face must be flushed with heat.

"I'm still so pissed, Den."

"I know." He walks down the steps beside me. "After what happened, my divorce, some other stuff, I saw the company shrink."

I feel the guilt warming my face. I did the same thing when I heard about his promotion—on the day after my first and only night in his bed. "You, too?"

"Yeah. I didn't get much out of the visits except this. She told me anger was a secondary emotion. You hit your thumb with a hammer, you get angry, but the primary emotion is pain. A car almost runs you off the road—"

"The primary emotion is fear," I recite. "We got the same shrink, Den. Why didn't you ever tell me you went?"

His face goes a shade deeper as we hit the asphalt and walk out, past the plant.

"Because now I'm your supervisor, I guess."

He says it in a factual voice, almost cold, but not quite. Bottom line, he's my supervisor. Bottom line, he chose it over me. Okay, I can live with that. I've lived with worse.

I spot his Volvo out in BFE, short for Bum Fuck Egypt, as the back parking lot beyond the plant is known to employees whose schedules prevent them from getting one of the primo places close to the building or along the curb.

"A secondary emotion." He gives me the look of one who has just gift wrapped a present and wants you to admire it. I'm not in the mood. Nor am I sure I'm in the mood for the coffee we'll soon be sharing.

"Secondary?"

"Yeah."

The Volvo waits just steps away. I look at him, look at it, then back at him once more.

"Where are we going?"

"Coffee. Some decent stuff, better than they have in the caf."

I nod. I even try to smile as he unlocks the car door and looks down into my eyes. "Tell me what I can do. How can I help?"

"You know."

He touches my arm, and I want to fall against him, the way I did that crazy night at the stupid holiday party, with too much champagne and too much Dennis. Just enough of both to make me want more.

"How, Rikki?"

"Killer Body." I feel as if I'm spitting the words in his face. This rage will kill me—or someone else—if I'm not careful. "Find out everything you can for me. Please."

"Use my connections through the newspaper, you mean, to acquire information about something that isn't a newspaper story?"

"It could be a newspaper story. Depends on what we find."

"But that's not what you're asking, is it?"

His car looks less dusty than usual. I realize he must have actually taken the time to wash it recently, then realize why; he drove it to a funeral last week.

Now, here I am, asking one of the most ethical reporters I've ever known—my supervisor—to compromise his ethics so that I can feel I'm avenging Lisa's death. I know it's not right, but I can't help it.

"I guess that's what I'm asking," I say.

"For me to spy for you?"

"For you to help me dig up background."

"That you hope will reveal something dirty about Killer Body?"

I meet his gaze. "Yes." Shame dilutes but doesn't destroy my resolve. "I can't help it, Den."

"Of course, any background I dig up for you on Killer Body, Inc. might help us learn more about what happened to Julie Larimore."

"That's true." We both know that's not why I'm asking. He opens the car door, and I wish I could apologize to him or to at least explain. "Den—"

"Yeah?" Those lie-detector eyes again, so pale in the harsh light that they're barely any color at all.

"It's a secondary emotion."

"Let's hope so." His scowl registers impatience. "Get in."

I do as he directs me, picking up a folder from the leather seat. The Volvo holds one of those medicinal vanilla scents indigenous to the car-wash business. He didn't just hose off the outside; he paid for an inside-and-out wash, complete with this well-meaning, horrible scent. Thank God he's going to the other side of the car. I don't want him to see me right now. I need time to rearrange myself.

To keep from thinking, I look down at the folder. I start to stick it in the back seat, but then I see the words he's scrawled on the outside. *Killer Body.*

I hear a soft moan, realize it is mine. It doesn't matter, not with this gift I hold in my hands. I open it up, and, damn, what a collection of research it is. Biographies of Bobby Warren; photos of him in his weightlifter days. Pages on Julie Larimore. Yellow sticky notes, in Hamilton's bold scrawl, many of them quotes. He did more than research; he talked to people. It hits me now that he's gotten in and is sitting here, beside me in the car, watching my reaction.

I turn to him, feeling incredulous, confused and so damned grateful.

"How did you justify doing all of this?" I ask in a voice so shaky I barely recognize it as my own.

"I haven't."

"Haven't justified it?"

"Not yet, but I'm hoping it'll happen. Otherwise, I'll have to jump off the fourth floor of the *Voice.*"

I fight tears. I fight throwing my arms around him and thanking him for me, for my family, for my cousin and my aunt. No, forget that—for me, me, me.

Instead, I say, "You're a good man."

"I'm a bastard."

"You're a good man." He starts the car, revs it, drowning out the rest of my words.

I wait until we are almost out of the parking lot, then try it again.

"Want me to tell you how I know you're a good man?"

The scowl that never really goes away deepens. "Your choice, Rikki."

"Because *you* make *me* want to be better."

He turns, and we look at each other in a way we never have before—not when we feared each other, not when we clung to each other, not even when we, by mutual, unspoken agreement, pretended our one evening together didn't matter the moment he became my boss.

"You're just fine the way you are."

Then he shoots out onto the street with such ferocity that I'm not sure that what I thought I felt and saw were real at all, or just what I needed at that moment. But that's more than I can allow myself to contemplate now. What matters—all I can allow to matter—rests in this folder in my hands.

And I know, after the coffee I don't need and the Hamilton fix I do—I know what has to happen next. I only hope I can pull it off.

TEN

Rochelle

She lay on the table, glad that this was one procedure for which she could remain dressed.

"Could you move up a little higher, toward the pillow?"

Rochelle sighed. Damn. Even the aesthetician was giving her directions.

An actress without a part; that's what she was. *Blondes fade fast, baby.* That's what Jesse always said.

Rochelle scootched her ass up along the narrow table, careful to keep the source of the scootching out of view.

"I love, love, love this place," she said. "No one in Hollywood loves anything anymore. Now we have to love, love, love it." She expected a laugh, at least a chuckle. Maybe even a tad of something that resembled respect. Didn't get zip.

"Enough," the woman said. "Now can you slide down just a bit?"

"Is this brain surgery, or what?"

"Sorry." The woman flushed, and Rochelle could tell

she didn't like it. So, let her. She wasn't dealing with just anyone.

"Close your eyes, please."

She did as she was told, focusing for a moment on the aesthetician's lack of expression, her curly red hair. There was a tightness to her lips she hadn't noticed before, though. Rochelle was way too old for attitude, but this was the land of attitude. Getting worse all the time.

"Your eyes, Miss McArthur. You need to close them."

"Okay, okay."

Maybe she should have waited a day, gotten in with the girl who did her hair. But Bobbo was calling the shots, and Bobbo made it clear they'd better be ready for the interview by Friday. She couldn't do it with granny-gray eyebrows.

"Is it going to hurt? Just tell me if it is."

"Of course not."

"My husband says it does."

"Is he one of our clients?"

"No, he goes to someone closer to where we live in the Hollywood Hills."

"There might be some tingling." A taut fingertip pressed between her eyebrows. "A little sting, and that's it. The results are very natural."

Was that a dig? Rochelle looked up, but the woman's expression remained calm, focused on her work.

"Close your eyes, please."

Damn, what she did in the name of beauty! Her eyes still burned from the extender that puffed extra fibers into her lashes while her mascara was still wet. She couldn't put it on without getting stray fiber on her cheeks or in her eyes. Now this.

The procedure proved painless, the way a mask felt

when being peeled from the face. This woman—wasn't her name Elizabeth?—was good. Why hadn't she thought to do this sooner? But she knew why, of course. What woman, what star, wants to admit she is so old she has to have her *eyebrows* dyed? And why were brows so different from hair? Because everyone, every age, dyed their hair, that's why.

"I got some new contacts, so I need a better match with the brows," Rochelle said.

"I mixed taupe and brown. If you want it darker, I can do another application."

The process was over in minutes. Just the warm application of a cloth, no odor whatsoever, and Elizabeth said, "That's it."

"I hope you did a good job." Rochelle used her best haughty voice, but it fell a little flat in the small room. She was better in front of a camera, or would be, if she could ever get in front of one again.

"Take a look and let me know."

The woman lowered a hand mirror at an angle that knocked off ten years from Rochelle's chin alone. The eyebrows curved and gleamed. Take off another five years, and that got her down to—what? Twenty-five, maybe? She'd lied so long she could no longer do the math in her head.

"It's great. I mean, I'm great."

"Guess you've got to be, right?"

"What do you mean?" Rochelle slammed the mirror on the table and spun around, facing her. "Are you talking about the television interview Friday?"

Their gazes held for a moment, then the older woman smiled. "One moment," she said.

She'd never been treated with this kind of disregard in the past. Just a year or two ago, the woman would be slavering, comping her the job, just so she could boast that she had Rochelle McArthur for a client.

She picked up the mirror again, looking directly into her face this time, seeing her bumpy chin, her eyes of distrust. Only the eyebrows perfect, as if she'd borrowed them from someone else, pasted them on. In spite of her rudeness, the woman, Elizabeth, had done a good job. Now, if Rochelle could just force the rest of herself to match.

This was how it began. The people who were supposed to serve you began to sneer, first behind your back, then to your face. It spread from bottom to top, up and out. Then, unless you had the luck of someone like Julie Larimore, you were history. She'd deal with it the same way she'd dealt with everything else, head first and balls out.

Rochelle yanked off the terry-cloth wrap, pulled on her blouse and was ready to get out of there. She almost collided with Elizabeth at the door to the lobby.

"I left the money on the table," she said.

The bitch didn't budge.

"You have a problem?"

"No, my dear." The woman handed her a newspaper and smiled again. "But maybe *you* do."

She did have a problem. The reporter from the party, Rikki Fitzpatrick, had written an article so damning Rochelle felt faint just reading it. The bitch had labeled the three of them, Princess Gabby, herself and Tania Marie, the Perfect Fit, the Near Fit and the Misfit, and that was just the beginning. Rochelle could barely walk outside to find a cab. But she didn't need a cab. Jesse sat in the Lexus at the curb. She jumped in and waved the paper at him.

"You're not going to believe this."

He didn't look at her, sharp features pointed straight ahead as he drove. "Oh, I believe it, all right. The question is, what are we going to do about it?"

She looked down at the article again. "What can we do about it?" She began to read it aloud, trying to convince herself the words weren't as horrible as they sounded. "Julie Larimore may be missing, but that hasn't stopped Killer Body, Inc. from recruiting her replacement. Not a replacement, exactly, says Killer Body founder and former Mr. Universe, Bobby Warren. 'An enhancement.'"

"I read it," Jesse said. "At least it makes it clear you're in the running."

"Yes, but as what? 'The Near Fit'?"

"Better than Tania Marie."

"The Misfit. That one's right on the money, at least. I wouldn't have called Princess Gabby the Perfect Fit, but it gets pretty nasty about her, too."

"I wouldn't be calling the kettle black," Jesse said. "At least that hick reporter didn't call Gabby over-the-hill."

"That phony royal pain in the ass should look so good when she's my age."

"She's supposed to *be* your age, remember?" He pulled onto Colorado and slowed down, looking for the street that would lead to their hotel. "I think I took the wrong turnoff."

He had absolutely the worst sense of direction of anyone she had ever known.

"I thought driving was genetic with men, part of the package, like balls."

"What the hell is wrong with you? There's no one listening. You mind turning off Rochelle the Bitch?"

"That's what got me where I am. You can't be a woman in this business and be anything else."

"So why take it out on me?"

What did she say to that? That she'd seen more than polite interest in his eyes when he'd talked to Princess Gabby at Bobbo's party? That she'd been treated like shit by a woman whose job it was to make her feel good about herself?

"I'm just tired," she said.

"Me, too, but we need to come up with something, a plan."

"That's your job," she said.

He turned and gave her one of the smiles that used to matter to her more than anything in the world, Hollywood included. "I think I have one."

Gabriella

Because she needed to get up early for the newest Killer Body grand opening, they ended up staying at the Westin in Pasadena that Thursday. Respectable for the money, Christopher said, and Christopher never lied. That was something her soon-to-be-ex husband didn't understand when he insisted that she kept Christopher around only because he kissed her ass. Being kind when one told the truth did not make one an ass-kisser.

The room was small in a cute, San Francisco kind of way, with a sectional sofa that stretched the entire width of it.

Christopher dismissed its peach-and-olive pattern with the same brief yet nonjudgmental frown he'd passed over the fake verdigris lighting fixtures.

"See there," he said. "If you travel with three very small people, you can place them end to end on that."

"You paid for the room, Christopher. You get the bed. It's only fair."

"Princess Gabby is not sleeping on anything that narrow. You wouldn't be able to sit up straight tomorrow at the Killer Body opening, let alone walk."

She looked at their remaining options: a queen-size, white-comforter-clad bed, a striped club chair right out of the fifties, a couple of small, round tables, that faux verdigris again.

"If I can do anything, I can stand up straight, let me assure you."

She did just that as she spoke, feeling that thread that pulled her up from these momentary setbacks into what she knew she really was.

"I'm having a drink later with my friend Frank," Christopher said. "I could probably stay at his place."

"I don't feel right about that."

"Frank's okay. Not my type, but I can count on him."

"And we can all count on you," she said. "Why can't I find a straight man at least half as decent as you are?"

"Because when they made me, they broke the mold?"

She sat down on the sofa, still concentrating on her posture. "The blush becomes you," she said. "Don't feel you have to stay at Frank's if it doesn't work out."

"I won't, but it will."

"Oh, Christopher." In the secret language they shared, it was her way of asking him what she was going to do.

He sat down beside her, and his eyes told her he'd heard the real question. "Your accent is slipping."

"It always does when I'm worried. You know he's going to have the other two at that opening tomorrow. I won't be the only one being interviewed."

"I wish I could do something." He laughed. "And I wish I weren't so damned co-dependent."

"At least you know you are. It's better, isn't it, when you know what's wrong with you?"

He gave her a sad smile and a big hug. "You're wonderful, you know that?"

"You think I ought to just call my soon-to-be ex and demand what I have coming?"

"Probably wouldn't do any good." He squeezed her arm. "Give him time. That's all he needs, all you both need. He's not going to let you starve."

"I wouldn't starve, anyway, not as long as there's a single french fry and an ounce of Baileys and a simple little Frostie left in Southern California."

It was brave talk for the humiliating poverty that sucked the pride from her at a soul level. How could anything in one's life feel right when one didn't have enough money?

"If I get this Killer Body job…" she began.

"I know." Christopher stood and picked up the newspaper, grinning like a Buddha, his shaved head glistening in the light of the gaudy floor lamp. "According to this Rikki Fitzpatrick, you, my dear, are the Perfect Fit."

The Perfect Fit. Christopher made her feel that way. And if she could just convince Bobby Warren, if she did a good job at the opening of his Pasadena Killer Body tomorrow and on the television interview after, she'd be able to support herself, get her own talk show. Lord knew, she'd been raked over the coals on enough of them that she'd be comfortable in charge, and she'd be kind to her guests, too. She'd never want to be a Rochelle McArthur, not even to get out of her financial trap.

Rochelle was her only competition, unless someone else surfaced at the last minute. Everyone knew Tania Marie didn't stand a chance. If the situation were different, she'd tell the poor thing how she lost her weight, not that the headstrong girl would listen to her or anyone.

Christopher had been gone less than ten minutes when the phone rang. She recognized Jesse McArthur's scratchy, way-too-sexy voice at once but couldn't imagine why he'd be ringing her up.

"How'd you know I was here?" The question sounded more abrupt than she'd intended, rude almost.

"Lucas Morrison told me."

Of course. She'd left her contact information with his assistant at Killer Body. All at once, she felt uncomfortable. Jesse was one of the most attractive men she'd ever met, so attractive and attentive she'd been thinking about him far too frequently. She'd done married once, talked about it on national television. She'd die before she did it again, especially with Rochelle McArthur's husband.

She aimed her acquired accent straight at the phone, a princess all the way. "What can I do for you, Mr. McArthur?"

"For starters, call me Jesse. And meet me for a little toddy."

"A drink? With you and Rochelle?"

"Just me. It could be important."

"But hardly proper."

"I understand how much you value propriety." Was that a ripple of humor in his voice? "But this is business. Important business."

Money, he seemed to be saying. Gabriella's mouth went dry.

"I will meet with you," she said, "but I won't drink alcohol."

"Whatever works."

"And my driver's out for the night."

"I'd be happy to pick you up."

There was something about the way that he said it, in spite of the tone of respect, that made her feel exposed, as if he knew a secret, all of her secrets.

"No, that won't be necessary. I'll make arrangements."

For a moment, she considered ringing up Christopher on his cell phone. No, that wasn't right. He wasn't the only co-dependent one in this happy little circle of two. He deserved a night in the company of friends. A night when he wasn't focused on trying to take care of her. She could deal with Jesse McArthur. She'd better.

ELEVEN

Rochelle

While Jesse went to meet Princess Gabby, Rochelle decided to play the Game. Not a decision, really. Just a toying with the keys of his laptop. What else was she supposed to do in this room that looked like every other hotel that had ever momentarily contained her life?

The site was easy to find, once she Googled it. She'd been there enough times. She scrolled past the first part, the medical definitions that made her cringe—the *exias* and the *limias,* the people who ate only at night, the ones addicted to exercise, the ones who craved sand or chalk. *Pica,* that one was called. So ugly these names, and the afflictions they represented. Then she found the one she was seeking. Clicked on symptoms. The answer flooded onto the small screen in blue and white, a wave of information. Now the game began.

Often have a history of abuse. She was free of that. A point for her.

Frequently have feelings of insecurity. Who in Hollywood wouldn't? Call it a draw.

Prone to shoplifting or breaking the rules. Another point for her.

Sexually capricious. Not for many years. Make it half a point.

She was okay. Every time she played the Game, comparing herself with the stereotypes, she knew that. She didn't even need to answer the other questions. Oh, hell, why not?

Frequently has excuses for missing meals, saying she or he has eaten earlier. Okay, maybe one point for the devil, but if you're not hungry, you're not hungry.

Regardless of weight, considers him- or herself fat. Another twinge. She got up from the computer and walked to the full-length mirror on the wall beside the window.

She wasn't slutted up, as Jesse called it. Just the jeans, just the soft heather-toned sweater over them. Damn, her ass. He was right about that. Her thighs. They weren't dangerous yet, but she could see the spread. The Clen wasn't working fast enough. She needed to increase the lunges and talk to Blond Elvis about his toys. Okay, give up a point. What woman today over thirty wouldn't feel the same way? Especially if her husband was having drinks with one of the sexiest women in the world?

Believes being thin is akin to power. You'd better believe it, baby. Guilty on that one, all the way. But who cared? She'd still won the Game.

That was why she liked to play the Game.

She always won.

She glanced over at the courtesy bar. There would be nuts in there, cookies, maybe crackers, along with the requisite alcohol. Perhaps she could just find something to chew. She wouldn't have to swallow it.

But first, where the hell had Jesse hidden her cigarettes? She just hoped he came back soon. And that somehow he didn't notice that Princess Gabby, and not his over-the-hill slob of a wife, was the one with the killer body.

Gabriella

Gabriella lucked out. The shuttle from the hotel was a black sedan. The young, buff driver looked as if he'd been cast for the role, and the Hilton was only six blocks away. She wouldn't have to be embarrassed in front of Jesse McArthur, jumping out of some Yellow Cab, the way she and her grandmother used to when they made a trip of similar length downtown.

"I could have walked it," she said to the driver.

"A princess shouldn't have to walk." He got out of the car and opened the back door for her. A well-meaning man, sweet, the way Christopher was sweet.

"How'd you recognize me?" She hated herself for trying to beg one more good moment out of this encounter.

"The story in the newspaper."

She looked up into his eyes but couldn't read whether or not there was sincerity there. What did it take to understand men? To know which ones were good, and which ones were rotten? It wasn't easy, not like shopping, where you could spot last year's fashion disasters on the sales racks, where you could identify the plastic-wrapped rotting vegetables on the kiosk at the grocery store.

She handed him the tip, fingers closed around the bill, pointed down.

"You have a way back?" he asked.

"They have a shuttle here, don't they? Besides, I can always walk."

His face seemed to go masklike. She, who prided herself on her ability to read people's moods, tried to slip into his thoughts and ran into a wall.

"Don't walk, not even six blocks."

"Why not? Why shouldn't I?"

He looked away from her, then back, into her eyes. "We've had calls at the hotel. I didn't think anything about them until I met you." Then, her money still clutched in his fingers, he seemed to snap to attention. "I shouldn't have said that. I'm sorry."

"Sorry? You tell me I should be concerned about walking six blocks, and you won't tell me why?"

His eyes became shadows, his posture even stiffer than before. "I can't tell you that, but I can be here when you're ready to go back. Just give me a call. You're a nice lady. I'm happy to do it."

"I want to know about the calls," she said, feeling that thread that ran through her bloodline pull her up to her highest stance. "Perhaps I should speak to your supervisor?"

"All right." He shoved the money into his pocket. "We've had phone calls asking when you were arriving and what room you were in. Of course, the front desk knows better than to give out that kind of information. One desk clerk said she was offered a bribe to tell. I'm just worried that she might not be the only one."

"The press." Probably the reporter, that damned Rikki Fitzpatrick. She was trying to track her down again. That was fine. She'd had tougher interviews. And if it wasn't the reporter? But it must be.

"I appreciate your telling me," she said.

"Just be careful. There are a lot of nuts out there."

She watched him return to the car, wondering if he was telling her the truth, or if he was one of those nuts he was talking about. Or both.

Lucas

"Jesse McArthur is meeting Princess Gabby in the cocktail lounge of his hotel."

Bobby Warren's voice sputtered through the phone. "How do you know?"

"First, Jesse called Ellen to find out where she was staying. Less than an hour later, the princess called. Just said she felt we should be aware, under the circumstances. There's no reason she shouldn't meet with him, I guess. She said she just wanted us to know in case it came up later on."

"Where's Shelly?"

"In their room, probably. Princess Gabby said he was meeting her alone."

"You *guess*, Luke?"

"Rochelle's in the room." Damn, the old man could be a pain in the ass. "Why does it matter where she is?"

"I just want to be sure she's okay."

"I've got the room number," he said.

"I never call a lady friend unless she asks me to."

Lucas sighed and looked outside at the falling gray evening. "Call her, Bobby. You know she'd love to hear from you. How many women get a call from Bobby Warren on a Thursday night?"

He could hear the self-satisfied chuckle under the reedlike voice. "I might just do that. How are you coming with the reporter?"

"She's exemplary," he said. "I can't find out anything to indicate why she'd be out to cause trouble for us." He stared out into the dusky light, trying to decide if he should share his suspicions, that he felt Rikki had other motives. No, Bobby didn't need intuition right now. "She got an award last year for a series on bulimia, so she may have an ax to grind. I'm still looking into it."

"And you're attracted to her, maybe?"

"My loyalty is to you." He spit out the answer before he could think. "If you don't know that by now, there's no way I could convince you."

"I know that." A sigh, maybe just a labored breath. "You're like my own son. You know that, too."

"Did you take your supplements?"

"Of course. Did you take yours?"

"I will, right after we hang up."

"Promise?"

"Promise. Good night, Bobby."

"Good night to you. Hey, Luke?"

It was Bobby W's way, that last question of the day. "Yeah?"

"I still think you're attracted to Rikki-Rikki."

"You're crazy," he said, then realized he was holding only a dial tone to his ear. The old bastard had hung up on him. But he'd tagged him first. It didn't make any difference, though. He wasn't about to act on his feelings. He didn't need to single out this woman. There were plenty to go around. Including the one in the next office.

He picked up the phone and pushed the button labeled *Horner*. Ellen didn't answer. Not like her to leave so early. Mild disappointment flitted through him. He was going to ask her to dinner, not a date, just one of those extended business days they shared occasionally. She'd made it clear from the start that theirs was a professional relationship only, and that made it possible for them to be friends without games or expectations.

Might as well leave for the day. He could pick up something on the way home, maybe drop by Bobby W's. No, the old man would be into the bourbon by now, and that was getting too sad to witness.

He had just turned off his computer when Ellen burst into his office.

"I was just going to call you," he said. Then he saw her flushed face and wide eyes.

"I'm glad you're still here." She shoved a tablet of scribbled notes into his hands. "I just got this from the people doing the background check. Rikki Fitzpatrick had a cousin."

"Had?"

"She died." Ellen moved next to him, jabbing her finger at the words she'd jotted down. "Just two weeks ago, Lucas."

The words on the page taunted him. It couldn't be. He felt Ellen beside him, was vaguely aware of her perfume, of the suddenly too-warm room closing around him.

"Lucas, what is it?"

"Oh, God," he said. "Not Lisa Tilton."

TWELVE

Gabriella

She had been wrong to speak rudely to Jesse on the phone. His behavior was above reproach, shy almost, as he ordered their drinks. She'd agreed to a glass of chardonnay, after all, not because she wanted it. Wine was loaded with sugar. Only one table remained unoccupied at the Hilton's lounge, heavy traffic for a Thursday. Must be a convention somewhere nearby.

They sat, tucked against the wall adjacent to the bar, probably the most private place in this darkened room that was anything but private.

"Why didn't Rochelle join us?" She felt it was the proper thing to say.

"She never accompanies me on business." That made her feel better. But then, he smiled and added, "In this case, I have to say the business is also a pleasure. You're looking wonderful, but then, you know that."

"It's always nice to hear." She tasted the wine. A compliment didn't hurt. It's not as if he were leering. And she hadn't put on this fuchsia ruffle-front dress to be ignored. "One never knows what to wear out here. The weather can change so suddenly."

"Rochelle says Bobby likes women to look like women. I'm sure he'll approve of that dress."

She started to say she wasn't wearing this tomorrow, but her cell phone surprised her with its embarrassing *William Tell Overture* ring. She'd have to get Christopher to program in a new sound. "Excuse me," she said, pulling it out, hoping Christopher was okay. "Very few people have this number, so it must be important."

It wasn't Christopher's voice that greeted her, however.

"Gabriella Paquette?"

"That's correct."

"This *is* Gabriella?"

"Yes, I just said so. What is this regarding?"

"My name is Courtney," the woman responded. "I'm calling regarding the delinquent balance on your Visa card."

Embarrassment flooded her in one hot wave after another. She looked across at Jesse, who watched with polite curiosity. "How did you get this number?"

"Ma'am, this is a collection agency. It's our business. Now, I want to know how much you can pay today."

"Today?"

"Right now. I can take a check, Gabriella, right over the phone. Can you pay the entire amount?"

Jesse continued to watch. Her mouth went dry. Pretend she was talking to a reporter; that was it. Make him believe it.

"Gabriella, are you there?"

"I'll need to call you back."

"Not until you make a payment. We've been patient with you for months now, and if we don't get something,

I'm going to have to turn it over to our legal department."

"I'll call you," she managed, her voice grating. Then she punched off the phone. Let this Courtney woman go to her legal department. At least they wouldn't find her tonight.

"Sorry," she said to Jesse. "Now, where were we?"

"Problems?" he asked, his expression quizzical. Again, she had the feeling that this was a man who could read her mind.

"The media never gives up." She forced herself to sound bored and reached for her wine with sweaty fingers that felt suddenly dirty. "This is excellent chardonnay."

"Would you like another?"

"Thank you, but one is my limit." She took another sip for courage, and because she was quaking from the inside out. "You said you wanted to discuss business."

He nodded and smiled again. "This is difficult, for a number of reasons. For one, you're not only beautiful, you're refreshing. I'm not sure I've ever met another woman quite like you."

Not a good beginning. Too much of a build-up. "Thank you. I'm pretty ordinary, actually."

"There's nothing ordinary about you, Gabby. You could do better than Killer Body. Much better."

So that was it. "Killer Body isn't an end," she said. "It's a beginning."

"But there are bigger beginnings, and I can help you find them."

"You invited me here because you want to represent me?"

"I'm good at hooking up people, and I have some contacts that would be perfect for you."

Then why didn't he use them for his wife? First, the horrible phone call, now this. A bad night all around. No reason to waste another moment here. She put down her glass.

"All I have to do to get you for an agent is bow out of the Killer Body competition, perhaps?" She pushed back her chair.

"Wait." He held up his hand. "Before you make a hasty decision, you should know there's money involved."

"How much money?"

"I'm used to advancing my clients whatever they need to set themselves up while we're launching them."

She sat back in her chair and forced herself to remain calm. "Isn't that a bit unorthodox?"

"Works for me." His eyes penetrated, reading her every doubt, driving away each one. "I know that you can do better than Killer Body."

"But your wife can't?" She felt herself flush at the mean-spirited response. But he didn't flare back, only nodded.

"Sadly, she's of an age where the possibilities are limited. Not like you."

The bitchy side of her tried to do mental arithmetic, wondering how old Rochelle really was. No, she shouldn't do that, and to ask would be below her.

"I think I'd be wonderful with a little talk show," she said.

"Better than wonderful, and you don't need Killer Body to get there." He reached across the table and squeezed her hand. "Why don't you let me see what I can get going, and in the meantime, I'll advance you some cash?"

Could it be this easy? Give up Killer Body, have

enough cash to bail herself out of this financial mess until her divorce settlement? Get her own talk show? Damn, she wished she and Alain were on speaking terms. He'd know what to do. He always did. Divorce was so rotten the way it sucked the friendship and trust away, along with the marriage. What would Alain say? she wondered, and as she did so, she heard the answer in her mind.

She patted his hand, removed her own and sat as straight as possible in the chair. "I don't know," she said. "I'll need time to think."

The hotel room looked friendlier than it had when she'd left it. She'd taken the shuttle back and had the driver stop for fries and a soft-serve cone, which, while softer than when it arrived in her hands, was still substantial enough to support the little topping of Baileys once she was back in the room. Marvelous—medicinal, almost—the icy cocoa, boozy cream swirling around the salty potatoes. Standing in the bathroom of her hotel room, she consumed every one of the fries. What the hell was she going to do?

She didn't know when she fell asleep, only that she had been jerked awake by an invasive noise of some kind. She sat up in bed. A bad dream? No, not a dream. A siren was blaring, reverberating in her head. Her first thought, halfway between consciousness and the other side, was that she still smoked, that she was still a rebellious high school kid in Texas. Crazy. This was real, and she had no choice but to deal with it.

She went to the door, opened it just enough to peek out, just to be sure she wasn't crazy.

Good Lord. The hall was swarming with partially clad men and women, many in the Westin terry-cloth robes, just like the one she'd put on earlier. Damned if she'd put it on again. She ran back and slipped her long, heavy macramé sweater over her Victoria's Secret T-shirt. As she stepped outside the room, frozen with fear, she heard an authoritative male voice announce, "The elevator's closed. Use the stairs."

Never had she seen so many bathrobes in one place. Strangers clattered down the dank-smelling steel staircase. They were all together here, all of them who'd been stopped in their pursuit of the evening—the ones getting drunk, the ones freshly or partially laid, the ones, like she, who had just been trying to sleep.

Down they ran, down the stairs. The faster ones burst ahead, as if speed were their right. The slower ones clutched the rail. At least a couple sobbed.

"We'll be all right," shouted a cheerful voice Gabby realized came from within her. "Just stay calm. We must all do that."

Somebody stronger than she slammed into her, knocking her out of the way. "Move faster, damn it. Do you want to die?"

She grabbed the rail and let the person in shorts and a gray sweatshirt shoot by. Man or woman? Who knew which at this hour? They were all terrified and driven by the noise pounding into them.

Frightened as she was, something told her that she'd live, that she'd be all right. This wasn't the end; it was a test of some kind. For all she knew, Bobby Warren could have set it up to see how she handled herself in an emergency. Yes, that was it, just another test. She'd had them since she was in elementary school, staring up at the monkey bars. She'd do now what her grandma had taught her to do then. Stand up straight, move carefully along these steel monkey bars, and she would do just fine.

At the end of the steps, the heavy mushroom-colored door opened onto the street. They flowed through it in a tidal wave of anxiety. Once outside, no one ran. They walked and waited outside the front of the hotel that had looked so glamorous only hours before.

"It's okay to go back to your rooms, folks," a soft female voice announced. "You can use the elevators."

A partially clad man, his Westin bathrobe barely belted, stepped up to the front desk. "I want to hear that from someone in authority."

A woman in a black jacket and slacks stepped forward. "You just did."

Before she thought better of it, Gabriella applauded. Others joined her. The woman smiled.

"We're sorry for the inconvenience," she said. "You'll all receive a complimentary room tonight."

Complimentary, as in *free.* Gabriella went up to the woman at the registration desk. She asked questions. She thanked her for the complimentary room. She walked back to the elevator, contemplating the irony of it all.

Gabriella rode the elevator, shoved between so many Westin bathrobes, that she felt ready to suffocate in white terry cloth at any moment. She'd never needed to talk to Alain the way she needed to right now. He'd understand; he'd tell her what to do, which was probably something like, "Get out of that bloody hotel, love. I'll be right there."

But she and Alain were finished. And even if she did call him, he'd probably be in bed with Judith. She was the real reason Gabriella had let the relationship with David get out of control. The bitch had pretended to be her friend, then bedded poor Alain the moment she got him drunk enough.

Poor Alain. That showed how bad off she was. To think of the cheating swine as poor anybody.

The elevator doors slid open at the seventh floor, and Gabriella stepped out.

She'd be okay. She wouldn't have to call Alain. Just room service, maybe, get herself that nice *ahi* salad she'd seen on the menu—balsamic vinegar instead of dressing. Yes, that would be lovely.

She started to slide her key in the door. Before she could connect with whatever type of electronic source responded to the key, the door slid open. How could that be?

She stepped inside. Everything was okay in the short, carpeted hall that led to the room. But the bathroom light was on. She was sure she'd turned it off.

She sensed the horror before she entered the room. The bathroom mirror had been shattered. Jagged pieces of glass gleamed from the sink and the pink marble vanity. What was going on? Her foundation lay in a broken glass on the floor. Had that been what had smashed the mirror? Whatever was wrong in this hotel went beyond a faulty alarm, into something more personal. She felt herself shrink beneath the sweater, unable to look at her defiled bathroom, her broken reflection another moment. She'd demand another room, damn the cost, get out of here right now.

She stepped out of the bathroom into the short hallway that led to the bedroom. Just find her suitcase. Just get out. Just...

She stopped with a gasp, refusing to believe what she saw. But there it was, taped to the wall above the sofa, almost as wide as the shuttered window. Red background, shiny as lip gloss, black dress, slit to reveal legs so perfect they must have been airbrushed on. And above Julie Larimore's flawless form, the slogan of which Bobby Warren was so proud.

You Have to Want the Body.

Julie Larimore.

Gabriella ran, grabbing the cell phone again, the key, running into the hallway. She'd be safer out there than in here. She almost collided with the in-charge woman she'd seen downstairs.

"I insist that you move me to another room," Gabriella said.

"Calm down, ma'am. It's okay. I apologize for any inconvenience."

"Inconvenience?" Dear God, don't let her start shouting at this poor woman who was only trying to do her job. "I need out of my room because someone has vandalized it."

"What do you mean? They just pulled one of the alarms by accident."

"Who pulled the alarm, if I may ask?" There. Now she was back on track, speaking softly, even though her teeth were all but chattering. "Who are these *theys?*"

The woman shook her head, and Gabriella could see the real story in her face. Too young for the job, twenty-three, she'd bet, and way over her curly little head. "An alarm," she managed. "Fire alarm."

"Which floor?"

"We're looking into that right now."

"So, you don't know?"

"We're pretty sure." She coughed, then looked her over as if trying to assess what motives lay behind her interest. "This floor."

"God."

"There's no fire, ma'am. It was a false alarm."

"My room's not a false alarm. Someone has destroyed it."

"Destroyed it, how?"

"Threw my cosmetics into the mirror, smashed them on the floor."

"Did you have a fight with somebody?" she asked through her squint. "Your boyfriend?"

"What boyfriend?"

"Aren't there two of you registered here?"

"Indeed, there are." Damned if she'd get into Christopher's private life. "He's not my boyfriend. And he isn't going to want to stay in the room, either. Surely you can get us into another."

"Only one problem with that," she said. "If the alarm really was set off on this floor, we need to talk to everyone on it."

"Are you saying you can't do that if I'm in a room without a shattered mirror and my personal possessions scattered all over the place?"

The woman's suntanned face took on a tinge, and for the first time, she spotted something more than her job in it, maybe even something decent. "I'm no cop," she said. "I don't know what to do here."

"For starters, please just get me out of that room."

She did it, too, and in less than an hour. New room, new life, new message for Christopher at the front desk. Now here she sat on the same bed with its white, down-filled comforter, its wonderful little pillows, its room-service menu, or as they now called it, "In-Room Dining."

Wine by the bottle or half bottle. She could use a drink. Maybe even some real food. She glanced at the menu. Farfalle, risotto, salmon. None was really that difficult to resist; she'd learned that when she lost her weight. It was all about choice; hunger seldom had anything to do with it.

She flipped the page of the menu. Temptation flashed past her. In two words, Dessert Menu. A cheesecake with chocolate chip cookies blended into it. A lemon tart. Bread pudding with apples and rum. Tiramisu made with coffee and marsala. Ice cream served in a brandy cup. Milk shakes, a classic hot fudge sundae, made with Häagen-Dazs, with additional hot fudge on the side. It was the additional hot fudge that got her.

God help her, she picked up the phone and ordered one of each. Just a bite, not what she used to do. She would have a bite of each one, and only that. After what she'd been through tonight, she deserved something sweet in her life. And desserts were cheaper than alcohol. This venture was more cost-efficient than a bottle of wine that would just puff up her face and make her look like hell tomorrow, anyway.

She picked up the phone and placed her order.

"You wanted the flan?" she called to an imaginary roommate. Then continued, "Yes. One flan, one crème brûlée, one lemon tart, one bread pudding, one California strawberry shortcake…" She continued down the list, all the way to the bottom.

"How many forks?" the voice on the other end asked.

"Why, one for each of us, of course."

Fifteen minutes later, her order arrived. The server was a woman, her eyes still dazed from the earlier alarm. She stood outside the door with her large tray.

"Where do you want these?"

"My friend, Christopher, will bring them in," she

said. "We're having a bit of a get-together. Our friends went back to their rooms to change." The server didn't alter her bored expression, and Gabriella realized she was talking too much. The young woman didn't give a fig who ate this stuff; she just wanted to get paid. Gabrielle extended her room key. "Is your tip included?"

"Yes, and I don't need your card, just for you to sign the bill here. You sure you don't want me to carry this inside?"

"No. My friend can take care of it. We'll leave the tray for you tomorrow."

The girl's expression softened. "Okay, then." The princess accent. It worked every time.

Gabriella stood outside the door, head held high, as the girl walked down the hall and into the elevator.

Once she dragged the tray inside, she twisted the dead bolt and slid the double lock securely into place. Where did she start? The smells, the textures, the fruit garnishes, the tiny knots of whipped cream, the gravelly sprinkling of nuts so minuscule she'd have to taste them to identify their origin? No; there was only one place to start.

She looked at her finger, pale and white, a creamy contrast to her lilac-toned nails. Then, slowly, she dipped that perfect fingertip into the silver cup that contained the additional hot fudge for the sundae. As the heat of the chocolate consumed her flesh, she felt finally free of the night's terror, and she reveled in the thought of what she would experience next.

Gabriella sat on the tile floor of the bathroom, head over the toilet, smelling the cool breath of the water in her face. Nothing more to expel, and probably nothing more to consume, if that act of human aberration were possible. She hadn't done this, had she? Not after being in control for so long?

No one answered. The toilet bowl just sat there. Oh, God, had it come to this?

THIRTEEN

Gabriella

She woke up a little after five, hating herself. That was the worst part, how it made you feel about yourself. She'd be okay, though. She'd been okay a long time, in control. That's what she needed to get. Back in control. Accountability, discipline, and for now, she needed to prove she was on the right track.

The hotel had threatened to crumble at her feet. She'd had to confront how alone she really was. But the health club on the fourth floor was open. On the treadmill, she faced the row of windows, shutting out the two or three other exercisers behind her on various pieces of equipment. She walked at a rapid pace, watching the dark hills against the light of the sky, only a few cars on Los Robles at this hour, and fewer still on Walnut. Safe-sounding streets in a city, a world, where it could all change just like that. How fragile our lives really are, she thought, despite how secure and indestructible we try to make them in our minds. Despite how we decorate them with desk clerks, elected officials, wedding vows.

Now here she was, absolutely alone, and having to face heaven knew what in only a few hours. Was it worth it, to risk her health? And based on what had happened back in her room, maybe more than her health? Maybe she should just accept Jesse McArthur's offer.

Rikki

They are all here, the reporters and camera people, on Los Robles, as Bobby Warren cuts the ribbon on his new Killer Body location. That it's a short, square building doesn't matter. That the three women can barely look at one another doesn't matter. That one of the reporters makes a crack about how he usually covers auto accidents matters even less.

"At least we're still alive," Bobby Warren croaks.

He is the true reason we're here—Bobby Warren, the ultimate living fitness pioneer. Bigger than Jack La Lanne; bigger than Joe Gold and his gyms; bigger than Harold Zinkin, who started the whole thing when he became the state's first Mr. California and, later, invented the Universal Gym Machine.

Bobby is dressed in a Versace T-shirt. I know that only because of the white-on-white linking initials embossed on it, the same pattern I saw in our newspaper the day we reported Versace's murder.

I have to admit old Bobby looks kind of cute, in spite of his cocky attitude, his paunch, his sparse, untinted hair.

"Welcome folks," he says, staring into the camera and speaking into a microphone he doesn't need for our tiny group. The scrappy old man knows no enemy. Behind him, though, I see angry eyes only partially hidden by scaled-down glasses, glaring at me as if he has a major bitch. Not thrilled at the article, I'm sure. I look away from him and focus my attention on his boss.

"We're happy to be here today, to welcome another Killer Body into the world." Bobby Warren's voice slurs a bit. He couldn't have had a drink this early, could he? I'll worry about that later. Right now, I'm mesmerized as I watch him introduce what he calls his "dear friends," who are there to celebrate the success of Killer Body.

A van pulls up as they are introduced. A cameraman gets out. The word must have spread that Tania Marie is here.

The women step forward as they are summoned. Princess Gabriella Paquette. Damn. At first, I am distracted by the head treatment, the intricate bandanna holding back all but a few dark blond spirals. But now, although the dress is a flattering violet shade, I realize it's the same dress, the Julie Larimore dress, my cousin's dress. Oh, damn, she's even wearing the belt, letting it slink down along her hips.

Before I can get over that, Bobby says to the camera, "I'd like to introduce my dear friend, Shelly McArthur." And up steps Rochelle, attitude a mile high and wide. The old man forgets his speech, obviously entranced by the way Rochelle moves across the back of the room in a black dress that has not only a slit over the right knee, not only a pale-pink V accentuating that slit, but a matching pink strap over the right shoulder.

"And another dear friend, I don't want to forget. Folks, let's welcome little Tania Marie Camp."

The audience hoots and hollers. Tania Marie is anything but "little," yet the ankle-length navy skirt and long jacket slenderize her a little. Either that, or she's lost weight since the party. She wears her usually flipped-up hair curved under, into a bob, that with her too-short bangs and John Lennon glasses makes her look an unlikely combination of vulnerable and hip.

The TV reporters and cameramen rush up the walk. Another van stops at the curb. Tania Marie looks ready to bolt.

Bobby tears his gaze away from Rochelle's espadrille-wrapped ankles long enough to give Tania Marie a reassuring pat and to whisper something in her ear. She nods then flashes him, us, the arriving reporters, her little-girl smile.

"Welcome, folks," Bobby says into the microphone. He's almost too smooth and spontaneous.

"Tania Marie," one reporter, an overweight male, asks. "Is it true you want to be the next Killer Body spokesmodel?"

"Who wouldn't?" She extends the smile, but I can feel her tension as if it were my own.

"What does Marshall Cameron think about that?"

She flushes. Standing between Rochelle and Tania Marie, Bobby Warren frowns, and Rochelle drops her gaze, not quickly enough to hide the amusement in her eyes.

"I'm sorry, but my attorneys have advised me not to discuss that subject."

"Are *you* on the Killer Body program yourself, Tania Marie?" A woman reporter this time, in her fifties, maybe, speaking in a patronizing tone.

"Okay, okay, I love the program." She bites her bottom lip, then finds the smile again. "Could you guys just give me some space? I can't answer any more personal questions right now."

Something makes me feel sorry for her. She has that quality that makes you want to cheer for her, something about the way she tries to do the right thing, even though she's visibly humiliated. Surprising myself, I step forward.

"I have a question for you, Mr. Warren." And before he can react to the sound of his own name, "Have you heard from Julie Larimore?"

Behind him, Lucas shoots a fresh supply of hatred my direction. I shoot it back. Bobby touches the quilted flesh of his throat. "No." He almost whispers it.

"Any idea where she is?"

"The police are treating it as a missing persons case. We're hoping for the best."

"The best, meaning what?"

"No more questions. Luke, get the girls inside."

"What do you think happened to Julie Larimore?" the older female reporter presses.

"I wish we knew. Sorry, folks. No more for today." He whisks the women inside the building. I come right after them, the other reporters behind me.

The entry is more elegant than the location I visited in the Valley. Glass and plants and that new-building smell give an impression of hope. The door to the rest of the facility is closed. Lucas stands in front of it overdressed as hell in the charcoal jacket the same color as his glasses.

"No more questions," he says. "Bobby and his friends would like to celebrate privately now."

The older reporter steps in front of the Julie Larimore poster and faces him. "What's the story on Princess Gabby? We heard her hotel room was vandalized last night."

That's a new one.

"I don't know. This is the first I've heard of it."

"How soon is Bobby Warren going to make a decision?"

"Very soon."

"Are there any other candidates?"

"The field's wide open, as far as I know." Lucas turns to his assistant. "Ellen, call Security, will you? I want these people out of here, now."

We have our stories. There's nothing else to be gained by sticking around, except for me. As the others begin to exit, I lock gazes with Lucas.

He walks over to me. "I want to talk to you."

"We'll talk, all right." I spit the answer back at him. "First I have a story to report."

He moves into my space, my face, forcing me to confront him, his voice still low. "The real story is about your cousin, isn't it?"

His words almost knock me over. I look around this room of glass and mirrors, not sure I can rise from the reality of those two words. *Your cousin.*

"She's part of the story," I say through quivering lips. "And so are you."

"You're looking for revenge, pure and simple. Were you the one who got those other reporters here?"

"No, but you don't have to be a brain surgeon to figure out that Tania Marie would show up at a Killer Body opening."

"Especially since you wrote a story saying she was one of the contenders."

Lucas looks at his assistant, poised by the front door, as if in charge of who goes in or out, a pretty little monitor in an all-white suit. "Is that locked, Ellen?"

She nods.

"Would you do me a favor? I want to talk to Rikki alone."

"Of course." Her voice is hushed like the voices on the telephones in law offices and courtrooms. "It's been a long night and a long morning, and I really ought to drive back to Santa Barbara," she says. "Unless you need me here."

"I'll be fine. You go."

"I'll check out of my hotel and head straight to the office. Are you coming back today?"

"I'll let you know."

He watches her leave, then turns to me. "Sit down, please."

I am too angry to sit, but I force myself to settle in one of the white wrought-iron chairs. He does the same, looking less imposing as he arranges his long legs on one of the loveseats.

"Don't men belong to Killer Body?" I ask.

"Some. Most of our members are women, but you know that."

"The furnishings kind of give it away," I say. Then, "Why did you ask her to leave?"

"Because I want to tell you something no one else knows, not even Bobby Warren."

Something in his eyes makes me believe he's telling the truth, but I can't imagine what he could say to me that he wouldn't say to his boss. "What could that be?"

"I knew your cousin."

Gabriella

The media had cleared out, and Rochelle McArthur had flounced off, her arm linked in Bobby Warren's, the pink strap of her asymmetric black dress slipping over her tanned shoulder. It would take everything she had to wrest the job away from that one. But then again, if Jesse was honest with his offer, if the sum was enough, perhaps it wouldn't matter.

So much for this little celebration. Gabriella stepped out the back door and walked around in front. Everyone except the hired help and poor Tania Marie had left the office, or the *center,* as Bobby Warren preferred to call it. A few hours later, they'd do it all again for the television audience. She was certain to be questioned about the mishap at the hotel. Gabriella felt her flesh grow clammy as she recalled what the real mishap had been last night, the one almost as terrifying as the smashed mirror. The one where the guilty party was all too clear.

Where was Christopher? She hated to stand alone like this, hated being alone, period. What had Alain said the day she left? "You want to spend your nights hugging air?"

And she had said, "I'll be hugging freedom."

"Hey, Gabby." She turned at the sound of the stage whisper to spot Tania Marie trying to press herself against the side of the building. Gabriella went over to where she stood.

Even in the stylish little glasses, the poor girl looked as if she needed a good cry. At least her hair had killer body, better than this frizzy mass she carried around. "What is it? Are you all right?"

"Totally screwed. My cell phone's all jacked up, and I can't call my bodyguard. Can I use yours?"

"Of course." At that moment, her sedan glided to a stop in front of the Killer Body center. "There's my driver," Gabriella said. "Why don't you let me give you a lift?"

"You mean it? Hey, that would be great." Tania Marie's lips, still as thickly polished and glossed as her fingernails, broke into a smile that seemed to come from her heart and not from a media trainer or makeup artist.

"I don't want to depend on this asshole bodyguard any more than is absolutely necessary, if you know what I mean."

"Of course," Gabriella said, although she didn't have a clue. Nor could she imagine why anyone, especially a pretty girl—and Tania Marie did have such a pretty face, not to mention that gorgeous burgundy hair—would want to, indeed even relish, speaking with the vernacular of a far less fortunate person.

Christopher played the chauffeur role with aplomb. How blessed she had been that this native Californian had decided, during the course of his world travels, to visit what she once thought of as her country. And she was more fortunate still that in that very city, his lover chose to desert him and Christopher sought employment as a driver.

She could tell Tania Marie was impressed as she directed him to her hotel. Arrogant cars cut them off at every corner. Gabriella couldn't abide these Southern Californians. Too brash—what Christopher would call too *ballsy*—they too frequently dealt with life the way they dealt with the freeways.

"Are you from here?" Gabriella inquired.

"Yeah, but not for a long time. My folks have been divorced for as long as I can remember. My mother lives in San Francisco. That's where her newest restaurant is."

As if Gabriella or most of the country didn't know that. "What does your father do?"

"He's back in New York." Tania Marie paused, and rushed out the rest of it, her voice defiant. "Probably the best damned bartender in the country."

"Indeed." That juicy tidbit was one the tabloids had missed. "I adore your mom's San Francisco place. Where do you live now?"

"Santa Barbara." She raised her eyebrows. "After my all-too-public problems in New York, I moved there about three months ago."

"Before the Killer Body misfortune?"

"You mean before Julie disappeared? Hell, yes. That wasn't the reason I moved." Her eyes darkened, or maybe it was just that the lighting changed as they pulled onto Colorado Avenue. "What about you? Where do you live?"

"Los Angeles, for now." She met the dark challenge of Tania Marie's eyes. "Like you, I suspect, I'm nursing a broken heart in the public eye. I don't like it very much."

Tears burst and spread along the bottom lids of Tania Marie's eyes. "Tell me about it. Don't you hate those bastards?"

"Sometimes," Gabriella said. "I'd have to say that sometimes I hate them, make that *him*. And sometimes I miss him with all my heart and soul."

Tania Marie wiped her eyes, leaving a raccoon smear from the corner of the right one to the side of her face. "I miss him, too, the bastard."

In that moment, Gabriella knew why Tania Marie swore. And she wished that she could swear, too.

They pulled onto Los Robles, and Tania Marie called to Christopher, "Look for Walnut. That's the cross street."

Something sent a small shiver down Gabriella's spine.

"You're staying at the Westin?"

She nodded. "It's a nice hotel. I like the robes and that double shower."

"You were there last night?"

"No, I checked in this morning. I heard about what

happened, though." She narrowed her eyes. "You know what I think?"

Gabriella looked into those deceptively innocent blue-green eyes and tried to swallow the knot in her throat. "Tell me."

"It's that bitch, Rochelle."

Another shiver shot through her. "What about her?"

"Like she's the one. Someone damn near killed me in the sauna at my health club. Someone trashed your room at the hotel. But nothing's happened to her."

"Maybe she's going to be next," Gabriella said.

"I doubt the hell out of that one. The bitch offered me her husband to back out of the competition."

"She offered you Jesse?" Gabriella couldn't stop the hot flush of embarrassment on her cheeks. She looked away, out the window.

"Not like *that*. As my agent. Jesse told me he might be able to get me some film work, something respectable. Take the attention off those recent events of mine."

"Did he offer you money, too?"

"No. I don't need money."

"No, you don't. Jesse offered you what he thought you *did* need."

Gabriella ached to tell Tania Marie about her own offer from Jesse, and her conversation with him, but she didn't dare take the chance. With a chill, she recalled that Tania Marie, not Rochelle, was the one who was staying at the Westin—the site of her room-trashing. Besides, Tania Marie was a loose cannon, with questionable regard for decorum.

"That reporter was right about you," Tania Marie said. "You *are* the perfect fit. I can lose to you, but I cannot lose to that bitch, Rochelle. You know she's screwing Bobby Warren?"

"Nobody knows that."

"The tabloids do."

"The tabloids also claim that you had sex with one of America's most respected news commentators."

"Had to tie him down, right? It was all me, and he was just overcome." Tania Marie wiped her eyes. "The man's not as pure as his image. You don't get to be his age and then just accidentally end up cheating on your wife with an assistant younger than your daughter. My problem wasn't what I did or even getting caught by that stupid housekeeper. It was believing him when he said he loved me." She bit her lip.

"We're not so different, after all," Gabriella said. "We've both been betrayed by the men we love."

"Like I said, I can lose to you, but not Rochelle. Have you ever really checked her out? She has those damned French manicured toenails. They're acrylics for sure, and her fingernails match. That's how all the manicurists wear theirs, just clipped down to nothing, and they paint that toxic shit on."

Gabriella glanced down at her own acrylics and the lilac frost that covered them. At least she had opted for tasteful polish. "How do you do your own nails?"

Tania Marie laughed. "Hey, in some ways, Mother Nature kicked me in the ass. But I've got great nails, great teeth and great hair." Across the narrow space in the car seat, she pointed a sharp, burgundy-coated stiletto at Gabriella. "Believe it or not, these are all mine."

"Believe it or not, I *believe* it."

"Good." Tania Marie turned to her and lowered her voice. "Now, what are we going to do about that bitch, Rochelle?"

At that moment, Gabriella decided to tell her about Jesse McArthur's offer.

FOURTEEN

Rikki

With that terrible beginning, Lucas and I find our own twisted path to peace and conversation. Now, here we are, only two hours later, driving different cars down the same freeway, having agreed to talk more.

In this darkening morning in a city that is never really light, I travel the freeway, afraid of what will happen or what I will learn, but afraid to do anything but keep moving forward. I can still barely believe what he's said to me.

We meet in the restaurant parking lot. And I know I have to ask before we go in.

"You okay?" he asks. He looks concerned but not too much so, with his short, dark hair, his cool glasses, the biceps beneath the Brooks Brothers.

"Why didn't you tell me you knew her?"

"I just didn't make the connection. You have different last names. Lisa went by Tilton."

"We were cousins. Lisa kept her father's name. I kept my father's name. Only difference is my father died before I was born."

That appears to surprise him. "I'm sorry." He's still just talking, though, not realizing what comes out of his mouth.

"Don't be. He was one of the final MIAs in Vietnam. I kept his first name as well as his last." I turn away from the teal sky, the crushing traffic, and look at him, just him, that face. "How did you meet Lisa?"

"A corporate trip. I saw her there, in the lobby."

"You knew she was engaged?" I can barely contain my venom.

"Not at first." He glances over at me. "Damn, I'm human, okay, and she was a beautiful woman. The minute I saw the ring, it was strictly business."

I am contemplating having lunch with a man who is attracted to me because he was attracted to my cousin. I don't want to be here, but I am committed. Later today, he has a television interview to monitor, an interview with the Killer Body candidates. I'd like to monitor it, too, but the press is excluded.

The balloon of anger that almost burst within me is slowly deflating. I'm not sure I like that. Hating Lucas Morrison has helped distract me from my true pain, my true grief. Not to mention my aunt's need for revenge.

The restaurant looks L.A. cute—bicycles parked outside, offerings like shredded-carrot-on-hummus sandwiches. I order the southwestern salad; he goes for the only red meat in the place. When I point out that the burger isn't Killer Body food, he admits the only times he's ever eaten the stuff is when Bobby Warren wants his input on flavors.

He tells me he wanted to be a writer. That he went to J-school, that he ended up with a job at the *Times*.

The way he speaks to me reeks of bad-date experiences in my past. It's the ultimate bad date with someone who talks only to fill the silence. Only it's not the silence we're trying to avoid here. It's the topic. Lisa.

I watch his face, the fierce eyes that his glasses only intensify. His thick eyebrows, his straight, thin lips. I always thought, as Hemingway suggested all writers should, that I have a built-in shit detector. But this man, if he is a liar, is a good one.

I need to make this fast, so that I can get to the TV station. Maybe I can find a sympathetic employee who will let me sit in on the interview with John Crosby. Yet, how can I leave what I've been struggling so hard to discover?

"You must visit many Killer Body centers," I say. "Why Lisa? What was it about her?"

He doesn't answer right away. Then, finally, the solemn expression lightens.

"I'm sure you're convinced that I use my job as chick bait, but the truth is, I rarely meet clients, just staff."

The food arrives before I can answer. Neither of us touches our plates.

"I should have known you were related," he says. "You look a lot like her, only—"

Only not gorgeous, I think. To him, I say, "Did you tell her she could have a shot at Julie Larimore's job?"

"Of course not." The statement almost brings him out of his seat; it's that forceful.

"That's what she told her mother."

"Are you sure? It's not what I said. I knew she idolized Julie, of course. I told her we could use her in some local ads, and I suggested she might want to go to work as a consultant at the center there."

Again, I try to lie detect. Again, I see only a sincere, little-bit-too-handsome man who claims his biggest mistake was being attracted to my cousin. I sort through disjointed conversations in my head, come up with Aunt Carey's desperate voice the day of the funeral. She told me Lisa was meeting a man in L.A., that she was being trained for television commercials. And when I insisted that only Julie Larimore was in the Killer Body commercials, she had said, "She didn't misunderstand. He told her Julie Larimore was quitting."

I pick up my fork and force a piece of lettuce coated with ranch dressing and barbecue sauce into my mouth. As if I've given him permission, Lucas picks up half of his burger.

I wait until he takes a bite and swallows. "She said a man told Lisa that Julie was quitting."

"I wouldn't have said it, even if that was the case." Now his candor is replaced by nervousness and eyes that dart from the dark booths to the shaded windows, anyplace to avoid looking into mine.

That alone makes me ask, "*Was* it the case?"

He shakes his head. "I wouldn't have talked to her or anyone else about Julie. I probably said there were positions in our company, and that she could be like Julie, but on a local level. There are others like that, at all our centers."

As the creepy reality sets in, I put down my fork. It clacks on my salad plate like a bad-manners alarm. All I can think of are all those centers, all those women, Lisa.

"Women who want to be Julie Larimore?" I ask.

"I know it's strange, but something about her inspires that kind of imitation. I've seen it at the centers. There's always at least one with some version of the dress and the belt, and they all have the pendant. Lisa had the look, though. It was organic with her. You, too."

I ignore the sudden rush of color to his cheeks, not

to mention my own quaking self. I am certain of only one thing. I am going to burst into tears if I sit here another minute.

"I've got to get some air," I manage, and get out of the booth, almost running by the time I hit the door. I stand on the sidewalk outside the restaurant, gulping air, realizing I'm not handling any of this as well as I thought I was. Now I've made a fool of myself in front of Lucas Morrison. I'll have to lie when I return to the table, make up some story about a dizzy spell.

I don't get a chance. He's beside me, hand on my arm.

"You okay?" he asks.

I nod and try to arrange my features. "I just couldn't sit any longer. I needed air."

He grimaces. "What there is of it. I don't know how anyone lives here."

"They get used to it," I say. "You can get used to anything." I look up at the putrid sky. "There are two Californias, three, if you count the Central Valley, and many don't. Perhaps because we're in the middle, most of the people where I live identify with either the Bay Area or Los Angeles."

"I can guess which one you prefer."

"What about you?"

He stops, lifts an angry chin to the sky. "I don't like the film-driven emphasis on style over substance," he says, counting off his complaints on his fingers. "I don't like all of the blue eyes, blond hair and pedigreed dogs. And I can't imagine why anyone would tolerate the endless tangle of freeway, that slow, claustrophobic crawl, even for the rewards of being close to Catalina Island or being able to spot Winona Ryder at the drugstore."

We take the narrow walk toward the parking lot in back. I have the feeling I could yell *rape* right now, and the people jogging by would just turn up the music they're mainlining through their headphones.

"So, where are you happiest?" I need to probe, to figure him out, to discover through these questions, answers to the ones I cannot ask.

"Out there." He points in the general direction of the ocean.

"Santa Barbara?"

"It doesn't matter. When the land slips away, and it's just the ocean, there's no place to hide from yourself."

"And that's a good thing?"

"A necessary thing, for me. Remember what Socrates said. The unexamined life is not worth living."

"And you know what happened to him." We reach the back lot, more gray and black, more dust. "Why did you stamp Lisa's card?" I ask.

He turns, his eyes narrowed, as if trying to sense a trap. Finally, he says, "I didn't."

"Well, there was a stamp on it."

"What did it look like?"

"It was marked Corporate," I say. "Red ink, and the type was in caps."

I can't read his thoughts, but I know he's trying to decide how much to reveal. "We do have a corporate stamp," he says. "Bobby likes to comp his friends. Amazing he ever got so rich with that empire of his. He's always trying to give away the store."

"Who can use the stamp?"

"Anyone in Corporate." He frowns. "Anyone who has Bobby's permission."

A chill travels along my neck as if a breeze has just ruffled my hair. "Where is it kept?"

"There's one at every center. Every comp is supposed to be logged, but they get pretty careless. Why would they comp Lisa?"

We reach my car in only a few steps, but I feel I've run a mile.

"That's what I want to find out. Can you check at the center?"

"Okay. I'll call later on, see what I can find out." I realize I'm starting to trust him in spite of myself, maybe even kind of like him.

He looks better outdoors than in. That's why the suits, the glasses, appear to trap him. He makes eye contact, and without a word, lets me know that he's aware I'm admiring his appearance.

I speak more harshly than before. "What kind of people are usually comped?"

"People Bobby Warren wants to impress. Old friends of his, public figures. They do it all the time for the media." Never ceasing eye contact, he waits a beat, then adds, "Bobby loves the media."

I groan. "You know what I need to do, don't you?"

His sigh is audible, even on this noisy strip of concrete. "You want to interview my boss."

"I really have to," I tell him.

He reaches in his suit jacket, toys with his dark glasses. "You know what I wish, Rikki? I wish you liked us better."

"*Us* being the royal us or the collective us?"

"Collective, I guess. Bobby. Hell, *me*. I wish, right now, that you liked me better than you do, okay?"

"I do like you." Damn, maybe Lucas Morrison really is as vulnerable as he appears right now. Not all beautiful women are stupid. Nor do all handsome men have to be liars, do they?

"But you don't trust me. Or Bobby, either, for that matter."

"I don't know, Lucas."

I find my keys, jiggle them, as he is jiggling his sunglasses. Two different escape routes. Will I drive away before he puts on the shades?

"Neither do I, Rikki." He gives me a look that brings new meaning to the word *guileless*. "I love the old man. My job, one of them, at least, is to publicize Killer Body. Still, I can't let you do a number on him."

"I don't want to do a number on him. I just want to know the truth about Julie Larimore."

"And your cousin."

It isn't a question.

"And my cousin."

I reach for the car door, insert the key. "You going to be at the TV interview?"

"If I can get in."

"Meet me there. I'll get you in."

My key still in the lock, I look up at him. He reaches for the glasses. His dark eyes spark out more light than this weary Southern California sky has for many years.

"I feel as if we're pulling on opposite ends of the same rope," he says.

"Me, too."

He pauses, holding his glasses the way another man might hold a pipe. "I have an idea."

"What's that?"

"Why don't we both try pulling on one side? We want the same results. Shouldn't we be on the same team?"

Now I'm the one reaching for the safety of my sunglasses.

"See you at the station," I say.

FIFTEEN

Tania Marie

Word of the day: *Crapulous:* Marked by intemperance in eating or drinking; sick from excessive consumption of liquor

Late that afternoon she met Princess Gabby, whose driver was going to take them to the television studio. This day sucked, and the dicey stuff hadn't even started yet. She didn't know if that was a good or bad thing. Good: it couldn't get much worse. Maybe the reporters had already *satiated* themselves. Bad: this might have just "hopped them up," as Marshall used to say. She hoped the son of a bitch fried in hell for all of his lying. She hoped every time he walked into a bar or turned on Bravo or popped in a CD, he'd hear that John Prine song—their song—"All the Way With You."

Shit, she hoped he'd call her.

She'd bought her outfit, like everything but her frigging jewelry, from either Chico's or Bloomies, online. No way would she trust someone in a shop to fit her and not mention her size to someone who would mention it to someone in the media. At least this outfit worked. Princess Gabby's sweet little sheath worked better, but anyone else, yours truly included, would look like a washerwoman with that sixties bandanna framed by all that stringy hair.

At least God was fair in one regard. No one had more fabulous hair than she, certainly not gorgeous Gabby.

The princess had everything else, though, looks and money, just for starters, not to mention a handsome ex, who'd probably do anything to get her back. She even smelled like frigging wealth, a hushed, understated scent. Tania Marie wanted to ask her what it was. Wouldn't that sound too crass?

Crass. Ass. That's what she was, what the media created, what she tried to live up to.

"I like your perfume," she said.

Gabby nodded in the direction of her very bald, very gay, very solicitous driver. "Christopher bought it for me. Banana Republic, I believe."

"It smells clean. Classy."

What kind of driver buys perfume for his client? She shifted in the seat, trying to get a better look at Christopher through the rearview mirror.

As if reading her mind, the driver shot off the freeway. In a moment, they were in Burbank. Everything was okay, but Tania Marie still had butterflies. "You sure he's a good driver?"

"Only the best."

"Guess I'm just nervous."

"Relax," Princess Gabby said. "As my grandmother used to tell me, they might can you, but they can't eat you."

Her words, her soft yet certain voice, forced Tania

Marie to listen. What kind of life would it take, how wonderful would your luck have to be, to get one bit of advice, true or false, from anyone?

"I can't imagine you with a grandmother who'd use that kind of language."

"Oh, she did, and she chewed snuff, too. Never touched alcohol, though, never wore lipstick, and I doubt if she ever told a lie." She turned to Tania Marie, her wispy curls starting to wilt beneath the bandanna; only that hair kept her from perfection. "You might try not to curse tonight."

Tania Marie felt as if her face had been slapped. "What's wrong with shoveling back a little of what's shoveled at you?"

Princess Gabby sat a little higher in the seat, distancing her from their momentary closeness. "Ladies don't do it."

"But they screw around on their husbands?"

Damn her mouth. The minute she said it, she wanted to gush out an apology.

"I guess I deserved that." Princess Gabby's eyes widened, and for a moment, Tania Marie could swear she saw tears in them.

"No, you didn't. I was being an ass."

"A bit testy, perhaps. I didn't mean to criticize, and your point is well taken. But if you do want this job—"

"You know I don't stand a snowball's chance in hell. It'll go to you because you deserve it, or Old Fake Tits because she traded Mr. Warren for a lifetime of blow jobs."

"You may be right." Princess Gabby lowered her voice, and Tania Marie realized she was trying to spare her driver the gory details of the conversation. "As you've perhaps discovered, those alliances don't always guarantee one woman any more power than the next. Just don't be your own worst enemy, dear. That's all I'm suggesting."

Something about her manner made Tania Marie feel like crying. She was taking time with her. No one, not even Virginia, had ever done that.

"By swearing?"

Gabby straightened her lips into a line that was a little too wise. "The F-word, in particular."

"It helps me blow off steam. My life's really…" She paused. "Really F'ed up right now. Is that better?"

"Still a bit coarse." The princess gave her a weak smile. "Sometimes I say *freaking* or even *flipping,* and under tremendous pressure *frigging,* but never in public, of course. It's a release for me. Maybe that would work for you."

"You have any kids, Gabby?" Now, what in hell made her ask that?

"We were trying before." Her eyes blanked out all emotion, and her accent became more pronounced. "Why do you ask?"

"Because I think you'd be a hell of a mom."

"Well, thank you very much, Tania Marie." Her expression softened. "We'll just have to see, won't we? In the meantime, think about what I said. I can't imagine Bobby Warren would give the job to Rochelle, especially when he finds out that her husband tried to get you to drop out of the running."

"She calls him Bobbo, for Christ's sake," Tania Marie said. "How the hell can anyone call *the* Bobby Warren Bobbo?"

"That's a bit extreme. But why do you, who swear like a stevedore, insist on calling him *Mr. Warren?*"

"I don't know." She didn't know how to explain it. But she remembered hearing on some TV show that the early Mouseketeers called Walt Disney *Mr. Disney.* It made sense to her. When you're the one in mouse ears out there doing the step-shuffle-step, you don't pretend it's an even playing field. And you don't call the man who can make it all happen for you *Uncle Walt.* Or Bobbo.

The princess wouldn't have understood it. Besides, they had arrived at the studio, and they didn't have much time. She wanted to hug Princess Gabby. She wanted to bawl her guts out. Most of all, she wanted to be thin, with big tits, fake or not, like that bitch Rochelle. How horrible was that as a life goal? Thin? Big tits? Rochelle?

Before she could think about it, the driver opened her door, and she stepped out into the studio lot. It looked like any other lot, blending into the monochromatics of the city.

"Thank you, Christopher," she said.

He took her arm, placed it in his and patted it. "Let me get the princess," he said.

There they stood, the three of them, facing the studio, which looked far less threatening from its parking lot.

"Ladies?"

Christopher squeezed her arm, as she knew he must be squeezing Princess Gabby's, as well. Tania Marie couldn't speak, but Gabby did it for her. "Let's go get the bloody bastards," she said.

"Hey," Tania Marie called around Christopher's slender frame to her. "I thought we weren't supposed to talk like this."

"We aren't," the princess called back, her limp hair like strands of ribbon one curled at Christmas with a pair of scissors.

* * *

They waited for the show to begin, the three of them, shoved like sausages on a stupid little sofa. Tania Marie knew she dragged down her end like a bag of cement in the back of a canoe.

Next to her, she could feel Princess Gabby's warm presence.

"This will be fine," Gabby whispered in her ear. "But please try not to curse."

Then it was lights, camera, Crosby.

At least John Crosby wasn't a nasty interviewer, not with most of the people on his show, at least. She tended to bring out the worst in people. She hoped this one would be different.

"Welcome to *L.A. Tonight,*" he said, his features accentuated by makeup much less subtle than Marshall wore on the air.

"Thank you," the three of them murmured in unison. Tania Marie only moved her lips, the way she did when forced to say the Lord's Prayer, or worse, sing the National Anthem.

Then Crosby's eyes, magnified by his glasses, sought her face. Of course. What else was new? "Tania Marie, the honey bee. How the hell are you?"

She started to tell him to take a flying one. She started to dissolve into tears, the way she usually did. Then she felt a gentle elbow prodding her. She flashed him the Tania Marie smile.

"Very well, John. And how are you?"

Lucas

On the sofa beside him in the back studio, Lucas felt Rikki stiffen when John Crosby referred to Tania Marie by Marshall Cameron's pet name for her. But the kid had bounced back. She was gracious, the one trait that worked, and the only one that could melt a tough guy like Crosby.

Obviously derailed, the bespectacled announcer turned his attention to the princess.

"So, Gabby. You talked to His Highness lately?"

"Not as frequently as I'd like, but Alain and I are in touch."

The close-up of the princess stopped Lucas. The sixties bandanna, the new millennium hair, the eyes for all time.

"She deserves it," Rikki said. "But she won't get it, will she?"

He wanted to lie but couldn't, not with Rikki this close to him. To pretend otherwise would only insult her, push her farther away from him, when he—okay, admit it—wanted her closer.

"It's difficult to say," he began.

Then, before Rikki could explain, anger exploded on the monitor.

Crosby had turned to Rochelle, who was beginning to explain her long commitment to fitness, in general, and Killer Body, in particular.

"I just like helping people reach their goals," Rochelle recited.

"Excuse me, John. Could I respond to that?"

The camera shot to Tania Marie's delicate features, which played better on television than they did in person.

"Sure," Crosby said. "You got a gripe, Tania Marie?"

She started to spring up, to shout, then just settled back in her chair. "Not a gripe," she said, her voice calm. "Just a question. I'd like to ask why Rochelle's husband, Jesse McArthur, offered to be my agent if

I'd drop out of the competition for Killer Body spokesmodel."

"That's ridiculous," Rochelle said.

Lucas watched the flush spread across Rochelle's face like a guilty cloud.

Rikki jerked to attention beside him. "Is that true?"

"I don't know." He concentrated on the screen, still on Tania Marie's face. The camera had fallen in love with her, accentuating her cheekbones, reducing the flesh beneath them.

"Maybe the princess could clarify," Tania Marie said.

The camera shot to the princess's face, a composed face, head held high, bright eyes like a cat ready to pounce. Gabby had been waiting for this, he could tell.

"Tania Marie makes an excellent point." Princess Gabby lifted her head, patted her sprinkle of curls. "Jesse McArthur contacted me, as well, offering me representation and a sum of cash if I would drop out of consideration for Killer Body spokesmodel."

The camera froze on Rochelle, her finely chiseled jaw, her prominent collarbone.

"I can't believe that's true," she said.

"Indeed it is," Princess Gabby countered.

The camera didn't budge. Rochelle licked at her lips like a dog at a water dish. "I have very little knowledge of my husband's business dealings, except those concerning my own career, of course."

"Oh, come on." Tania Marie just couldn't restrain herself, Lucas thought.

The camera knew what she didn't, though. Just stay poised and let the clock tick, give Rochelle enough rope to hang herself. Lucas felt sweat break out on his own brow, as if he were the one facing the judgmental camera and Crosby's scrutiny.

"It's a matter of ethics." Rochelle smiled into the camera, as if explaining something elementary to a backward child, that child being Tania Marie. "Show business is extremely competitive, every aspect of it. For my husband to share confidential information with me could embarrass or otherwise harm his clients."

"So you had no idea he approached these two ladies?" Crosby asked.

Rochelle blinked into a close-up. "Absolutely not. And, since he isn't here to defend himself, I have no way of knowing who approached whom, if anyone."

"Not bad," Rikki said.

"You're right." Lucas wiped his forehead. Damn, how he hoped Bobby W wasn't watching, because right now, Rochelle McArthur was in deep trouble.

SIXTEEN

Rikki

Back to Santa Barbara. Glad to be here.

Hello, sterile room; hello, upside-down glasses on ink-blotter paper coasters. Welcome, queen-size bed.

Staying away from the day-to-day of the *Voice* and the Valley is almost preferable to facing those routines without Lisa.

I don't know what to make of the accusations against Jesse McArthur or the way Lucas reacted to them. His concern was to save Bobby Warren any pain. He phoned Bobby on his cell and woke him from a nap. Relieved that he hadn't witnessed the finger-pointing interview, he explained what had happened and agreed to set up an appointment with Rochelle for today. Right now. Which is where I come in.

The interview with Bobby is going to have to wait. I'm not about to miss this opportunity with Rochelle.

The Killer Body offices are decorated with more care and thoughtfulness than Bobby Warren's home, and I wonder if that's because they are his home. He and Lucas have the views, on opposite ends of a long hall of shiny parquet covered with a Persian rug so tight and finely toned that it must have taken many Killer Body memberships to finance.

Ellen, Lucas's assistant, has the office in the middle. She's already at her desk as I pass. Across the office from hers, a large room contains about six, seven desks, all occupied by people with what could very well be described as killer bodies. Bobby Warren hires workaholics, Lucas said. Don't these people have lives away from here? Don't they have something better to do on a Saturday morning?

"Can I help you?" Ellen stands in the doorway I've just passed on my way to Warren's office. Her voice is as friendly as her smile, but I know she's playing monitor again.

"Lucas knows I'm here," I say.

She crosses her arms across her white knit top. "He hasn't come back from Los Angeles yet."

"Actually, he got in late last night." I match her well-mannered tone. "We both did."

"Oh." Is that a flush spreading along her cheekbones?

"Yes. He told me Rochelle was meeting with Mr. Warren at seven-thirty, and that I could interview her after that."

"Okay, then." She gives me a too-cheerful smile for this time of morning. "Why don't you step in the reception area until she and Mr. Warren are finished, and I'll have someone get you some coffee while I give Lucas a call."

Her point is not lost on me, couched as it is in high school cheerleader perkiness. After this, I won't need the coffee.

She starts back for her office, and the heavy door to

Bobby Warren's office opens. Out steps Rochelle. For the moment before she spots me, I see her face as it really is, the thin lips twisted into a pained line, her body, depleted and too thin except for the distracting breasts. A black bra strap has slid along one shoulder of her tanned arm. When she sees me, she instinctively straightens and pulls it up.

"What are you doing here?"

"Lucas said I could talk to you."

She pauses between me and the closed door of Warren's office, and her eyes look trapped. "I thought it would be a phone interview."

"I'd rather talk to you in person."

"I have an appointment."

"This won't take long." I launch into my questions without negotiating further. "What was Bobby's reaction to what happened last night?"

"He's fine with it." Her voice is huskier than usual, as if she's been doing a lot of talking since Crosby's show last night. Or a lot of smoking. "You know how I feel about Mr. Warren. I—"

"Love, love, love him," I say.

"Whatever." She's not at her best today, ready to snap. "Mr. Warren respects my ethics, because, as I'm sure you know, he is also an ethical person."

"And your husband? How ethical is he?"

"Hold on a minute, lady." I'd heard she was a bitch in her heyday, and I see it flashing in her eyes right now. "Who the hell are you to insult my husband?"

"I'm just trying to understand how he could have made offers to both Tania Marie and Gabriella Paquette in order to help you land the spokesmodel job."

"We don't know that he did." She reaches into her purse, shoves her sunglasses into her disarray of hair.

"If you want to talk, we can do it on the phone." She darts past me toward the elevator.

I take off after her.

She's inside, slamming her finger against the lobby button when I pull the doors apart and scoot inside.

"I'll tell Bobby Warren," she says.

"And I'll tell him you didn't cooperate with his marketing director's request."

"Somebody should have notified me. I made another appointment."

"There's just one thing I want to know," I say. "Then we can finish up on the phone, if you like."

"What's that?"

"About Julie Larimore. You introduced her to Mr. Warren, right?"

"How'd you know that?"

"You told me the night of his party."

"It's no secret." She shrugs. "Basically, I got her the job." The elevator doors open. She strides out, into the lobby. Its glass windows reflect a jacaranda-studded street and buildings with adobe tile and exteriors so white they could have just been painted yesterday, a place stuck in a time warp, as perhaps is the man who owns the view.

At the door, she turns to me, and I feel, more than think, *lioness*. Her mass of brittle blond hair is almost that fierce, and even with the fake contacts, the rage in her eyes makes me wonder which of us is the stalker and which the stalked. "Is that all you wanted? Am I free to go now?"

As if I or anyone could keep her anyplace she didn't want to be.

"All I need to know is whether you and Julie Larimore were friends."

"I told you I as much as got her the job."

"But you didn't tell me if you liked her."

She presses her lips together, fighting a smile but not successfully. "Do you really think I can answer that, when you probably have a tape recorder in your purse?"

I lift my bag from my shoulder, unzip and open it, showing her the contents. I need to make a decision, fast, and I wish Hamilton were here to advise me of the wisdom of what I'm going to say. Or maybe I'm glad he's not here. Maybe what I'm after isn't about the newspaper or my story, at all. But it's too late to consider my motives now, the magic words on my lips.

"Off the record."

"Are you serious?"

"Off the record. Were you and Julie Larimore friends?"

"You think I'm stupid, don't you?" The lioness look returns, and she is in my face again. "Don't make the mistake everybody else does. And don't judge me—" she shoves her chest at me "—by these."

"I'm not judging you by anything except your answers. You know I can find out whatever I need to. I never give up. If you can make my job easier for me, I'll keep what you tell me off the record."

She moves close enough that I can see the filmy circle of her contacts, feel her breath in my face. Mint first, then, yes, the unmistakable scent of a smoker. "Contrary to what you may have heard, no one was friends with Julie Larimore."

The hoarse honesty of her voice shoots chills through me. I was right.

"She criticized Princess Gabby in an interview after those photos of her were printed, and I don't even know what she did to turn Tania Marie against her. Again, no one was her friend."

"Not even Bobby Warren?" I ask.

"I won't discuss Mr. Warren with you. Not on the record, not off, not over or under. He made the right decision for his business, and Julie's done a great job for him." She sighs and shakes her head. "I'm really tired. My husband's waiting outside."

"You're not the only one who hates her," I say.

The smile spreads. She nods. "I know."

"Why?"

She leans close to me, and her cigarette breath overpowers the fading mint, the too-strong perfume. "You ever meet a perfect person?"

"I don't think so."

"Well, meet Miss Julie. She's smug and sanctimonious, but she thinks she's earned the right because she's perfect. And she is, damn it. Perfect skin, perfect shape, perfect voice, perfect dedication to her job."

"What else?"

"Off the record?" Her stare is greedy; she doesn't want to stop. I remember Hamilton telling me that all an investigative reporter needs to do is find an angry person for a source.

"Yes, off the record."

She turns away from me, says it to the wall. "I thought she'd be grateful for my help. Instead, she stabbed me in the back, tried to make Bobbo distrust me, made unflattering statements about me to the press. And they say *I'm* a bitch?" Then, still looking at the wall, she says, "I have to leave now."

"I'll walk out with you."

I hate to admit it, but there's something almost likable about Rochelle, something you have to dig for underneath all of the makeup and, yes, the anger.

"Another off the record," I say. "Why are you always so ready to attack?"

She digs the glasses out of her hair, shoves them over her eyes. Jesse drives their Lexus up to the sidewalk, and I can sense her relief. There's no parking place, however, and he drives down the street, away from us.

"Why am I such a bitch? Admit it. That's what you're asking."

"No, it's not." I join her outside, beneath a jacaranda, still green, not yet in bloom.

"You know how the lofty princess says everything she doesn't like is *so California?* Well, I *am* California, honey. I'm every battle every woman in this state and this industry ever fought. If a man my age had fought the battles I have, you'd call him a war hero, or maybe like Bobbo, a pioneer."

"Maybe." I start to say more, but the Lexus pulls up to the curb and Rochelle brightens. "I have to go," she says. "Call me if you need more. I don't want to appear uncooperative."

She's like a pendulum, swinging from anger to the media cooperation I'm sure Bobby Warren insists on.

I walk with her to the car. "You've been very helpful," I say.

"Call me if you have any questions." She's focused on her husband now, moving like a sleepwalker toward the car.

Every time I see Jesse McArthur, I'm struck by the same thought. He doesn't look married. All scrunched-back ponytail and photogenic smile, he leaps out of the car, runs around to open the door for Rochelle.

For one moment, outside that open door, she tilts her face to his, and I think, no, they can't really be going to kiss. But it's something else, some shared exchange of emotion that maybe only people who have been together as long as they have can share. Whatever it is, it changes what I think about both of them.

I want to move forward, to ask more questions, but I hear someone calling my name. I turn.

Ellen stands outside the door, holding up a cell phone. She joins me on the sidewalk and gives me her cheerleader smile. "There seems to be some confusion," she says. "I have Lucas on the line. He'd like to talk to you."

"Hi, Lucas," I say, smiling back at her as I press the phone to my ear.

"What the hell is going on? Ellen says you told her that I gave you permission to interview Rochelle McArthur this morning."

I'm aware of Ellen's inquisitive eyes, the fact that she, as well as Lucas, is waiting to hear my excuse for this intrusion into their safe little world.

"I lied," I say.

"You lied? Why would you do that? I thought we were getting along."

"I had to, Lucas. And I'll explain why when I see you."

An exasperated sigh. "And when might that be?"

"Right now, if that works for you."

SEVENTEEN

Rochelle

"Give me a cigarette. In fact, give me the whole damned pack."

"You know you'll hate yourself later. Besides, we're barely off the street. That girl could be following us."

She slammed open the glove box, took out a safety kit, flipped open its tin lid. Underneath the couple of bandages, the two cigarettes lay hidden, wrapped in a piece of gauze.

She could feel his glance as, fingers shaking, she lit it.

"That's not very healthy."

The smoked burned its comfort into her lungs. "Healthful." Her voice sounded like someone's who'd taken a hit of weed and kept most of it down. "People are healthy. Things are healthful."

"Or not." He shot the window down a crack, which she hated. Turned on the air conditioner. Foul air crept into the refrigerated car. She sank back against the leather seat, unable to deal with one more confrontation. First, Bobbo, then Rikki Off the Record. They'd see about that one.

Beside her, Jesse navigated the freeway, coddling it as he did her. Then forgetting he was supposed to be driving, he turned as if they were in some damned coffee shop, his singsong voice touching upon the subjects of lung cancer, emphysema, secondhand smoke.

"So what's health?" She exhaled a hearty stream out the window he'd cracked for her. "It's just one more thing you'll lose when you die."

"Now, that's a cheerful thought. I take it Bobby knows you too well to be convinced by whatever you said or did up there today."

How could he always reach right into her head and come out with her secrets? The car bumped beneath them. Bad road or he'd drifted over a divider again. "Watch your driving," she said. "I did my best back there. And, no, he was not thrilled that you tried to buy off Tania Marie and Princess Gabby."

"You didn't admit it?"

"Of course not."

"You sure? You're not changing sides, are you, not trying to blame the whole thing on me?"

She gulped smoke. Exhaled. "How long have we been a team?"

"Maybe you're the one who should remember that. I stuck by you after the show folded. I'll always stick by you."

"As long as I keep bringing home the bacon."

His gaze left the road once more. If he did this one more time, she'd get out and walk. Shiny gray hair made its own part as it fell across his face. Immediately, she wished she could take back her last retort. Instead, she took a defiant drag.

"I hope that's just the Rochelle McArthur bitch role and not the real you," Jesse said. "You couldn't be stupid enough to believe that you're the one supporting our lifestyle."

"I'm not stupid, Jesse, and, yes, I'm supporting a good deal of our lifestyle. If I get the Killer Body deal, we'll be set. Even if I don't, I know Bobbo will give me the Ass Blaster. He said it again today. He just wants— no, he demands an untainted public image. Those are his words exactly."

"Meaning you can't have your husband trying to buy out the competition."

"Exactly. That's what I told you in the first place."

"It was our idea, babe, and it could have worked."

"Might have worked." Her mouth tasted like an ashtray. She flipped the remains of the cigarette out into the air, watching it shoot past the car in tiny sparks. "Didn't work."

"Why?"

"Because those two teamed up. Can you believe that? Princess Gabby and Tania Marie, the honey bee? Who would have thought they'd compare notes?"

"I'm so seldom wrong, and I missed that one all the way."

"Your turnoff," she said as she covered her eyes. "Damn it, Jesse."

She felt the careening motion, that threat of their tiny little world spinning out of control. She didn't want to see.

"We're fine." He patted her leg. Squeezed, not a sexy squeeze, a doctor squeeze, like the little silver hammer on the knee. "You're turning into a regular bone fuck, you know that?"

"Now, there's a lovely term." She forced herself to sit up, relax into the seat, no broomstick posture like a certain princess. "Would you rather I look like Tania Marie? Or Gabriella Paquette, perhaps?"

A smile crossed his lips, then disappeared faster than you could say *Princess Gabby.* "I like you just as you are," he said.

How many years had he said it? Why could she still not believe it? Because he only said it; he didn't demonstrate it, and every time he mentioned Gabby's name, he all but salivated.

This was the worst part of going home—not the back-to-back traffic, not the lost hours—but all of the doubts that manifest themselves when two people who should love and care for each other find themselves together, in a car, on a freeway that may never end.

This is the place you remain silent or you attack. She decided to remain silent. She had plenty to think about, anyway, especially if cute little Rikki decided to forget that what they discussed was off the record. Then she'd have big-time problems. And if Gabby were remotely interested in Jesse, she might have even bigger ones.

"Is Bobby on our side?" he asked.

"I think so, although no one really knows for sure with him."

"You should."

"Why? Because of something that happened years ago? I was a kid, and he was gorgeous. What did I know? I cared about him for a long, long time."

"I know."

"Then, what's your point?"

No answer. She hated it when he did that, as if someone had just pulled the cord out of the stereo.

"He's not what you think," she said finally. "Under all of that body-builder stuff, he's a good guy."

"He's a drunken tyrant."

"Sometimes. He's the last person I'd choose for a boss, but I'm not in a choosing position. I just hope this mess with Tania Marie and your friend the princess doesn't hurt my chances."

"So do I."

"It was an idiotic idea, anyway, thinking you could buy them off."

"It's never idiotic to appeal to someone's greatest need."

The way he said it chilled her, made her study his face, the angular thrust of his jaw. For that moment, the sunlight washing over his features, he looked like a stranger.

He slowed for the turnoff.

"I don't suppose you'd like to stop for lunch?"

She'd like to slap that knowing smile from his face. But they were a team; they'd been a team a long time. And he looked like himself again.

"No. I think I'd like to get home. We can grab a bite later."

With that they moved from one stretch of freeway to another, on their way to home and a world where "later" never came.

Rochelle opened the glove compartment again, reached for the first aid kit.

Lucas

He had vices, but vanity wasn't one of them. He'd seen too much of it when he was competing. His pride in his home bordered on vanity, however. Now, for the first time since his divorce, he viewed this haven he had created for himself with critical eyes.

Would Rikki think it overdone? Would she scoff silently at a thirty-two-year-old man living in a town house big enough for a family? He'd opened the curtains, and the views of the city, the ocean and the islands looked like a living photograph on a wall of glass.

Although he'd considered safe music, he decided to go balls out, as Bobby W would say, and play the CDs he loved. Instead of soft jazz or elevator music, Lyle Lovett, the poet laureate of root music put to a big band beat, sang "If I Had a Boat." After that one, he had Iris DeMent, and then, if Rikki survived those two, it would be Rod Stewart singing love standards, and then another sweet Lyle.

Doorbell, damn. Too late to worry about the room or the music. He had to just let her in and hope for the best.

He studied Rikki's face as she stepped inside, but he couldn't evaluate her impression of his home. She must have run up the four flights of stairs. Her short reddish-blond hair had been ruffled like little feathers by the breeze, and her chest rose and fell slightly. The large blue eyes reflected no emotion whatsoever. Up close, her similarity to Julie Larimore and even Lisa ended. There was an arrogance to her that they lacked. But it wasn't arrogance she was trying to conceal right now. No. Then he knew what it was. She'd been crying, and not long before. Let her know he'd figured that one out and he'd be finished before he started.

"You could have taken the elevator."

"How do you know I didn't?"

"That flush of health, as Bobby would say. You work out?" He could tell by her body, the way she moved, that she did. He just wanted to see how she would answer.

"Sometimes." She crossed her arms across her chest as if trying to conceal as much of herself as possible from him. "We have a gym at the newspaper."

She wore jeans, low cut, with a white shirt where most women would show skin beneath the long-sleeved black sweater she'd layered over it. Was she dressing modestly in response to her cousin's death and the whole Killer Body image? As they stood, looking at, no, evaluating each other, he wondered how she really dressed when she wasn't making a statement.

"Come on in, have a seat. Bobby will be right down. He's making a phone call." He didn't add that Bobby W was responding to an emergency message from Rochelle McArthur, who would not leave him alone.

Rikki sat on the edge of the black leather chair. He took the sofa, across from the view, and watched her look around the room, the bookcases behind him, the layered ebony coffee table that his housekeeper had spread out into five tiers and topped with an oblong pewter dish.

"Very nice." She glanced over at the view, then back to him. "Killer Body must have been good to you."

"Bobby has. He's a generous man. I was doing an internship at the *Times* when I met him on an interview. I guess the timing was right." He glanced up the sweep of stairs, wondering what was keeping him. "We shared the same values."

"Was that before or after his son died?"

She spoke quickly, attacking with her question, then searching his face as he answered.

"You did your homework."

"Part of it."

"I never met Greg. Bobby has a strong nepotism policy. He figures anything that applies to his staff members applies to him."

"And his son died in ninety-nine?"

"In an automobile accident, as you obviously know. I'm happy to discuss it with you, but I'd rather not do it now. It's really hard on Bobby W."

She watched his face, frankly examining him. "You're very loyal."

"Bobby W says your greatest strength is your greatest liability."

"In weightlifting? Business?"

"In anything. What's yours?"

She looked as surprised by the question as he was. "My greatest strength?"

"Bobby W also says when a person repeats a question, it's a good indicator she's lying."

That got an embarrassed laugh out of her. "I have nothing to hide."

"So what's your greatest strength?"

"According to my boss, Dennis Hamilton," she said, "tenaciousness."

"Like a dog with a bone?"

She nodded. "Perhaps."

"And that's not always pretty."

"Not to the bone, at least."

It was as if someone had lifted a screen from her face, and the sadness, the arrogance disappeared. Lucas knew without trying that he didn't have a line in his entire repertoire that would work on her. And he didn't care. He on the sofa, she on the chair, they sat locked in a perfect moment of Lyle's voice and eye contact, and, yes, a smile. Rikki was smiling, and she probably didn't even know it.

"When this is over," he said, "do you suppose we could spend some time together?"

"What kind of time?" She'd shut him out again, and he realized how he must sound to her.

"I'm sorry. You're probably seeing someone. It was a rude question."

"Not that rude." She met his gaze and leaned forward.

"I was seeing someone, sort of." She flushed. "I'm not anymore."

"Why not?"

"It's complicated. Something out of our control."

"Do you still care about each other?"

She shrugged. "As I said, it's complicated. What about you?"

"Just your basic workaholic without a life." That should have been enough, but something in him drove the rest of the truth—the truth he hadn't even shared with friends like Ellen—through his lips. "Before I went to work for Killer Body, I was married to my high school sweetheart."

"Married?" She hadn't expected that one, he could tell. What would Bobby W say in a situation like this?

"For five minutes. It was the biggest mistake I ever made."

She frowned. "How nice for your former wife to be described in such terms."

Why couldn't he do anything right with this woman? He leaned forward on the sofa, trying to regain the previous magic. "She'd probably say the same thing about me and be right."

"Okay, if you say so." But she had withdrawn. Her posture was straighter, her expression more guarded. "Speaking of Mr. Warren," she said, "how much longer before I can talk to him?"

The same question had been buzzing in his head. "Let me check on him."

He took the stairs two at a time, remembering a night when his instincts had saved the old man's life. That had required a trip to the emergency room.

Maybe he'd gotten sidetracked on the phone. He seemed to be doing more and more of that, calling his old friends and lovers at all times of the day and night.

Bobby W sat in the upstairs office, his back to the door, facing the window.

"Hey." Lucas knocked softly on the open door. "You okay?" Then he saw the bourbon bottle sitting on the glass desk, catching the light.

Bobby W turned, his eyes blurred with alcohol and tears. He held out his phone, fingers trembling. "She called me."

"Who called you? Rochelle?"

He shook his head and stared down at the phone as if it were a person, or the ghost of one. "Jules."

EIGHTEEN

Rochelle

At least Jesse hadn't killed them on the freeway. He dropped her off in the driveway, leaning over the seat when she got out.

"Get something to eat," he said. "I'll grab a sandwich on the way to the office."

She walked slowly inside, glad the nightmare of the last two days was behind her. Not much mail, mostly bills, but there would be an e-mail from Megan. Her baby never missed a day.

She entered through the front door, trying to keep the bills from slipping off the catalog. Damn. Jesse had forgotten to set the burglar alarm before they left for Santa Barbara.

She dumped the mail on the white-tiled bar and stopped for a moment to look at the large framed poster beside the black refrigerator. Admit it, she had looked pretty good; no wonder the poster was a collectors' item now. If you had a Charlie's Angels and you had a Rochelle McArthur, you had two of the most important looks in the past two decades.

She'd like a cigarette, but she hated to smoke in this home she loved as if it were a living thing. No, just resist the urge. Go through the mail, first this stuff, and then the computer.

A creamy envelope slid out of a Victoria's Secret catalog. An invitation to something? She tore open the envelope and reached inside. What the hell? A card of some kind. She pulled it out, staring into Julie Larimore's enigmatic smile. She turned it over. On the left side was the printed slogan: *You've Got to Want the Body.* To the right, where the address should be, someone had printed in large capital letters, "Don't try it."

She dropped the card. What a cheap shot, a prank. Was this amateur threat really supposed to scare her off? The prankster didn't know who she was dealing with, and it was a *she,* of course, someone petty, like Tania Marie. Still, she felt violated to receive something like this in her own home, her sanctuary.

She picked it up again, thinking she'd have to talk to Jesse. Maybe they could turn this around to get her back on Bobbo's good side, point the finger back at Tania Marie. Only she would stoop to something this childish.

As she started to put it back in the envelope, she realized something else was in there. She turned the envelope upside down, and two pieces fell out. It looked like a photograph, torn from a magazine.

Holding them side by side, Rochelle felt a tremor. It *was* a photo. A photo of Megan.

Rochelle clutched the phone and leaned against the kitchen sink, looking through the window at the vine-covered fence, tiny yellow flowers trailing along the wood. It all looked so safe, but it wasn't. She wasn't.

Megan answered on the first ring.

"Are you all right?"

"Of course. What's the matter, Mom? Your voice. You're not still smoking, are you?"

"Listen, baby, because this is really important." She felt as if someone were strangling her, as if she were speaking through a crushed windpipe. "I want you to come home, right now."

"What's wrong? Is it Dad?" Always Daddy's little girl. He was her first concern.

"We're okay, honest," she said. "I just want you with me at home."

An audible sigh, and then Megan's voice returned to normal. "I'm in the middle of finals, Mom. I can't give you that four-point average if I drop the ball now. Has something gone wrong with your Killer Body gig?"

Still pressing the phone to her ear, Rochelle reached out to close the blinds. "Yes, something has, and I want you home, finals or not."

Rikki

When I hear Lucas close the upstairs door, I know I'm in trouble, and I'm ready for any excuse as to why Bobby Warren won't be joining us.

I've taken the moment of his absence to stand at the window across from the sofa and admire the view, something I wouldn't allow myself with Lucas in the room. Nothing like being in someone's home to level the playing field. Just a day before, I'd contemplated how well he and I might have gotten along if we didn't have our separate loyalties standing between us. Something about his reserved sexiness appeals to me, surprising considering the self-imposed hiatus of my love life after that one night with Den.

Now I'm thinking it's more than Lucas's loyalty to Bobby Warren and mine to my aunt that stand between us. It's the difference between this condo sanctuary of black leather and chrome, this island-dotted ocean view, and my home in the San Joaquin Valley. A nice-enough home, except for my crazy neighbor to the left, who uses his big black pickup as a living room, where he can be seen reading the newspaper every morning.

Except for the 106-degree heat in the summer that would drive anyone but a native to saner climates.

Except for my too-small backyard, which shrunk to postage-stamp status after I got a wild hair and planted it with tomatoes, bell peppers and jalapeños, which immediately took over.

Except for the vacuum cleaner that stands like a greeter just inside my front door, and the piles of paper—bills, magazines, hand-written notes to myself for stories yet to happen.

Except for all of that, a nice-enough home. But what would Lucas think?

It's flat-out depressing when you view your life through the eyes of a man you're contemplating whether or not you should get to know better.

Besides, I haven't thought about anyone like this since that disaster with Den, and I just can't anymore. I learned the hard way that a man who requires too much thought, too many questions about yourself and your relationship, is like a boulder. There's no way you can rise above the problems and complications of life when you're hanging on to that big, all-consuming rock.

Why hasn't Bobby Warren come down those stairs? Just when I'm ready to go up and find out for myself, I hear footsteps and turn to see Lucas. I can tell by his stern expression that he's going to try to weasel the old man out of this interview. And I resolve to climb over him and his posh Italian leather sofa if that's what it takes to get to what I was promised.

Then he tells me.

"Bobby's really upset. Julie just called him. That's where he's been, talking to her on the phone."

I sense a lie there, an omission, at least.

"Julie Larimore? You really expect me to believe that?"

Lucas shoots me a look so irate that I want to duck. Then his eyes change, and he looks like the other Lucas again. In a flash, I remember Hamilton's words. *Anger is a secondary emotion.* Pain. Fear. Which one have I triggered?

"He believes it happened. He claims it was her voice, even though it was muffled."

"Then, let me talk to him. Maybe I can help."

"That's impossible." In a smooth couple of steps, he blocks my way to the staircase, and I realize for the first time how large he is.

"If Julie Larimore really did call him, we need to find out everything we can."

I move closer. The stairs are my goal. Surely he won't grab me if I maneuver around him, and I must. This is too important. No way am I going back to the motel until I hear what happened from Bobby himself.

"Don't, Rikki." Lucas blocks me again, stepping to the side just before I can skirt around him. I wanted to kiss this man just a few minutes ago. Now he's ready to go to blows with me. "We'll talk to you before we talk to anyone, but for now, a couple of hours at least, Bobby W and I need some time to discuss this. You understand, don't you?"

Through his glasses, through his dark eyes, I see the

truth. He is scared, and I—a woman whom moments before he made feel desirable for the first time in a long time—am suddenly his new worst enemy.

I move closer, try to make him hear me through the fear. "We don't have the time for private meetings, Lucas. You don't, and neither does Mr. Warren. If Julie Larimore was really on that phone tonight, she may not have much time, either. I have to go up there and talk to him."

I see the resolve in his features, realize how he won those weightlifting titles. He simply doesn't give; he'd drop before he did.

"I'm sorry. I really am. But if you don't leave right now—"

"Cut the crap, Luke."

At the top of the staircase, Bobby Warren, dressed in a sea-foam-green sweatsuit, stands erect as a monarch before his subjects.

"Mr. Warren," I begin, but he interrupts me before I can continue.

"Get the hell up here," he says. "You're right about timing. We can't help Jules if we sit on our butts around here all day. Isn't that right, Luke?"

Lucas doesn't reply. I don't have to look at his eyes to feel the fury in them. But he steps back, almost sinking into the chrome rail.

By then, I'm already on the stairs, smelling Bobby Warren's bourbon breath beneath his Obsession or whatever high-powered, upscale scent with which he's doused himself, following him into the second bedroom that must serve as Luke's office.

Once there, I don't know what to do next. The desk, on large black casters, turned to face the ocean, is glass with a greenish cast to it. Bobby Warren heads for the teak-backed, black upholstered chair behind it. Then he just collapses—all of him, not only his body, but his skin, his gaze, his attitude.

"I can't help you," I say, "if you don't let me help you."

"Rikki." I feel Lucas at my back before I hear his voice, a voice that, at this minute, I'm not sure I can trust.

"She's right." Tears squeeze out of Bobby Warren's eyes. He jerks his head toward Lucas. "I have to talk to someone, Luke."

"We can discuss that later."

"No, I do. I really have to talk to someone right now." He returns to me. "Jules called me just now on my cell phone. Do you believe that, or do you think I'm a crazy old man?"

How do I answer? I stand before him, trying to tug down the sweater I wore because I wanted Lucas to notice it. He did. Bobby Warren hasn't, thankfully, and now he's far too distracted to be interested in it or me.

"If you say it's true, I'm sure it is."

He nods, his dark eyes so unfocussed that, for a moment, I consider calling 911 or taking him to an emergency clinic. He's aged a decade easily since the first time I spoke with him. And he's worried.

"No one will believe me," he says. "Not even Luke believes me."

Then it comes to me, how to know for sure. I move closer to him. "She called you on your cell phone?"

He nods, picks it up from the glass desk. "I know it's my Jules. She said she missed our calls. She always called me every morning for motivation before she started her day. The voice was muffled, but I know it was hers."

"There's an easy way to prove that." I can barely breathe, so I turn away and stare at the safe black-gray-white painting on the opposite wall. "Your cell keeps a record of all phone calls, doesn't it?"

"I guess so." He holds it up, in front of his nose, the way my uncle George, Carey's late husband, used to hold a magazine when he was trying to read without his glasses.

"Bobby." Lucas's voice booms behind me.

I move closer, put out my hand. "Do you mind?"

"Bobby, we need to talk about this."

"Why? I have nothing to hide, and this girl's trying to help."

"She's trying to get a story."

"Maybe she'll get the right story this time, and help us find Jules." He hands me the phone. "You'll help us, won't you?"

"I'll try." I can't help shooting Lucas a look of triumph.

I press the up arrow on the black keypad and the rectangular screen lights green: *01 New Calls; 21 Total Calls.*

"Do you see anything?" Bobby asks.

"There is a new call on here." I hear a sigh of what sounds like relief from Lucas. He must have thought Bobby made it all up, that it was some alcoholic fantasy. It still could be, of course. That one call could be hours old. "We'll find out in just a second." I press the arrow again.

Wireless Caller.

"Do you know this number?" I offer the phone to Bobby, then realize he can't see. Vanity. The old man won't wear glasses.

As he fumbles, I lean down beside him and am almost overcome by heavy aftershave unsuccessfully masking bourbon. It reminds me of Rochelle McArthur's overdone scent, her attempt to hide the smell of her nicotine habit.

I take the phone from him again, press the talk key and put the phone to my ear.

"It's ringing."

That surprises me. Not a telemarketer, a real phone number, connecting me to a real person. Maybe.

I hear the click of an answering device. No, not a real person, after all. A machine. I walk back to the painting, unable to face the hope in Bobby Warren's suddenly alert eyes.

"Hi. You've reached Julie. Leave a message, and I'll call you back soon as I can." The soft voice leaves no doubt as to its authenticity.

"What is it?" Bobby gets up from his chair. He and Lucas form a wall between the desk and me. "Did you get anything?"

I hand Lucas the phone. "I think you'd better listen to this, and then we're going to have to call the police."

NINETEEN

Tania Marie

Word of the day: *Formidable:* Alarming, frightening, fearsome

If she hadn't gone to the Weight Watchers meeting, she would have eaten every chocolate chip in Santa Barbara that Friday night. She didn't want to go, either, first, because she knew she'd taken another trip up old Pork Chop Hill. Second, because someone might recognize her, might take her photograph, might make her feel even fatter than she already was.

One thing she loved about this place was its lack of music. At Killer Body right now, "Personality" would have played countless times. Right about now, Faith Hill was probably belting out some sexy, lick-your-body song, and if she looked like Faith, she would, too.

As she waited in line to step onto the formidable scale, Tania Marie considered removing her straw hat; even straw, probably even her damned tattoo, weighed something. Everything weighed something. Besides, this was a support group. They shouldn't give a rat's ass who she was, and Mr. Warren shouldn't give a flip, either. Who the hell cared how she lost weight? At least this program had worked better than the others, Killer Body included.

Finally she reached the scale. No pride here; kick off the shoes, take off the gold watch from Virginia. Dump it on the fake wood-grain table and smile at this slender woman before her.

"Hi, hon. How'd you do this week?"

Annie, her absolutely favorite group leader, a petite brunette, spoke in an exaggerated Brooklyn accent that made Tania Marie miss her dad. Annie was deceptively disarming, with her short, springy curls and a trim little form that no one could miss in her fitted, ankle-length dress about the same color as her indigo eyes.

"I didn't do shit." No need to worry about the kind of lecture she got from Princess Gabby. Annie understood.

"That's okay, hon. I bet it's not as bad as you think."

Tania Marie stepped up onto the black step of judgment, then squeezed her eyes shut so that she wouldn't see what Annie's table monitor registered in its damning digits.

"You're only up point-nine," Annie whispered.

"Holy shit, a whole pound."

"Not quite, hon. Don't give the power to the pound you gained. Give the power to the twelve you lost."

Twelve. Had she really lost twelve pounds, just by subjecting herself to these awful weigh-ins and trying to lay off the Milanos and the snacks Virginia sent? She wanted to grasp Annie by both hands, thank her repeatedly, but instead, she stepped down, into her shoes.

"Thanks," she said. "I have to go."

"You sure?" The friendly smile took on another dimension.

"Why do you ask?"

"It's crazy, hon, but the people who stay for the meetings tend to lose more. We've done studies nationwide. It's not just the plan, but the reinforcement."

Tania Marie decided to stay for the meeting. "By the way," she asked, once she had crammed the straw hat back on her head and was ready to leave. "What do you think of Killer Body?"

Annie scrunched up her face—thinking, judging, judging, thinking. "Guess you could call it the perfect program," she said with exaggerated sarcasm. "With Killer Body, you can buy a life membership. With us, you have to earn one."

And now she was home, in the sprawling Santa Barbara apartment that seemed to lose rather than contain her, that seemed too bright in the morning and too dark at night. Like now. This kitchen, specifically.

She had to do something in this monochromatic mess, had to look into the fridge and at Virginia's labeled packages, for something, anything good. Just not that damned gorgonzola and raspberry salad dressing, though.

Tania Marie pulled open the stainless-steel door, trying to ignore the fridge and its labeled contents. Noisettes of lamb, whatever the hell that was, with mashed Yukon golds and roasted garlic. Vegetable strudel. Salmon in *beurre blanc*. No.

She slammed the door shut, forced herself to think about what Annie had said at the meeting. "Sometimes in our lives, treading water is really doing well. Just hanging in there can be awesome."

She had to hang in there, for herself and no one else. This wasn't hunger, she knew, not food hunger. It was a gnawing of a different type, one she might not ever understand or overcome. But she was learning the tools to keep it from overcoming her.

She stepped into the pantry, located just off the kitchen, a dark little walk-in with shelves on each side. Maybe she could just nibble some dry fruit. The angel food cake mix beckoned. Angel food. No fat. Perfect. In fact, Annie had handed out cake recipes today— chocolate with diet cola, angel food with fruit. Didn't she have any fruit in this frigging place? Crushed pineapple. Hell, that was fruit. Just stir it into the cake mix and shovel it in a couple of loaf pans.

Tania Marie prepared the cake batter, then dumped the pineapple in and began to stir the mixture with a wooden spoon. Wouldn't Virginia be horrified to see her actually trying to cook something? Tania Marie scraped the effervescent mixture into the shiny cake pans. Then she allowed herself a tiny lick of the spoon.

The sweet fizz, like champagne and cookie dough, sent her spinning as surely as if it had been a straight shot of booze. If Ben & Jerry's could patent this one, they'd have a winner. Tania Marie couldn't help herself. She raked first the spoon, then her knuckle around the inside of the mixing bowl until it was as shiny and clean as if she'd just washed and dried it. And she had, taste by greedy taste.

The cake batter had increased instead of quieted her aching dissatisfaction. She stared at the two loaf pans glistening on the counter, ready to go in the oven.

Tania Marie picked up one of them, bringing it close to her face so that she could inhale its earthy sweetness. Did she really need to bake both of these?

Something stopped her. A noise, a sound just different enough to make her pause and stare out the kitchen window through the miniblinds. Nothing moved. She slowly returned the loaf pan to the granite counter. A familiar feeling settled in her chest, the tight, constricted pounding of her heart the night she was locked in the sauna, a week ago. Was it less than a week ago? She couldn't go through that again, would die if she had to.

So, did she embarrass herself and call the cops, have big, fat photos of herself slapped on the front of every tabloid in the supermarket? Or did she stand here, ready to pass out, unable even to eat, because she was afraid of whatever she felt out there?

A memory flitted through her mind. Her father's voice when she'd had a bad dream.

Next time you have it, just ask the monster, "Who are you really?"

And what if he doesn't tell me, Daddy?

He will. They always do.

She knew she'd locked the back door, but she ran through the house, just to be sure. Yes, it was fine, dead bolt in place. And the front door? She hurried down the hall again just as the doorbell chimed.

She opened the front door, her fingers sweating, and called through the security door, "Who is it?"

"Me, Jay Rossi."

"Leave me alone."

"I can't. Virginia wants to see you."

She stood to the side of the door so that he couldn't see her. "I'm not letting you in. Go away now or I'll call the police."

"Don't be crazy. I'm trying to help. Your mother's worried about you."

"So you say."

"Call her if you don't believe me."

"You know she doesn't take calls at work."

"Damn it." He hit the security door with a smack. "We don't have time to screw around."

She heard the jingle of keys, the click of metal on metal. The brass knob of her security door began to turn. Surely Virginia hadn't given him a key to the apartment. But how else could he have gotten one? The door inched open. Tania Marie ran for her cell phone on the kitchen table, but he was already inside. A firm hand stopped her before she could get there.

"Let me go, you bastard." She tried to struggle, to pull free of him, but he had both of her arms now, holding them together from behind her. She managed a scream. One hand clamped over her mouth.

"Calm down, it's okay."

She tried to scream again; the hand pressed harder.

"Don't." His voice was firm, calm. He pushed her toward the kitchen door leading to the garage. "I'm not going to hurt you, but I'm not leaving without you. Think about that, and let's move out here and get in the truck."

Tania Marie thrashed as best she could, but he was stronger than she. Her face shoved against him, she felt her feet being dragged along the floor. She began to cry, unable to breathe, afraid she might suffocate against his shoulder.

His grip on her eased just slightly. She sobbed again, gulping air.

"Now," he said. "Are you ready to listen to reason?"

Tania Marie nodded slowly.

TWENTY

Lucas

Bobby W looked almost like his old self as they got off the boat in Avalon. He always perked up on the ocean, the way flowers did in water. The shore patrol nudged up next to them, and Bobby W hopped on. The sail had smoothed years from his life. They both stood, and for the first time in a long time, Bobby W didn't appear one step away from collapsing.

"Sea air. I love it." His voice attracted the attention of others on the boat. A couple nudged each other. A few women smiled.

"Hey," a young blonde, maybe nineteen, her fine hair fanned and tangled by the wind, said. "Aren't you the Killer Body guy?"

"And a few other forgettable titles along the way." Bobby W flexed through his black turtleneck and gave her what Lucas had come to call the look of assessment. Boobs, legs, then, finally the face. "Sometimes," he said, "especially when we're young, nature is kind. Later on, less so. May I say nature has been extremely kind to you, my dear lady."

"Thanks." She nudged her friend and preened in her tight black top, full breasts threatening to spill through the deep, keyhole-shaped neckline.

The old man's charm never failed him. His rosy cheeks caught the glow of the harbor lights. His eyes glinted as he chatted with the blonde. Lucas hoped this was the right move, a positive move, and that it might be able to get Bobby W's mind off his obsession with Julie and whether or not she'd return.

What will Rikki think?

The thought arrived unbidden, followed by the image of her intense, annoying gaze, staring him down, chin uplifted, blatant accusation in those amazing blue eyes. For the first time since his brief marriage, he was thinking about a woman more than he thought about his job.

"So." The blonde turned to Bobby W, offering up her chest like a plate of buffalo wings at happy hour. "When are you going to pick another Julie? My boyfriend and I love Princess Gabby."

Bobby W steadied himself on the rail. "I can't really say. There will never be another Julie, and she'll be back very soon, you know."

His voice drifted off. The blonde frowned. As they neared the pier, Lucas could see she'd lost interest in the conversation.

"So," she said to her friend. "You want pizza or pasta tonight?"

Bobby W shook his head and gave Lucas an indulgent smile. "Your greatest strength is your greatest liability," he said, low enough so that no one heard him this time.

"So what's that young lady's?"

"She thinks she'll be like this forever."

"That's a strength?"

He raised a cagey brow. "Can be. Depends on which side of the screen you're viewing the movie from."

They ended up in a café eating bowls of minestrone and yeasty bread, from which Bobby W ripped out and discarded the centers. He gnawed at the crust between sips of bourbon.

"So, what are we going to do, Luke?"

"About?"

Another sip. Another nibble. "About getting Jules back, of course."

Lucas looked out between the blue-and-white-checked curtains of the café's windowpanes, where boisterous visitors strolled toward any number of locations, all ending with food, drink, entertainment. No one came to this side of Catalina Island with any longer-term goals.

"Don't you think Julie will come back when she wants to?"

"No." He shook his head. "I don't think she can, or she'd already be here. There was something fake about that conversation we had on the phone."

"Fake how?" As always, he tried to discern how much was real and how much was just Bobby W being Bobby W.

"As if she was reading it, maybe." He took his credit card receipt and rose. "Something's wrong with her. Maybe where she is, she can't get back."

They'd seen different sides of Julie, so there was no point in telling him that Julie would do what she damn well pleased, when she damn well pleased to do it.

They stepped onto the sidewalk.

"So, where next?" Lucas asked. "Luau Larry's? The Marlin Club?"

"The Marlin, of course, with that wonderful fish-shaped bar. Dolores and I used to go there a lot in the eighties, you know. She had the cancer then, but she was still the most beautiful woman in the place. On the whole damned island, for that matter."

Off they walked, to visit the past. Lucas hoped, as the bracing air hit their faces like a tonic, that Bobby W had forgotten the subject he'd raised at dinner, but, of course, he hadn't.

"We need to hire someone to find out where she is." He said it as if ordering a drink.

A niggling itch spread along Lucas's spine.

"Like a detective, you mean?"

"Or a reporter." Bobby W stopped, arched an eyebrow. "That little girl impresses the hell out of me."

"Rikki?" In the rush of night air, his face felt hot. "Forget it."

"Okay, so the chopped-off hair can be a turnoff, at first, but on her, it's cute. And her body, Luke. Have you taken a look at that?"

"So what? I know lots of attractive women."

"Like Ellen?"

"Ellen and I don't have that kind of relationship."

"So all of those dinners and lunches, and you're not getting any?"

"You know it's against the Killer Body code of ethics. No relatives, no dating, right?"

Bobby W's parchment lips tightened. His eyebrows rose. "Would that stop you?"

"It would stop me with Ellen. It's stopped me with people in the past. Boring, aren't I?"

The door of the Marlin Club was opened. He turned to Bobby W, about to ask if the fraternization policy would stop him.

Instead, a tightly wound guy in a stocking cap almost collided with him, then shoved him out of the way.

"Watch where you're going, asshole."

He looked like a power-boat owner, or maybe just someone who traveled on one.

Lucas stepped back in his path. "Maybe you're the one who'd better watch where he's going."

"You think so?" The sailor raised something that looked like a thick, gray wand.

Lucas tried to block it with his upraised hands, but the weight of most of it assailed him. He felt a hard hit from which he couldn't quite recover. Felt himself crash into something solid. No, God, not Bobby W.

Yes, it was. Bobby W moaned beneath him.

"Careful, you pricks." The man's voice, a hoarse whisper, was the most frightening sound Lucas could recall in his adult life. He tried to open his eyes, but he couldn't. Oh, God, he really couldn't.

"Leave this thing alone," the man said.

"What thing?" Lucas choked out.

As he did, a sharp pain caved in his right side.

"This thing, asshole. Don't ever ask no one about Julie Larimore, not you, not this old dead-ass man. Understand?"

The pain rang through him again, sharper, closer to his kidneys.

"Yeah, I understand."

Another kick, sharper and more splintering this time. Lucas knew, as his body jerked to protect himself, that the assault was more directed to the pleasure of the one inflicting than to the fear of the one receiving.

He heard a retching sound beside him, knew it was

Bobby W. That alone forced him to fight the blinding blackness, open his eyes. As he did, he heard a woman scream.

Tania Marie

Word of the day: *Instauration:* Restoration after decay, lapse or dilapidation

Finally, after breaking every speed limit and not taking even one pee or food break, they parked in front of Virginia's, as evidenced by the purple neon sign in small lower-case letters.

Rossi told Tania Marie to wait in the truck, but he could kiss her ass. As he slammed the door of the driver's seat behind him, she opened the other door. Damned lucky she didn't break a leg having to scramble out of the pickup.

"I told you to stay put."

"Fuck you."

She'd refused to speak to him on the horrendously long drive, planning what she'd do once they got here. Now she stormed past him into the restaurant, past bald Max at his glass-brick station, past the hostess in her long black gown, right into the sacred, frigging kitchen.

Late as it was, the place was packed with customers lingering over drinks and conversation. Let them linger over this!

Virginia presided over the line in her white jacket, looking like a crazed, brilliant scientist. Her hair, an angled bob about the same color as Tania Marie's swished like filmy fabric around her face as she turned from the line.

"He brought you *here?*" She shook her head as if correcting one of the line chefs. "The idiot!"

"Watch who the hell you call an idiot. And I don't care if you are my boss." Rossi stalked in behind Tania Marie and went straight up to Virginia, who was almost his height.

"So, why don't you tell me why you brought my daughter inside this restaurant when you knew she'd throw one of her fits?"

Rossi didn't flinch. "Did you expect me to tie her down, lock her in the truck, maybe?"

This was fresh. No one talked like that to Virginia.

"Certainly not. And that's not what's upsetting me."

"Hey, Gin, you told me to get her. I got her. You told me you were scared. I believed you. Now you're telling me I should have made her stay in my truck." He looked from her mother to Tania Marie, then back again. "In case you haven't noticed, your daughter has a mind of her own."

"I've noticed."

"Since when?" Tania Marie demanded. Now she was really steamed. She nudged up next to Rossi, close to Virginia's flushed, angry face. "Since when have you noticed one thing about me?"

"Keep your voice down, Tania Marie."

"I won't."

"You *will*. This is my kitchen, my restaurant."

Tania Marie took a look around, surprised by how in control she felt. At the shrine of Virginia—all sauté pans and bubbling water ready for the next pasta order—the white-clad line cooks pretended this nasty little scenario was invisible. Tania Marie guessed everyone in Virginia's life did that. Everyone but her.

"But it's my life." Tania Marie walked along the

line as each cook turned away, like cartoon characters, heads down, waiting for the next command. "It's my damned life. Why did you hire him to yank me out of it?"

Virginia leaned back against the counter and lifted her right hand, motioning to Rossi. "Take her to my place, okay? We can discuss this later, after we close up here."

"I'm not going," Tania Marie said.

"Of course you are, dear. But I have lots to do before I can leave. I can't spend that time battling with you."

"Didn't you hear her?" Rossi touched Tania Marie's arm. "She said she's not going."

"It's your job to see that she does, dear Jay." That was the sweet Virginia voice, the engaging voice that, along with a shitload of talent, had made her the most famous female chef in America. Not even Rossi would be able to stand up to that one.

"I'm out of here," Tania Marie said. "You two wasted my night. You robbed me of my evening, and I'm going back to Santa Barbara." She shot a glare in Rossi's direction. "With or without him."

"It's *with* him." Rossi squeezed her arm again. "I shouldn't have brought you here. I thought she was afraid for you."

"Afraid? You want to see afraid?" Virginia grabbed Tania Marie by the wrist, her fingers so cold that Tania Marie felt as if her hand were being amputated by an icy metal vise.

After that initial shock, Virginia let go, then marched into her tiny office, set off from the kitchen by a short glass-brick screen. Tania Marie followed her in. The small room held a small glass desk. On the desk, papers and sticky notes engaged in a competition that the sticky notes just might win.

"Okay, Miss Perfect." Virginia reached into the pile of papers and pulled out only one envelope.

"What is it?"

"Why don't you take a look, since you know so damned much."

The envelope had been resealed and taped. Tania Marie slashed into it with her fingernail. Inside was a note, written in block letters that should have been easier to read than they were.

Get Her Away From Killer Body.

Tania Marie reached in again, pulled out something odd. She stared at it, trying to figure out why it looked so familiar.

Then she realized it was a photograph of the lower part of her body—shorts, shamrock tattoo above the ankle, strappy little shoes.

The photo had been torn in half.

"What does this mean?" She shook the ragged partial photo at Virginia.

"I don't know." For the first time Tania Marie could remember, Virginia looked on the brink of tears. "I want you to come stay with me for a while. I don't want you all those hours away."

Virginia was actually crying, crying for her. Tania Marie threw her arms around her. "I'll be okay," she said.

Virginia lifted tear-streaked eyes. "But you won't stay?"

"I can't. I'm sorry." She hugged Virginia—her mother, damn it, her mother. "It's just too late for that."

Tania Marie huddled in the passenger seat of the horrible pickup, still seeing Virginia's face.

"Well, I guess you told her." Jay Rossi seemed to be hiding a smile, and that pissed her off even more. He wore the windbreaker over a pair of khaki pants and boots. The lenses of his glasses only partially concealed his eyes.

"I don't think it's very amusing that you kidnapped me and dragged me from my home, Mommy's permission or not."

"Maybe I made a mistake. She's scared, though, terrified. You must have seen that."

"More like a guilty conscience, if you ask me." She still couldn't figure out how it felt to know Virginia actually gave a damn about her, but she wasn't going to share that with him. She settled back in the seat as they flew down the freeway, its shadowed tangles of traffic and car lights. At least he was a good driver. "So she gets some postcard of Julie Larimore and a torn-up photograph of me? It's one of the others, probably that bitch Rochelle, trying to scare me away from the Killer Body gig."

"You hope that's all it is."

"When you've been through everything I have in the last year, you don't let an anonymous note scare you off."

"But you don't have to fight the person who's trying to help you." He rubbed his cheek, and Tania Marie realized she'd left a scratch there during their earlier struggle. Good.

"Anyone who breaks into someone's home deserves anything he gets."

"I'd do it again," he said, "and I don't agree that you should go back there."

She wondered, for a moment, if he was right. Were the threats coming from the same person, as Virginia feared, who'd locked her in the sauna at the gym? That dizzy, spinning feeling as she realized she was trapped, and as the heat sucked her breath and her hope from her, was one she'd never forget.

Rossi glanced over at her, but his gaze was more analytical than casual. "Having second thoughts?"

"Of course not."

"Want to talk about it?"

"I don't talk to kidnappers." She crossed her arms and slid down in the seat.

"Virginia's right. That place you're staying is too open. You need to move."

"To a Virginia-approved apartment? What do you know about the place, anyway?"

"You don't have an alarm system. You have that door off the hall, no proper lighting in the back. That backyard's the size of a postage stamp. You go out there at all hours, water your plants, dressed in a hell of a lot less than anyone should wear outside. You leave the bathroom window open. The screen of the patio door in the bedroom has a hole in it. Anyone could just reach inside."

She shivered as she heard her apartment and her habits so adroitly described.

"How long have you been spying on me?"

"It's not spying. Virginia was paying me to keep an eye on you. That's all I've been doing."

"Without my knowledge." Now she was doubly pissed. "Why couldn't you have told me?"

She raised her voice, and he matched the tone. "Because you would have raised hell, okay? Get off my back."

"You could have at least tried talking to me."

"I did, remember? You told me to go to hell. You got yourself damn near killed in your gym, photographed wearing not much more than a towel, and now your mother gets a note all but threatening your life."

She felt cold all over, reached to turn down the air conditioner.

"What can I do? She wants to pack me off to Europe again. That's what she did when the shit hit the fan before. Do you know how lonely it is to be scuttling around Paris with a broken heart, scared to death, just so you can avoid the media?"

Some of the anger left his face, and he seemed to be thinking. Finally, he said, "No, I can't imagine."

Was that actually a note of concern in his voice? She looked out again. They must be getting close. The air smelled cleaner, the way it did when nearing the ocean. Her body ached from all of the hours she'd spent cramped in his truck.

"This time you might be risking a hell of a lot more than exposure to the media," he said.

"Why me?" Remembering Paris, the sauna, the last miserable year, brought tears to her eyes. "It's not fair, everything I've been through, and now, finally a chance at instauration."

"At what?"

She recited from the word-of-the-day definition. Damn, she missed Marshall. Missing. Hating. They balled together in a tight knot in her stomach.

"Instauration," she said. "A chance at something decent, and now it's all starting up again. The talk shows won't leave me alone, but all they want are the gory details." *And to look at my thighs,* she thought.

"Do you have any idea who set you up at the gym like that?"

The question that had been driving her crazy. No answer made sense. "Rochelle, maybe. Maybe even her husband, Jesse."

"What makes you think it's one of them?"

"Jesse McArthur talked to Princess Gabby and me both, remember? He offered us representation if we'd step out of the running for the position. Besides, we've both had bad things happen to us, and nothing's happened to Rochelle, not a frigging thing."

She tried to wipe away her tears, but more took their place. So much pain inside of her; it would take years to cry it away.

Rossi drove with one hand, the other spread across the seat, the way farmers drove their pickups. This pickup he called Blackie was a farmer's truck, if she ever saw one.

"Maybe there's another reason," he said. "Is there something you and Princess Gabby know? Something that Rochelle doesn't?"

She tried to block his question, to block any answer that might try to escape her. "About what?" She felt queasy. She'd been trying to shut out the last year for too long. She hurt too much, was too scared to do anything else. "I don't know what Princess Gabby knows."

"What about you?" The moan of the traffic increased in volume. Too loud for questions or for answers.

"I don't know anything that would put me in danger."

She forced herself to breathe evenly, anticipating his response, the probing, familiar way he conversed with her. Instead, he said nothing, and the traffic noises blended into a comfortable hum once more. She leaned down farther in the seat, wiping her eyes again.

Finally, he spoke, as if an afterthought. "There's always the possibility that what you don't think puts you in danger may threaten someone else. Sometimes it helps to run it past another person."

"You, for instance?" So he could run to Virginia with it.

"I don't care who. Just talk to someone you trust. Tell them what you know."

But she hadn't told him she knew anything. She would never say that to anyone. Worse to defend herself, though. She'd appear even more suspicious. Instead, she said, "Don't you tell anyone I cried."

"I won't tell anyone anything."

"Yeah, right."

"That's the reason Virginia wanted me for this job. She knows most people would talk to tabloids or at least gossip about you."

"What makes her so sure you won't?"

"Come on." He glared at her across the seat. "Do you really think I'd lower myself to do something like that?"

"I don't know."

"Well, I wouldn't. I was raised not to kick people when they're down. I just wouldn't do it."

She hadn't expected a speech like this from such a full-of-himself asshole. She felt the tension ease up.

"No shit?" she said.

His thin lips spread into a smile. "No shit."

They drove in silence, Tania Marie afloat in memories. Marshall and her together, loving each other, swearing that they were forever. How stupid could she be to believe that word, *forever,* from the lips of a married man? How stupid was she to believe the war was between the wife and her, and that one could actually win? The only one who won these three-way wars was the man.

"The worst part of this," she said aloud, "is that everyone thinks I'm a tramp, and I'm not."

"I don't think you're a tramp," Rossi said.

"You don't?"

"No. You were new on the job. You fell for the wrong man. That doesn't make you anything but normal. Someday, you ought to tell your side of the story."

"You mean write a book or do one of those tell-all interviews?" She could never expose herself that way. "Virginia doesn't want me to," she said.

"That's natural. But this is your life, not hers." He started to go on with the sermon, then stopped himself, shaking his head. "Big talk coming from a guy who lets his father dictate his college degree." The self-ridicule in his voice was raw and far harsher than anything he'd directed at her.

She patted his shoulder. "Don't be so hard on yourself, Rossi. You were pretty cool back there with Virginia. I'm amazed she didn't fire you on the spot."

"Screw her." He slowed the truck as they neared Santa Barbara and cracked the window. "With all due respect, I'll make it with or without her. I'm that good."

She hoped he was right. More than that, she hoped Virginia would keep him around. Insane. She was confiding in a kidnapper, her mother's stooge.

"Got any music in this kidnap-mobile?" she asked.

"Delbert McClinton work for you?" Without waiting for an answer, he punched a button on the dash, and a raw, bluesy voice reverberated through the pickup, singing about the blues, moving with and through the blues, not making light of it, but coping.

"Rossi," she said. "You have potential."

"Yeah?"

They'd been in the pickup almost all night. Soon it would be sunup. The ocean stretched out to her right, illuminated by boats and starlight. He didn't look short in this light. He looked caring and handsome, in a cocky kind of way. Then he smiled.

"So, now that we wasted this night, what do you think about stopping for a glass of wine?"

The Interview

Who were your role models when you were growing up?

No one. I was my own role model, and it wasn't easy. I had this voice I couldn't get rid of driving me on.

Perfect. I always had to be perfect. It was the only way out. I did it in school. I did it with my looks, the looks that were the reason for my shame. I made myself perfect. If it hadn't been Killer Body, it would have been somewhere else. I was athletic; I went to work for a gym, met Mr. Warren through a friend there. I always called him Mr. Warren. And then I started working for Killer Body. I became Killer Body. Perfect.

I shut the doors on the past. My life started the day I became Killer Body. The doors are open again now, and I can't close them. Weak as I am, I'm glad to be back, to be cared for. A child.

TWENTY-ONE

Rikki

Julie Larimore's cell phone was missing, but someone had used it to call Bobby Warren. He told us she'd said she was coming back to Killer Body, but I'm not sure how much was fact and how much was hope fueled by alcohol. Lucas insisted we postpone the interview, and when I asked if the Killer Body spokesmodel search was still on, I got only tears from Bobby Warren.

I don't think I could live in Santa Barbara. There's something wearing, even decadent about constant perfection of climate and scenery. On the way back to my hotel yesterday, I stopped about one-thirty at a Trader Joe's to pick up a sandwich. My choices were roasted red peppers or turkey bacon, lettuce and tomato. They worked for me, but I wonder how they'd play outside this comfort bubble that Princess Gabby calls "*so* California." Outside the store, I saw a bearded will-work-for-food guy, sign in hand, drinking a bottle of carrot juice. Even the street people here are politically correct.

I told Hamilton that on the phone, when he called from his car, and it made him laugh, not always an easy task. I felt glad he was coming, not only because we needed to compare notes, but because in this world of faces, figures and fitness, I missed the everyday reality of him.

I was up half the night, reading through the reams of material he and I collected on Killer Body. Interview after interview with Julie Larimore, transcripts from talk shows, Q's & A's from Killer Body corporate, reprints of articles. The woman's life before she disappeared must have been one long interview.

"I'm not sure I like her," I say as Den and I drive toward the gym where Tania Marie was locked in a week ago.

We're in his Volvo, so I can look around at the beach as we go, the boats stretching along it forming their own society. I know Lucas has a sailboat out there somewhere, and looking at the white sails, dark wood and variations of fiberglass, I wonder which one is his.

"Based on?"

Hamilton always likes his raw opinions served up with boiled-down facts.

"All of those interviews. She has an opinion on everything and everyone, and yet there's not a lot of humanity. She can get pretty judgmental. If I can do it, you can do it, and if you don't, you're a slob. That kind of thing."

"So, what does she have that inspires so many people?"

"Looks, intelligence. And a killer body, of course."

"What else?" His gaze intensifies, makes me feel I'm back in college, or on a job interview, maybe.

"Do you know something that I don't?" I ask.

"Maybe." Before I can say more, he gives me that unreadable smile that got me in trouble with him in the first place. "What would you say if I told you there is no Julie Larimore?"

"I'd tell you I thought you were missing a screw," I say.

Although he's staring at the road now, I still feel the heat of his gaze.

I turn sideways in the car, giving myself a full view of his stubborn, stubbled face, his slightly slumped profile. He turns, meets my eyes.

"Well, there's not. Julie Larimore, at least with the data we've been given, does not exist and never has."

Hamilton and I were told we'd have to talk to the night supervisor at the gym. That gave us a day in Santa Barbara to kill. We spent much of it talking about Julie Larimore and how the trail to her had run into a dead end prior to her job with Killer Body, how Hamilton could find no trace of her before that. I told him I'd talk to Lucas Morrison at once, and I was furious that this man I liked more than was wise had probably lied to me, by omission, at least.

Hamilton and I had lunch, walked State Street, in and out of the galleries, eyeing the assortment of types brushing past us on the crowded sidewalk. When the ninth or tenth braless, panty-challenged woman in halter and shorts jiggled past us, I finally said to Hamilton, "Not quite like the Valley, is it, Den?" and watched him color as he pretended he didn't know what I meant.

Now we visit the gym again. I've learned, in my short time here, that the city changes on the weekends, swelling with visitors, taking on a noisier, more frenetic pace. It's like that tonight. The commingled scents from the restaurants tangle in the sea air. The sidewalks look automated, like the ones in airports. If one person were simply to stop, everyone behind would crash like dominoes.

The night manager is only slightly friendlier tonight than she was the evening of Tania Marie's mishap. She informs us at the front desk that men are not allowed, and the three of us go outside into the still air of early evening.

"We don't have anything to say," she tells us, crossing tanned, well-muscled arms across her black T-shirt imprinted with the name of the gym. "I hope you'll keep the club out of the paper."

"You didn't know it was Tania Marie Camp?" Hamilton asks.

She shakes her head. "I was as surprised as anyone. She registered as Mary Warren. We don't run checks on our members, and nobody recognized her."

"How did she get locked in?"

"An accident." Although it's dark, I can almost see the sheen of perspiration on her smooth forehead. When neither of us speaks, she adds, "A new employee who didn't understand the procedure."

"Would it be possible to talk to the employee?" Hamilton asks. "Maybe she saw something that would be helpful."

"She's no longer with us."

Hamilton pounces on that. "You let her go?"

"No, she resigned." More silence from us. She wipes her hand across her forehead. "I guess it was too much for her. She never came back to work after that night."

Hamilton and I exchange glances. "Surely you have contact information for her," I say, suggesting with my voice that it's her duty to turn it over to us. She's not buying it. The gym-teacher stance again, the voice of finality.

"I'm sorry."

"If we had her name—" Hamilton begins.

"I said I'm sorry." She stops at the open door. "She was a new employee."

"We're not blaming the club," I say, but before I can continue, she goes inside, letting the door swing shut behind her.

"Want me to go after her?" I ask.

Hamilton frowns. "Why piss her off more? We can always come back."

"What next? Julie Larimore?"

He nods. "Think you can get hold of Lucas?"

"Let me try."

I take out my cell but get only Lucas's answering machine. "It's Rikki. Please call me as soon as you get this." I'm still shaken by Hamilton's news that there is no Julie Larimore, and the fact that Lucas might have withheld that information from me.

We're in the middle of the club's parking lot, which it shares with a wholesale liquor store, a coffee kiosk and assorted small businesses. As I return the phone to my purse, I'm aware that Hamilton is staring at me with his odd, pale eyes, his lips set. It's that same feeling I get when someone points a camera at me.

"What is it?" I ask.

"Nothing."

"You have that reporter look. Did I do something wrong? You think maybe the message I left on his machine was too rude?"

"It was fine."

He starts for the car, but I can't let it go. "I want to know what made you stare at me like that."

"I was just noticing that you didn't need to look up Lucas Morrison's phone number."

I feel a guilty flush that I know he can't miss. "I'm good with numbers, I guess."

He gives me a vague smile and opens the car door. "I didn't mean to unnerve you. It's none of my business, anyway."

I meet his smile with one I hope is equally enigmatic. "No," I say. "It's not."

"If it ever is my business…" he begins.

A sudden flutter of hope makes me feel more foolish than I must look. "What?" I ask.

I've gone too far, pressed too hard against the supervisor-employee wall. But he started it. I stare up at him for an answer.

"For starters," he says, "I'm going to make you pay for the lunch. How can the company come down on us for that?"

I can't look at him any longer. Instead, I say, "I might just offer to buy your lunch one of these days."

"You've already promised to," he says.

Rochelle

She kept the treadmill in the garage, for emergencies. Not that she needed to run today. She'd been to the gym early this morning, worked out under the watchful eye of Blond Elvis, but she'd also eaten. Jesse had forced her to share part of his scrambled eggs when she'd returned, and watched her chew every bite, even though she'd tried to steer around the yolks. Finally, she'd thrown down the fork, gone into bitch mode and said, "You know I hate eggs." But the damage had been done.

Now, wearing a long T-shirt over her shorts, she

pushed the treadmill to its limit, feeling the rush as the endorphins kicked in and the sweat bled from every pore.

When she worked really long, really hard, she could hear music in the noise of the treadmill, sometimes almost voices. Today it sounded like *banana yogurt, banana yogurt, banana yogurt.* She sped up; the sound continued.

God, this was good. Another hour and the eggs would be history. She needed to get some extra time in now. Once Megan got here, she'd be under scrutiny, but at least she'd have her baby. She'd know she was safe.

A chill touched her slippery arm as if someone had tapped her. She wasn't alone in this dim room. She slowed her pace, trying to glance over her shoulder. A shape filled the door between the garage and the kitchen.

"Damn it, Jesse. You scared the hell out of me."

"Haven't you been at it long enough?" The noise of the treadmill gobbled his words. He was on edge, too, had been since she'd shown him what had come in the mail.

"When I need another personal trainer, I'll advertise for one."

"I thought you might be interested in knowing I got you a part."

"A part? Why didn't you say so?" She jumped from the treadmill and threw her arms around him. "Oh, baby, you are the best."

"Now, hold on." He struggled to untangle himself from her, but she covered his face with kisses.

"I knew you could do it. You never give up on me, do you?"

He sighed and patted her the way you'd pat a child. "No, I don't."

Lucas

He had been hurt worse than Bobby W. He was grateful for that. They talked to the police, who chalked up their attack to too much drinking on the island, and Bobby W seemed eager to agree. Lucas wasn't so sure.

His aching body still attested to the anger of his attacker, and he'd have to concoct a story to explain the bruises and cuts on his face. He'd told Ellen the truth, of course, and now he was going to have to do something about these messages from Rikki.

He found Bobby W in the gallery, as the old man called it. Ironic, because every room in Bobby W's life was a photo gallery. Some of the photos were collectors' items—Mr. Universe John Grimek, Harold Zinkin, the first Mr. California, Jack La Lanne—all of them in shorts that looked clunky, regardless of how brief. They posed while doing handstands or balancing women in swanlike poses. In one bookend pyramid, a young Bobby W balanced on Zinkin's back and held a white bathing-suit-clad woman in a handstand.

As he entered the room, he thought he heard voices, then realized Bobby W was whispering to the people in the photo.

"You feeling better?" Lucas asked in a louder-than-usual voice.

Bobby W turned from the black-and-white display with the face of a younger man. His cologne created a wall of scent between them. "Those were the days, Luke. We did things a lot differently back then. No AIDS, no palimony."

"I doubt that it's as simple as that."

"It never is." He pointed to a photo of him and his

two partners, twisted into one unit of amazing proportion. "You see that pose? No one has ever duplicated it."

How many times had he told him that? How many times had Lucas nodded in affirmation?

"You guys were the best, Bobby W."

"No, those guys were the best. I was lucky to learn from them." He flexed unconsciously, lifted his chin, gazing off at a beach in a time as old as the photos. "I took their drive, their discipline, and put it into this business. I'm proud of what we do."

"You ought to be."

"Now that Jules is coming back, we'll be the way we were before. Better, by God." His voice rose slightly. He looked at Lucas as if waiting for an answer.

"You are sure that was Julie on the phone?"

"I'm not senile. I talked to her every morning, even though I didn't see her all that often." His dark eyes held Lucas's gaze. "I'll let you in on a little secret."

He turned from the past and walked to the window with its view of the red tiles and white buildings, stretching off into a rising skyline of wealth.

Lucas followed, standing as close beside him as he could without being overwhelmed by his scent, something heavy with sandalwood.

"You thought I was crazy to announce a new spokesmodel so soon after Julie's disappearance." His smile was tender, but his gaze was Bobby W at his sharpest. There had been no Dutch courage, as he called it, for breakfast today, no Bloody Mary, hold the tomato juice.

"I questioned your judgment, I'll admit."

"That's because you don't know Jules the way I do. You don't know what makes her tick."

"Which is?"

"She *is* Killer Body, and she's proud of it. It's not just the money, either."

"I know that." It's the ego, he wanted to say, the drive for perfection, but he knew better.

"By announcing a search for a new spokesmodel, I was gambling that I could drive Jules out of hiding, whatever the reason." He crossed his arms and smiled out on the view, as if he owned it, which in a way, he did. When he turned to Lucas, tears glistened in his eyes and his lips quivered. "It worked."

"It appears to have. When did Julie say she was coming back?"

"She didn't say when, only that everything would be all right now, that we'd talk every day, like always." Cold fingers clutched Lucas's wrist. "She told me to hold the job for her."

"You think we should call off the competition, then?"

"I keep changing my mind on that one, Luke. Even before I knew Jules was gone, I wanted to have a second spokesmodel for the Ass Blaster, but now I don't know. What do you think?"

He didn't know. They'd generated considerable publicity with the search. Now, if Julie returned, if she really did, would they need a second spokesmodel, especially if it turned out to be Rochelle, as he suspected?

"What do you think about what that bastard said when he jumped us? Do you think he knows anything about her?"

"A drunken bully." Bobby W waved his words aside. What was he feeling? Shame that he couldn't flatten the guy the way he would have in his youth? "I totally discount everything he said."

The door swished open behind them.

"Sorry to interrupt." Ellen's pained expression belied her soft voice. "That pushy reporter, Rikki Fitzpatrick, has been trying to reach you all morning."

Lucas tried to hide an unbidden smile, but he wasn't fast enough. Bobby W's sharp eyes caught it, and he chuckled.

"I probably should take it," Lucas said.

At least he'd deceived Ellen. She pushed a strand of blond hair behind her ear and handed him the phone. "Good luck."

How was he going to talk to Rikki with the two of them watching, Ellen with professional concern and Bobby W for entertainment? He turned his back on both of them and walked to the window. If he couldn't see them, he could pretend they weren't there. He hadn't seen Rikki since Friday and that emotional scene in his house. If he was lucky, maybe he could talk her into lunch.

He pressed the speak button and looked out the window. Santa Barbara never looked brighter, more inviting or full of promise. "This is Lucas." Might as well try to sound professional.

"I've been trying to phone you all weekend." Her voice was flat, edged in anger.

"If I'd known, you wouldn't have had to phone more than once, believe me. Bobby W and I were out of town. Ran into a little problem. Have you had lunch yet?"

"This isn't a personal call."

He'd seen pride in her face, arrogance. He'd never seen the anger he heard in her voice. This was the woman with whom he'd shared something. A woman who felt something for him. It wasn't his imagination. He knew she felt something, even now.

"What's the matter, Rikki? What happened?"

"You lied to me."

He felt the heavy presence of Bobby W and Ellen behind him. Lowered his voice even more.

"What are you talking about?" Then, in a voice a shade shy of a whisper, "We're on the same side, remember?"

"Then tell me this." He could feel her take a breath, and he took it with her, picturing her face, the lifting of her chest.

"What is it?"

"Just tell me. Who the hell is Julie Larimore?"

TWENTY-TWO

Rochelle

"So tell me everything about the part." Back in the house, she'd managed to let go of Jesse long enough to ask the question. Her head spun with plans. She'd have to up her workout routine, get rid of her ass, make sure it could be photographed from any angle.

"It's television, of course," Jesse said.

"Nothing wrong with that. Television is what made me. That and Clenbuterol."

"The three-week miracle. You won't need it for this."

He'd insisted she take Clen before and pretended not to know she still did now and then. She'd never even known what it was until he explained that, in addition to being an asthma medication, they could melt body fat at amazing speed. Sure, they stopped working after three weeks, but that was all it took.

"Are you sure I won't? At least it's not a steroid, and in case you don't remember, I lost nine pounds in ten days the last time. That's why that baby sold more copies than any of the others from the jiggle series, thank you very much." She pointed at the poster beside the refrigerator. Had she ever looked anywhere close to as sexy and in control as that girl?

"I said you won't need the Clen."

He went to the refrigerator door and filled a wineglass with water, frowning as if trying to decide what to say next. Worried about Megan, she knew, as was she.

A basket of popcorn sat on the counter. It was the only food she trusted, and she planned on rationing out the entire bowl to herself today, through the night, until they met Megan's plane and had her home safely with them. At the moment, she'd like to shove the whole thing into her face by the fistful.

"Stop playing games, Jesse. I want to hear about the damned part."

"I'm not playing games. I'm just trying to think." He sat at the counter, patted the stool beside him, but she was wired too tight to sit.

"The part," she repeated. "Tell me about it. How much thinking does that require?"

Bitch mode, but she couldn't help it. He was expecting far more patience than she could deliver.

He nodded, acknowledging the jab.

"It's a drama, based loosely on real life, ripped from the headlines, they call it. A spokeswoman for a national weight-loss program is missing, and three women vie for her position."

A shudder passed through her, but no, she couldn't think that way. Opportunity was opportunity. She needed to accept it, be grateful for it. "Tell me about the three women."

"One's divorced, a royal of some type. One's been dumped by a media figure, and one's an actress."

"Just an actress?"

He sipped his water. "An actress with a weight problem."

"Weight problem?"

An image of Shelly Winters, whom she'd met when she was just getting started, emerged in her mind. Shelly—gritty, tough and wonderful—had been a rarity, a fine actress who put her gift before her self-image. A large woman. Rochelle wasn't a large woman; she just had a big ass, a *problem* ass, okay? If she played an actress with a weight problem, people would notice and figure it out. All they'd see when they looked at Rochelle McArthur would be what Rochelle saw. Her ass. And her career would be over, if it wasn't already.

She got in Jesse's face, every muscle in her body tensed. "No one has ever said I had a weight problem, and no one but you and Blond Elvis has ever known about the fucking Clen."

"Of course not," Jesse said. "It's television, remember?"

"I don't know how I feel about that."

"How you feel about it doesn't matter," he said. "Carley Steel's playing the actress. She doesn't have a weight problem, either."

That one stopped her like a clanging bell inside her head. "As I'm sure you've noticed," she said back to him.

"What's that supposed to mean?"

He'd flipped the switch in her brain. Now it was too late. She'd gone straight to bitch mode again. "Carley Steel with her Botox and her boobs, who brands herself the new Rochelle McArthur. I've seen you looking at her. How could you let her have this part?"

"I'm not in casting, babe." His gaze was even, untroubled. "And there's nothing wrong with looking, if it's all I do. I'm no Bobby Warren, you know."

The remark stung, as he had intended. Cruelty was always his best defense. She forced herself to look away from the penetrating gaze, and wondered if he was telling the truth, wondered also if he *looked*—as he put it—at Carley, and now Princess Gabby, because he didn't like what he saw at home.

She leaned against the counter. The exercise that usually energized her had left her drained. She couldn't ignore the waves of nagging anxiety. Something was wrong here. Jesse's deliberate motions, even the way he held the glass of water, were too calm, like a doctor who had to tell a patient the illness was fatal, not an agent imparting good news to his client, wife or not.

"So, if I'm not playing the actress?" she began.

"You wouldn't want that role, anyway. She's over the hill." Then, looking up at her, "By Hollywood's standards, anyway. Besides, she's the killer. It wouldn't be good for your image, considering the similarities to real life."

Carley Steel, over the hill? Rochelle didn't think so.

She faced him at the bar, so close she could smell the popcorn's now suddenly repugnant scent. "Who the hell am I playing, Jesse? Just tell me."

Another sip of water. She wanted to smash the glass on the tile floor.

"The actress has a mother."

He said it tenderly, his voice husky, the way it used to be when he said he loved her. "She's important to the story line, and it's a great part."

For a moment Rochelle couldn't react, couldn't move. She'd heard him wrong. She had to have heard him wrong.

"The mother?"

He nodded, sadness, maybe even embarrassment

pulling down the corners of his mouth. "It will give you a chance to stretch."

"I've been stretching my whole damned life." She slammed her fist on the tile counter, knocking the basket of popcorn onto the floor in a shower of white. "I'll die before I play Carley Steel's mother."

"Your choice."

Avoiding her tantrum, he looked down into the glass.

She'd be a laughingstock. They'd talk behind her back, say she was losing her looks, her figure. They'd point out the broadening of her ass.

"Never," she whispered.

Jesse got up, poured more water. "You know what happens when you turn down roles."

"I don't care what happens. I will not do it. I will not."

He opened the freezer, staring inside for a moment, looking far younger than he deserved in his jeans and taut torso beneath his polo shirt. Just when she was about to ask what he was doing, he pulled out a six-inch, foil-wrapped package.

"My stash," he said. "We're both feeling a little stressed right now. How about a cigarette, baby?"

It was that or dinner. It was still early. She had plenty of time to make a decision.

She put out her hand.

"Fire me up, Scotty. Just don't tell the fans."

Rikki

When did I become obsessed with Julie Larimore? It's the interviews, I think, trying to hear her voice through the answers on the page. Her favorite color: white. I knew only one other person with white as a favorite color. Lisa. Her favorite beverage: water. Her favorite singer: Diana Krall, especially Krall's remakes of Nat King Cole songs like "A Blossom Fell" and "Maybe You'll Be There."

How could two people be so similar? They couldn't, I think with a chill. Lisa, too, must have pored over these articles. She must have hated her own life so much that she tried to absorb Julie Larimore's. Why hadn't I known? Why hadn't Aunt Carey known? Or had we known and tried to hide the truth from ourselves?

Hamilton and I sit on the patio of my motel, the files spread out on the round table with our coffee cups and Hamilton's ashtray. I've told him I think there's some enormous, cosmic fire alarm that will go off if it detects cigarette smoke in the vicinity of Santa Barbara, but he makes it clear he's not up for my humor this early on a Monday morning.

I'm not sure I can read another word. Each interview brings back Lisa, makes the loss fresh and raw again, flooding me with more questions.

"You're putting in too many hours on this." Hamilton gives me a look of assessment, his eyes a watery hazel in the sunlight.

"I don't have a choice, Den. There's got to be something here that will tell us who she is."

"Only your buddy Lucas Morrison can do that."

A sad tugging within reminds me of the momentary hope I'd felt with Lucas, the beginnings of trust. But then the anger sets in again. "The more information I have, the less he'll be able to lie," I say.

"Want me to stick around and go with you?"

I feel it's a test. He's fishing, trying to figure out if I want to be alone with Lucas.

"If you'd like to," I say. "Depends on how soon you

need to leave for home." He lights a cigarette. I've made him nervous. I watch him blow a translucent stream out into the clear day. "Den?"

"Yeah?"

"I think we ought to break the story about Julie Larimore."

He scowls down at his cigarette, then back up at me. "We don't even know for sure it was Julie Larimore on the phone."

"I heard the voice mail. It was definitely her cell phone."

"So, what you observed was Bobby Warren calling Julie's cell, not Julie calling Bobby, right?"

"It's still a story."

"But not *the* story." He smashes out the cigarette and gets up, moves his chair out of the sun, closer to mine. "I suggested you take time off. I thought you needed it, and I still do."

"What would I do with time off?" My voice chokes out the words. Hamilton frowns as if to say he told me so. "I have to do this, Den, and I'm close. If I can get Lucas to tell me who Julie Larimore really is, we might be able to figure out what happened. And if it's big enough—"

"You can bring down Killer Body?"

"Maybe not bring them down, but expose them."

"Make them pay for what happened to Lisa? Give your aunt the revenge she wants?"

"Why not? And it isn't revenge. It's closure. That's all she wants." I realize how crazed I must sound to him. I never should have told him about Aunt Carey, never trusted him with my feelings. "Okay," I say in his face, so close I can almost taste the cigarette he's just smoked. "I may have started out that way, but I feel compassion for Bobby Warren, and there are things I like about Lucas, too. The fact remains that someone is trying to harm the women Bobby's considering for Killer Body spokesmodel."

"Harm or frighten?" he asks.

"Good question. Either way, there's a story there. And now Julie's called Bobby. That's part of the story."

He leans back in the wrought-iron chair, apparently unconvinced. "So, why print it now?"

"To keep readers focused on the story?"

"Why else?"

To keep Killer Body in the news, I think. Damn, is Hamilton right? Is my interest in this story motivated by revenge? Suddenly I can feel the sun on my face, too hot and unrelenting. I put my head in my hands, feel the heat on my skin.

Hamilton touches my bare arm and I jerk up, meeting his eyes. "It's too damned hot out here."

"Talk to Lucas Morrison." His voice is low, yet harsh. "See what you can find out. After that, we'll get together again and decide what to do next."

"About the Larimore story?" I ask, knowing better.

"That and the rest of it."

"Den, please don't make me take time off." He narrows his eyes, the lines around them carved deep, as if etched in clay. "Please, please let me stay on this story," I say.

He looks away, then gets up, scraping his chair on the concrete.

"Let's talk about that later, okay? After you've heard what Morrison has to say."

I can take gruff from him. I can take pissed off. But I can't take pity. Immediately, I regret pleading. The only thing that works with Hamilton is what he saw in me from the day he met me, back when I knew what I wanted.

I yank my chair out, too, facing him. "My guess is Lucas has plenty to say, and I'm the one person who can get him to say it."

"That's more like it." His tough face goes tender on me, and I'm reminded again what attracted me to him in the first place. I know he feels the tug, as well.

"What is it?" I ask.

He shakes his head. "Just thinking." Then, with a grin, "Like maybe I should apply for a job writing obits, anything to get out of being your boss."

"I was thinking about that opening in features," I confess.

"No, you're ideal for this."

"You mean it?" I ask.

"Yeah, I mean it." His gaze doesn't waver. "When we—when I applied for this promotion, I had no idea you and I were going to—"

"I know that, Den."

"Sometime down the road, once you're finished with this story, you and I need to sit down and have a talk."

I feel myself break into a smile. Even if it never happens, just the fact that he's said it, thrills me to the soul. "I hope we can do that," I say.

TWENTY-THREE

The Interview

What happens when you get too old for the job?

Age is the last thing I fear, and no one else needs to fear it, either. Age is a bully, when you think about it—all bluff and bluster, that can distract you from the joy of being alive. Killer Body isn't about age. It's about lifestyle, about choices, about giving yourself the freedom to choose. Inspiration and accountability. That's what Killer Body is about.

And Julie Larimore is Killer Body.

It's not age that scares me now. It's this draining strength, this pain. No one can ever know. Promise me that no one will ever know. Stop the others any way you can.

Tania Marie

Word of the day: *Vehemence:* Forcefulness, intensity, fervor

Since there was no parking on Third Street, they found a place on Fourth, where she expected Jay Rossi to wait. She'd agreed to an interview and photo shoot for *Woman* magazine, and she had to find something to wear.

She should have left Rossi behind, but he refused, saying he'd feel better if he could just keep an eye on her. The fact that someone worried about her, even though he was being paid to do so, softened her, and she agreed.

Damned if she didn't know better. He'd done nothing but harp at her since they left her place. She was keeping something from him, he said. She was a lousy liar. Neither accusation was news to her, and the second had been witnessed by the entire country the year before.

"Even if I did know something, what makes you think I'd tell you?" she'd said as they drove into Santa Monica.

"Because I care."

"Can it, Rossi." With that she'd turned up the music, drowning him out in a joyous blare of Van Morrison.

That's what she got for having dinner with him Saturday. She was glad that was all they'd had. For a moment there, when it had been just the two of them, a bottle of Frogs Leap zin and the foggy slice of moon, she'd considered breaking her short-man rule.

"About an hour?" she asked. "I won't be long."

"This is my first time here," Rossi said, ignoring her request.

Instead, he followed her past the art galleries, jewelry vendors and street performers that made up the center of Third Street Promenade. Restaurants, clothiers and coffee shops lined the sidewalks. The smells of cotton candy, funnel cakes and churros were so real she salivated.

She stopped in front of a cotton-candy concession. "No one has ever seen me shop," she said. "It makes me too nervous."

"So, try me. If it doesn't work out, I'll wait in your car." He grinned and walked up to a tiny studio of a store, its windows filled with Asian designs. "Come on. I shop with my sisters all the time. Sometimes, a second opinion can help. Otherwise it's just you and the mirror."

She pulled her straw hat lower and pushed up her dark glasses. "How many sisters do you have?"

"Four."

"That's obscene."

"My mother would probably agree with you."

"You're the only boy?"

"Yeah, the oldest. That's why women don't intimidate me." He grinned at her. "Not even you."

"You don't intimidate me, either." She tried to move past the shop, but he remained planted in front of it.

"My number three sister was a designer for Ralph Lauren. She's living in Paris now."

"She should buy her brother a new truck," she said. "And some shoes without pointed toes."

He looked down at his boots. "What's wrong with these?"

"You ever hear the term *shit kicker?*"

"I'm not ashamed of my roots. And Blackie's fine for me."

"Offhand, I can't think of any famous chefs who drive old pickups and wear cowboy boots."

"So, I'll be the first." He looked at a variegated blue dolman top in the window. "You could wear that."

"No, it's smocked."

"But the fabric's light. And the color will bring out your eyes."

That made her smile. "I'll bet you don't even know the color of my eyes, Jay Rossi."

Her sunglasses were no protection from the intensity of his look. "I know more than you think."

"Like what?"

"Like that it's a shamrock tattooed to your ankle, not a clover like the tabloids say."

That was a surprise. "I'm Irish," she said.

"I know that, too."

She caught a sweet, hot whiff of cotton candy. She had to have some, to feel the way it melted the moment it touched her tongue. That's what she ought to be doing, eating cotton candy, not flirting with her mother's lackey.

"A very thorough bodyguard," she said. "Virginia will be pleased."

His gaze didn't waver. "This isn't about Virginia."

"She's paying the tab."

He started to say something else, then shook his head in apparent disgust.

"Come on," he said, taking her arm. "Let's go check out that top."

Before she knew it, there she was, a makeup mask pulled over her face, the dolman sleeves at her side. She looked like Bat Woman From Hell.

She kept the makeup mask on. It made her look even more ridiculous—Bat Woman From Hell wearing a blue old-lady shower cap over her face, short little clumps of hair sticking out at all angles.

The designer, a Japanese woman wearing a plum version of the same top, frowned. "I can lengthen it for you."

For a moment, Tania Marie was afraid she might have recognized her through the mask. Then she realized the designer was thinking of ways to minimize the maximum. "It looks better on you, that's for sure," she said.

"It's lovely on you," the woman said. "Perhaps we should lengthen the sleeves."

Tania Marie felt ready to pass out with only the designer, the close quarters and her reflection in the mirror.

"Why the hell not?"

Gabriella

She sat in the back seat as Christopher drove the town car north on the I-5. The rearview mirror indicated NW in turquoise digits. Northwest. Such a comfort to know where one was going. Although the weather outside had been a little on the warm side, within the car it was colder than she preferred. Christopher kept it that way because he always wore a jacket, today one matching the gray leather seats and upholstery. At least the car was paid for. She couldn't bear to give it up, although heaven knows, she'd given up a great deal more.

"Do you think this is a good idea, meeting with Tania Marie again?" he asked.

"I don't know, but I couldn't turn her down." She wasn't sure how she felt about it, either. "I don't think she's a bad person," she said.

"But it can't help you to join forces with her." He was always gentle in his suggestions; maybe that was part of the reason she always listened to him.

"I don't plan to join forces, only to hear what she has to say. And what Rochelle has to say, too, for that matter."

"You think she'll even show up?" Christopher asked as they passed the first of the San Clemente exits.

"I think she'll be afraid not to."

It was a springlike day, and the clumps of purple and pink along the highway added to the illusion. Rain was predicted for the following week, but you wouldn't know that now. She'd dressed accordingly in white and a floral print top and the wonderful bandanna Christopher had to buy for her that horrid day at the hotel gift shop.

"Maybe Tania Marie's going to withdraw," he said. "She's suffered enough embarrassment."

"So have I, but neither one of us is a quitter, and I doubt that Rochelle is, either."

They drove a few miles more, and Gabriella knew he was chewing on something, as her grandmother would say. Right after San Juan Capistrano, he cleared his throat.

"What is it, Christopher?"

"What do you mean?"

"There's something on your mind. The air in this car is thick with it."

"As a matter of fact, there is, but I want to wait until we stop."

"So, let's stop."

"Not until we get closer. I want to hear what Tania Marie has to say first."

"What difference should that make? I'm more interested in what's bothering you, and I don't want to wait. After all we've been through, we shouldn't be keeping secrets."

"It's not my secret. It's yours. How much do you really want this Killer Body thing?"

She leaned forward in the seat. "It's not Killer Body I want. It's the talk show and the wherewithal, of course. I've got a really good chance if I gain some exposure, and Killer Body will do that for me."

"Why don't you go straight for the job, don't even mess around with Killer Body?"

"You know why." She couldn't even speak the words, so shamed she was by her financial situation. "I just can't bear living like this any longer. And I can't keep begging Alain for money. I'm not going to give him that kind of power."

"I don't think it's power he wants."

"Of course it is. He loves to see me beg. Thinks it's what I deserve for cheating on him in such a public way, regardless of what he did to instigate said cheating."

Long Beach. They were getting closer. Finally Christopher coughed again.

She leaned forward over the too-cold air, on the wide console that separated the two seats.

"You might as well just tell me."

"I can't lie to you, Gabby. I talked to Alain."

"What do you mean you talked to him? How did he find you?"

"He didn't."

"You mean you contacted him? Oh, Christopher, you didn't."

"I'm sorry. I didn't know what else to do."

It was impossible to get angry with Christopher. This was the closest she had come. "For starters, you could have talked to me about it first."

"I knew what you'd say. I know how proud you are."

She pulled the bandanna down over her eyes, sinking into the seat with a moan. "You didn't ask him for money, Christopher. Please tell me you didn't do that."

Gabriella spotted Rochelle right before they got to the beach.

"Park here," she told Christopher, indicating the line

of snack bars and a pipe shop whose only clientele appeared to be tattooed skaters and potheads.

He parked in front of an old-fashioned liquor store, meeting her eyes with his sad ones as she stepped from the open door. As upset as she was, she gave him a hug. "I hope this won't take long," she said. "When I get back, we'll talk."

The rest of the drive had been frosty, as her grandmother would have said. She loved Christopher dearly, but she was happy to get out of the car and let her anger dissipate in the cool Santa Monica breeze.

Rochelle walked up to meet her, wearing a pair of low-cut jeans and a shirt that appeared to have shrunk along with her rib cage. She seemed to be growing thinner all the time, all except her chest, that is. Thank goodness for flowing fabrics. Gabriella might not have much up there, but at least hers was real.

She still couldn't believe Christopher had talked to Alain, not to mention asked him for money. She couldn't bear the thought of Alain knowing she was destitute, convinced that she'd gotten what she deserved.

"Well, isn't this cheery?" Rochelle said. "Tania Marie the honey bee insisted on neutral territory, but this is pushing it, I'd say."

"Is she here yet?"

"I haven't seen her. Thought I'd wait out here and decide if I really want to meet with you. My daughter just flew in from school, and I'm too busy to play Tania Marie's little whacked-out games."

"Try to be nice to her," Gabriella said. "She's not a bad sort. What she's been through would finish most women."

"Oh, it's *finished* her, all right." Rochelle did a terrible imitation of Gabriella's accent. "She just doesn't know it yet."

A mini SUV pulled up across from Gabriella's town car. She spotted the straw hat and dark glasses behind the wheel. "Here she comes."

"Good," Rochelle said. "Maybe we can settle it right here. The last thing I want is a walk on the beach with you two."

"You have something against the beach?" Gabriella asked.

"I have something against wasting my time."

"You needn't be unpleasant."

Gabriella started toward Tania Marie. Unlike Rochelle, she looked better each time Gabriella saw her. Trimmer. The wind had tossed her short little flip into something softer and less funky, and from the tiny blue sunglasses to the tattoo on her ankle, she looked—well, jaunty.

In spite of the floppy hat, knee-length pants and jungle-print top, closer fitting than usual, Tania Marie's manner was serious.

"I'm glad you could make it," she said.

Rochelle made a huffing sound and unknotted her sweater from around her waist. "I should have my head examined for it after what you two pulled on Crosby's show."

"We had a point to make, and we made it." Tania Marie slipped her macramé bag over her shoulder and began to walk toward the beach. "In fact, that's what I want to talk about today."

Rochelle sighed and she wrapped the sweater around her, looking as if she needed all of the warmth she could get. "I knew it. If this meeting is another excuse to knock my husband, you can go to hell, both of you."

"I agree with her, Tania Marie," Gabriella put in. "We said what we had to on the Crosby show. I have no desire to cause more problems for Jesse."

"Big of you." Instead of appreciating her support, Rochelle struck back as sudden as a snake. "I'll be sure to let him know that you don't want to cause any more problems for him."

"Back off." Gabriella had just about had it. "All I meant was Jesse's a nice man, and he's been kind to me."

"I know what you meant." Rochelle's face had gone dry and tight in the sun. Gabriella felt her own cheeks burn. "Too bad for you he likes big tits."

"Big ones or fake ones?" she inquired. "Only a very insecure woman would be this threatened by someone who means her no harm."

"I thought it was the insecure women who went after the married men."

The heat in her cheeks burned through Gabriella's entire face. "How dare you suggest—"

"Cut the crap." Tania Marie stopped on the sand, facing both of them. "Listen, you bitches. Don't you see this is what they want? The only way we're going to get out of this is to stick together."

The harshness of Tania Marie's command stopped the retort on Gabriella's tongue. Heart slamming, she stood face-to-face with Rochelle, humiliated at what she'd been engaging in. "They?" she managed. "Who?"

"Whoever's doing these things to us. Gabby's hotel room. My thing in the sauna, a threat to my mom." She sat down on the bench, removed her glasses and gazed up at Rochelle with those wide blue-green eyes. "We can't be the only ones. Something has happened to you, too."

Gabriella expected Rochelle to fly into a fury again, but instead, she sank down on the bench beside Tania Marie. "You say someone sent a threat to your mother?" she asked.

"Yes. A picture of me torn up, and a postcard with Julie Larimore's photo on it."

Rochelle's hand flew to her sunglasses. "Oh, my God," she said.

Tania Marie

They ended up at a bar, with a menu offering one page of tacos and three pages of tequila. Tania Marie would have preferred tacos to booze, but she wasn't about to start that again. What had Annie said at the last meeting? Nothing tastes as good as thin feels. Tequila it was, and damned if they didn't serve it with chips.

Sitting on tall stools around a small, round table, they all avoided looking at the basket in front of them and pretended not to notice the salty fried-corn smell wafting from it. Tania Marie had wussed out with a margarita, but the other two had straight shots.

"The tequila bar must be to Southern California what the martini bar is to San Francisco." She sucked the tart liquid through the way-too-small straw, giving herself an instant headache.

Rochelle hadn't spoken. After her outburst on the beach, she had shrunk inside herself and moved almost zombielike. Now she reached for her shot glass and, ignoring the ritual of lime and salt, drained it.

"I thought it was you," she said to Princess Gabby.

"I thought it was *you*."

"That's ridiculous. How would I be able to lock Tania Marie in a sauna, let alone stage that fiasco at the hotel?"

"You seemed like the one with the most to lose," the princess said.

Tania Marie pushed away her drink. "Let's face it. We all have a lot to lose."

"Indeed." The princess nodded. "But if it isn't one of us, who is it?"

"That's what we have to find out," Tania Marie said. "We need to stick together instead of trying to screw one another over at every turn."

"I've never—" Princess Gabby huffed.

"You know what I mean. We have to keep in touch with one another. We need to report anything unusual to one another, even if it seems minor. And we need to tell what we know about Julie. She's the only thing we all have in common."

"Who should we tell it to?" Rochelle caught the server's eye and pointed at her empty glass. "The police aren't all that interested. They don't even think there's foul play involved. When I reported getting that threat in the mail, they didn't even send anyone out. They took the information over the phone."

"What about the reporter?" the princess asked.

"I don't trust her. She doesn't care about what happens to us."

"She was nice to me," Tania Marie said. "She saved me from the nightmare inside the gym that night."

"But then she wrote that story about us." Rochelle's second tequila arrived, and she lifted it to the light, studying its amber glow. "Let's toast," she said, and with a harsh laugh, "You've got to want the body."

They shrieked, then clinked glasses. Rochelle swallowed, then turned to Tania Marie. "You're the last person who ought to trust the press."

Tania Marie felt herself flush. She slammed her sunglasses back on, indoors or not.

"True. But I think we should talk to Rikki Fitzpatrick, and I think we should talk to Mr. Warren, too."

"That'll be a cold day in hell," Rochelle said. "If

Bobbo thinks there's a chance of bad publicity involved, he'll call off the competition."

"Have you ever thought—" Princess Gabby paused, staring down at her untouched glass.

"Thought what?"

"Have you ever thought that perhaps Mr. Warren should do just that?"

Before they could respond, Tania Marie was aware of voices behind her.

"Don't look around," the princess whispered above the din. "There's a guy behind you with a camera."

"Oh, shit." Tania Marie felt the familiar flush of humiliation that blossomed into full-blown fear. What was the point in trying to do the right thing when you got the same results as when you didn't? She should have eaten the damned cotton candy, the tacos. She would, by God. She'd get out of here right now, run for it, then eat every taco in the whole damned town.

Rochelle drained her shot glass. "Let's just leave. You get in the middle, Tania Marie." She slid off the stool gracefully, as if she'd rehearsed the movement dozens of times.

"Hey, Tania Marie." A bald man with a sunburned face and wrinkled tan slacks brandished a camera as if it were a weapon. "That is you, isn't it, Tania Marie?" He looked more tourist than paparazzo, but that didn't make him any less dangerous. The tabloids would buy from any bastard who could find the shutter release.

She shoved her hat over her head, turning away from the tiny red light that blinked at her.

"Could you hold it a moment, Tania Marie? Don't move." The bastard had his nerve.

"Fuck off."

She jerked past him, squeezing between the tables,

the princess to her right, Rochelle to her left. The man
stepped behind her. How many times had photographers shot pictures of her ass and thighs? Tears choked
her. This was so unfair. "I'm going to make a run for
it," she managed to whisper to the others.

Princess Gabby linked arms with her. "Take the high
road," she said. "Don't let anyone dictate your exit. The
photographs will be there, anyway, whether you run or
walk or curse. That's how I finally had to come to think
of it. Either that, or go crazy."

"She's right." Rochelle reached for her other arm.
"Just pretend we're going out for a shopping spree.
There's no reason to run from that weasel."

"Except that he's photographing my fucking ass
from behind."

"Asses are the worst." Rochelle squeezed tighter.

"At least he's not getting the satisfaction of seeing
you run from him," Gabby said under her breath.

The man caught up with them on the sidewalk.
"Come on, Tania Marie. Smile for the camera."

The asshole's own snakelike smirk radiated so much
self-love that it was almost lewd. Tania Marie made the
mistake of looking directly at him. The neatly trimmed
little strip of colorless hair beneath his nose sickened
her. Marshall would have called it a metaphor.

Marshall thought everything was a metaphor for
something else. If she wore a black thong instead of a
red thong, it was a metaphor for her mourning their relationship. If she wore a fucking red thong, it was a
metaphor of her sexuality and her anger.

If she forgot a thong in his car, that was a metaphor
for her hoping they'd be caught, as, of course, they ul-
timately were, meta-fucking-phor or not.

Now this bastard and his spiky little moustache. It

was a metaphor, but of what? That the trenches kept getting lower and lower, perhaps?

"Excuse us, please," the princess said in a crisp but pleasant voice that probably took years of voice training to achieve.

And they—all three of them—fueled by Princess Gabby's voice, walked briskly past him.

The princess retrieved a cell phone from her straw handbag and pushed a button. "Christopher, dear, my friends and I need your assistance," she said, her voice as sweet and delicate as the flowered dress she wore. "We're just leaving the beach, the tequila and tacos place. Wonderful. There you are. Can you see us, dear?"

Tania Marie sighed with relief as the sedan swung around the corner and pulled to a stop. The three of them scurried in, leaving the bald asshole standing on the sidewalk, clicking away.

"They say everyone in this godforsaken place is a wannabe actor or writer," Princess Gabby said once she slammed the door behind her. "I'd wager there are as many wannabe paparazzi, wouldn't you?"

"Sure," Rochelle answered. "Cameras are a hell of a lot cheaper than acting lessons, and you don't have to put up with the cattle calls."

"Fucking bastard." Tania Marie knew the princess hated that kind of talk, but that's what the bald pig was, damn it. Tears started coursing down her face. Tomorrow there'd be another story about her yo-yoing weight. But at least she was safe now, thanks to Princess Gabby and her driver.

She took comfort from that and settled back in the seat, feeling strangely at peace between these two women who were supposed to be her rivals. Maybe she wouldn't need the tacos, after all. Maybe she still had time to make the Weight Watchers meeting. Yes, before she resorted to anything more drastic, she'd at least check out the meeting.

And she'd call Jay Rossi.

Knowing someone would listen to her and care about what happened today softened her still-raw fear. The fact that it was the first time in a long time—maybe forever—that anyone had cared, caused her to sob with even greater vehemence.

Rochelle reached in her bag and handed her a neatly folded tissue. "Don't do that, honey. It's not worth it."

"I know, but I can't help it. I can't." Tania Marie wiped her eyes. "Those photos are going to be all over the fucking tabloids tomorrow."

The princess cleared her throat and shot her a pained look.

Tania Marie returned it. "The *F-ing* tabloids," she said.

TWENTY-FOUR

Rikki

I'm not sure I'm ready to do this, but I have no choice. Difficult as it is to see Lucas, I have to remember why I'm here, walking along this upscale pier toward the slip where his sailboat is docked.

These weather-stained slats of wood beneath me are about as safe as this entire relationship with a man I admit I don't really know. I remind myself that my last relationship, if you can call Hamilton that, was all of one night. The one before that was with a near stranger, who, two days after I moved in with him, decided co-habitation was too much work and went back to college. Two men, same result. I know I can't trust my own instincts, and I vow to be careful this time.

Looking down at the kaleidoscopic water makes me dizzy, so I stare straight ahead at the boat. It's smaller than I thought it would be, a sloop, I think, of shiny white fiberglass and a blue tarp-covered cockpit.

I haven't wanted to come here, where it would be just the two of us, but he said he needed to work on his boat, and if I wanted to talk, it had to be here in the marina.

Lucas appears from below, and I know he's been watching me approach.

"Here, let me help you," he says, and reaches for my hand.

At once, I spot the purple welt under his sunglasses, the jagged little scabs along his jawline.

"What happened?"

"A drunk attacked Bobby and me. I'd like to say if you think I look bad, you should see the drunk, but I'm afraid that's not the case. He got away."

I climb up, then down, hanging on to a blue tarp covering the cockpit, so that I won't have to hang on to him. In jeans and a black T-shirt, he looks younger, and that somehow makes this meeting more intimate. His pale amber glasses wash his face with light.

"What's the matter?" he asks. "Do I look that bad?"

"No. I just realized I never saw you without a tie before."

"I wear too many of them. Bobby W likes a formal image. Says too many in this business dress like wrestlers, and he's right." He moves past me and the cockpit. Says, "Come on. I'll show you around."

I hold my ground, as much of it as I have on this little vessel, and say, "I'd rather talk out here."

"At least have a cup of coffee. I just made some."

I'm at once aware that I left so early that I didn't have food, coffee, not even my usual tomato juice. Damn, I now detect the aroma from below, along with Lyle Lovett's voice. I can't let myself be sidetracked, though. I can't.

"First we need to talk."

He shakes his head and smiles. "Your greatest strength is your greatest liability, all right. If I looked up *stubborn* in the dictionary, I'll bet I'd see a picture of you."

"This is important to me," I say. "More than coffee. More than nautical etiquette."

His expression grows thoughtful, less friendly. "It's important to me, too. I told you I didn't know Julie Larimore wasn't her real name. Neither did Bobby."

I feel relieved every time he says it, and I think I believe him.

"It's not," I say. "We couldn't find a trace of her. Didn't you check her out before she was hired?"

"Bobby did. She was Julie Larimore from the beginning, as far as our employment records go back, from her first job at the first Killer Body."

He seems sincere, but I've been fooled before. I move closer, study his eyes, which are frankly examining mine. I get another whiff of coffee, cutting the cool air.

"Do you know what she did before she went to work for Bobby?"

He shakes his head. "Modeling, I think. Minor stuff. Rochelle McArthur might know. She's the one who introduced her to Bobby W, which I'm sure she regrets."

"Why? She didn't want to be the original Killer Body, did she?"

"No, but Rochelle and Bobby W had been close even before Dolores, his wife, died. She was always Bobby W's confidante—until he met Julie."

"Were he and Julie romantically involved?"

He starts to answer, then stops. "Never," he says finally. "He was her mentor. Look, I want Julie to be found, but I don't want to embarrass Bobby W with the media."

"I'm more than the media. This is more than an assignment to me."

"I know that." He's distant now. "I don't know about

you, but I'm going to go down in the galley and have a cup of coffee."

With that, he goes below. I follow down into the cozy galley, all wood and chrome. A kind of sofa that's obviously also used for sleeping covers most of one side of the space. A sink is fitted into the end of it, and shoved into a tiny corner beside it is the stove. A coffeepot sits on it. I take the sofa.

"Does Julie have any family?" I ask as I watch him pour.

"She mentioned a father, but I don't know if she sees him. She doesn't have family, doesn't have close friends."

"No men friends?" I ask. "Didn't she date?"

He brings the coffee and sits down beside me. The boat rocks gently with occasional little splashes hitting its hull.

"You'd have to know her to understand."

"After reading a folder full of her interviews, I feel I do know her."

"She wasn't into men," he says.

"Was she gay?"

"No. She's never married, and anytime I saw her with a man, it was a friend. She was in love with being the girl with the Killer Body. She didn't have time or energy for anything else. I don't think anyone was perfect enough for her."

"Do you know any of the people she dated?"

He ponders that one for a moment. "She went out with her personal trainer sometimes, but you could see it wasn't anything serious."

"Are you good at detecting that kind of thing?"

He looks at me steadily. "I don't think chemistry between two people is something you can hide. Do you?"

I take a swallow of coffee to avoid his gaze. "Probably not."

"Then take my word for it. There was nothing between her and her trainer."

I reach for my notebook. "What's his name?"

"He's one of the best in L.A.," he says. "We send him to our clinics to motivate the troops. I'll have to look up his name and contact information for you."

"You don't know the name of someone who works for you?"

"He's a freelancer. We hire him by the job, refer clients to him, that kind of thing. And I don't know his real name. All of his clients call him Blond Elvis."

"Blond Elvis?"

"Because of the way he used to wear his hair. He's a good guy, though. Takes his job very seriously."

"Where can I find him?"

"He works out of a couple of different clubs." He puts his coffee cup on a white table attached to a pole beside the sofa.

"There's a place for everything here, isn't there?" I say. "No wasted space."

"That's one of its many advantages over reality. Do you sail much?"

"Are you kidding? In the Valley? All we have is a couple of Clorox lakes where the rich people live. We won't have waterfront property until after the big quake."

"I'd like to take you sometime."

I'm aware of how close we are, pushed together here on this pillow-lined bed posing as a sofa. I know what I would like to happen and how easy it would be to let it. Everything is moving that way—the boat stirring against the quiet urging of the water, the unobtrusive breeze, the patch of sunlight on the wooden floor. Lyle Lovett's voice.

I straighten on the sofa and hold my coffee cup with both hands. "This is the first time I've ever been on a boat."

"Do you like it?"

"Yes." I realize that it's true. Realize that if I never set foot on one again, he's given me a gift. "It feels more natural than land in some way and much more natural than a plane."

"That's how it is for me, too." His gaze is intense. "Come with me. I'll show you the Channel Islands first. And then—"

"Lucas." I touch his arm, and the contact surprises both of us. I take my hand away, staring at it as if it is not part of me. "I can't."

"Why not? You want to."

"Yes," I say. "Yes, I do." Sitting this close to him, pressed against the pillows, I don't even consider lying. "I can't, not now. *We* can't."

"When this is all over, then?"

"Maybe." Did I really say that, and worse, did I really mean it? "Maybe when it's over."

He moves closer to me. "There's nothing like waking up in the morning and smelling bacon cooking on another boat, or someone making coffee before the sun is even up. Or sailing to Catalina, before the island comes into view yet, and Los Angeles just fades from sight as if it's dropped into the water." He takes my coffee cup and places it on the table with his own. "I want to show it to you. Want you to have that feeling of just you and the sea, no land before you or behind you."

It's one of the sexiest things anyone has ever said to me, maybe because he's saying it, maybe because he could read last week's newspaper to me, and I'd think it's sexy.

"Maybe." It is the only word I know.

I've barely spoken before his arms slip around me, and he leans down to kiss me. My arms go around his neck, slide down around his shoulders. It's like embracing a rock. His body must be pure muscle.

He tastes of coffee and desire. The kiss flattens us down, among the pillows, against the upholstery. My fingers dig into his flesh. *So long,* I think. *It has been so long. But not now, I can't.*

I tear my lips away from his and come up gasping for air. He releases me.

I reach for my cup with shaky hands, trying to quiet my breathing. He looks stunned and lurches for the stove, his back to me, fiddling with the coffeepot. Finally, he turns.

"I'm not sorry that happened."

I look at his lips, freshly kissed, swollen and flushed. "Neither am I."

His expression makes me want to run to him.

"But it can't happen again. Not now."

The light in his face fades as rapidly as it appeared. His nod is almost curt. "If that's the way you want it."

"It's the way it has to be until we get to the bottom of what happened to Julie Larimore. That has to be our focus."

"Then tell me where we need to start." He's a strictly business Lucas now. No suit and tie required; it's all there in his voice.

"With the personal trainer, maybe? How can we find out where he is?"

He paces the area before the stove. Then he says, "We could go through Julie's bank statements."

I jerk up, suddenly alert, the moment of the kiss lost. "You have her bank statements?"

He nods. "I have all of her mail."

TWENTY-FIVE

Rikki

I could have kissed Lucas for telling me about Julie's mail. Truth be known, I could have kissed him, anyway, wanted to, more than I've wanted anything with any man since that crazy night with Den Hamilton.

There's a humming in the back of my head now, like a love song playing softly in the next apartment, just loud enough to hear if you stop to listen. I don't just *look* at myself in a mirror now. I *examine*—wondering if my minimalist makeup plays all right, if my manicure-scissors-clipped hair is really *fun,* as my stylist insists, or just weird. Is my natural peach-fuzz color honest or bizarre? Then there's my hair, in general. Should I keep it defiantly short like this, or let it grow?

And my body of course. Damn. I make even myself ill. Thank God no one else can hear my sudden detour into Vanity Land.

I've dealt with this delicious indecision only one other time in my life, with Den Hamilton. And when he became my boss, and that relationship ended before it began, I paid big-time dues. Swore I'd never revisit that

Fantasy Island again. Now here I am, ready to head there tomorrow, on a sailboat, no less. It's the worst and best part of being a woman.

I hate it.

I love it.

And I can't stop wondering if Lucas Morrison really likes me.

It has to be business today, and I will see that it is. We are going to Julie Larimore's home. I'm sure Lucas hasn't shared those plans with Bobby Warren, but I could be wrong. Loyalty is his strength, just as tenacity is mine. It's good to know your strength, as Lucas pointed out, so that you can also know your weakness.

I meet him there, because as much as I'd like to ride in the same car with him, I feel more secure with my own wheels. Embarrassed that I spent so much time self-evaluating and primping, I pulled on, at the last minute, all-black everything, without stopping to think which or what.

Now I stand outside a discreet condominium complex, vaguely visible through what look like castle gates. I see his smooth gray little car, something retro that's supposed to remind those who can remember them and those who'd like to of the Datsun 240Zs. It slides up beside me; I jump in, smelling crisp fabric and that citrus scent of his before we can as much as look at each other.

"I appreciate this," I say. How formal and stupid is that?

"I trust you." I can almost taste the words, and I can feel the sweet decency that caused him to speak them.

"I'll earn that trust," I say, looking straight ahead into the jungle of this remote complex. "I promise."

"Bobby W insisted we pay all of Julie's bills and her

house payment, as well as the lease on her Mercedes, which is a company car, anyway. That's why I have a key. It's his way of gambling that she's coming back."

"If he really talked to her on the phone, she might be."

"If."

Now I have to turn, but his face is stone, all profile and posture. "I'm sure she will," he says.

I go the friendly reporter route. "I'm glad you're letting me take a look at it. Once I see the place, maybe I'll think of something I didn't before."

"That's what I'm hoping," he says.

He stops to retrieve Julie's mail, and we pull into the garage in front of the gated unit. He's dressed down, as well, in a shirt that skims over his muscles and jeans, with which he's wearing what I can only call boat shoes. The bruise still welts the area beneath his eye.

As if feeling my gaze, he stops, and even with the dark glasses, I can see his eyes soften into the way they looked yesterday when we were on the sailboat.

"What is it?" he asks.

"Nothing. I was just thinking this is the second time I've seen you without a tie."

"But not the last time, I hope."

His voice makes it sound erotic. I don't answer, moving instead into the living room.

From the moment we close the door behind us, I feel like an intruder. This sequestered place is not used to visitors. Its white carpet bordered in blush-toned tile is so pristine that it's disturbing to imagine someone living with it.

I move along the tile, not wanting to sully the carpet with my shoes. The small kitchen, also tiled, with its brushed stainless-steel refrigerator and stove, looks as though it has never been used.

"Julie didn't do much entertaining, I take it." I realize I am almost whispering.

"She's pretty reclusive." Lucas carries the briefcase he's taken from the car. "The gym is at the end of the hall."

I follow him down more tile and into a room that looks larger than it is because three of its four walls are floor-to-ceiling mirrors. Exercise equipment gleams in the center. I turn away from my reflection, but there is no place to hide. On the single unmirrored wall, the Killer Body poster hangs, framed. *You've Got to Want the Body.* What must it be like to work out here every day with only one's own reflection and that poster?

"The personal trainer worked with her here?" I ask.

"Yes. It's not unusual, especially not for high-profile people. Julie's a perfectionist about her body."

I survey the minimalist decor. "And apparently everything else." He's still holding the briefcase. "You brought her bank statements?" I ask, hoping he hasn't changed his mind.

"I brought everything."

He walks past the mirror into the room across from the gym. It, too, is immaculate, with an L-shaped glass desk, a computer on the short end of it and three white laminate bookshelves. I go straight to them—motivational books with titles like *Go for the Gold,* tapes with similar titles. I pick up a magazine, her photograph on the cover, then put it back down on the shelf. She must have photographs, letters, mementos. No one can live with just books and exercise equipment.

An aluminum-toned file cabinet squats on casters beside the desk.

"Have you checked that out?" I ask Lucas.

"Of course not." His disapproving look reminds me

how much he's already compromised himself to let me in here, and I don't want to push it. "The police went through the place, of course, because they wanted to determine if there were any signs of foul play."

"There weren't?"

"No. And the Mercedes is gone, as well. There's no reason for them to think she didn't leave of her own accord."

I have to restrain myself from touching the file cabinet. Instead, I ask, "Did you open any of her mail besides the bank statements?"

"Just the bills," he says. "Bobby W doesn't want to intrude into her life more than necessary. He just wants to make it as easy as possible for her to return."

"He's convinced she's alive?"

He nods and opens the briefcase. "Since the phone call, more than ever."

We spread the contents out on the surface of the glass desk. Each bank statement has miniature photocopies of her checks, all neatly printed with her flourish of a signature, a name that is drawn rather than written. *Julie Larimore*. No middle initial.

Most of the checks are recurring. PG & E, mortgage company. A second mortgage company. Utilities, routine obligations not so different from my own. Among them, a credit card payment, several to Whole Foods Market, a couple to a doctor's office and several made out to Raymond Scott. I begin to shuffle the statements, checking the dates and amounts. One hundred, two hundred, two fifty.

"This must be the trainer," I say. "How much does he charge?"

"Probably a hundred an hour, anyway." Lucas leans over me, and I can feel his breath on my neck. "Yes, that's Blond Elvis, the personal trainer, although I didn't know she worked with him that often."

I look up at him. He still hasn't moved. "I guess," I say, "we'd better start making phone calls."

"It won't be difficult to find him."

He straightens up, and I can tell he's having second thoughts.

"I'd also like to borrow those bills," I say.

"I don't know how Bobby W would feel about that."

"He doesn't have to know. I'm sure you're not going to tell him that you let me in here."

He zips the briefcase as if to protect it from me. "Showing you the condo and the bank statements are one thing. To turn over Julie's personal mail is another."

"Why?"

He clenches his jaw. "Because, regardless of how I feel about you, you're still the press. You've written damaging stories about Bobby W's business, a business that's helped a lot of people."

I feel my face get hot and look away from him. I know I'd write those same stories again, given the same circumstances.

"I'm not trying to hurt anyone, and this is what I do for a living, Lucas. I'm used to looking for needles in haystacks. Maybe there's something in there you missed."

"There could also be personal information Julie doesn't want made public."

"Like what?"

"Her balance at Macy's, her shoe size. Anything. I told you she's a private person."

"We aren't intruding into her life," I say. "Bobby Warren wants her found. That's all we're trying to do. Just find her."

"I know." But his eyes remain unconvinced. "What if she doesn't want to be found?"

"Is that what you think?"

"It's what I wonder." He opens the briefcase again. "Nothing about this is typical behavior for her. There was no reason for her to take off. Bobby W lets her get away with anything she wants."

"Anything, like what?"

"You name it. She can miss appearances, take off for weeks, months at a time. As long as she checked in with him, and they had their daily conversations, he didn't care what she did."

"You don't like her, do you?"

He starts to deny it, then meets my gaze. "No."

"Why not?"

"For the usual reason people don't like other people. She doesn't like me. Didn't want Bobby W to hire me and was never happy that he did."

I feel myself grin. Why am I relieved? "I thought may-be—" I stop, not sure how to continue. "It occurred to me that maybe the two of you might have been close."

"Never. The only love affair Julie has is with herself. No one else is perfect enough for her." A smile spreads across his face. Sitting there, at Julie Larimore's glass desk, in the full light of day, I know I am blushing like an adolescent at her first compliment. "She isn't my type, Rikki."

"No?"

He starts to bend down, but I can't do this, not in Julie's home, and not now, not with Hamilton still on my mind, unresolved.

I put out my hand, feel his firm body beneath the soft cotton of his shirt. "We've got to find this Blond Elvis guy."

He takes my hand, brushes his lips across my knuckles. "Exactly what I was going to say." He's still smiling, and although I'm not sure why, I smile, too.

"Twenty-four hours," he says, his voice low.

"For what?"

"That's how long you can keep this stuff." He hands me the briefcase. "I want it all back by this time tomorrow, okay?"

TWENTY-SIX

Rikki

I'm not in the habit of ogling men, but with Blond Elvis, I'd be almost rude not to. He walks toward me with the air of someone who is so used to standing out that he gives it little thought, like the only swan in a duck pond. His enormous arms confirm his credentials, and the rest of him, clad in those butt-hugging shorts, is just as impressive.

The hair isn't really Elvis, shorter on the sides, and the pompadour in front is flatter, secured by spray. The half smile that borders on a smirk makes me wonder which came first, the attitude or the nickname. So, this is the rich women's personal trainer. At least, you'd be motivated to show up for class.

He has one of those Laguna complexions that some have been known to deride as boring, only on him, it works. His blue eyes and shock of white-blond hair illuminate a tan that looks as if it was acquired the old-fashioned, politically incorrect way—in the sun.

"You're Raymond Scott," I say.

"Only when I'm having a bad day."

His voice is a surprise, soft, borderline effeminate, although he is anything but. It's the secretive, musical voice of a confidant, someone who's witnessed as many confessions as a family priest. His accent is more rainy night in Georgia than California dreaming. Although he may have embraced the accoutrements of our state, he's no native.

"And what kind of day are you having?"

"That depends on what I can do for you." He gives me a friendly and somehow asexual undressing with his eyes. "You're in good shape. What are you looking for? Upper body?"

Now I'm embarrassed, but I'm also tempted to continue the charade. Instead, I put out my hand and say, "Rikki Fitzpatrick. I'm a newspaper reporter. And you're called Blond Elvis, aren't you?"

"A reporter? Cool." He shakes my hand, lowers his conspiratorial voice. "Blond, for short."

"I want to talk to you about one of your clients," I begin.

"No can do. Believe it or not, my job is as confidential as a shrink's, and probably just as weird at times."

He smiles, and I am struck by the fact that even my car when it was new was never as white as his teeth.

I look around the open gym, the assortment of shapes and sizes on their machines, the generally friendly atmosphere.

"None of these people seem ashamed to be seen here," I say.

"Most of my clients aren't. Those who are hide out in the posing rooms." He starts moving in the direction of the waist-high wooden desk at the front counter, a polite way of kicking me out before I can ask any more questions. "You, for instance. If you decided you wanted to work with me, and it was okay with you, I'd use you as a reference. But even then, I'd never, ever share anything you told me with anyone."

"You must be very good at your job," I say.

He accepts it as his due. "It's why I can charge top dollar. That and the fact that I get results. If I can do it, you can do it. That kind of thing. Think about it. I know journalists aren't exactly in the high-income bracket, but an investment in your body is an investment in your life."

"You sound more like a young Bobby Warren," I say.

"Bobbo's good people. He's the one you ought to interview. Has a million stories about bodybuilding in the old days, and he just loves the press."

"I've talked to Mr. Warren." We've reached the front desk, and I stop. "This isn't a very good time for him."

Not only is his face pretty; it's also as easy to read as a book with oversize print. Right now, it telegraphs panic.

"I don't know anything about Bobbo's problems. Haven't seen him for several months, now that I think about it."

"When was the last time you saw Julie?"

"Julie, who?"

"Come on, Blond. I know you're her trainer. Do you want to talk to me, or do you want to talk to the police?" I don't know where the threat came from, but I let it push me through the question. Based on his expression, it seems to work.

"You tell the cops I don't know nothing, lady. I'm just her trainer."

"That's what I want to talk about," I say.

* * *

After my mention of police, Blond Elvis decides to grant me an audience, after all. He leads me into a small room in the back, past the Employees Only sign, and we settle on a horrendous turquoise bench that reminds me of those that used to line the balcony of the public swimming pool when I was growing up in Pleasant View. Mirrors line every wall. More mirrors on short stands fill the middle.

"So this is a posing room," I say, trying to avoid my own reflection.

"Spare me the stereotype," he says. "We don't come in here to admire ourselves. We come to see if we're doing it right." He's dropped his people-pleasing role and cuts to the chase before I can answer. "Don't cause trouble for Julie, okay? She doesn't need any more shit in her life right now."

"Do you know where she is?" I ask.

"I can't tell you that."

"Can you tell me if she left on her own?"

He licks his lips and shakes his head. "Not if you're going to put it in the newspaper."

I realize he must think I work for the *Times*. I don't correct him. Instead, I turn to face him and press my palms into the bench.

"I'm not looking for a sensational story," I say. "I just want to know that Julie's okay."

Damn. I realize I mean it. I really am past that blind, limiting need to help my aunt avenge my cousin. I've been all the way out, and now I feel I'm part of the way back.

"I think she is. Julie's a fighter."

"What's she fighting?"

"Do I look like *Unsolved Mysteries* to you?" He gets

up, impatient, I can see, to be out of here, away from me. "I can't tell you much about her, couldn't if I wanted to. That's because I don't know her that well, not that I didn't try."

There's no mistaking the gleam in his inky-blue eyes.

"You were interested in her?" I ask.

"Interested, shit. I dug her, okay?" The gleam disappears into pools of anger. "I'm good at my job, you know? Maybe twice I got interested, as you put it, in someone I was training. Walked away from more than most men get in a lifetime."

"Was the interest returned?"

"Not in Julie's case." He sits back down on the far end of the bench. "That's okay with me, though, because I got myself something better out of it. I got myself a friend."

"You consider Julie Larimore your friend?"

"Damned straight." He lifts his chin, threatening me to challenge him. "I helped her, and she helped me. We're friends. Best thing for her if she doesn't come back."

"Why not?"

"Too much pressure," he says quickly. Then, more slowly, "Can you imagine what a bitch it is to be in the spotlight like that, day and night, not to mention at old Bobbo's beck and call?"

"You don't like Mr. Warren?"

"I love the guy, but, hey, he's a tyrant."

I catch sight of myself in the mirror and turn away, but not before I realize I need to make an appointment with a real hairdresser instead of my own scissors. Damn, how do these people live with the constant self-scrutiny?

"Julie obviously had great respect for you," I say. "Don't you know where she is?"

"I don't, and I don't want to. It's her business. When she's ready—*if* she's ready—she'll come on back."

Our exchange is so rapid, and his staccato responses so distracting, that I'm unable to detect how much is honesty and how much is him blowing smoke.

"Do you know where she was from, what her real name is?"

His sweet little face caves in. "What do you mean her *real* name?"

"That's all I know for sure. Her real name is not Julie Larimore."

"But it was on her checks. Printed right there, with her address and phone number."

"Doesn't matter. You can sign your checks Elmer Fudd, if you're not doing it with criminal intent. Doesn't bother the banks in the least."

"No shit?" He rests his chin in his left hand, raking his thumb across his lower lip, left to right, left to right.

"Hey, Blond. Where the hell you been?" A trim African-American woman stops just inside the door, not sure if she should venture farther.

"I'm here now, so what do you need, Shirley?"

"You, baby. Rochelle's on the phone for you and not about to hang up. Can you take it?"

He lifts his hand to block the thought. "No way."

"She said it's important."

"Important to Rochelle could be chipped toenail polish. Tell her I'll call her later." Then, as an afterthought, in a more gentle voice, "And tell her to give Megan a big hug for me."

"Will do." The woman departs as abruptly as she arrived.

"Clients," he says to me, but my head is spinning with what I've just heard.

"You work with Rochelle McArthur?"

"She's not ashamed of it, so why should I be? I've been her trainer for more than a year."

"Does she know you're Julie's trainer, as well?"

"That's between them. I never talk to clients about other clients. Got to be that way since I do a lot of the Killer Body people."

He says it with pride, and I can tell he's committed to his job. That pride might be one way to get him to talk.

"It's clear your clients trust you. I'll bet you hear some stories."

"You wouldn't believe it."

"Has Julie ever talked to you about her life before Killer Body?"

"You mean like where she worked?"

"Anything. Has she ever talked about it?"

He shakes his head. "I think she went to school in Santa Barbara, but that's not where she was raised. She told me she grew up in a small town between there and Santa Maria." He frowns and closes his eyes. "You know the place. The Davy Crockett guy started a winery or something there, bought a hotel."

"Fess Parker?" I ask.

"That sounds right."

"It's Los Olivos, isn't it?" Although I've never been there, I've seen it touted on press releases from the Santa Barbara Visitors Bureau. "Isn't it kind of an artists' colony?"

"You mean like Solvang?"

"I'm thinking more rustic," I say. "Barns, old buildings converted to art galleries. That kind of thing."

"I don't know about that. She said it was laid back, not very many people, didn't even have a high school.

Her dad worked in a winery." His eyes lapse into sadness. "But if she lied about her name, maybe she lied about the town, too."

"She'd have no reason to do that," I say. "She might have had a reason to lie about her name."

"Then it was Los Olivos, right off of 101," he says. "Why is it so important?"

"Because someone there might remember her. They might know who she really is."

"I thought I knew." His pumped-up body seems deflated by our conversation. "They can get anyone to be the Killer Body spokesmodel. I've met several who could do it. It's Julie I care about, and I hope she dumps the gig."

"What do you think makes a good spokesmodel?" I ask.

"Drive. Ambition. And willingness to do whatever it takes, including kiss Bobbo's ass. Julie's got all that, but she has all the money she needs. She ought to just step down, let someone else take over the pressure cooker."

"And you really don't know where she is right now?"

"Couldn't tell you if I did. It wouldn't be ethical."

He stands up, gives me the Elvis sneer-smile, and I know I've gotten all that I'm going to out of him.

"If you ever change your mind about training with me, just call." He makes one of those tongue-clicking noises I don't usually associate with anyone over the age of twelve. "You could be awesome."

"Thanks." I follow him to the hallway. "I do have one question, though?"

"What?"

"Your teeth?" I say. "I have to ask."

"Trade secret." He gives me the grin again. "But because I like you, I'll give you the card of the chick who bleaches them. Debra's her name. We trade services. Nothing unethical about that. Everyone does it in this business."

At the door, he reaches out, touches my arm. It's a far cry from physical contact with Lucas, more like being touched by the brittle branch of a tree you pass on a narrow sidewalk. There's that little life in it.

"Tell me the truth, okay?" If homeless people could learn how to plead with their eyes like this, they'd all be earning what he is and could afford to laminate their Will-Work-For signs.

"About her. Are you absolutely sure she isn't Julie Larimore? Is even her name a lie?"

"Damned straight," I say, and walk out onto the street, leaving him to return to the room of mirrors and think about what it all means.

TWENTY-SEVEN

Tania Marie

Word of the day: *Chagrin:* Mortification, vexation, disappointment

"Didn't I tell you it would work?" Jay Rossi surveyed the dolman top and pants, and nodded a smug smile. "Bet they use this as a cover shot."

"It'll be a cold day in hell before I'm on the cover of any publication that doesn't smell like ink and rub off on your hands."

She'd insisted they take her car, but Rossi said only if he could drive. Now here they were, carrying in garment bags for the photo shoot. They told her they wanted her in her own clothes, so readers could see the real her. Rossi had said that was good, that the last thing she needed was the long-gloves and feathered-hat routine.

She couldn't believe she'd allowed him to accompany her, but it was easier to let him come along than to try to stop him.

"*Woman* magazine is no tabloid," he said.

"That's why you won't see my smiling face or any other part of me gracing the cover. But that creep who recognized me at the tequila bar's probably already sold his photos. I don't know what I would have done without Rochelle and Gabby."

"At least you three aren't dead set on destroying each other anymore."

"No. We check in on one another every day. No more threats, so far. Rochelle's daughter's here from college."

"You don't think they were involved with what happened to you in the sauna?"

She'd gone over it in her head. She'd been deceived before. She'd been betrayed by the most trustworthy man in America. She wasn't exactly a human lie detector, but she believed these women.

"No," she said. "You should have seen how they backed me when that creep came after me."

"I wish I'd been there. I would've kicked his ass."

He said it with pride. For a moment, she thought of Marshall, who would never dream of uttering anything so crass, but who would carry on one affair after another while conveying an image of trust and dignity to the public. She'd bet Jay Rossi wasn't a cheater.

"You're wearing the right shoes for it." She looked down at his shit-kickers and couldn't help giggling.

"Hey, now," he said. "I want you to know I did my share of brawling back in my drinking days."

"Did you like it?"

"Good question." He checked the address of a building with only a glass door and a gold-embossed number. "Come on."

In the elevator, she asked again, "So did you like fighting?"

"It was a high at the moment, because, of course, I was drunk. But no, there's nothing satisfying about breaking another human's flesh with your fist. That's one of the reasons I quit drinking."

"You were doing okay with that zin the other night."

He stood back, sizing her up, his secretive smile like that of a man remembering a fine meal. "It was a good night, and that had nothing to do with the zin."

She tried to look away, but there was only the reflection of her in the elevator's glossy interior. She couldn't deal with that much reality right now, so she gave him the little-girl Tania Maria smile and said, "I had a good time, too."

"And I would have kicked that guy's ass. I mean it." The elevator stopped. They walked out onto the polished tile. Tania Marie's shoes dug into the tile like brakes, screeching her to a halt.

"Oh, shit," she said.

"What's the problem?"

"I can't do this."

"You *are* doing it."

"I'm not sure, Rossi. I've been screwed over too many times."

"And if you don't do it, right now, today, you'll never believe you can."

His eyes were so fierce that she couldn't turn away. She needed to grab some of that ferocity for herself if she were going to survive this session.

"So who appointed you lame-ass cheerleader of the month?"

His eyes didn't change, but a weak little smile replaced the street-fighter scowl. "I appointed my lame-ass self. Now, let's find this photographer before he changes his lame-ass mind."

Gabriella

"Don't get mad, okay?"

There was only one reason that would cause Christopher to initiate an exchange in such a fashion. Now she knew why he'd driven to the television studio in silence.

"If this is what I think it is, please don't tell me until after I meet with John Crosby."

Christopher gave her a sad smile. His shaved head glinted in the sun, and in his white linen shirt, wrinkled as only good linen can, he looked as if he were already the writer he aspired to be. He'd do it, too, working days at the clothing store and nights on his novel. The universe couldn't ignore his kind of dedication.

Neither could she.

She touched his cheek. "Tell me I look okay, dear, and we'll talk as soon as I get out of this meeting."

"Princess Gabby looks wonderful."

He ought to know. He'd helped her pick out the white denim skirt with its asymmetrical raw hem, that not only slenderized but created an off-center V-shape when she walked, revealing her legs. He'd also found the wedges—large X's of cognac-colored leather, so soft she could dance in them if she had to.

The crochet halter, with its built-in bra, was her find, however. Its vivid cantaloupe hue made the rest of the ensemble stand out in a way that was well planned without looking that way.

She didn't have to lean up to hug him. The shoes were higher than they felt. "Now then, give me a kiss for luck."

"Just don't get mad, okay?"

"I know you did it again, Christopher. You talked to Alain, didn't you?"

He sighed and looked down. "Worse than that."

"Worse?"

"I saw him."

"You can't mean he's here?" She saw the truth in his eyes. "He's in Los Angeles?"

Christopher nodded. "I'm supposed to take you to his hotel when you're finished tonight."

Rochelle

She had to hear about it from Jesse. She wished there'd been an easier way.

"You know this for a fact?"

She kept her voice low. Megan was asleep—she hoped—in her bedroom down the hall.

Propped up on three pillows, stark naked on the bed, he channel-surfed a silent television screen, pausing only at porn movies and sporting events. In her next life, she would not marry an insomniac.

"I talked to John Crosby's press agent," he said.

Rochelle decided to go for a little test. "So what did she have to say?" It would be a *she*, that nameless press agent; Rochelle knew it.

Jesse didn't notice. He'd just found a multiracial ménage on the screen. He reached down, not for her, but for himself.

"She said Crosby's interested in helping Princess Gabby. He likes her. Gabby told me he's going to ask her to sit in while he's on vacation. If that goes as he thinks it will, he's going to lobby for her to have her own show. Wonder how many blow jobs that took."

"Not a one." She was startled at the anger his words

elicited. That wasn't an emotion she allowed to surface very often. The bitch routine often dispelled any true emotions. "Gabby's amazing, and she deserves her own show. Why can't you just give her that?"

"She *is* amazing. You're right there."

She poked his arm, trying to nudge his attention back from his friend under the covers to her. "Besides, if she gets the talk show, she won't want anything to do with Killer Body. I don't think she ever did, anyway."

He clicked off the television, right in the middle of an act that would have left even the media's cartoonish version of Tania Marie gasping for breath. They sat together in the darkness. Husband and wife. Agent and client. Rochelle had never felt more alone.

"Which means you'll have it for sure."

"Exactly." Why didn't she feel more victorious?

She slid down under the comforter, which left her feeling anything but comforted. "I guess I'll try to sleep now."

She rolled over, away from him.

"So you see all of this as a positive?" She couldn't identify what bothered her about his voice.

"About Gabby? Sure. I'm happy for her, and I hope it works out."

"Even if I'm her agent?"

Her body froze on the bed. "What are you talking about? You're not her agent."

"I offered to be, if you'll recall. After I talked to the press agent, I got in touch with Gabby and told her I hoped she was still considering my offer."

His glib response was too pat, rehearsed. She rolled over again, studied his profile, hoping even now that she was wrong about him. "But you offered only to get her to withdraw from the Killer Body competition. You weren't serious about wanting to be her agent, were you?"

"I was, and I am."

She felt control slipping away from her, like a thin string she could no longer continue to grasp.

"And she accepted your offer?"

"Yes." He patted her hip. "Take it easy, baby. She'll have her talk show and you'll have Killer Body. Everybody wins."

"You son of a bitch," she said.

"Baby." He reached out to pat her again.

"Don't touch me," she said. "Don't talk to me. Don't *anything* me." She couldn't control the words, the anger that had been banked too long.

Jesse must have heard the difference in her voice. He backed away to the opposite edge of the bed and turned from her without another word.

Once she was sure Megan was okay, once this stupid Killer Body competition was over, she was going to have to figure out what to do about her life. She couldn't go on like this.

The Interview

What were your goals prior to Killer Body?

I remember watching a tape of an interview Barbara Walters did with Barbra Streisand. Walters asked her if when she was a child, she knew she was going to be Barbra Streisand one day. And Streisand, looking on the brink of tears, said it was the only thing that could have happened, the only way it could have been.

I understand that.

When I was a child, I knew I was someone special,

that I wasn't like the others. Some of us are born with the knowledge. That's what I believe.

I was never a child, not really. I was waiting for time to pass, for this. And now that I have it, in these moments of clarity between the darkness and the pain, my only goal is to keep it, no matter what.

TWENTY-EIGHT

Rikki

Los Olivos reminds me of the San Joaquin Valley. Instead of stubborn, sun-baked fields, grapes grow from gentle rolling hills. It's a place that has embraced its history, either that or just not grown out of it. The feeling, as I drive down the street with the flagpole in the middle of it, is charming but cloistered.

Blond Elvis was right. With a population of about one thousand, there's not a high school to be seen, but there are two elementary schools. Armed with no name, only my file and photos of Julie Larimore, I hit them both.

I'm not sure what to expect. Towns like this can be genuinely open, like Fort Bragg in the Mendocino, California, area. Or they can be closed. This one seems to fall in the former category. All of the people I talk to at both schools are helpful, but none can help me. One directs me to a retired art teacher who operates one of the town's many galleries.

Roberta Matlock looks as though she never left the sixties. With long gray hair and no makeup, she is still as unassuming yet striking as the wheat-colored linen dress that almost covers her sandals. I meet her in the backyard of her gallery, which is an extension of the business itself. Wild sculptures—some decidedly western, some impressionistic—spill out onto the fenced-in lawn, among the pots of cactus and pansies. Standing there, still and straight, in the middle of them, she could be another sculpture.

I introduce myself and tell her I'm looking for someone who might remember someone who attended elementary school here in the late seventies or early eighties.

"That's like yesterday to me," she says. "I can remember far back or close up. It's the middle that gets murky sometimes." In spite of her low-key appearance, she has a school-teacher voice.

"The principal's secretary said if anyone could remember a student, it's you."

"That's because I was smart enough to retire before my brain was completely stewed." She settles down on a wooden bench, so crudely fashioned I'm sure it was carved by hand, then painted white. Above the back, which is painted to resemble white bones, three skulls sit, mounted on red strips of wood, barely wider than sticks. The legs and base are fashioned to resemble those of a skeleton. "Join me, and let's see what you have here."

"I don't know," I say, regarding the skulls. "Those guys don't look too friendly."

"It's a Day of the Dead piece," she says. "From Guatemala, although most associate Día de Los Muertos with Mexico. Comfortable as all get-out if you don't let your mortality issues get in the way."

I could tell her a thing or two about mortality issues.

"That's one way of putting it." I sit beside her on the bench. "Are you aware of Julie Larimore, the Killer Body spokesmodel?"

"We do get an occasional newspaper out here. Have they found her?"

Dread tinges her voice. She knows there's only one way such disappearances usually end, and so do I, although I don't want to think about that right now.

"This may sound strange," I say, "but her name isn't really Julie Larimore. We can't find a trace of her before she went to work for Killer Body."

"I'll be." She frowns and nods. "Kind of sounds made up, now that I think about it."

"Julie told someone she went to elementary school here. I know it's a long shot, but I thought maybe I could find someone who remembers her."

She closes her eyes. "So many pretty little girls. I run into them, those former students, around town, ages later, and I can't see any of those little girls inside them anymore. They're all used up."

"Maybe if I showed you some photographs of Julie, it would help."

I open the file and take out the promotional shots, along with a portrait and a couple of candids of Julie and Bobby Warren.

"She would have been a beauty, even back then. When did you say, late seventies?" She rubs her palm over her chin. "Looks like she's frosted her hair. That's what they call it, isn't it? So, it would have been brown back then, right? What we used to call dishwater blond?"

"Probably," I say, pushing away thoughts of Lisa.

"Son of a gun. If the hair were different—" She grabs the portrait, pulls it close to her face.

My arms prickle, and I realize I have to get off this bench right now. "Do you recognize her?"

She nods slowly, unable to take her gaze away from the portrait. The look in her eyes showers me with more chills. "The girl wasn't lying about one thing. Her name was Julie, all right."

Tania Marie

The photographer's name was Garza, whether first or last, she didn't know. He was the kind of man you could be alone with and forget he was a stranger. Part of it was his ability to remove any intimacy from the experience. He could tug her collar, move her arm and look at her as if she were a piece of artwork in progress without making her feel violated.

Unlike the paparazzi, his goal was not to expose her, to reveal her flaws, but to uncover her. His dark hair and intense gray eyes made him good-looking, in an innocuous, preoccupied way.

Tania Marie felt comfortable with him at once and hoped to hell she was getting better at judging character. She hadn't done badly with Jay Rossi, at least so far. She felt better knowing he was in the other room, although for a moment there, she was afraid he was going to march right in behind her.

He waited outside while Garza posed her on a stool so small she was certain she'd slip off of it.

"It's not going to show," Garza said, as if reading her mind. "It will just give us some interesting angles to play with. In a minute, I'm going to have you sit on the floor."

Shit. That's all she needed, to have her thighs spread out like butter on that black tarp. She held the gaze of

the camera. Smiled. And even though it wasn't showing, sucked in her gut.

He clicked and moved in, turning her head, ever so
slightly, with his thumb.

"Do we have to do the floor?"

"I think it might free you up a little. Now, big
smile. Good."

He had a point; the floor did free her, whatever the
hell that meant. With the camera pointed down at her,
she felt less inhibited.

"Another smile, Tania Marie."

For months, people with cameras had been asking
her for smiles. And for months, she'd been running
from them. Maybe Rossi was right, and it was time for
her to take charge and tell her story, her way.

Garza seemed pleased with his efforts, and they made
plans to meet the following week for an outdoor session.

"You don't look too bad off," Rossi said after they
were outside.

She'd heard the term *golden complexion* all of her
life, seen it in beauty articles and on makeup contain-
ers. His was the first deeply burnished skin tone that
qualified as the real thing. Golden. In this light, Rossi's
eyes were golden, too. And interested. Interested in her.
That made the whole day worth it—to return to someone who actually gave a flying flip.

"It wasn't as horrible as I thought it would be. Different from my usual experience with photographers."

"That has to be a bitch." He spoke in the same tough-
kid voice he'd used when he told her he would have
kicked that stranger's ass at the tequila bar.

"You can't imagine."

"So, why are you still protecting the bastard?" he
asked. "Why don't you tell your side of the story?"

She felt the flare of heat in her cheeks, as if she'd been slapped. "Watch it, Rossi. There are some lines not even you can cross."

"Have it your way." He marched into the elevator, holding her garment bags like a barrier between them.

They didn't speak until they reached the sidewalk. She opened the back of her car, and he slid the bags inside into the empty taupe compartment. Whatever kinship had developed between them had been killed by his reference to Marshall. He had no fucking right, and she ought to tell him that right now. Better to just let him go. She'd let go of plenty in the last year. What was one more man?

"Thanks for your help today," she said, not making eye contact.

"Anytime."

Great. He was finally out of her life, walking in his shit-kickers, toward that battered embarrassment of a truck, which would no doubt carry him back to her mother's restaurant and a career as star chef or star lackey, depending on how good he really was in the kitchen. She could let him go, or she could speak. Silence would be best.

"Only one thing." Rossi turned, his arms stiff and fisted. "Why do you have to take the heat for that affair, anyway? Cameron's the one who's married, not you. You're looking out for too many people."

"And what about you? Who the hell are you looking out for?"

"You."

She started to tell him to go to hell, but that hypnotic, caring light in his eyes stopped her before she could. So what did she tell him?

"I don't want to share my secrets with anyone," she said. "Enough of me has been spread across the headlines. They say I almost destroyed Marshall Cameron's reputation. But I'm the one who was destroyed, no 'almost' about it."

"You could even the score. Hell, even write a book."

"I've had offers, and I might one day."

"One day means never. You won't do it, because you still love him. That's the reason, isn't it?"

"Of course not. Now, get out of here."

"Fine. But first, tell me how you could love anyone who said what he did about you."

She slammed the back door of the car shut. "You don't know he said it."

"But *you* do."

She closed her eyes to stop the sudden tears.

"You think I'd believe anything his wife said in some pathetic interview, especially then, with all of the pressure on both of them? She could have lied."

In reality, Lucy Cameron had wounded her in her frigging magazine interview Princess Gabby would call *so California.*

Lucy had said their marriage was stronger than ever. Tania Marie expected that. She had said she loved her husband. Good luck, lady. But the quote that sent Tania Marie on a week-long Milanos binge still hurt so much she tried to forget she ever read it.

"Indeed, my husband made a mistake, one that was probably based on pity. He started out really wanting to help this girl, his assistant, and he had no idea, until it was too late, that she was infatuated, obsessed with him. He also told me, and I believe this in my heart, that he could never, ever carry on a serious relationship with someone with a weight problem."

Rossi came back to where she stood. "Forget the son of a bitch. Can you do that?"

"For Virginia? Is that what she sent you here to do? Are you just another…?"

The rest of her anger was crushed against his lips. The middle of Los Angeles, broad daylight, and she was kissing the hell out of this man who worked for her mother. She broke away, pressed her forehead against his.

"Let's go," he whispered.

"Not so fast." She ran her fingers over his thin, rose-colored lips, sexier than Marshall's full, lying ones.

"Come on." He pulled her closer. She fought the internal signals of attraction that had proved to be lies the last time. She couldn't fall head-first again, not physically, not metaphorically, thank you very much, Marshall Cameron.

"I can't."

"You don't want any baggage going into Killer Body?" he asked.

"As if I have a rat's-ass chance." She leaned against him again, and for some reason, they both laughed.

"What's really bothering you?" He breathed the question into her ear.

She forced herself to step back, look into those golden eyes. "I already have baggage, Rossi."

"What kind?"

"Big-time baggage." Might as well just say it. "I saw something that might not mean anything. Or it might mean everything. It could save somebody's life or ruin it. I don't know. But if I tell it, I'll have to admit something else about myself."

Now the tears escaped, warm as his arms back around her, but not as a potential lover this time, as a protector.

"What did you see?"

"Julie Larimore."

His arms tightened. "You saw her? When?"

"I don't want to go into that."

"After she disappeared?"

"No, right before." She pulled away from him, trying to erase the image from her mind. "It was Julie Larimore, but it wasn't."

The Interview

Do you really think you'll go back, or will Bobby Warren find a replacement?

Of course I'll go back. I wasn't running away from Killer Body or Bobby Warren. I was taken away by a problem that has since been solved. He will never know what happened during the Secret Hours. He'll welcome me back. That's my face, my figure on the poster, my dress that the stores can't keep in stock, that soft sweep of black wool jersey. He will never replace me. I'm like a daughter to him. You don't replace your own daughter. You wouldn't, would you?

Do other women do this? Do they engage in imaginary interviews in their own heads, interviews so real they can hear them? They're shorter now, the questions less connected, but I continue to answer. I always answer.

Will he replace me? The question brings tears to my eyes, and I burn from the inside out, unable to writhe away from the pain that drains my strength. No one replaces me. Don't let them. Stop anyone who tries.

TWENTY-NINE

Rikki

Roberta Matlock has taken me inside, nearly dragging me because she's as overcome with excitement as I am with shock. "I have newspapers," she says. "We can find yearbooks. I'm just floored that little sad-faced girl grew up to be Julie Larimore."

We go down the narrow wooden hall that leads to the staircase. A couple of customers browse. Roberta pays them no mind, lifting her long skirt as she steers her large, graceful body up the carpeted steps.

"If I don't have anything up here, I'll have it at home."

The upstairs office is a conglomeration of statues and flowers, much like Roberta's backyard. File cabinets line every wall except the one with a window. It's open, and the sun fills the room with yellow light, the same color as the organdy curtains that look as if they belong in a nursery. Roberta goes to one of the files and begins digging. "Computers don't keep track of the newspaper stories worth a tinker's dam, so I've got my own filing system."

"What are you looking for?" I ask.

She turns, gives me a wild-woman stare, and for that second, I feel as if I'm back in third grade. "You're a journalist. You want proof, don't you?"

"You think you can find a photograph of her?" I indicate the haphazard stacks of yellow paper. "In there?"

"I didn't say I could do it in five minutes or even a day. It's going to take a while. Can't remember her last name, either, but I can remember the story. She left after that. Went to live in a foster home in the Santa Barbara area, and he—darn, can't remember if he finally died or if he just left after they sold the house."

"Calm down." Now I'm the one with the schoolteacher voice. "I'm not sure who you're talking about."

"Sorry." She sighs, for the first time looking her age. "This has me so rattled. You must think I'm an old dingbat."

"Of course I don't. Just take it easy. You said you didn't know if he died or not."

"That's right."

"Who's he?"

"Why, Julie's father," she says, back on track again. "She tried to kill him."

Tania Marie

Almost an hour passed, and Rikki didn't return her call. Tania Marie's courage passed along with the time. Why had she listened to Jay Rossi? If she told Rikki Fitzpatrick about seeing Julie Larimore, she'd have to tell the truth about herself, too.

She picked up the remote, pointed it at the open armoire containing her television. She needed to relax, channel surf, maybe watch wonderful Wolfgang Puck create some amazing dish.

She heard Marshall's voice moments before she saw his face. Damn her luck! The bastard was ubiquitous, not to mention gorgeous, with the gray hair, the sad, wise eyes. She couldn't get away from his image, his voice, his memory.

She'd stumbled upon some history channel showing his elder-statesman pose. His gaze, thoughtful, yet certain, he talked about the Wright brothers, Charles Lindbergh, Amelia Earhart, Chuck Yeager, John Glenn, Sally Ride. "The wonder of flight," he called it, then with that trademark wiseass chuckle, "and all since 1903."

"Fly home to your skinny wife," she shouted at the screen. "Fly back to whoever took on my job after you got me fired."

One click, and his image disappeared as abruptly as if it hadn't existed in the first place.

The refrigerator beckoned.

What had she heard at the meetings? Put the healthful foods in front so that they are the easiest to reach?

She opened the stainless-steel door. All of the veggies and the Laughing Cow one-point cheese were right in front, so that she couldn't possibly ignore them. Could she? She even kept her mini-bagels in there, next to the tomato juice. She could stick one in the toaster, spread it with the Laughing Cow.

As she thought about it, she opened the freezer, digging far back, past Virginia's care packages, finding what she needed, by touch, knowing it the moment she connected with its smooth surface. Frigging Milanos. She could taste the sweet shortbread outside, the bitter chocolate bite of filling. Her trigger food, as they called such things at the meetings. She'd put them in here months before, to save for a special occasion. Well, this was it.

Tania Marie washed down the package with icy cold milk. What was it about standing up that made one feel less guilty, as if the food eaten that way didn't count? What made it count even less if you left the refrigerator door open when you did it?

Now, with every delicious crumb licked away, she felt stuffed and shamed, and not at all ready to talk to the reporter.

So, that of course, was the moment she chose to call.

"What took you so long?" She felt like sobbing again. Jay Rossi had deserted her, and now Rikki Fitzpatrick had, too.

"I was following a lead on Julie Larimore."

"I might—" She swallowed hard, still tasting the Milanos. "I think I might have one, too."

"I'm parked in front of your apartment," Rikki Fitzpatrick said. "Come on out."

Rikki

It's late by the time I leave Tania Marie. I'm still trying to figure out what I should do next. I need to visit the San Diego hospital and try to confirm her story about Julie Larimore. I need to go back to Los Olivos and talk to more people who might remember Julie and the childhood scandal that sent her away from there.

The hospital is first. I call from the car that night. As I suspect, there's no one to talk to me. I'll have to wait until Monday and go in person. I'm still not sure I believe Tania Marie, although I know she's convinced the person she saw was Julie Larimore. I just need to find out, and I can't do that until Monday.

There's something else driving me as my car moves instinctively toward the freeway, as if it already knows something I don't. I need to talk to Pete. That's crazy. I can just call him. A sure instinct pushes me forward all the same. He would have been my cousin's husband. I must sit down with him face-to-face. And I must ask the questions neither of us wants to hear.

Why now? I've waited this long. Why not wait a little longer until the pain of loss dulls, as it must, the way all pain does? But, no. I have to ask, and I have to ask now. I can be there in under four hours, and then, once I have my answers, I can decide where to go next.

Before seeing him, though, I have to visit someone else. I've put it off too long.

The Interview

What if they find out?

They can't find out. You can't let that happen. There's too much at stake. Only one person knows. She recognized me at the clinic. I saw it in her face before she turned away.

And the reporter? She's digging into your past, trying to ruin your name.

Her, too. She has to be stopped.

The doctor?

He'll never say anything. He's afraid for himself. They're all afraid. I won't go back there. I'll be all right if everyone will just go away.

And the other women?

Leave them alone. It's Tania Marie. She's the one.

The cramps swallow up everything but the fear. No one must find me. No one. Just go away now, if you love me. Leave me alone in the Secret Hours. I'm hungry, and there's so little time before dawn.

Rikki

I hadn't expected it to get dark so fast. I make my visit, anyway, following the tenuous black ribbon of Belmont Avenue. It might be easier at night, I reason, without that verdant, sunlit reminder of everything that remains behind when someone we loves leaves this earth.

The cemetery is the brightest place on the abandoned street. Perhaps that's why the looters and trashers loot and trash the fast-food places and tire shops, instead. They don't want to step into the spotlight of this world. Neither do I, but I have no choice.

The ribbon gets skinnier and darker. Damn, would she want me to do this? Of course she would. She'd expect it. I try not to register the graves that stand like stark road signs. I just move, realizing I'm not sure where it is. I don't even know where my own cousin is buried.

Then I see the car. Black. Understated. Clean as rain. Pete's. I stop, trying to decide if I should invade his life while he's out here, mourning. As am I.

No. I'd better drive on.

Then I hear a noise. See him approaching me. I stop, roll down my window.

"Sorry," I say. "I just felt it was time."

"I'll leave you alone, then."

Tears shine on his cheeks.

"I need to talk to you," I say. "I wanted to stop here first. I didn't think—"

"I come every night."

Do I really want to go through with this, put both of us through more than we're already suffering? "I'll call you tomorrow morning. We can get together before I go back."

"Let me buy you a drink," he says.

"Where?"

"I don't know. It's Friday night all over town."

"I'm not sure I can deal with that."

"Me neither. Junior Pacheco's little brother's got a match out at the casino. I promised Junior I'd meet him there."

Ringside Lewis, Lisa used to call him. "You love your boxing."

"I love Junior." His voice catches.

Junior was to be best man, and Troy, one of the groomsmen at the wedding that death called off. Lisa and Pete never missed one of Troy's fights, even before he was a contender. Now Pete is probably going as much for Lisa, for the memory of the two of them, as he is for Junior Pacheco.

"I know. You and I can talk tomorrow."

"Meet me there, Rikki."

"I don't think so."

"Come on. You've gone with us before, and you liked it. We'll be sitting with Junior."

Pete is about as subtle as Troy Pacheco's fists. He and Lisa had been trying to set me up with Junior for the last year.

Junior, although no more interested than I in that cozy combination, had been gracious when they announced he would be best man and I maid of honor at the wedding. Pete and Lisa had never gotten it. I don't want to spoil the illusion now that it is the only illusion remaining.

Somehow, I segue from graveyard to ringside, the only constant being Pete, clutching a paper cup of beer in one hand. Junior's doing his version of table hopping, up and down the aisles in the casino's indoor stadium, and the Pacheco fan club swells to fill the seats and cheer for their man. *One of us, one of us,* their rhythmic applause seems to say.

Every time I watch Troy box, I remember the less-than-sober night he told me once that fighting for three minutes was like fighting for eternity. That's what hell would be, he'd told me. One long round and no bell. That's how I feel now, how I've felt since Lisa's death.

We're on round number four, halfway through, only worse than that, if you consider he's fighting three minutes a round with only one minute between. He sags against the ring, white shorts collapsed against him in shiny, sweaty folds. His head lolls, as he lifts his parched lips to his manager.

Pete nudges me. "He'll be okay. He always comes back, just wait."

Pete is the definitive kid. That's what Lisa always said. He has to sneak into his Christmas presents early. He tries to make those he loves do the same, even if he has to help them with the unwrapping. An ethical attorney, he can't, when it comes to family, keep a secret.

I'm hoping that is still the case.

"We have to talk," I say. "You know what I'm asking."

He gulps his beer, jerks his head, just in case I'm missing the angry storm in his eyes. "No, I don't. I thought we were here to cheer on our *compadre.*"

"You know exactly why I came here tonight, Pete."

"You think I'd invite you if I knew you were on one of your missions?"

"Maybe that's the reason you asked me. You knew there'd be too much noise, too much action, too many people we've both known since high school."

He shrugs. "You're overreacting. You're still grieving too hard to make sense of what's happened."

"Can you make sense of it, Pete?"

I hear the bell, watch Troy dance in a flash of white, out into a rain of fists. Troy doesn't let up. Neither do I.

"You knew her better than anyone, even better than I knew her."

"Maybe," he whispers through dry lips.

"In all of that perfection, something wasn't right. I felt it, but you know it, Pete. Why did Lisa have to die?"

Blows fly; Troy tumbles, finds his feet and the music of his movements again. Cheers and applause envelop us. I don't move, waiting for my answer.

Pete looks as if he's been bitten by a vampire. In a way, he has. I'll pay big-time guilt dues for it later. Right now, I just have to know.

"Pete?"

"Fuck it. I'm leaving."

He jerks up, stalks, in his slacks, his crew-neck gray sweater, up the aisles, to the exit.

I dash behind him, no longer caring about anything but the truth.

Finally, I gain on him. Grab his sweater from behind.

"I wish it would go away, but it won't. You have to tell me."

The anger in his eyes is hot enough to blast this stadium of noise to splinters. I match it with my own anger, my own need. I'll die before I as much as blink.

"Okay." He chokes out the word, looks around as if someone can hear, but they can't hear. They're all on their feet, dancing, cheering for Troy. "It's my fault."

Perfect diction, no sign of tears.

Through the cheers of *Viva Troy,* I ask, "Why?"

"I'm a perfectionist."

"So was she."

"I made it worse."

He's thrown me a line I'd love to hang on to, but I know better. That's why I'm here. He's not the one to blame, not the reason. At worst, he's a symptom.

I take his arm, say, "Come on," and lead him down the steps to our seats. He's no longer fighting me.

"She thought she had to try too hard," he says.

"She always thought that, long before she met you. It's the way we were raised."

I can't think about it, or I'll be the one who falls apart. Just think about the stairs. One step, then another. We'll be down there soon, ringside. Another round, another eternity, is over, and Troy sprawls in his corner, a satin dot on the black night of the ring below.

"You know about Julie Larimore," he says.

"You mean that Lisa wanted to look like her?"

"If it hadn't been Julie, it would have been someone else." His voice offers no hope. His eyes are dark shields of pain, curtains down, no visitors, please.

Then the bell, and Troy goes for it. And so do I.

"When we were growing up, I knew what she did, even though I didn't see it."

"I didn't see it, either," he says. "She was too careful."

I feel as if I'm the one who wants to vomit now. As we near our seats, I know what he's going to tell me. Worse, I know what I should have told myself years before. We've both seen the truth. We've both managed to avoid it. And now, with Lisa gone, there's no reason to lie.

I slide my arm down and squeeze his hand. "Lots of people have eating disorders," I say.

"It wasn't a disorder. She was just too much of a perfectionist." He shakes free of my grip, rubs both hands together.

The hairs on my neck ripple with the recognition of what he can't admit.

"She binged. She ate and ate and ate, then tried to eliminate the consequences."

"I didn't figure it out for a long time," he says. We're back in our seats, the fight before us only noise now. His voice comes out exhausted, yet relieved. "Then I found the syringes."

I hadn't expected this, but I let myself absorb his words, trying to keep from trembling, trying to pretend it is an interview, that I am an emotion-free reporter. "What then?"

"I had to confront her. She said they were some high-tech weight-loss drugs the Killer Body trainer had picked up in Mexico. I was worrying over nothing, she said. All she wanted was to be perfect by our wedding day."

"And you believed her?"

"I thought I did. I couldn't let myself think that she had a problem, not even when she'd go days at a time without seeing me."

The sickening reality settles in my body. "She did the same thing to me. She told me she liked her space, and I could never let myself get close enough to question her."

"Neither could I."

As the magnitude of what we're admitting to each other sinks in, one jagged piece stands out.

"Which Killer Body trainer got her the drugs?" I ask.

"I don't know. Some guy with a funny name."

"Lucas?" My mouth is so parched that I can barely speak.

He shakes his head, as if impatient to connect to the memory. "Something weirder, like a color. Beige? No, that's not right."

"Blond?" I offer.

"Yes, that's the guy. Blond Elvis. If those sudden drops in weight didn't bring on the heart attack, they had to weaken her. What did she do on those days we were apart? Binge?"

"Or get her weight back down." I shudder as the possibilities float through my mind. "It's not your fault, Pete, and it's not my fault. We have to keep reminding each other of that."

He grabs my arm and nods, and although he cannot speak the words, I know he understands.

Then, Troy Pacheco's fist connects; the man in black goes down. And as the victory is counted down, the crowd surges to its collective feet in a mantra of *Viva Troy, Viva Troy.* Because it is expected and somehow easier than remaining seated, I stand, too, Pete beside me.

We don't talk about it again. We don't need to. Pete goes off for another beer while we wait for the next match. Someone moves close to me. I smell cigarettes, beer. I turn into the harsh whisper. "Some people get the best seats in the house."

"Den." My first reaction is guilt. I've begged him to let me stay on this story. Now, here I am, at a boxing match.

I want to hug him, want to sob out everything I've just learned. Before I can, Den Hamilton's flushed face breaks into an embarrassed smile. "I came with a date. Couldn't believe it when I saw you here."

Date? Well, why not? The newspaper doesn't say its editors can't date, only that they can't date the reporters they supervise. I crane my neck to see if there's a solitary woman standing nearby, but it's impossible with this crowd. "I haven't been in town long, but I've got good stuff for you."

"Lord, woman, when do you sleep?"

I ignore the compliment, wanting to prove to him that I've been making progress. "I found where Julie Larimore's from. I'm going back there tomorrow."

"On a Saturday?"

"Why not? The town doesn't close up on weekends."

"Want some company?" he asks.

"I'm leaving early in the morning." I feel myself blush as I say it, asking questions with the implication that they are none of my business.

He flushes for both of us. "The earlier, the better. Shall we take my car?"

"It's probably better if you ride with me and fly back," I say. "I need to go to San Diego Monday. There's a medical clinic there I need to check out."

"You don't give up, do you?"

The admiration in his voice warms me, makes me realize how emotionally numb my conversation with Pete has left me.

"I can't give up," I say. "This clinic, Den. Tania Marie told me she saw Julie Larimore there, at least someone she thought was Julie Larimore."

"She couldn't tell? Was Julie in some kind of disguise?"

"Just dark glasses, but that wasn't the problem. She said Julie was huge."

He frowns, and I can see him trying to make sense of it, recalling the image on the Killer Body poster. "Overweight, you mean?"

"Grossly overweight," I say. "Tania Marie said she was obese."

Lucas

She found him on his boat that morning. He'd come down to do some work and ended up sleeping there. His first thought when he spotted her approaching the slip in casual pants and a lace-up burgundy sweater was that she'd come because of him, because of *them*. But her unsmiling expression, the look of determination, told him otherwise.

Now they walked the pier, and Lucas tried to make sense of what she had told him. There must be another explanation.

"It can't have been Julie," he said. "It makes no sense."

"Not to me, either, but Tania Marie insists it was Julie. She talked to her, she said. Didn't you tell me Julie would disappear for months at a time?"

"Weeks at a time. Months this last one. But she had too much self-control to go off like that. She had too much to lose."

He paused at the pier railing, wondering how much he should say. Would Rikki be able to help? Or would she spread this story all over the newspaper?

"There's something you haven't told me." She tilted her head, and the sun glinted off her hair, so shiny she must have just washed it. "I know it."

"I'm trying to tell you everything. I just don't know what's important."

"Is that true, Lucas?" Her unyielding eyes narrowed on him with lie-detector precision.

"Of course it's true." He hesitated, unable to look away from her. "There is something. I'm just not sure how important it is."

She touched the tender place beneath his eye where the drunk had hit him. "Tell me."

It was down to a simple choice, his loyalty to Bobby W or his belief in her.

"Bobby W has a trust," he said. "If Julie violates the Killer Body code of ethics before or after his death, it's going to cost her and her survivors a lot of money."

She shuddered, and for a moment, he regretted saying it. "Ever the controller, isn't he? Even beyond the grave. So, did he also dictate her personal life? Does the Killer Body code of ethics include dating, marriage, maybe?"

"I believe it does."

"You're not kidding, are you?"

"No." He turned toward the ocean, wished he were out there on it, where it was easy to make the right decision, where he had only himself and the stars to depend on. "Bobby W doesn't have a family. Killer Body is it. I told you this only to prove that it would cost Julie a fortune to violate something as basic as control over her weight."

"Maybe it was out of her control." Her eyes looked wet, catching the reflection from the sea. He questioned again his wisdom in trusting her.

"She's controlled everything else. Lived her life by the book."

"Perfect. She was perfect." She clenched her fists. "Damn. That's why she disappeared."

"Why? You think she's hiding until she can get the weight off? Come on, Rikki."

She glared at him. "You really don't get it, do you? Even the most rigid people can lose control, and when they do—"

He reached out for her, wanting to stop the pain that shimmered in her eyes. She jumped at his touch, pulled away.

"I have to go. There's something I need to do."

"Wait. I'll go with you."

"No."

He hated the way she could shut him out like this. "Have it your way, only I think you owe me something before I go. The briefcase with Julie's bank statements in it."

"Damn." She threw her arms around him. "The briefcase, of course." And she was gone, dashing toward her car, calling over her shoulder, "I'll phone you."

"Wait," he called.

"I can't. Den's waiting for me in the car."

Den?

Lucas watched her until she disappeared into the parking lot.

Her boss, Dennis Hamilton.

A voice that might be Bobby W's, a voice he was ashamed to acknowledge, whispered to him, "He's probably a slob. Please let him be a slob."

THIRTY

Rochelle

"**D**amn it, Blond, I'm desperate." Rochelle gulped her water bottle, shivering as the air teased the sweat from her flesh.

"Then, that's another reason." He held his ground, intent in his tiny white trunks, unconcerned with the attention he was attracting. Most of the women at the club, more than usual for a Saturday morning, had found excuses to amble by and check him out at closer range. "Desperation is the worst reason for getting involved with the toys."

"What was your reason?"

"Competition." He pulled a shirt over his head. His sprayed hair emerged unscathed.

"My point exactly. Don't tell me you weren't desperate."

"You got me on that one." He opened his own bottle of water. "I knew I'd only be doing it for a certain period of time."

"My situation's exactly the same." She made herself

speak slowly, as he did, forcing the agitation to remain beneath the surface.

"You're in good shape. If anything, you're too thin."

"Have you looked at my ass?"

"Of course. You think I'm dead? I never miss an opportunity to look at your ass." His soft-spoken drawl failed to calm her as it usually did.

"Then, tell me the truth." She turned her back on the floor-to-ceiling mirror.

"Most of that's the fabric of your pants." He pinched her butt. "You could maybe tighten it a little more, but you can do that with the lunges."

"I don't have time for lunges. The spokesmodel's going to be named any day now. My husband—" She couldn't put those fears into words, not even to Blond Elvis. "You said you could get toys."

He nodded. "Lasix injections are the fastest way. You can lose ten, fifteen pounds like that. It's a diuretic used for congestive heart failure. There are side effects, though. Your legs will cramp up."

"I don't care about frigging side effects. What is it, Blond? What do you want from me?"

"A reporter tracked me down," he said. "Her name's Rikki Fitzpatrick. She was here when you called."

"So?"

"I can't afford to get dragged into some scandal. I can tell she's not the type to back off. Cute as hell, but a real bulldog."

"All she cares about is what happened to Julie Larimore."

His expression lost some of its tenseness. "It's not that I don't want to help you, Shel."

"You think I'm so stupid that I'd take chances with my own body?" Her voice was steady now, the pleading and the fear buried in the iciness of the bitch voice. "You want me to be fat? You want to look at a client of yours and know, in your heart, she's a lard ass?"

"You're not fat, and you're not stupid. I know you respect your body. It's not that."

"What then? Surely, you don't think I'd ever reveal to anyone where I got it? You couldn't have so little trust in me, not as close as we've been."

"I trust you." He spoke in a low voice. It never failed. Rochelle the Bitch always got what she wanted, when the real Rochelle could not.

"The toys," she said.

"We need to discuss dosage."

"Sure thing."

"And you can't say a word to anyone."

"You know I won't, Blond."

He looked over his shoulder and smoothed the shellacked sweep of hair across his forehead. "Come on, then."

She'd won. At least, Rochelle the Bitch had won. As she followed him to the lockers, she caught a glimpse of her ass in the wall mirror. She must have been out of her mind to wear white.

The toys would soon be hers. And not a moment too soon.

Rikki

We're almost there, and I'm still trying to deal with the look I got from Lucas when I left, as if he knew something I didn't. I'm also trying to figure out what to say to Blond Elvis, how to scare him enough to tell me the truth—about Lisa, about Julie. Hamilton leans back in the passenger seat and says he's going to put on some music. Instead, my CD case in his lap, we talk nonstop about Killer Body and Julie Larimore.

I tell him everything except the nagging suspicion I've had since I woke up at after three in the morning, sweat-drenched and chilled to the bone. I can't say anything until I have more than intuition to go on. But I do have more. I have Tania Marie's convincing story, her impassioned eyes haunting me with their guileless honesty. I have what Lucas revealed about the Killer Body code of ethics and what it would cost Julie Larimore to break it.

Hamilton calls me a "lead foot," but I know he's okay with my driving. He seems relaxed, as if he's gotten a good night's sleep, and I think, with only a little remorse, that whatever he did after he left the casino must have been good for him.

Our first stop after leaving the harbor is Roberta Matlock's gallery in Los Olivos. She's as drifty as she was the first time, moving back and forth between clarity and ambiguity. She greets us, carrying a large magnifying glass. With her gray hair spread out over a long black tunic, she looks like the Good Witch in a fairy tale.

"You can tell what I've been doing," she says with a laugh. "Didn't realize how much stuff I've collected."

"You haven't found the news story yet?" I ask.

"Not yet. I've been concentrating on the yearbooks. Once I remember her name and the dates she was in my class, it will be easier for me to find the newspaper. It just takes a heck of a long time."

I accept a cup of tea from her. Hamilton declines. I can feel his doubt, even when Roberta tells us she remembers where Julie and her sister were raised.

"It was sold years ago," she said. "The current owner is renting it out."

"Do you know who lives there now?"

She shakes her head. "He's not a patron of the arts, I'm afraid. I've seen him a couple of times at the market."

"We could drive out there." It's Hamilton's way of telling me he wants a smoke and an excuse to get out of here. In the car, he fumbles for a cigarette, lights up and pulls down the window. "We can find the story faster ourselves."

"You never know," I say.

"Are you sure a little girl named Julie ever shot her father?" he says. "Are you sure the child that Matlock woman remembers was really Julie Larimore?"

"No," I admit. "But even a possible lead is better than no lead at all."

Having had his fix, and knowing how much I hate it, he tosses the cigarette out the window.

"Have you smoked forever?" I ask.

He flashes me a sour look. "For about six months when I was fifteen. Then, after my divorce. It's only temporary."

"That's good."

"You ever try it?"

"Are you kidding? My aunt would have strangled me."

Remembering the stern perfectionism in which Lisa and I were raised, I shudder. Aunt Carey wants me to find out what really killed Lisa, what caused her to get in such terrible shape that she died from a heart attack. If I told her what I suspect—that Lisa's compulsion, like my running away with the first boy who looked at me, was an attempt to escape herself—she'd think I'd lost my mind.

We turn off Grand Avenue and find the address on

the mailbox easily. The red barn-type building sits off the road guarded by a large tree on each side. We park on the street side of the trees, before a boulder-lined path. I stare at the house and try to imagine Julie Larimore growing up in it. Impossible. Not that it's bad, just ordinary: a red barn of a house with white-framed windows and porch supports.

"So," I say to Hamilton. "I guess I just walk right up to the door and announce who we are and what we want."

"Won't be the first time," he says.

Some strangers are helpful when you knock on their doors in the middle of their weekend. Others are not. The man who lives in the red barn is one of the latter.

Maybe I'm judgmental, especially in these hawkish times, but there's something about camouflage gear that unnerves me. Thus, I'm not surprised when this guy, clad from cap to toe in it, doesn't warm up to us.

"Can't a man cut his grass in peace?" he demands. "I don't have no money to donate for whatever it is you're collecting for."

"We're newspaper reporters," Hamilton says. "We've heard that Julie Larimore might have grown up in this house."

"Who?" His voice echoes the same cigarette rasp of Hamilton's, only multiplied by many more years of nonstop puffing.

"Julie Larimore," I repeat, "the spokesperson for Killer Body. She's disappeared."

"I heard about that." He pulls off his cap, scratches the gray stubble on his head. "I'm just the tenant. Been here about a year. I hope they find that little girl."

"She lived here as a child," I say. "Perhaps your landlord might be able to give us more information."

His gaze takes me in as if for the first time. "I'll help anyone who asks, but not no newspaper, and not you, lady." He moves forward, leading with his hip, as if imagining a rifle balanced there. "Get off my property before I call the cops."

Hamilton touches my arm, to let me know he's here. Then he steps in front of me, confronting the creep. "There's no need for that."

"Then get out of here." He looks at me, eyes narrowed to two glittering pricks of light. "I hate reporters."

I start to give the son of a bitch a short lecture on what *I* hate. Before I can decide if he's worth my rage, the door slams in my face.

Hamilton grabs my arm. I shake free. My impulse is to smash my fist into the door. That's the horror of being degraded in a time that's supposed to have outgrown it. Every instance feels like the first one. Instead of wearing you down, each assault provokes you, kickstarts your anger, all over again. I'm a woman. I'm a reporter. And this asshole doesn't trust me.

I force myself to stay put, turn off the Sexist Pig Channel in my own mind, block out Mr. Camouflage and head down the walk, Den Hamilton behind me.

"Rikki."

"Not now, Den."

Another day, I may come back to smash down this door and spew my rancor on anything or anyone that answers it. For now, I have to get out of here, to follow this undeservingly lovely path to my car. I just do.

Gabriella

The word *sip* was invented for martinis. You could guzzle beer, even wine, and live to tell about it. Martinis were lethal, the heroin of the drinking world. Thus, one sipped; one did not shoot up.

She calculated the calories, which even if she avoided the olive, which she couldn't resist, were more than the tin of tuna fish and the tiny bit of toast she'd had for lunch.

She remembered something her grandmother had told her. "Your thoughts are your destiny." Thoughts lead to action. Action leads to habits. Habits lead to destiny.

Gabriella's thoughts were somewhere between this fat, glistening olive, the same color as her eyes, Alain once said, and the biggest Frostie and saltiest French fries in Orange County. Not much of a destiny there.

She didn't see him enter the room, but she felt him. Instinct aside, Alain was never late and abhorred anyone who was. Gabriella lifted her glass, feeling vain, knowing that he watched her, as she watched the smooth olive through the glass, contemplating its contrasting smudge of pimento.

She wore a skirt Alain bought her right before the breakup, a series of bias-cut, floral-print panels that joined to form a handkerchief hemline. The top was new, a sky-blue stretch halter with a keyhole neckline and narrow rows of smocking skimming her midriff. Between the skirt and the smocking, only smooth skin. And darned taut skin, thanks to her workouts with Christopher and the Killer Body nutrition plan.

It hit her like a jolt. She'd never felt this much in control of her life. She was alone, she was broke, but she was in charge and something close to happy, no longer the unsophisticated little Texas urchin rescued by the prince.

"Damn, you look lovely."

She'd forgotten how she liked his voice, the passion with which he addressed everything from the marmalade on his toast to children at a school he was visiting. She steeled herself and looked up.

He was dressed so that no one would recognize him, and she could see Christopher's guilty hand at work. Light-toned pants and a matching zip-up jacket, trimmed in black, no tie. His face was the same, though. The dirty-blond hair, like hers without the frizz, parted in the middle. His eyes, the color of the ocean when it goes gray at twilight, revealed, as always, little of what he was thinking.

"Someone will recognize us," she said, as much to cover her nervousness as anything else. "We shouldn't have risked this."

"Last I heard, you were still my wife." Alain pulled out the chair across from her and sat. "We could always move to a booth, or to my room, for that matter."

"I think I expressed myself to you on the phone yesterday."

"You told me, as your grandmother would say, how the cow ate the cabbage."

Hearing his accent wrap around her grandmother's words both pleased and saddened her.

"I miss her."

"She knows you're okay. She lived long enough to see that you were going to be fine."

Gabriella felt her hackles rise. "I was fine to begin with, Alain. I just fell in love with a man who betrayed me."

She hoped for a reaction, an admission, a begging of forgiveness. Instead, she saw only his cold gray eyes of hostility.

"She's waiting," Alain said, and Gabriella realized

why he'd suddenly shut down. She looked up to see who *she* was.

The waitress stood at the table, her slender hips hitched beneath a long black skirt. A server, waiting for an order. Gabriella had screwed up again.

"I'll need a moment."

She could swear she heard the waitress sigh. Before she was certain, the woman spoke, but not to her, of course.

"Could I get you anything?" Her glossy lips cracked into a smile.

"One of those." Alain pointed at Gabriella's glass. She decided to take a swallow. Not bad, a frenzied, flowery scent, before the cold teeth of booze bit into her.

As she clicked off to fill the order, Gabriella said, "She's going to call someone. She recognized you, I'm sure of it."

"All of this publicity has made you paranoid." He leaned forward on the table. "I like that thing you're doing with your hair now. Sixties, right?"

"It was Christopher's idea. Hide a bad feature with a current trend."

"Your hair's wonderful. Why do you buy into that rubbish that everyone has to have a spiky little Tania Marie flip? What good did it do her?"

"Don't put down Tania Marie. She's sweet, actually." Goodness, had she said that? Did she feel it? Indeed, she did.

"She doesn't have a chance at the Killer Body job, does she?"

"I don't know. Bobby Warren's behavior isn't easy to predict. But the Killer Body job doesn't matter anymore." Relief flooded his face, and he couldn't control the smile that spread across it. She felt cruel delivering the rest of the blow, but that was crazy. She owed him the truth, and now. "I'm going to be taking over John Crosby's show while he's on vacation. If it works out, I may get my own show without having to detour through Killer Body Land."

"And if you don't?"

"I'll keep trying. I have an agent who believes in me. I have John Crosby's support. The more I think about it, I don't believe Killer Body is for me."

"I won't quarrel with that." Alain looked stunned, unaware that the drink had arrived and the server had departed. Gabriella knew that astonished, bewildered feeling, had lived with it from the moment those photographs of her had hit the tabloids. She hurt for Alain, but she knew what she had to do. She pulled out her chair and stood.

"I've dealt with my weight problems as honestly as I know how, but I don't want to make a career out of them. I'm going to tell Bobby Warren that."

Alain rose, too, ghostlike, his face pale and unsmiling. "It was my fault. I know that now. You never would have done what you did if I hadn't gotten drunk and made an ass of myself with Judith."

"True. But it was my fault, too. I had a very small life. You made it larger. Then it got too large, too out of control."

"And now you don't need me."

A commotion from the front of the bar commenced as two men with microphones and a woman, wearing too much makeup and a suit the color of a hydrangea, entered the room. She and Alain had been recognized, and now here came the media. She could flee or meet them head-on. She didn't have to think about which it would be.

"I don't *need* anyone." Gabriella crossed the small patch of carpet separating them and took his arm. "But I've never stopped *wanting* you."

THIRTY-ONE

Rikki

Hamilton flies back home, and I miss him at once. When we're working, I forget that he's my supervisor. I even forget he's a man I could have cared for.

I arrive in San Diego that Monday, using my famous last name—*Valley Voice* newspaper—when asking for the director of the clinic. He isn't in, but the office manager, a Ms. Potoroff, no first name, gives polite, no-nonsense answers to my questions from behind her computer.

This is a room of *no,* I realize, a room where one is cut off, not admitted. The white counter and its waxy pink roses serve as a barrier, and the woman behind it serves as a sentinel.

"It's absolutely against policy to reveal patient information," she says in an officious tone that reminds me of Lucas's assistant at Killer Body. Those attitudes only make me more determined.

"I would think there would be an exception in a case such as this, when someone's life could depend on it."

She reaches for the coffee on her desk. I notice that

although she wears dark lipstick, not a trace remains on the white cup. "I hardly think anyone's life depends on whether or not I give you information about that patient."

I lean over the marbleized solid surface of the counter between us. She's younger than she looks, not much older than I, although the skinned-back black hair and prim little glasses do a fine job of hiding the fact.

"This isn't just any patient. She's a public figure who's disappeared. Her health could be a significant factor in the investigation."

"You're a reporter, not the police."

"I'm a reporter trying to uncover leads that, once I print them, the police won't be able to ignore. Not everyone judges all information with equal importance. The police are conducting their investigation in the way that they see fit. I believe that Julie Larimore's health is a major factor in her disappearance."

"Well." She enters something into the computer and watches the screen, her cheeks the color of the roses on the counter. "If that were a factor, she would have returned here, wouldn't you agree?"

"Not necessarily. Perhaps she's unable to."

"Nevertheless." She stares back at the screen, which she clearly prefers to looking at me. "Our policies are in place to protect our patients."

It's been a long drive with no payoff. I make one last attempt.

"Could I at least speak to Julie Larimore's doctor?"

"Dr. Bledsoe isn't available today." Spoken too fast to be the truth.

"Could you leave him a message that I want to speak with him?"

"I seriously doubt that he'll want to discuss a patient with you."

"A high-profile patient," I remind her, "with a high-profile problem. I'm sure he'll want to talk to me, on or off the record."

She hands me a notepad with the name of a drug company stamped on it. "Write down what you need, and I'll see that he gets it." Then in a softer voice, "I'm not trying to be difficult. I'm just trying to protect her privacy. She entered the hospital under a pseudonym. That's an indicator that she prefers to remain anonymous."

"She did that before she disappeared," I say. "If she's in danger, she'd want us to do whatever we can to find her." I scribble a note, attach my card. "I'm going to write my story with or without speaking with the doctor," I say. "Tell him that for me."

Ms. Potoroff rises, her expression as set as her hairdo. "I will."

It's all I can do to keep from dashing across the parking lot full of expensive vehicles. Instead, I walk briskly, trying to contain my excitement. At least she admitted that Julie Larimore was a patient. At least I have the name of her doctor.

Her doctor. I run the rest of the way to my car and the briefcase Lucas has entrusted to me. I've seen doctor bills in there.

I lock the door, look around, feeling as if someone is watching me. But no, that's guilt manifesting itself as fear. There's no one anywhere around, only late-model automobiles, the kind indigenous to this community. My own white Toyota, less than neat, just barely fits. My jacket hangs like a shapeless black drape on the back of the seat, hiding Lucas's briefcase, which I didn't dare leave in a motel room. I'm late in returning it to him. I wonder if that will be the final straw in this tenuous allegiance of ours.

My suitcase on the passenger seat, now a base for my laptop, makes me realize how far away I am from the life I have come to think of as normal. How long will it be before I can do something as simple as bathe in my own tub and sleep in my own bed?

Since Lisa's death, my nomadic existence has isolated me in this car, always moving. I realize how much I want it to be over, how ready I am to go back, regardless of what I must face when I do.

I touch the smooth black surface of the suitcase, my only connection with what I've left, and get out my cell phone.

I take out the packet and begin sorting. Yes, Dr. Wayne Bledsoe, The Bledsoe Clinic.

I can find no mention of what the bills are for. Under the column for procedure, only numbers are listed.

Then I look at the clinic bill. This was major surgery. I feel as if I've just drunk a gallon of coffee. I grab my cell phone and call the number on the bill.

"Bledsoe Clinic. How may I help you?"

"I'd like to make an appointment with Dr. Bledsoe."

"Are you a new patient?" The receptionist at The Bledsoe Clinic is friendlier than the office manager I encountered inside.

"I've been referred by my family doctor."

"I'll need to get your insurance information," she says. "What's the nature of your visit?"

"The surgery."

I hold my breath in the moment of silence.

Then she says, "Gastric bypass? Has your physician already consulted with Dr. Bledsoe about it?"

"Yes. That's Dr. Bledsoe's specialty, isn't it?" A wild guess, fueled by what Tania Marie told me and what I have come to first suspect and now believe.

"The clinic handles more gastric bypass surgeries than any other clinic in the state. Dr. Bledsoe can answer any questions for you. I'll need to get your name and insurance information. Let's start with your name, last one first."

I clench the phone in my sweaty fist. Why am I shaking now? This was what I guessed, the reason for Julie's disappearance. Tania Marie was right. She'd seen Julie at the clinic, the *before* in a before-and-after nightmare. What is *after,* and where is Julie now?

"I'll need to call you back," I say, and I press the button to disconnect the call. Then I make another one.

"Dennis Hamilton." His voice sounds far away.

"Den, it's Rikki. I know what happened to Julie Larimore."

"What happened? Where is she?"

"I don't know where, but I know why. She had gastric bypass surgery."

"Holy shit. Are you sure?"

The Interview

And how do you feel about that?

About what? That everyone is looking for me? I'm too tired, too weak, to answer. Instead, I think of forgiveness. I forgave my family, my father. Bought him this house so that we could all be together, so that we could be a family again. I forgave. Will I be forgiven, as well, for my sins?

My energy bleeds from me like water right now. But your question is almost as important as the answer.

How do I feel about that?
I feel nothing.

Lucas

Bobbie W was talking to the photos in the gallery again. Lucas didn't want to hear what he was saying.

He walked up behind him, put a hand on his surprisingly frail shoulder. The one-way conversation stopped in mid-whisper.

"How's it going?" Lucas asked.

"Tough right now."

Bobby W continued facing straight ahead, his head held aloft, like that of a younger man's. His neck looked old, folded in tight little pleats. The entire hall smelled of heavy after-shave. Maybe that's how guys had done it once, just doused themselves in scent, held their heads up and hoped for the best.

"What can I do to make it less tough?" Damn, if he could have talked to his own father this easily.

"I just received some horrible news. It's not certain, but—" He reached for Lucas to steady himself. His eyes were rimmed in red, the way they were after a bout of drinking, but Lucas could smell no liquor on him, only the cologne, almost medicinal in its intensity.

"What's happened?"

"Come, sit down, and I'll tell you. Regardless of the outcome, I'm canceling the competition. I want to see all three girls, not out in public. Somewhere safe, the boat. Ellen's making the calls right now."

"Are you sure?" Lucas asked. "What made you change your mind?"

The old man put his head in his hands. "I can't do this anymore."

A sickening realization started in his stomach and spread through him. This wasn't something minor.

"Julie?" he asked, already certain now.

Bobby W nodded, meeting his eyes with a look that could mean only one thing.

"Where?"

"L.A. Harbor. Washed up." He shook his head. "They want me to identify her, Luke."

Gabriella

"So, are you going back to him?"

Christopher opened the door of the car for her, and Gabriella slid inside. "In case you failed to notice, I didn't renew my wedding vows. I just spent the night with the man."

"Two nights, if I may be picky." Christopher gave her an indulgent smile but didn't close the door. "And, last time I checked, the man was your husband."

She hoped she didn't look as goony and love-logged as she felt. "Two nights, okay? And the press is going to have a proverbial field day."

"With you landing on your sweet little *huaraches,* as usual, I might add."

"They do like a good love story."

"So do I."

"I know you do." She glanced at her watch, as much a distraction as to check the time. "We'd better get moving."

As was his style, he didn't mention the subject again. As was her style, it continued to gnaw at her. She'd be glad when this next step was taken. She owed Christopher the truth about her decision.

"Whatever happens, I'm still filling in for John

Crosby," she announced to the silent car. "If I like it, and it likes me, I'm going to try to get my own show."

"Good for you."

She leaned forward, tapped the back of his smooth neck. "Whatever I do, I'm taking you with me, Christopher."

"Gabby, please."

"I mean it. You stuck by me when I didn't have the proverbial pot, and you're the only family I have now."

"You're my family, too." His voice was so low and tear-choked that she could barely discern the words. She hadn't wanted this to get emotional, but how could it be anything else?

"I want you to be able to quit your day job," she said, "to write, the way you were when you were working for me full-time. Whatever I decide, that won't change."

He adjusted his dark glasses and drove in silence for a moment.

"What about Bobby Warren?" he finally asked.

"I'm going to tell him today."

"Before or after he announces his choice?"

"Before, of course. I've got to take the high road."

"I'm glad." He turned around, his grin wicked. "I'm also glad we don't have to spend the day on a sailboat with Bobby Warren and Rochelle McArthur."

"Shel's not that bad. That whole bitch thing is just an act. Can you imagine how terrifying it must be to be losing everything when you're just approaching your prime?"

"That's Hollywood, the ugly side of a city that's driven by the film mentality, an oxymoron if I ever heard one."

Her cell phone rang. "Alain, I'll bet," Christopher said.

"Anyone ever tell you that you're a hopeless romantic, my dear?"

"As a matter of fact, yes," he said.

She pressed the phone against her ear. "Alain?" Goodness, she was eager to hear his voice once more.

But Alain was not the one who answered. Only Tania Marie, a frantic Tania Marie, at that.

"I went to the boat, but no one's here," she sobbed. "I tried to call Mr. Warren and got Ellen, his assistant. They changed the meeting place at the last minute and didn't tell me."

"That's fine with me." As Christopher pulled the car into the marina, Gabriella spotted Tania Marie, her short hair blown by the wind into a glistening black-cherry sheet. "I can see you from here."

"Oh, I can see you, too." Tania Marie began to wave frantically.

"Where are we going? Is it near here? If you like, we can ride together."

Tania Marie turned, telephone smashed against her ear, and began walking down the pier in a long crinkle-pleated black skirt, totally unsuitable for anything but a cruise ship, poor dear. "That would be so cool. It's not far at all. Just up the 101."

THIRTY-TWO

Rochelle

This was it, the moment of truth, according to the gospel of Killer Body.

Rochelle sat in her car and fluffed her hair. Not that the wind wouldn't destroy it, anyway. She pressed the magnifying mirror close to her face. Shit. The sprinkles from her eyelash extender looked like dark lint on her face. She brushed at them with her finger.

Her wrinkles stood out as if they'd been painted in neon. Damned irresponsible of Blond Elvis to wait until after she'd started on the toys to mention they were hell on anyone who'd had Botox. But, as Blond had asked, in self-defense, "Would it have made a difference?"

Probably not, although she needed everything on her side, especially now. Although he couldn't distinguish between a green or a red light at a crosswalk, Bobbo could spot the wispiest of crow's feet or a minuscule pinch of flab in the dark.

Blond Elvis had better not have been lying about her ass, because it would turn Bobbo off faster than anything. Better to have the body than the face; the face was easier to fix.

Besides, Bobbo's decision had been made. This meeting would be pure Bobbo—making the losers in this little-contest-that-wasn't feel good about themselves, possibly offering them token rewards. Bobbo hated nothing on this earth except *being* hated, and he seldom was, even by his former lovers. She could attest to that. How could you hate a man who made you feel good about yourself just being around him?

Just the Ass Blaster.

The thought drifted through her as she spritzed her cleavage with a final spray of Ellen Tracy's new fragrance. Bobbo loved scent, the more, the better. If something happened, and this spokesmodel job didn't come through the way she hoped, he'd sure as hell better give her the Ass Blaster. Damned luck that it had to be an ass machine, though, instead of an Ab Blaster or a Thigh Blaster. She had killer abs and thighs. Still, she could pull it off—give that Marilyn Monroe smile, stroke the machine, say only a few words, maybe just, "Ass Blaster. I love, love, love it."

Rochelle got out of the car and shivered as the tingling breeze hit her exposed midriff. The hell with her hair. Bobbo wouldn't be looking at it, anyway. She pulled on her baseball cap and adjusted her gold bikini chain right below her exposed navel, above the top of the drawstring salsa pants, a gift from Jesse in his ongoing quest to keep her looking young. Little distractions, like the chain and matching anklet, just might divert attention from her ass.

She'd taken only a couple of steps when a familiar black sedan rounded the curve. Princess Gabby and Tania Marie waved from the back seat. Rochelle stopped and crossed the landscaped dividers, waiting for the car to return from the other direction.

Princess Gabby's bald, cute driver was behind the wheel. He slid out and opened the back door, and Rochelle squeezed inside.

"What happened?"

Tania Marie's thighs almost nudged her out the door. She might be thinner, but not thin enough, at least not yet. "A change of plans. We're meeting them a few miles north of here."

"Good thing I saw you, then. I would have been left clueless."

"Mr. Warren's office didn't call you?"

"No, and it's damned thoughtless if you ask me."

"They didn't call me, either," Princess Gabby said from the other side of the mountain of flesh that separated them. "I wouldn't have known about the change if Tania Marie hadn't told me."

Rochelle tried to get it straight, narrowing in on Tania Marie. "There was a change in plans, but you were the only one who was notified?"

Her cheeks flushed. The girl did have creamy skin, absolutely flawless. And her blush was more vibrant than anything in a compact. She flashed that sweet, little-girl smile and tried to look perky.

"I've probably been eliminated, and they don't want me there for the final announcement, some half-assed attempt to save my pride, as if I have any left."

"Don't put yourself down, dear," Princess Gabby said. "It's just a mix-up on the administrative end. We're all supposed to be there, aren't we, Rochelle?"

"We must be. There were nothing but seagulls on that damned boat."

"It's too weird." Tania Marie appeared to shift her

weight in the seat. "I'd better phone Ellen back and find out what's going on."

"Good idea."

Rochelle kept her voice low and husky. Inside, she was screaming.

Jesse had demanded to come along for the announcement, and Rochelle had refused because she wanted him at home with Megan, and, okay, because she didn't want him sniffing around Princess Gabby. She thought Bobbo would be easy to handle. Wrong. He was betraying her—again. First, almost eight years ago, he'd dumped her and taken Julie for his confidante, made her a rich, respected woman, a woman who wouldn't lose her career once she committed the sin of aging.

Julie with the perfect body, the perfect ass.

Now Bobbo was trying to pull something with Tania Marie, an innocent kid, in spite of her bad press and poor decisions.

"Where are we supposed to be going, anyway?" Christopher, the driver, asked from the front seat.

Tania Marie looked up from her overstuffed bag. "Place called Los Olivos. I've never been there. Have you?"

Lucas

He was the one who had to identify the body. Bobby W had insisted he could do it, but Lucas didn't want to push him any closer to the edge than the news already had.

She had been weighted down, Keith Ota, the coroner, had explained. They'd scheduled an autopsy.

"Did Julie Larimore wear a necklace?" Ota asked.

"The Killer Body pendant," Lucas said. "She almost always wore it. Mr. Warren had it designed to replicate her figure."

"Could you describe it?" Ota asked.

"Silver chain. Red-enamel pendant in the shape of a woman in high heels, arms at her side."

Ota nodded. "Sounds similar to the one we found."

The body on the slab didn't look like Julie Larimore, even remotely. Gray, chalky, distended; the only way Lucas could keep from reacting violently was to force himself to forget this thing he was looking at had once been a person.

He looked up at Ota's unsmiling face, his hopeful eyes. "I don't know."

"Perhaps if you take a little time."

"I have. Can't you go with dental records or DNA?"

"We're working on that. Positive ID from you can help expedite the process."

"Was she—" He forced his gaze down at the corpse again. "Did someone kill her?"

"That's a tough one. We may never know."

They walked out into the fresh air. What was he going to tell Bobby W? He needed to offer him some hope or the old man would cave in, the way he had after his son's death. Maybe worse. Lucas had never seen him more vulnerable.

"When are you making this public?" he asked.

"We're scheduling a news conference for tonight," Ota said. "We're going to say we're trying to make a DNA match between the body and Julie Larimore, but that it could take weeks."

"But it's Julie, right?"

Ota gave him a blank look that said it all. "We'll see."

"And you don't have any idea how she died?"

Ota stopped at the glass door. "Unless there's a bullet or something that damages the bone, cause of death is pretty difficult, even after a short time in the water. Whoever did this probably chose that way for a reason."

"So, we may never know?"

Ota shrugged and put out his hands in a noncommittal gesture. "We'll do our best. That's all I can say."

Rikki

I get the call from Lucas that afternoon.

"I'm on my way to Los Olivos," I say. "Roberta Matlock's found Julie's photo."

"I'll meet you there."

His voice is strangled and tight, like that of a stranger's.

"No need for that," I say. "We can get together and compare notes as soon as I leave there."

"I said, I'll meet you," he repeats, harsher this time. "I've got to do something. I can't just stay here."

"Okay, then. The road's ending. I need to get off the phone."

"Rikki?"

"What is it?"

"I wasn't sure when I saw her, what was left of her. But now, the more I think about it, I believe the body they found really is Julie Larimore."

What do I say? What do I feel? I hate the platitudes I've heard, even in my own family.

Now you can heal. Now you'll have closure.

Closure? Someone is dead. But that's not the end of anything, certainly not the pain. The identification is just the beginning of a wound that may never heal.

But I'm not thinking about Julie Larimore, am I? I'm

thinking about Lisa, Aunt Carey. Doing so has almost forced my car off this road. I put on my brake. Slow down.

"I'll meet you at Roberta Matlock's gallery," I manage to say.

Tania Marie

Shoulder to shoulder in the back seat of Princess Gabby's sedan, Tania Marie pulled out her phone.

"It's half-assed nice, isn't it?" she said. "All of us together, kind of like sisters."

"You ever had a sister?" Rochelle demanded from her right side. "It's not all bunk beds, blind dates and Aqua Net, especially not if you're raised in a house with one bathroom."

A nauseating wave of shame forced Tania Marie to look out at the thick tree-lined vineyard they'd entered. She'd been an only child, and they'd had four bathrooms at home, even after Virginia left her dad.

Head ducked, ostensibly peering into her purse, Tania Marie asked, "Where's your sister now?"

"Last I heard, she married some truck driver." When Tania Marie couldn't help giving Rochelle a look, she got a sharper, more narrow one in return. "If you hang out with your past, you'll never rise above it, right?"

What a cold chick. How could she answer that one?

"Hey, folks. I think I'm lost."

Princess Gabby's driver gave Tania Marie the excuse she needed. And he was right. This road was supposed to lead them to a winery, where Mr. Warren would greet them. Instead, they were losing light and direction by the moment. All that remained ahead was an abandoned-looking brick building with some antique equipment and a couple of rotting barrels in front of it—definitely not the kind of place Mr. Warren would pick for a meeting.

"I'm phoning right now," Tania Marie announced with more enthusiasm than she felt.

Only a machine answered the phone. She didn't bother to leave a message.

"What's wrong?" Christopher demanded. "Is anyone there?"

"No problem. I have the cell number for Mr. Warren's assistant right here."

If usually unruffled Christopher was concerned, maybe there was a reason. Tania Marie knew she must talk to Mr. Warren, or even Lucas Morrison. She was starting to get what Marshall, damn him, used to call "the creepies." She was starting to get them bad.

Then they approached the old, brick-faced building, hidden beneath a facade of trees—dirty, dusty and abandoned as far as she could see into the side and back.

"This is Ellen Horner," the crisp voice answered.

"I think I wrote down the wrong directions," Tania Marie said. "Where are we supposed to be right now?"

"*We?* What do you mean, *we?*" Ellen's voice sounded angry.

Tania Marie laughed as much from nervousness as anything else. "The Killer Body crew. Rochelle. Princess Gabby. That's what Mr. Warren said. Didn't he?"

In the pause that followed, she felt stupid again, stripped naked, the way she'd felt when Marshall's wife had made those horrible statements about her.

"You're bringing *them?*" Ellen's response was more shriek than statement. "It's supposed to be just you."

"Well, they're here with me, wherever in the hell

here is." Tania Marie looked back at her friends and suddenly realized that this tree-covered place might not be the safest for any of them.

"Get out," Ellen screamed into her ear. "He's going to kill you, all of you."

Then another scream, then smashing silence.

A white pickup appeared behind them, coming too fast, blaring its horn. They skidded to a stop in the dirt, clouds of dust rising around the car.

A large, angry-looking man in camouflage gear swung down from the pickup.

From the other side, a young woman—Ellen Horner—ran, screaming, into the brick building. The man had a rifle balanced on his hip. He glanced at Ellen, then returned his attention, and the gun, on them. He motioned to Tania Marie. "Out."

THIRTY-THREE

Rikki

I believe it, but I don't. Sitting between Lucas and Roberta Matlock on her Día de Los Muertes bench is easy, especially with the floppy hollyhocks drunkenly climbing the pole beside it. We look at a yearbook, but I can only think about Lucas and what he told me.

Is Julie Larimore really dead? I won't believe it until it's confirmed through DNA.

I'm a journalist. What's my instinct?

Tears burn my eyes. Damn, it's just too close. I don't want to know.

"Told you she'd have to be a beauty." Roberta scoots closer to me on the bench and points at a photo in an old, yet still shiny yearbook. "Took me hours to find this, but I knew I would. Got the newspaper stories, too. She tried to kill her father. Talk was he was abusing the girls, but she never said. Both girls got placed in a foster home, anyway."

"What happened to the father?" Lucas asked.

"I don't know if he's even alive. He'd been in Vietnam. His wife took off and left him with the girls, and his mother helped raise them until she died. He fought to get them back, but I can't remember how it all worked out." She taps the photo with her finger. "I remember her, though. A perfect student."

"Damn." Lucas must see what I do.

There's no mistaking her identity, even with the darker hair, minus the streaks. I read the name under the photo. "Julie Horner." As I speak, an image flashes into my mind: blond, perky, efficient to the point of irritating.

I clutch the yearbook. "Lucas, what's your assistant's last name? Ellen?"

I see the answer in his startled eyes. "Horner."

"Ellie Horner. That was the little sister," Roberta Matlock says.

But we already know that.

Lucas is on his feet. "Ellen's gone. I haven't been able to reach her since she contacted the women this morning."

"What women?" I ask.

"Tania Marie, Princess Gabby and Rochelle McArthur."

Holding the yearbook, inhaling its musty scent, I feel ill. "Why did she contact them, Lucas?"

His eyes look sick, too, and worried. "To set up a meeting with Bobby W."

"When?"

"Right about now, I think."

Gabriella

The man with the rifle moved so fast that it took her a moment to realize that he was reaching for the door next to her, where she huddled on the other side of Tania Marie.

"My God," Rochelle said as the door flew open.

Hard fingers clamped Gabriella's left arm, yanking her into the dusky air. She tried to struggle, and he slapped her across the face, searing her with a bright flash of pain.

She gasped, struggling to stay conscious, knowing he would kill her if she collapsed. This man in the horrible camouflage clothes and the eyes of stone was a killer.

A bolt of energy hit them full force.

"Let her go."

Out of the car now, Christopher broke the man's grasp and set him off balance. Gabriella scrambled away from the car. The man came back at Christopher full force.

"Run," Christopher shouted, but the pickup blocked their exit.

She ran, nevertheless, flew to the other side of the car, where Rochelle and Tania Marie huddled. Christopher wrenched the man away from him. But without even looking, the attacker darted out his hand for the rifle.

"No." Gabriella heard a scream she knew must be her own. But she saw only the rifle, its dark angry shape swinging into position. The exploding shot was the loudest noise she'd ever heard in her life.

Christopher flew back, his body exploding before her eyes, in blood and dust.

Sobbing, stunned, knowing that her life was over, that she was dead, Gabriella stumbled after the others into the building.

Rikki

"Ellen's gone," Lucas says. "No one knows where she went. That's not like her. And Bobby W says the women didn't show up to meet him at the boat."

I barely hear him. The briefcase lies open on the seat of the car, and I hold the bills in my hands. The answers are here, I know. The doctor bills, the statements from the clinic, yes. But something else that stuck in my mind now seems more important.

"The mortgage company," I say. "Julie Larimore made payments to two mortgage companies."

He kneels down next to the car, watches as I open the envelope I've been seeking.

It was here all along. I just haven't known where to look for it.

I touch the address of the property as the truth sinks in.

"Los Olivos," I say. "She owned the property the old winery is on. That's where she went when she disappeared."

"So, who lives there?" Lucas asks, and I shudder with the knowledge.

"Julie's father."

Gabriella

She crouched on concrete, on all fours. Someone had vomited. She could smell it, taste it. She could hear now the words that came from her mouth. "No. No. No."

"Shut up."

Tania Marie half dragged her behind a looming vat that smelled of wine-soaked wood.

"Where's Rochelle?" she managed to squeak.

"Shut up," Tania Marie repeated, then reached down along the ground. "Look for a rock, for anything. I've got one, and I'll smash the bastard's head in."

Gabriella trembled and pressed her forehead against

the wood. She had fallen apart, like a bundle of sticks, and at this moment she most wanted to live, she was going to die, the way Christopher had died.

A door opened, not the one they had run through, but far to the right side. The light waited outside. The man came in, closing the door behind him.

"Ladies?"

Gabriella bit her lip to keep from screaming. Tania Marie squeezed her shoulder. Please don't let him move this way.

"Ladies, we need to talk. There's been a misunderstanding. There's nothing to fear here if you just listen to reason."

The voice was rich, commanding. He talked like a police officer directing traffic around an accident.

"Let me escort you back to your car," he said. "The driver will be fine."

Fine? Gabriella choked back tears. Tania Marie's fingers dug deeper.

She felt him pause, as a stalking animal does. He'd heard her, smelled her fear.

"You have a choice, ladies." Then a click in the darkness. "You can come out, let me help you get back home, or you can make me come looking for you. Not a good idea, let me tell you. You don't want to make me mad."

"Don't do it." Another voice, high-pitched with the lunacy of fear, rang out not far from them. Whoever it was had also hidden behind a vat. Not only could the woman see them; she could direct the monster to their hiding place.

"Shut up, Ellie."

"And what if I don't? Are you going to kill me, too, Daddy?"

"I said, shut up." He began to thrash in their direction. "Do you think I'd ever hurt one of my daughters? Haven't I always tried to take care of you and your sister?"

"No, Daddy. Jules was the one who took care of us."

"She never stopped loving her daddy, even though we both made mistakes over the years. That's why she bought me our old place, why she came here when she needed help." He spoke softer, hypnotically, moving closer all the time. Soon, he'd see them, yet there was no place they could dare to move. Tania Marie didn't even appear to be breathing, but she continued to squeeze Gabriella's shoulder. "It wasn't my fault what happened to her. I'm a medic, ladies. I took good care of my daughter, but something happened and she got real sick."

"You *know* what happened, Daddy."

"I mean it, Ellie. Shut the hell up or you're in for it."

"Jules wouldn't want you to do this, she wouldn't."

"She told me what to do, just as she told you what to do."

"She didn't say to kill them."

"She told me what to do. Now, leave me do it or you'll have hell to pay." He moved a little closer. Gabriella could make out his silhouette, right down to the rifle.

"She didn't mean it. She knew how sick she was. She didn't want anyone to know why. She didn't really want you to kill Tania Marie. She'd be horrified at what happened here."

Tania Marie gulped. Now Gabriella clutched her. The entire cellar lay quiet, submerged in the silent, surreal world of scent. Earth, oak, wine, time.

Then movement. The crunch of heavy shoes, combat shoes.

"Ladies, don't listen to my little girl here. She's just had a terrible shock. We both have. Come on out, now. Don't make me pick you off one by one."

"She ate, Daddy. She ate, even after the surgery, because she had a hole in her life that couldn't be filled, regardless of the size of her stomach."

"Liar."

Now he'd find them. He stood inches away, panting like a bull.

The woman stepped out. Walked to face him. Yes, it really was Ellen Horner, Bobby Warren's assistant. And she saw them. Even in the darkness, Gabriella could make out her blond hair and slender form and knew that Ellen saw Tania Marie and her. She moved away from them, and the man followed.

"Her stomach was this small." Ellen clenched her fist. "It couldn't hold even a cup of liquid, but that didn't stop her. She ate herself to death. The stitches exploded, and she died. He got rid of her body in the ocean so that no one would know what killed her."

"I warned you, Ellie."

"In case you really are here," she said, looking away from them, "I want you to know that my father made me call Tania Marie. He wanted to get her here alone because she saw my sister at the clinic, saw what had happened to her. He made me do it."

"I don't care what they think." He was drawn to her, though, following her through the shadows of the winery. "They can't leave now, anyway."

"I was the one who tried to scare you," she said. "Jules was still alive. She didn't want anyone else to be Killer Body." She sobbed. "It was her life."

"Get out of here," the man demanded. "Leave me to take care of this."

"He's sick," Ellen said. "He did try to help Jules, but no one could help her." She stood with her back to them, addressing the wall of barrels, her voice harsh with tears. "She didn't want you to hurt them, Daddy. She just wanted to scare them." She turned to him. "Come on. Let's leave now."

"No." He pulled back the rifle, turned it on her. "Get out of here."

"I'm not going. You killed that man out there."

A short silence, and then his voice, strangely distant. "Well, then. You don't leave me much choice, do you?"

He hit her with the rifle, as if swatting a fly. A loud smash, a moan. Ellen collapsed into a heap. Gabriella gasped, unable to control her trembling, in spite of Tania Marie's strong fingers digging into her. Tears coursed down her face.

The silhouette holding the rifle stopped and swung slowly toward her.

THIRTY-FOUR

Rikki

"What are you going to say to him?" Lucas asks as we pull in front of the winding drive.

"I'm not sure."

I'm not even certain what is propelling me right now—the anger, that secondary emotion, that the man who must be Earl Horner evoked when I was out here the first time?

I called Den on the drive over, telling him what I suspect.

"Don't go there" were the last words he spoke to me. But I can't wait for the police, for polite questions and answers.

"Let's park down the road and walk back," I say.

A brown fence with scabby paint delineates the house and yard from the spiked vines and the brick-faced stone building in back. A ghost winery, Roberta Matlock had explained, deserted during the phylloxera epidemic. The trees look black silhouetted against the light of the sun.

Barbed-wire coils along the top of a chain-link fence.

The gate is closed. We move along the side of the fence toward it.

I peek through the links. All I can see is a white pickup and the back of a car in front of it.

"Someone's back there," I say. "Do you have a weapon?"

"Pistol. In the car."

"Go get it."

"I'm not leaving you." His face is grim, his eyes behind the glasses unrelenting.

"I'll wait here for you. I just don't think we should go poking around without some protection."

"I don't think we should go poking around, period. The police will be here anytime."

He has a point.

"But if they have the women in there—" I don't finish the sentence. "We have to find out, Lucas."

He touches my arm. "I'll be right back. Promise you'll stay here."

"Halt!" The gate jerks open, and I go numb. He's there, Earl Horner, grimacing down the barrel of a rifle. "Inside." He bellows it, as if commanding soldiers, the word ejected from his throat in two harsh syllables.

I move through the open gate, knowing he will kill me if I don't, knowing he will kill me, anyway. Each step is just buying time, an additional moment so that I can think. I just need to think. Lucas walks behind me. He's in top shape and probably twenty years younger than the guy. He might be able to take him if we can get the rifle away.

"I want to ask you something," I say.

"Move." He scurries alongside me with the rifle. "Past the truck. In there."

We walk around the truck and the black sedan that

is, I'm sure, Princess Gabby's. Both driver and passenger doors stand open. Sprawled before it, in a still, blood-spattered heap, lies a body.

"God, no." It's Princess Gabby's driver. He shot a man in his own driveway. There's no hope for us. He's not sane enough to listen to anything I can say.

"Shut up. Keep moving."

But I can't move, not staring at this brutally disfigured body. His hand shoots out, slams against my cheek.

I cry out, and as I do, Lucas tackles him. I scream again, run for the winery, where I know the women are. It's like stepping into a refrigerator. The air slips over my flesh like a cool film of oil. My face is numb where he slapped me. I taste blood on my lips.

Ellen Horner leans against a barrel, rubbing her head. I run to her, ask, "Are you okay?" She rubs the bloody gash above her eye. "He's going to kill them. You have to help."

I hear the rifle, and pain and fear pierce me. *Lucas. No.*

"Hide," she whispers. "I'm his daughter. He won't hurt me."

"He already has."

"Hide," she repeats, her eyes fierce and unfocused. I scramble up the wooden stairs to a loftlike platform full of implements, equipment that must have once been used to make wine. They smell of oil, dust, age. I look for anything heavy, anything with a sharp edge, find it with a heavy, spool-shaped piece.

The winery door swings open. He steps into the slanted sunlight, the rifle in his hand. *Lucas,* I think again, remembering the body of Princess Gabby's driver. The man points the rifle at a barrel and fires.

Ellen screams.

"Leave now, honey, or stay. I don't care."

"Daddy, please."

He fires again.

Another scream, not from Ellen. He laughs and moves sideways until he is standing almost directly below me. "That's more like it." He takes aim with the rifle, starts to move toward the barrel. I have only one chance. I must make it perfect. I aim, as well, then send the heavy piece of iron down over the edge, in the exact direction of his head.

Rochelle

She clamped her hands over her mouth. *Don't scream, no matter what. Don't let one sound escape.* Her heart hammered, the way it did after one of the injections. The toys, all of her rituals, seemed a lifetime away. Now she thought only moment to moment. The man who'd just fired at her. Not a sound, though. She must not move. There might still be time. Time to live, to get out of here, to make everything right.

Rochelle heard a thud, a sharp outtake of breath, a guttural retort, like someone being kicked in the stomach. She peeked around the barrel. The man lay jack-knifed on the dusty floor, hazy sunbeams lighting his form, the blood on his head. A few feet from him, Ellen Horner stood, as if unable to move. She hadn't done this to him. Someone else, someone upstairs, must have. Rochelle glanced up the stairs, trying to make out a shape among the shadowed shapes. A woman. She could see a woman there. The reporter. She'd found them.

"We're down here," she shouted to her. "Help us."

A loud explosion thundered through her head, her

body. She felt as if she were being cut in half. Pain sliced into her, bringing her to her knees, as the camouflage man knelt, the rifle in his arms, blood gushing out of his head.

He dropped the gun now. *See.* He was dropping the gun. They were going to be all right, all of them. She was going to have a chance to go back and make her life all right. She could do it, too. She wasn't a stupid woman. Not just another stupid woman with a killer body.

Rikki

Rochelle McArthur's shuddering breath reverberates up here, and I know it is her last. She crumples next to the wine barrel that has hidden her but not well enough. Earl Horner makes a noise of satisfaction, a noise that is mostly throat, a noise that says he isn't finished yet. He reaches for the rifle, leans against it, pulling himself up.

He knows I'm up here. Rochelle looked directly at me. I've wounded him, I know. The stench of blood and fear and death almost overcomes me. I have to hide, but my only chance is to hurl something else at him. Once he's up here, I'm dead. Like Rochelle, I think. Like Christopher. Like Lucas.

He makes it to his feet. In spite of his age, he is amazingly agile, and his military man's bearing is unmistakable.

"Daddy?" Ellen Horner again. More sob than voice. He ignores her, scanning the top of the loft where I crouch behind a crate, lifting his rifle once more.

It's my only chance. I push the crate down over the edge as the rifle explodes again. I feel the shot tear through me, ripping fire through my flesh. His agonizing shouts filling the air, I crumple into the dust, try to flatten myself on the floor.

"Ellie, help me." He struggles under the crate. His voice is still strong, a harsh voice cut by a history of giving commands. I cannot lift my arm, a fiery slice of pain along my side. But I'm able to lift my head. To see him trapped there. To see her standing before him, dazed. "Get over here, girl."

She moves, not really walking, stumbling as a child might. "That's right, baby. Get this off me, then get me the rifle. Good girl. That's right. You're a good girl."

"Don't." Tania Marie steps from behind a vat. "Leave him there for the police."

Ellen pauses, looking as if she has just awakened. "The rifle," he bellows. "Give me the rifle, Ellie."

Ellen turns, bends.

"No." Tania Marie moves closer to her now, her expression wild, tears streaking her face. "Julie didn't want this. You said so yourself. You don't have to do what he says anymore. Not ever again."

"Ellie, *now*." He pushes the crate from him, his arm extended. My whole body throbs with pain as the crate falls away. I try to shout, to beg Ellen to help us, but my voice comes out a weak gasp.

Ellen reaches down for the rifle.

"Don't." Tania Marie makes a run for her, but Ellen already has shouldered the weapon.

She turns, points it at Earl Horner's head and fires. Then she collapses to her knees in tears.

The last image I have is of Tania Marie, long skirt torn and stained, her arms wrapped around Ellen's sobbing form.

THIRTY-FIVE

Rikki

"**P**ersonality," the Killer Body theme song, plays as I walk into the chapel for Rochelle's memorial service with Lucas, our last date, in a way. Two services too close together, but I need to be here, afloat in this sea of grief. I hold on to Lucas as an anchor.

Lucky. That's what they tell us we are. Lucky that my shoulder is only a dull ache now. Lucky that Lucas didn't lose a leg when he tried to save my life. Lucky that Earl Horner murdered only two people. *Only* two.

In the front row of this small chapel, Rochelle's husband and daughter also hold on to each other. Blond Elvis, looking like a family member, sobs openly, his arms around both of them. Outside the chapel, he told me Rochelle's sister did not choose to attend. I shudder at how horrible that must be—to have a family member so estranged that not even your death beckons her back.

In the back row, Princess Gabby buries her face in Prince Alain's shoulder. Seeing the way the Prince holds her—as if she is a precious jewel he's been allowed to touch—gives me pleasure and just a little envy.

Only Tania Marie, her bodyguard at her side, stands outside the group of mourners, her head held high, dark glasses hiding her eyes. If we *were* lucky, those of us who survived that nightmare, Tania Marie was the luck. Her courageous appeal to Ellen is probably the only reason we're alive. I intend to say that, in print. She's since come forward about recognizing Julie at the clinic. When reporters asked what she was doing there, Tania Marie said, "Gathering information. It's a procedure that saves a lot of lives. I decided to go a different route."

Ellen Horner's plea of self-defense will be corroborated by all of us who witnessed what happened. She will inherit Julie's estate, which Bobby Warren has insisted will include the Killer Body trust.

We will never know if Earl Horner's motives were money, or if he was really trying to protect his daughter's image. Nor will we know why Julie Larimore, who excelled in so many areas, could not break her ties with her father or with what Ellen called the hole in her life.

Ellen told us later that it was Julie's idea to buy their former home for their father once he was discharged from the psych ward of the veterans hospital. If Earl Horner was an example of what gets discharged, I'd hate to see what's still inside.

Lucas recognized him at once as the man who attacked Bobby and him on Catalina Island.

"She said one time that she couldn't even remember when she ate, let alone what," Ellen told me, her words coming out in little gasps. "Can you believe that?"

In a voice that didn't sound any more certain, I told her I could.

"That was the only thing in her life she couldn't control. She'd come back to us, time and again, and we'd take care of her when it got too bad."

"You and your father?"

"First me, then us." She glanced over at my fingers as I tried to scribble down her every word. "Go ahead and write it. Maybe if I'd read about something like this, I would have recognized what was happening in my own family. People need to talk about it."

"Yes, they do," I said.

Pete may hate me. Aunt Carey may never speak to me again, but I'm going to have to talk about it, too. As long as I—we—remain silent, the monster that destroyed Julie, Lisa and countless others will continue to claim new victims.

Bobby Warren stands before a tabletop shrine that includes photos of Rochelle and her family, publicity shots and, on the wall behind them, the famous poster that captured her at her most gorgeous, when Rochelle McArthur was the face of the moment.

"Shelly was more than a beautiful woman," Bobby says in a wavering voice. "She was an intelligent woman, an intelligent person. And she had personality. I'm going to miss her every day of my life."

The last word ends in a high-pitched wheeze. He is unable to continue. With shaking hands, he reaches into the pocket of his jacket and brings out something, that, at first, I think is a crucifix. But as the sunlight reflects from its red-enamel surface, I realize it is the Killer Body pendant, hanging from a silver chain.

Bobby Warren presses it to his lips, then places it on the table, beneath the poster.

An involuntary shudder chills me to the bone. That pendant, that image, is what caused Rochelle's death, and Julie's, as well. I look up into Lucas's eyes, and he squeezes my arm.

"Rochelle would have loved it," he says. He doesn't have a clue.

In front of us, Princess Gabby collapses into sobs.

The service has left me drained, with an inner pain greater than the one in my shoulder. There's nothing more for me in this town. All I can do now is write the story and hope that, in doing so, I can start to heal.

I talked to Aunt Carey again this morning and told her what I learned. The man who met with Lisa in Los Angeles was Julie Larimore's trainer, a bodybuilder known as Blond Elvis, who knew about Julie's weight problem and didn't think she'd return to Killer Body. He told Lisa more than he should. He also supplied her with the drugs she used to lose weight.

"He's lying," Aunt Carey said. "Lisa would never take drugs. That girl wouldn't even swallow an aspirin."

I didn't try to convince her otherwise, yet when I heard the denial in her voice, I couldn't help wondering how I was really raised, and if I got out in time.

Maybe I did. I was able to confront Pete at the boxing match that night. I was able to confront my own knowledge, my own guilt—a guilt so entrenched in the tangled roots of the past that it sometimes forces us to look away from what we know is true. Here, I'd written articles on the subject, and I couldn't see it in my own family.

The truth is that my perfect cousin lived like the crystal she collected. Tap it, and it rings. Tap it too hard, and it shatters. Damn, will I ever get over that? No, but I will no longer deny it, not to Pete, not to my aunt, not to myself. Acknowledging it saved two women's lives, three, if you count me. And I do.

* * *

Because I cannot drive yet, Hamilton is coming tomorrow, around noon, he said. I'm ready to go, to leave Killer Body behind. But I'm not ready to leave Lucas.

He asked me to have dinner with him tonight, but I said I have to pack. It's more than that, of course, and we both know it.

On this late Friday afternoon, perched on the edge of dusk, a teasing breeze stirs the scents of Santa Barbara into a tantalizing aroma. Soon, the tourists will arrive, and the laid-back city will pose and preen. The tile rooftops will gleam in the sunlight. The jacarandas will bloom, and the ocean will whisper its promises to anyone willing to believe.

Instead of returning to my motel, Lucas drives along the beach. He's taken off his jacket, and his soft, linen shirt drapes across his shoulders.

"A detour," he says when I question him. "I can't give you much of a walk along this beach today, but at least we can look at it."

He stops the car and we get out. I lean against the car's cool surface, staring out at the ocean.

He moves slowly, trying not to limp, I know, then stands beside me, takes my hand in his. I am reminded that he risked his life for me, and that he'll always carry the evidence of it in his leg.

"I'm leaving Killer Body."

That startles me. I look up, see lines around his eyes I haven't previously noticed. But I also see certainty there, resolve.

"What are you going to do?" I ask.

"That depends."

"On what?"

"What do *you* think?"

He's asking much more, of course. I don't know how to answer. "What *would* you do?" I ask. *If I weren't part of the equation.* That's what I mean, what I can't admit.

"Take some time off. Try to make some of my boat dreams come true."

"You mean sail to Mexico or Hawaii?"

He gazes out at the blue-green ocean, then back at me. "Probably the South Seas, Tahiti. I crewed there once, and I'd like to do it again, solo. That's every sailor's boat dream."

"Why don't you, then?" I feel as if I'm tearing the words out of my heart.

"I guess you answered my question." But he doesn't look away, his gaze more intense than ever. That he's not willing to settle for my platitudes makes me even less certain of my decision. "Is it that guy you work for?"

"No." I don't think so, but I'm not sure. "It's too soon." I can barely hear my own words, not sure, as I speak, that any of this is right, at all. "Too soon after a lot of things, and, yes, Den is one of them."

"'Soon' isn't a constant state. It can change."

"Yes, it can."

"I have something else to discuss with you." His set expression softens. "Although I know what you're going to say."

"What?"

"My last official act on behalf of Killer Body." He flashes me an indulgent smile, too perfect to matter. "At Bobby W's request."

"I've got to report what happened, Lucas. I can't soften any of this."

"Bobby W knows that. He's fine with it." He looks awkward, standing there in his linen shirt and penetrating gaze, like a man about to propose marriage. But that's not what this is about. This is about endings, not beginnings. This is about cutting one's losses, as I am trying to do right now.

"What does he want of me?" I ask. "Just say it."

"He thinks—hell, he wants you to be Killer Body's new spokesmodel."

For one moment, I feel a flush of flattery. But only for one moment.

"You can't be serious."

"I mean it," he says, speaking rapidly, as his words register. "Real life. That's what Bobby W's decided we're missing, and I think he's right."

I look at him, listen to these words that would have made Lisa's life, her world, probably even have taken her from Pete. I want to ask Lucas what a Killer Body spokesmodel does all day, what the office hours are, or if one's whole life is just handed over in return for a generous chunk of change, a poster and a red-enamel pendant.

"You're insulted," he says.

"No, not insulted. Sad."

He puts his arm around me, and I pull away, refusing to give into tears and grief once more.

"You want real life this time?" I say.

"That's what Bobby W wants. And, okay, I think it's a good idea, overall."

"You'll probably never go for it," I tell him, "but I know who your next spokesmodel ought to be."

Tania Marie

Word of the day: *Boeotian* (bee-O-shuhn): Relating to Boeotia, in ancient Greece, noted for its thick air and the dullness of its people or its citizens. Boorish, dull, lacking culture.

"Real life. That's what Killer Body is missing."

Tania Marie sat next to Mr. Warren at the conference table in his office. Someone had brought in a pitcher of Bloody Marys and two glasses. Mr. Warren had used his to down a fistful of supplements, but Tania Marie couldn't drink, and she wasn't sure she could talk.

She'd left Jay asleep at her apartment and driven over here as soon as she got the call, and she hoped she looked all right in the clear, honest light that flowed in through the open glass door with the breeze from the ocean.

Better than poor Mr. Warren, at any rate. The tragedy of Julie's death had deepened his hawkish features, and his dark eyes seemed to have sunk deeper into his head. His voice was as powerful as a young man's, though.

"Real life," Mr. Warren boomed again. "Not unattainable glamour. Someone who's overcome challenging obstacles and taken charge of her destiny. That's what we need."

His eyes lit up, and he squeezed her thigh with his caliper fingers, no doubt tallying exactly her percentage of body fat.

"Do you mean—"

She didn't know how to ask the question, didn't dare, in case she had misunderstood. She'd be damned before she humiliated herself again, not for Killer Body, not for anyone.

"Yes, my dear." Mr. Warren's dark eyes glittered, and she knew that he saw himself as some kind of studly, refined yet still sexy Santa Claus. "We'd like to offer you the position as Killer Body spokesmodel, effective immediately."

"You want me to be your spokesmodel?"

"Yes, my dear Tania Marie. Real life. That's what you can share with our Killer Body members."

She looked down at her thigh, and his fingers on it. "I don't want to see this body on any damned pendant."

"Of course not. The world is changing. We must change, as well." He took the final gulp of his juice, and Tania Marie detected the mean scent of alcohol on his breath. "No one can take the place of Jules, of course. We're not trying for that. We're trying to do what Lucas calls updating. As happy as I am that Princess Gabby is getting an opportunity on television, I want someone less refined, a survivor—the same kind of street-smart survivor I am—for the new Killer Body."

Tania Marie stared out at the ocean and forced herself to hold back the tears. It was really happening. Really, really, really. But, as much as she wanted it, she couldn't, wouldn't go back.

She glanced down once more, pushed her fear out of the way.

"Thank you very much," she said, as if it were one long word. "I'm honored, I really am. But Bobbo. If we're going to work together, let's get it straight right now. Take your F-ing hand off of my leg, okay?"

Rikki

Lucas and I said our goodbyes yesterday, so I'm surprised to see him as I'm lugging my suitcases to the front of the motel. When he shares Tania Marie's news, I'm glad he's come, and I tell him so.

"It's going to be a different Killer Body," I say.

"Tania Marie's already calling him Bobbo." He looks down at the bags. "You need some help with these?"

"Hamilton can do it. He just called from the road. He'll be here any second."

"Then I should go." He pauses. "Sure you don't want to apply for a job with the *Times?*"

"I hate Los Angeles, remember?"

"Maybe I could help you like it better."

"You already have, Lucas. Los Angeles. Santa Barbara. My life. You've made me like all of it so much better."

He starts to say something but, instead, pulls me into a kiss. Arms around his neck, I absorb the heat and power of him. When we break away, I go for a hug.

I hear Hamilton's Volvo before I see it. My cheeks hot, I break away from the hug, still squeezing Lucas's arm, feeling the tenseness through his jacket.

"Send me a postcard from Tahiti," I say.

Hamilton stands outside his blue Volvo. His face looks more florid than usual, probably because it's in contrast to his wrinkled denim shirt. His paunch protrudes slightly, and I hope Lucas isn't evaluating him as I am.

"Want me to come back later?" Hamilton asks, not taking a step toward me.

I glance over at Lucas, the swell of muscles under his sport coat, his unmussable hair.

"No," I say. "I'm ready now."

Hamilton's face changes, charged with surprise, mixed with something I can't read.

"Have a safe trip," Lucas says. "Be careful, Rikki, will you?"

"I'll try. You, too."

He picks up my suitcases and moves toward the car with sure steps that I know must pain him.

"I've got those." Hamilton yanks them from him, puts them in the back seat.

Then it's all polite conversation and best wishes and no body contact whatsoever.

I watch Lucas drive away in his silver car, and I look at Hamilton, letting him know that we can leave now.

I get into the Volvo, wanting to cry.

The jacaranda trees lining the walk in front of the motel have burst into purple flowers overnight, so dramatic they look as if a designer has placed them there. The interior of the Volvo has been cleaned again. That vanilla scent indigenous to car washes covers the darker smoke smell.

As we drive away, Hamilton takes out a cigarette. "You feel like lunch?"

"Not here." My voice says what my words can't.

"Gotcha."

He pulls onto the freeway, then lowers his window. A burst of air blows into the car. He tosses the cigarette, raises the window.

"What's that about?" I ask.

"I think I just quit."

"Really?"

"Yeah, I think so." He looks over for my reaction. "Maybe we'll stop in Bakersfield. Does that work for you?"

I think ahead, of the Grapevine, of Bakersfield and the scrubby flat land of the San Joaquin Valley that waits for me. My job. The hole Lisa has left. The hole I can feel in my own life. Questions. Answers. The newspaper. Hamilton. The whispered hope of the future.

Real life.

"Works for me," I say. "And, Den, I'm buying lunch."

* * * * *

MIRA Books invites you to turn the page
for an exclusive preview of
DOUBLE EXPOSURE

the next bestseller
by Bonnie Hearn Hill

Available in paperback April 2005

One

Reebie

Everyone in San Francisco was drunk that night, so drunk that I had to drive the taxi.

St. Patrick's Day. I was raised to be proud of my heritage, proud to be Rebecca Mahoney, otherwise known as Reebie. Still, I was always amused, in a smug kind of way, to see this entire, mismatched city pretending, for twenty-four hours, to be as Irish as I am all year long.

I was working a temp job. After the fiasco with my ex and losing my beloved winery, I couldn't settle. Instead I bounced from cosmetic saleswoman to various temp jobs to my newest assignment-working through my temp agency, this time for the local newspaper. My job? Coordinate the food at this event. I'd coordinated dozens of events at the winery, so this would be no problem.

The eclectic Celtic wanna-bes at the pub were already in their cups, as my dad would say. I should have been, too, crooning *Danny Boy* and forgetting about the laptop I'ddumb lugged in like a bad date, at the insistence of my panties-in-a-wedge supervisor, who had insisted I keep her posted, via e-mail, regarding my whereabouts.

Alberts, the newspaper's HR director who'd interviewed me, had explained to me that the paper was trying to drive down its demographics-translated, get more young readers-by sponsoring the vent. *Dumb* down sounded more like it, but I needed Alberta's approval for only a short time.

Since I lost the winery, I didn't care what I was or what I did. I had a second part-time job at a cosmetics counter, but this one would give me a little extra money and an excuse to hang out with my photographer friend, Daphne Teng.

The television above the bar was broadcasting footage of former President Remington, who'd died this morning. The revelers seemed to be paying little attention. Daphne and I snagged the coveted corner booth, the only one with a good-sized square table just large enough for our two pints. Daph snuggled in against the wall and lifted her glass.

"Cheers," she said in the clipped accent of one who had been taught English somewhere other than America. "We don't have to start for thirty minutes. Let's get a nice little buzz on and check out the guys."

I should have left it at that, focused on the pub crawl, a little beer, another easy temp job-just hand out the corned beef, make the drunks think they were having fun, collect my money and go home. But, no. Instead of joining Daph in the consumption of a Harps Lager, I had to unfold the laptop on the edge of that tiny table, e-mail Alberta that I'd arrived early, then pull out my cell phone and check my answering machine. When I heard the commanding, yet strangely familiar voice of a woman named Jeanette Sheldon on my voice mail, without weighing the wisdom of the move, I called her back.

Clearly disgusted, Daph sighed, picked up her glass and headed for the bar where, if the noise level was any indication, most of the fun was taking place. I didn't blame her.

Jeanette answered. I introduced myself.

"Rebecca Mahoney?" She dragged it out, in a velvety, almost-amused voice. "And I'm Jeanette Sheldon. Perhaps you've heard of me."

I drew a blank. In which of my many temporary situations had I offended this woman? And when? Perhaps the Saturday I was hired to make snow cones in the park? The week I tried to hang wallpaper?

"I've never heard of you," I said.

"I forget how young you are. You must have bypassed the rumors. I want to talk to you about the president. President Remington."

A dead former president. So Remington's death today was the reason I was letting my Harps go flat beside me. I took a bitter swallow and smacked my lips, half hoping she heard.

"I'm here with a photographer for the newspaper, but we're only covering the pub crawl today. I'm sure the paper will be running a number of stories about Michael Remington tomorrow, but I don't have anything to do with that. I'm just a temp."

I felt as much as heard her clear her throat. "They'll print interviews with his son, his son's wife, and of course, June."

"That's right. I'm sure they will."

"But you'll be the one talking to the president's mistress."

I shook my computer house to life, nearly tipping

over my pint. I Googled as fast as I could, doing a Web search for Jeanette Sheldon. Maybe she was just a nut. She had to be if, out of everyone in the Bay Area, she'd picked me to confess to.

"You were President Remington's mistress?"

"You heard me. The old rumors are true. I'm telling you this only so you'll agree to talk to me."

I hadn't hear the old rumors, but if there were any, I'd find them online. "Why are you coming forward now?" I asked.

"That's part of what I want to talk to you about."

The revelers at the bar launched into *An Irish Lullaby*, Daphne's lilting accent soaring over the others. My laptop screen filled with several promising links. This woman might be for real, after all.

Too-ra-loo-ra-loo-ral, too-ra-loo-ra-li,
Too-ra-loo-ra0loo-ral, hush now, don't you cry.

"Leo Kersikovski works in the newsroom at the paper, and I'm sure he'd be interested in talking to you," I said over the song, which seemed to grow in volume by the moment. It would be a good break for hunky Kersikovski. If Jeanette were on the level, he might even scoop the *Chronicle*. Of course, if she were on the level, wouldn't she be calling the *Chronicle* anyway? "Mr. Kersikovski might still be at work. If you hang on a minute, I can get his direct extension from the photographer."

Too-ra-loo-ra-lo-ral, too-ra-loo-ra-li,
Too-ra-loo-ra-loo-ral, That's an Irish lullaby.

"I said I want to talk to *you*."

The certainty in her voice sent a tiny chill through me.

"And I told you I'm just a temp," I said. "My only connection with the newspaper is setting up the St. Patrick's Day pub crawl. How did you get my name anyway? Why-?" I couldn't finish. A photograph of her on the computer screen choked off my words.

Beautiful, so amazingly beautiful, but it wasn't her arresting eyes, or her flawlessly sculpted features that stopped me; it was those dates beneath her photograph, the second one in particular. *Jeanette Sheldon, 1945-1976.*

"What is it?" The imperious voice lowered to a murmur now.

I stared at the screen of my laptop. "You're supposed to be dead."

"Things are not what they seem. Do you know that poem?"

"What poem" I sat frozen to the photograph of her on the laptop. Damn, why was this happening to me, and why couldn't I shake free of it?

"*The Emperor of Ice Cream.* A marvelous poem by Wallace Stevens, one of the president's favorites." I could hear the wistful smile in her voice, the softening. "It's time, Reebie Mahoney, for us to talk, and I have something very important to tell you. Now, how soon can you get over here?"

From the remarkable author of *Leah's Journey*

Gloria Goldreich

For Rochelle Weiss, everything in life has come easily—
good looks, professional success—until her life is turned
upside down by the news that her beloved parents are
dying. Determined to care for them in their final days,
Rochelle loses her job, the support of her lover and her
lifelong belief that everything will turn out okay. Finding
herself alone and nearly broke, she has nowhere to go but
into the depths of her own unexplored soul. The closer
Rochelle comes to truly understanding what lies in her
own heart, the more she realizes that all the pieces of her
life must somehow fit together: her parents, her life
before their deaths and her search for a new beginning.

Walking Home

"…an absorbing and often moving narrative,
written with sensitivity and compassion."
—*Publishers Weekly* on *Leah's Journey*

Available the first week of January 2005 wherever books are sold!

MIRA®

BONNIE
HEARN HILL

2001   INTERN   ___ $6.50 U.S.   ___ $7.99 CAN.

(*limited quantities available*)

TOTAL AMOUNT $_____
POSTAGE & HANDLING $_____
($1.00 for one book; 50¢ for each additional)
APPLICABLE TAXES* $_____
<u>TOTAL PAYABLE</u> $_____
(check or money order—please do not send cash)

To order, complete this form and send it, along with a check or money order for the total above, payable to MIRA Books, to:
In the U.S.: 3010 Walden Avenue, P.O. Box 9077, Buffalo, NY 14269-9077; **In Canada:** P.O. Box 636, Fort Erie, Ontario L2A 5X3.

Name:_____
Address:_____ City:_____
State/Prov.:_____ Zip/Postal Code:_____
Account Number (if applicable):_____
075 CSAS

*New York residents remit applicable sales taxes.
 Canadian residents remit applicable GST and provincial taxes.

MIRA®